D0497833

GOOD HUSBANDS

Ray, Cate, author.
Good husbands

2022
33305254837226
ca   06/15/22

GOOD HUSBANDS

CATE RAY

PARK
ROW
BOOKS

PARK
ROW
BOOKS™

ISBN-13: 978-0-7783-8701-5

Good Husbands

Copyright © 2022 by Cate Ray

All rights reserved. No part of this book may be used or reproduced in any manner whatsoever
without written permission except in the case of brief quotations embodied in critical articles
and reviews.

This is a work of fiction. Names, characters, places and incidents are either the product of the
author's imagination or are used fictitiously. Any resemblance to actual persons, living or dead,
businesses, companies, events or locales is entirely coincidental.

Park Row Books
22 Adelaide St. West, 41st Floor
Toronto, Ontario M5H 4E3, Canada
ParkRowBooks.com
BookClubbish.com

Printed in U.S.A.

Recycling programs
for this product may
not exist in your area.

For Bec Vaughan, with love

GOOD HUSBANDS

Yes, injured Woman! rise, assert thy right!
—Anna Laetitia Barbauld, *The Rights of Woman*, c. 1795

It starts out as curiosity—the temptation to peek behind the door. Just one look and maybe that will be enough to satisfy it. But that's never going to happen because the door is always locked. They know what they're doing.

Before long, the desire has grown so sharp it's difficult to sleep through. Nothing dulls the pain. I carry it everywhere I go.

I begin to have the same dream, night after night... Someone opens the door for me and I turn to thank them, but they're gone. A stranger who has done me an enormous kindness, perhaps without even knowing.

I don't have time to think about it because the clock's ticking. I'm taking in the palm leaf wallpaper, inhaling the scent of lilies, knowing that at any moment they will spot me, eject me back to the streets.

It happens all too soon. And I wake to a smell that isn't lilies, to walls that aren't palm leaves, and to bones that ache and creak. The longing becomes hostile in those moments; I hatch all kinds of plots, none of which will see the light of day.

And then one night in my dream, everything changes. The stranger reveals her face to me and suddenly the way forward is clear.

Maybe there's a way inside, a way of staying longer, after all.

PART ONE: THE LETTER

JESS

I'm 100 percent average, said no one ever. Yet that's what most of us are, myself included. I know the sum of my parts and it equals ordinary and there's no shame in that. In fact, it's a strength. My parents were ordinary too, and as their only child they raised me to respect being a leaf on a tree, a grain of sand on the beach. You get the picture. But it doesn't mean being insignificant, anonymous. It means being part of a community, a clan, a cause greater than yourself.

I realize this kind of thinking isn't very now. The idea of being average scares my girls to death. I wouldn't accuse them of it outright, yet it's probably in their DNA too, and at some point, they'll have to confront it. Mediocrity isn't something they can deal with, and perhaps that's where we're going wrong, because ordinary is what gets you through. Ordinary is noble, life-affirming. It's the heart of humanity, and somehow, we've forgotten that.

And then the letter arrives, and I know as soon as I read it that I'm going to have to rethink everything. Because I'm fairly sure that ordinary people don't get letters like this.

———

It's the first day of autumn and I don't know if it's actually colder or whether I'm imagining it, as though a door closed yesterday on summer and a chillier one opened, but I'm definitely feeling it today. The tip of my nose is icy and I would get a hot water bottle for my lap, only I'm leaving the house in twenty minutes.

I'm meeting Duane Dee, my favorite sculptor—the only sculptor—on my client list, and anything could happen. You never know what you're going to get with artists, which is why I like working with them. They're up and down, but more than that, they're honest. I've never known a profession like it. My artists talk about integrity and authenticity all the time, and I lap it up. I love that the men don't shave for meetings, the women don't dye their grays, no one bothers ironing anything.

The investors are another sort altogether. People who buy and sell art are very different from those who create it. I know whose company I prefer, but I keep that to myself because even I know not to bite the hand that feeds me.

Max thinks it's funny that I work for Moon & Co.—he calls them the Moonies—even though he was the one who got me the job. He knows everyone in Bath because he grew up here, whereas I'm originally from the East End, London. I've been living here for twenty years and it still makes me laugh that locals think it's urban, even though I can see cows from our bathroom window.

I've just got enough time for a quick look at Facebook. I don't know why I do it to myself, but sometimes I feel that if I don't keep up, I'll be left behind. Which is odd because it's not as if it's a race, is it, being human?

I'm forty-six years old and still looking for friends. I'm pretty sure I won't find them here in this endless scroll of happy images. People work so hard to make themselves look perfect, it's hard not to try to find faults. I don't enjoy it. It makes me feel bitchy, but still I return and peek.

I glance at the time: ten minutes until I have to go. Outside, red leaves are hanging on the trees as though they've gone rusty and can't move. There's no wind today, the air completely still.

Duane Dee doesn't use social media. He thinks the tech companies are using us to get rich and that it's odd I'm willing to be a pawn in Silicon Valley because I strike him as militant.

It's probably because I still have a slight East End accent, which can sound blunt, tough, but I like to think of it more as plain-talking. My late dad used to say that the EastEnders wore their hearts of gold on their sleeves. A firefighter all his life, he believed in helping people out, especially along our street of identical row houses where no one could set themselves apart.

Enough of Facebook. I shut it down, telling it I won't be back, knowing I will. And then I gather my things, ready to take off.

In the hallway, I sit on the stairs to put on my sneakers, wondering when I started dressing like a teenager, and that's when the postman comes. There's only one small piece of mail, which slips in like a piece of confetti, drifting to the mat. I pick it up with interest because it's handwritten, and I can't think when I last received one of those.

Then it's out of my mind because I'm locking up and putting on my puffer jacket as I walk to the car. And then I'm driving to town—the sun a pale wedge of lemon above me—running through what to say to Duane Dee.

Is he well? Is he pushing himself too hard? Is he sleeping enough? He always looks chronically tired.

I ask too many questions. Intrusive. That's the little bit of feedback my boss always gives me. *Jess, here's some feedback you didn't ask for...*

When people say you're intrusive, assertive or direct, they're basically telling you to be quiet. Are men given feedback like that? I don't know. But I'm thinking about this as I enter the Sicilian café, which is my personal preference and not Duane's.

Whenever he chooses, we end up somewhere too dark to see our food, sitting on tasseled mats.

The service here is very good. Within seconds of my sitting down, the waitress hands me a menu even though I always have an Americano and an almond pastry.

Glancing in the wall mirror beside me, I note that my expression is severe. A semifriend told me recently that I carry a lot of tension in my face. It was a bit passive-aggressive of her to say so, but I know what she means. I have bony cheekbones and thin lips that can look mean if I'm not careful.

So, I've been making an effort lately to smile more, worry less and unclench my hands. I also tend to tap my teeth together, and I'm doing that now in time to the café music as I wait for Duane.

And then I remember the letter.

It takes me several minutes to find it, as well as my reading glasses. Since hitting my midforties, I misplace things all the time. I normally ask myself, where would I have put it? And it's never there.

The letter is in the front compartment of the rucksack that I haven't used for so long, there are crumbs and bits of foil in there from the primary school-run. Flicking the crumbs off the envelope, I examine the handwriting, feeling a pang of nostalgia at the idea of someone putting pen to paper just for me.

The writing is tiny and in capitals, internet code for shouting, but in this case is more like whispering. Something about it gives me the sense that it's trying its hardest not to offend or take up too much space. I have to pry the paper out of the envelope, where it's wedged, folded into eighths.

THURS 1ST OCTOBER

DEAR JESSICA,
I HOPE YOU'RE SITTING DOWN TO READ THIS
AND THAT YOU'RE ALONE.

THIS IS SO DIFFICULT. YOU WOULDN'T BE-LIEVE HOW OFTEN I IMAGINED TALKING TO YOU, BUT I DIDN'T KNOW HOW TO GO ABOUT IT. AND NOW IT'S TOO LATE.

For what? I check the postmark on the envelope: Monday 5th October, 5.00 p.m. That was last night. Shifting uneasily in my seat, I turn over the letter to see who sent it: Holly Waite.

I'VE KNOWN FOR SOME TIME THAT I WON'T MAKE OLD BONES, BUT NOW IT'S URGENT AND I'VE ONLY GOT A FEW DAYS LEFT. SO, I'LL JUST COME OUT WITH IT.

ON 22ND DECEMBER 1990, MY MUM NICOLA WAITE WAS RAPED BY 3 MEN IN THE MONTAGUE CLUB, BATH. THE MEN WERE ANDREW LAWLEY, DANIEL BROOKE AND MAXIMILIAN JACKSON.

MY MUM FELL PREGNANT WITH ME. SHE ASKED THE MEN FOR HELP, BUT THEY DIDN'T WANT TO BE INVOLVED. SHE NEVER RECOV-ERED FROM WHAT HAPPENED AND DIED 9 YEARS AGO OF AN ACCIDENTAL OVERDOSE.

EVERYTHING I OWN IS AT STONE'S STORAGE, UNIT 21, 156 CLEVEDON ROAD. IF YOU GO TO THEM, THEY'LL GIVE YOU THE KEY. YOU'RE WELCOME TO ANYTHING. I HAVE NO ONE ELSE TO LEAVE IT TO.

WE NEVER KNEW WHO MY FATHER WAS. SO, I'M ALSO WRITING TO:

PRIYANKA LAWLEY, 32 WALDEN WAY, HIGH LANE, BATH.

STEPHANIE BROOKE, 7 SOUTH AVENUE, BATH.

I'M SORRY TO DO THIS. I KNOW IT'LL BE A SHOCK, BUT I COULDN'T GO WITHOUT TELL-

ING YOU. YOUR HUSBANDS WENT UNPUNISHED,
WALKING AWAY COMPLETELY FREE. I ALWAYS
HOPED THAT ONE DAY I'D SEE JUSTICE DONE,
BUT I COULDN'T THINK OF A WAY TO DO THAT
WITHOUT DESTROYING MORE LIVES.

NOW THAT I'M OUT OF TIME, I CAN SEE THAT
IT WASN'T MY CHOICE TO MAKE. SO, I'M PASS-
ING IT OVER TO YOU, TELLING YOU WHAT YOU
SHOULD HAVE KNOWN FROM THE START. IT AL-
WAYS FELT SO PERSONAL, BUT IT WASN'T, NOT
REALLY. YOU CAN'T DRAW A LINE WHERE ONE
LIFE STARTS AND ANOTHER BEGINS.

ONCE AGAIN, I'M SORRY.

I HOPE YOU DO THE RIGHT THING.

YOURS TRULY,

HOLLY WAITE X

The kiss throws me the most. I stare at it. It's like she's trying to add a softener, after making the worst possible accusation.

I read the letter again, my eye lingering on *Maximilian Jackson*. No one ever calls Max that. It doesn't even sound like him.

"Jess?" I glance up to see Duane standing there, untying his Aztec scarf, clay stains on his sweater. "All right, darlin'?"

I can't pull out a smile for him. I'm not great at hiding my emotions. It's one of the things Max has always loved about me, and I like it about myself too. Yet, suddenly, it feels like an impairment; a liability, even.

Slipping the letter into my bag, I stand up robotically and we exchange kisses. He smells of autumn air, and his cheek as it brushes mine is so cold it makes me shiver. "Hi, Duane."

We sit down, and Duane scans a menu before tossing it aside. "Who am I kidding? I'm gonna get the calzoni. I always get the calzoni."

"So…how are you?" I manage to ask. "How's the new project going?" I sound uptight, formal. I clench my hands, trying to stop them from trembling.

The waitress takes our order. And then I sit rigidly in my chair, listening as Duane describes his latest creation—how it embodies technoculture, hyperreality, paranoia.

When the coffees arrive, I drink mine too quickly and burn my tongue.

"You okay?" He cocks his head at me.

No, I'm not. How could I be?

"Actually, I just need to pop to the ladies. Could you excuse me a minute?"

Out in the restroom, I stand with my hands against the sink, trying to breathe, feeling dizzy. Closing my eyes, I see *Maximilian Jackson* again in that tiny handwriting.

It's not Max. It's some sort of mistake. Holly Waite…whoever that is…is wrong. And perhaps, dead.

I don't think I've ever felt happy before to hear of someone's demise, but as I open my eyes it occurs to me that if this woman is deceased, then there's no one present to make any accusations.

I return to the table, where Duane is tucking into his calzoni, a thread of cheese hanging from his lip. Normally I wouldn't hesitate to tell him, or anyone, so they could set themselves straight.

But something strange happens and I just sit there, silent, watching the thread dangle as he chews and talks. It seems to me that I don't know who I am. Or more to the point, who my husband is.

When I get home, Max is out. I pause in the hallway, noiselessly taking off my shoes because I don't want Eva to know I'm back. At some point during the last year, I started tiptoeing around the house, stealing moments of peace. Sometimes I sit in the dark so no one knows I'm there. Tonight, though, I have more reason than usual to sneak.

"Mum? Is that you?"

Damn. A door opens, followed by footsteps across the landing.

"Hello, my lovely," I say.

"Hi, Mum." Eva recently turned fifteen and was gifted very long legs. From this angle, they're all I can see until she emerges fully at the top of the stairs. "You're home early."

"Am I?" I pretend to be surprised. "I've got some work to do. Are you okay carrying on with your homework?"

She nods. "That's fine. I've got Spanish revision."

"Good." I feel guilty. Eva normally likes a chat as soon as I get home. "Can I get you anything?"

"No, thanks. Call me when you're done. I want to tell you what Charlotte said."

Charlotte only reaches Eva's elbow in height yet somehow manages to bring her down every day. They've been friends since primary school, despite my efforts to break them up. Just hearing her name makes me waver, assessing Eva's face. But then I think of the letter, my body tensing resolvedly. "See you in half an hour," I say, making for the kitchen.

"Okay, Mum."

I make a cup of tea while waiting for the laptop to wake up. It's slow and old, but it's the only one that doesn't talk to the others and doesn't have child safety blocks on it.

With the letter hidden on my lap, I enter Holly's name into the search engine.

Holly Waite, Bath, UK, is an osteopath and a makeup artist. She could be either of them, or neither. I look up Stone's Storage instead. It exists, seems innocuous enough, but then storage is storage.

I bend my neck to read the first of the men's names. Andrew Lawley. I've never heard of him, which is odd because I thought I knew all of Max's friends. He's a very sociable, open sort of person. His mantra is to treat people the way you'd want to be treated yourself. I don't know whether I've mentioned that I adore him, but it probably should have been the first thing I told you about me.

I type *Andrew Lawley, Bath, UK* and tap my teeth together as an image appears. His eyes are deep-set, his hair bushy—set away from his head as though you could lift it off. I don't hate or love his face; it leaves me neutral.

He runs his own IT company, based in an attractive Georgian square in the city, a short stroll from the Montague Club.

I sip my tea, thinking of the unmarked door that's the club. I've never really given it much thought. I don't need to know everything about Max, not on the business side of things. We've reached a point where I smile and nod when he talks about fixed rate mortgages, just like he does when I tell him about the Moonies.

He doesn't go to the club very often; maybe once a month, if that. Born in the mid-nineteenth century, it was once a lavish gentleman's club for the landed gentry. But gradually, it evolved into an exclusive social club for businessmen and professionals. And then, during the eighties it caved and allowed women to join.

I've never even set foot inside the place. I'm not into private clubs. I don't like private schools either, or anything exclusive. It irritates me that some people can't cope unless they're on the top tier, looking down on the rest of us. But these days the Montague is full of entrepreneurs, according to Max; excellent for networking. He arranges most of the members' mortgages, so I can't argue with that.

He started going there during his teens with his dad. He could easily have been there in—I look at the letter on my lap—December 1990.

Upstairs, a door closes and the pipes whisper as Eva comes

out of the bathroom. I wait for her to return to her room and for everything to go quiet again.

I take a closer look at Andrew Lawley's picture. How old is he? I guess at fifty. Max is fifty, but a lot better looking. Maybe this guy is slightly older. Either way, they'd have been about twenty in 1990.

So, I'm doing this? I'm taking a stranger's word for it? Why don't I just show Max the letter—confide in him like I do with everything else, ask him outright?

I don't answer myself—not yet, anyway. Instead, I look up the next man. Daniel Brooke. The moment I type it, a light goes on in my head.

Brooke Prestige Cars is a large dealership in the city center. Everyone knows it. You can't sit in traffic in Bath without having to look at one of those window stickers.

I'm surprised, though. I had no idea Max knew him.

I find Daniel Brooke's photo on the company website page, and again, he looks about fifty. Unlike Andrew Lawley, I have an immediate reaction to this man. His hair is spiky, cropped short like an army cadet's, and there's the hint of a smile on his lips as though he thinks he's smarter than you.

The front door rattles and I jump. I completely lost track of the time. Quickly, I grab the letter and stuff it into my bag, and I'm just deleting the history on the laptop and slamming down the lid when Poppy enters the kitchen.

I can smell the chlorine from here. "Hey, Mamma Mia," she says, going to the fridge, the back of her sweater wet where her hair has dripped onto it. "What the—" She spins around, her face like a screwed-up newspaper. "Who drank all the juice?"

She's scrappy, like me. You shouldn't typecast your kids. We all know they're their own people, but still, we look for ourselves in them and I always see myself in Poppy.

"Oh for God's sake!" She stamps her foot.

I should say something. She's always shouting, and I'm sure

our elderly neighbors can hear her. Yet I'm too busy watching Max, who's just come in with an armful of swimming bags and coats, as though he's taken five twelve-year-olds swimming and not just one.

"What's all that lot?" I'm glad of the distraction. I wasn't sure how I'd be with him.

"Sasha left her things," he says, dropping the bundle onto the table. "I've texted Marie to say we've got it. It's no biggie."

He's so easy with it all… Sasha… Marie… I couldn't pick these people out in a lineup, but then he's been taking our girls swimming since they were toddlers. I'm happy not to be involved. There are parts of my daughters' lives that are nothing to do with me because they fall under his jurisdiction. It's the way we've always done it: fifty-fifty, right down the middle. That's how partnerships are supposed to work.

"Everything okay?" he asks, catching sight of my expression.

I'm still sitting at the table, chewing my thumbnail. "Yeah, I was just doing some work."

"Think I'll take a quick shower, then. It's always so bloody hot in that pool." He loosens his tie, unbuttoning his tight shirt, arms bulging.

I try to imagine what the swim mums think when they look at him, maybe mistaking his friendliness for something else…subtly checking out his frame, his heavy eyelids and long eyelashes, weighing up whether the lack of height would be a problem.

He works out most days. And in all honesty, I like it. I like having a man who others find attractive; a man who is strong and capable.

Capable of what?

As he draws close to me, pressing a kiss onto my lips with a flutter of his cartoon eyes, I feel mistrust for the first time.

"What's wrong?" He frowns.

"Nothing. Just tired." One of the benefits of being middle-aged is that you can use this line to cover pretty much anything and no one ever questions it.

He kisses me again. And then he's off upstairs, whistling an empty tune.

———

Just before lights-out, I tap on Eva's door. She's in bed, duvet drawn to her chin.

"Hey, lovely." I sit down on the edge of her bed. "Sorry we didn't get to talk. It's been one of those days. Do you want to tell me about Charlotte now?"

But she's already sleepy, the night-light casting a peach glow over her face. "Okay, then. You get some rest." I nudge her hair from her eyes, kiss her cheek. "Night night. Love you, sweet-heart."

In the doorway, I turn back to gaze at her. She looks just like she did as a baby, and I regret the time that's passed so quickly. Closing the door softly, I think for the thousandth time how my mum would have loved watching her grow, turning into a woman; Poppy too. Yet life has a way of taking your beautifully drawn-up plans and red-inking them.

———

In our bedroom, Max is undressing. He takes off his T-shirt, swapping it for a pajama top that fits snugly over his chest. I feel a familiar swirl of pride and lust, followed by that nasty mistrust again. I hate this. I've never hidden anything from him before.

Just ask him. Give him a chance to explain that it's a huge mistake. A terrible lie.

I practice it.

Max, hon. Do you know someone called Nicola Waite? Did you rape her in 1990?

I can't do it. If he lies, I'll know. He gets a look, a tension around his mouth when he fibs. I have a strong radar for these things and have called him out on it before, on little lies like whether it was him who tracked mud through the house.

On something this big, he wouldn't be able to hide it. We'd both know the truth and it would hang between us. Maybe I don't know him as well as I thought I did, but I know me. This letter, this accusation—if endorsed—would destroy our marriage in an instant.

My life. Our girls. Our home. Everything ruined.

Switching off the bedside light, he spoons me and I breathe heavily, pretending to have fallen asleep in record time. Within minutes, he loosens up, his limbs slipping away, softening.

I can't confront him about the letter yet. I need more time, more information.

Drawing up my knees, I curl into a ball, my body tight. Sometimes, before you do something really big, it helps to make yourself small. That way, if it all goes wrong, you're not an easy target. That's what I'm thinking as I fall asleep.

PRIYANKA

There's a reckless part of me that I struggle to contain whenever I arrive at Tadpoles. It's the same sensation I used to get when the opening chords to a brilliant track boomed through the speakers and I would slop my pint in the race to the dance floor. The same excitement, the same burst of energy where I don't know what to do with myself. You could say I've swapped partying for parenting, and I'm more than happy with that. Look what I've gained.

Turning off the stereo, I jump out of the car, locking it over my shoulder. I can see Beau waiting for me behind the wooden gate, holding up a single red rose, and it's all I can do not to run to him.

On my way across the car park, I catch up with a mum whom I see most days, wearing a velvet blazer and ballet pumps, even in a frost. She probably knows me as pink hair, Doc Marten boots.

"All right, me duck?" I'm thirty-six and haven't lived in the Midlands since I was twenty-one, but sometimes I still talk like we did at school: terms of endearment like me duck, me cocker. It's not something I seem to have much control of, breaking into it like a nervous comedy routine.

"Hi there." You can tell she's itching to get away—eyes already fixed on the other blazers queueing to collect their treasure. She's probably worried I'll try to make friends and is making a mental note to come five minutes earlier tomorrow to avoid me.

I'm at the wooden gate now, at the back of the queue. Ballet Pumps has slipped away. "Hey you," I call to Beau, waving at him.

"Hello, Mummy." He holds the rose higher so I can see it.

This is the bit where I struggle the most to rein it in. I want to grab him and throw him up to the sky and catch him again.

"Nippy, isn't it," I say to the dad next to me. "Wish I'd brought me cardy." He's on his phone and looks at me in surprise as though he didn't know I was there. He doesn't seem to know what he's doing here or which child is his. I'm not like that. Even when I'm not with Beau, I'm with him. I won't have to use a GPS tracker when he's older; I'll know where he is.

I'm at the front now. The day care staffer introduces me to a new colleague who'll be looking after Beau from now on. She's petite—on my eye level—and her name's A-na-ees, although it won't be written like that. As a teacher, I have to come up with quick ways to remember names. Spelling it phonetically helps, so long as I don't write it that way on school reports.

"Is this for me?" I bend down to talk to Beau, who glows with pride as he hands me the rose.

"It's chocolate," he whispers, tapping his nose to indicate a secret.

I inspect the rose. It really is chocolate: red foil on a green stick.

"My boyfriend works for a chocolatier," A-na-ees says.

"Well, lucky you. What a result!" I lift Beau and kiss him, propping him on my hip. He's only three, but it won't be long before he's taller than me; no joking.

"I love your hair," she says.

"Thanks. I do it myself."

"Really? It looks so professional." She clocks the butterfly tattoo on my wrist, her gaze falling to the neon laces in my Doc Martens.

"Mummy colors her eyes too," says Beau, touching my nose stud. He always presses the emerald as though he thinks it's going to fall off.

She looks confused. "I wear colored contact lenses," I explain. Today, my eyes are violet, one of my favorites.

"Oh." She clasps her hands together. "That's so cool." I can see that she doesn't know what to make of me.

"I like to mix things up. Keep everyone on their toes. Isn't that right, Beau?"

He nods. "Mummy knows if Daddy hasn't looked at her today."

We both laugh, and I can see Ballet Pumps watching me out of the corner of her eye. I set Beau down because he seems to weigh more than he did this morning. And then we go, Beau skipping alongside me, telling me about finger painting and sausages for lunch.

In the car, I strap him in and turn the music from Kiss FM to "Wheels on the Bus." Beau kicks his feet and gazes out of the window with his big brown eyes, curls catching the sunshine. Sometimes, I can't believe that he almost didn't make it. He's the most beautiful boy on the planet, and I'm so lucky to have him.

———

"Hello!" I call out, setting Beau's day bag and my pile of schoolbooks on the table. There's a letter in the rack, sitting there on its own. It'll be from one of my nieces in Leicester.

I push it into the pocket of my tunic and call again for Andy. "We're home!"

He's going slightly deaf and says it's because he's fifteen years older than me, but I think he's too young for it to be age-related. More likely, he gets absorbed in what he's doing. He always seems to hear me when I say I'm in the mood for sex, or can't manage the rest of my chips.

Deaf or not, he can surely feel Beau, who's thundering down the hallway, floorboards shuddering. Anyone would think they'd been separated for years, not a handful of hours.

I poke my head around the study door. Beau is perched on Andy's lap, telling him about the chocolate rose and how much his new teacher likes my pink hair. "Well, what's not to love?" Andy says. "Everyone loves Mummy... We do, don't we?"

"Aww, stop. You'll make me blush."

In truth, I can't get enough of hearing things like this, as the only woman in the house. Growing up, I was the youngest of five—*little Pree*—and I'm used to being the one who everyone looks out for. Of course, the flip side is that no one thinks you can cross the road without supervision. My mum still rings to ask if I'm eating properly and when I'm coming home.

"So, how was it with Saffron?" Andy asks, setting Beau down.

"Not great. He's permanently expelled."

His face falls. "Oh, I'm sorry, my love."

"It's okay." I reach my hand out for Beau, who trots forward happily. "He kept pushing his luck. It's like he wanted it to happen, but I didn't even get a chance to say 'bye."

I teach RPE—Religion, Philosophy and Ethics—plus PSHE—Personal, Social, Health and Economic education. My parents think that because I teach subjects consisting of letters, they aren't substantial, like math or science. It's a running joke in my family. They also think I teach in a rough school and have to wear a ballistic vest, just because it's a state school and all boys.

Yes, we have our challenging students. Saffron was one of them. Yet, somehow, I always managed to get on with him. He used to say that I was one of the few people who didn't talk down to him. To be honest, it's difficult to talk down to anyone when you're five foot one.

"Have you got much more to do?" I ask Andy. He looks so tired—his hair stuck on end where he's been ruffling it, his eyes sunken and dark. The light in here doesn't help. I click on a lamp.

He shrugs. "Just an hour or so."

He works from home most days, only goes into the office when necessary or if he feels like it. It's his company after all, so he gets to choose.

I turn to go. Beau has already taken off, running upstairs to start the bath.

"Wait a sec." Andy taps a computer key, then moves stiffly toward me. "Sorry about Saffron." He draws me to him, my head reaching the middle of his breastbone. I sigh, inhaling the comforting scent of stale cologne on his sweater.

"It's fine…really." My mind moves to Beau. I don't like him running the water on his own. "Tea will be on the table for six," I call over my shoulder, and then I'm gone, bounding up the stairs.

Beau has steamed up the bathroom. He's pouring in bubble bath as though we have an endless supply and has emptied his entire plastic bucket into the water. There are animals and Lego everywhere, bobbing in a primary-colored stew. I crouch down to undress him, something crunching in my pocket, and I remember then: the letter.

I set it on the windowsill and help Beau into the bath. And then I sit down on the closed toilet seat to open the envelope. It'll be from Surina, my sister's little girl. She's always sending me adorable notes like this. The day she grows up and stops will be a sad one.

As I read the note, I'm so certain it's from Surina I don't even absorb the words. I'm still wondering why she's writing like this.

Then I start to skim-read, racing ahead. Everything's getting confused and a strange dislocation seems to be happening, as though I'm watching myself and Beau from a great height.

"Mummy, look!" He's standing up, pouring water from a cup in a torrent, droplets spraying over the side of the bath.

I read the letter again, slower this time. I don't know who any of these people are. I've never heard of them. The blood rushes to my ears, making them buzz so loudly I can't hear Beau's water cascading. I grip the towel rail and the floor tiles start to shimmer beneath me: a black-and-white chessboard.

The bathroom handle turns then, making me jump, as Andy enters the room. Hastily, I crumple the letter into my tunic pocket.

"Thought I'd finish early and help with the bath, so you can—" He breaks off, looking at me in concern. "What's wrong?"

"Just Saffron," I say, catching my breath.

"I *knew* it would be bothering you." He holds open the door, ushering me out. "Go. I'll see to Beau. Get yourself a cup of tea, and then we'll make dinner together."

"Okay." I hope I don't sound as unresponsive as I feel. Leaving, I glance back at Andy, who is carefully crafting Beau a large bubble beard.

Downstairs in the kitchen, I pull a bottle of vodka out of the freezer and pour myself a tumbler full, staring at the butterfly tattoo on my wrist.

I take the letter from my pocket, smoothing it flat on the table, thinking for a few minutes, and then my mind is made up. I don't know what kind of sick person would write a thing like this, but it can't stay here. Creeping through to Andy's study, I feed the letter into the shredder, which gives a conspiratorial whir as it swallows it whole.

STEPHANIE

"Oh my God! Steffie *Chivers*?"

I lower my reading glasses as I look up. A woman is staring at me over the reception desk, out of breath from taking the stairs.

"I don't believe it! You haven't aged at *all*!" She hitches up her leggings with a wiggle. "We were at school together—Shelley Fricker...used to have long hair?"

I gaze at her, pursing my lips.

She smiles. "Don't you remember me, Stef?"

No, I don't. Leave me alone.

The door to the consultation room opens and one of our new specialist endodontists appears, talking to his client—a tall lady in a beautiful rose trench coat.

"Do you have an appointment?" I ask Shelley Fricker.

She gapes at me in surprise, denied the expected Midsomer Norton camaraderie. A poky town ten miles away, everyone knows each other's business.

"Yep, two o'clock," she replies. "Gotta get in and out quick to pick up the kids. You got kids, Steffie? You don't look like you do, mind. But then you always were immaculate, like a Barbie doll."

Her voice is so loud, everyone in the waiting room is looking at us. I'm embarrassed; this is *the Circus*—a ring of historic town houses, a renowned masterpiece of Georgian architecture—not a fish market.

I stare at the screen, pretending to be looking for her booking in the system, even though it's right in front of me. "Ah. Yes. Please take a seat. Dr. Fitzpatrick will be right with you."

She leans over the counter toward me. "I've never been in a building at the Circus before. Fancy, innit? Makes the dentists down Norton look a right dump! You worked here long, then, Stef?" She rubs her nose vigorously with the palm of her hand as though it's itching.

We get National Health Service referrals from time to time; that's why she's here. If I ignore her, she'll soon get the message.

I keep my eyes on the screen. The endodontist is heading back to his room, smiling at me. I return the gesture fleetingly, in case Shelley Fricker thinks it's for her. She's waiting for an answer to her question. Thankfully, the phone rings and I turn away. "Hello, Chappell and Black. How can I help?"

When I hang up, she's still there, rubbing her nose. "You turned fifty yet? I did, last month... I honestly can't believe it—you look *exactly* the same, Steffie!"

I'm not Steffie. No one calls me that anymore. I'm not Chivers either. I'm Brooke.

Standing up, I smooth my skirt flat, tugging my cardigan straight.

The new endodontist has reappeared from his consulting room and is handing me a client file. I take it with a little nod and go to the filing cabinet, ensuring that Shelley notices my elegance. Maybe then she'll realize we're not from the same drawer after all.

I take longer than usual with the paperwork, running my tongue discreetly over my teeth. I always wear a red lipstick, and black clothes more often than not. I don't like to stand out, but nor do I like to be dismissed.

All of which Shelley will have taken in. And sure enough, when I turn around, she's moved away, hovering in the corner by the fish tank.

I sit back down at my keyboard, acrylic nails tapping soothingly as I type. I love working here, where everything is clean and orderly. I've been Chappell and Black's main dental receptionist for ten years, and in all that time, I've never seen anyone from school…until now.

It feels as though someone's outed me, but I'm not sure from where or what. The thought troubles me, and then I'm distracted by Shelley, who's going into the treatment room.

As she hitches her leggings again, she glances sideways at me, grinning as though we've both been given after-school detention.

I look away.

———

I'm listening to the stereo on low as I wait for Georgia. I like old soul—Marvin Gaye, Otis Redding, Gladys Knight—back when things were graceful, dignified. I'm the first to admit that I'm old-fashioned. I overheard my sister-in-law telling someone at my wedding to Dan that I looked like an eighties throwback. I could have killed her for saying that, but I never let on that I heard. Besides, she got it wrong. If anything, I'm a sixties girl.

I tap my nail on the wheel to a Randy Crawford song, watching the girls approaching down the school driveway, muddy legged, hockey sticks over shoulders. True to form, Georgia's last, looking at her phone, not concentrating on where she's going. She has splashed through two puddles already and has a giant leaf stuck to her sock.

She doesn't look up until she's right on top of the car, checking she's not getting into the wrong one.

"Hello, darling," I say.

She chucks her sports bag and rucksack onto the back seat and clambers in beside me, smelling of cold air and perspiration.

"Did you have a nice day?" I start the engine and pull away. I'm a slow driver. I can't understand people wanting to dash around like maniacs. It's so stressful, and stress is so aging. I make a conscious effort not to encourage wrinkles and don't even laugh unless something is really funny, which isn't often in the normal run of things.

"Whatever," Georgia says into her collar, slumping in her seat.

"Sit up straight, please." I turn on the windscreen wipers as a handful of rain hits the screen.

"Why? Not as if it matters."

"What doesn't?" I'm not sure what she's referring to.

"Me sitting up straight. I'm in the car. I'm tired. It's only me and you. Who the hell cares?"

I gaze at the rain on the windscreen, watching the wipers go back and forth. "I care. Posture's important."

"Oh, *right*." She stares at her phone, her face glowing ice-blue. "The Queen has spoken."

Silently, I count to ten. She's thirteen, so I'm trying to be understanding.

I hated being thirteen. I started my period that year and never told anyone at home. My mother would have cried at the extra expense. Instead, I stole sanitary pads from my sister's room, and when she ran out, I used toilet paper.

"Do you have much homework?" The traffic is moving, at last. I turn down the stereo to hear her answer.

"Fuck knows."

My mouth falls open. I don't know how to respond. I've never heard her swear before. "Georgia…"

"Don't start." She turns away, putting as much of her back to me as her seat belt will allow. "And do we have to listen to this crap?"

I turn off the radio obligingly, and we travel the rest of the way in silence.

Parking the car outside our garage, I leave Georgia to sort herself out and assemble her things, a memory suddenly appearing as I approach the house.

I'm in the school toilets. There is blood in my knickers and I'm petrified, trying to breathe.

There's a voice on the other side of the door, telling me that everything's all right. A huge sanitary pad snakes along the floor, underneath the cubicle, edging toward me. It's gathering dust on that dirty floor, but still, I'm glad to see it and I say thank you.

Don't mention it, Stef. Anytime. We're all in the same boat, eh?

That was Shelley Fricker.

It's dark in the hallway. I'm always the first one home. Dan won't be here for an hour, enough time for me to clear up and get the dinner ready for when he gets in.

I wait to see if Georgia's coming inside, but she's still in the car, looking at her phone. I leave the front door ajar and turn on the table lamp. There's a cluster of post on the mat, which I take through to the kitchen.

I always do the same thing each night: pour a small gin and tonic, and rest before having to deal with my two eldest girls and Dan. They all come home in a noisy rush. Without my quiet time, I don't think I could face them.

Georgia's the only one who knows about this—gives me space and respects it as though it's a church service with candles and prayers. She may be going through a difficult phase, but she's still my girl at heart.

I fix my drink and pry off my heels as I sit at the kitchen table, tutting at the amount of junk mail. I almost don't spot the little envelope nestled between pizza flyers.

Using my thumbnail, I tear it open. As I begin to read, the front door slams; Georgia has come inside at last.

I listen. She's stomping upstairs. Turning back to the letter, I sip my G&T. I'm only halfway through when my skin starts to goose bump.

What on earth is this? I stare at the signature. I don't know a Holly Waite, nor any of the other names. What does this have to do with me? If Dan were to see this, he'd hit the roof.

Suddenly the front door slams again, making me jump. "Hello?" Dan calls out. "Stephanie?"

Panicking, I hurry to the cupboard, reaching for my mother's old cocoa tin. Dented, worthless, it was one of the few personal items I kept when she died. She used to hide things from my father inside the tin.

I'm just shutting the cupboard, when Dan enters the room. "Hello, darling," I say. "I wasn't expecting you home yet."

He approaches, his hair spiky and hard with day-old grooming clay, raindrops trembling on his coat. "I said I'd be back before six."

"Did you?"

"Don't you ever listen to me?" He says this jokily, almost as a whisper. Often, his voice is so quiet I have to stop what I'm doing to hear him.

As he kisses me, I picture the letter inside the tin, but can't say how I feel about it. I always need a long time to think, even about small things like what to wear or cook.

Breaking away, he tosses his smoothie container into the sink. Every morning, he blends a blueberry-and-hemp smoothie—a green concoction with kale and ginger that makes Georgia roll her eyes and imitate a gagging motion.

"Did you have a good day?" I ask.

"Yep." He smiles. "Sold the new Panamera Porsche."

"Oh, well done!"

"I knew I was—" He breaks off, scowling up at the ceiling.

"For Christ's sake." Georgia's music is blaring, a signal that she knows quiet time is over with the return of her father. Sometimes I think she does it purely to aggravate him. Their relationship is very much a work in progress. "What the hell...?" He leaves the room, coat fanning behind him, feet pounding up the stairs.

I hope a fight doesn't erupt. There always seems to be someone shouting in this house, and it's never me.

Finishing my drink in one go, I start preparing dinner, thinking again of the letter inside the tin. No one will ever find it there; the most humble domestic items are always overlooked, especially by men. No wonder witches flew on brooms. Growing up, my mother's cocoa tin felt magical to me—a surprise weapon of sorts, an unlikely source of power. The secrets that went inside there never came out.

JESS

I'm normally the first one up, but this morning at five o'clock there are no other contenders. I've barely slept and my eyes feel gritty. Reaching in the dark for my dressing gown, I sneak as quietly as I can into the hallway and down the stairs. When the girls were babies, I had to retreat silently after night feeds without their hearing me or they would cry out, knowing I had left them. I know every creaking floorboard in our house and can navigate my way like a criminal.

Familiarity makes crime easier to commit. I read once that 90 percent of victims knew their rapist prior to the offense. Does that mean that Max knew Nicola Waite?

It's the question I've been asking myself all night, so much so that I was worried I'd say it out loud.

In the kitchen, I shut the door and then, as an extra precaution, push a chair in front of it.

I start the laptop to give it time to warm up and make a coffee while I wait, taking the letter from my bag and reading it through again, this time my eye lingering not on Max's name but on *pregnant* and *father*.

I raise the window blind. The garden is glowing as the sun

rises, berry-purple clouds above the chimney tops. Autumn's my favorite season, but I've a feeling I'm not going to enjoy this one.

I search for Priyanka Lawley first, the laptop whirring wearily. You'd think it would be easy to find people these days, what with privacy being dead, but that's not the case. The only people who are easy to find are those who want to be found.

The laptop's still whirring, waking up. I sip my coffee, nibble my fingernails.

So, does Max know Nicola Waite? If I said her name, would he panic, drop whatever he was holding, the blood draining from his face?

If he knows her, then he must know who Holly is, or was. What if he changed his mind about helping Nicola with the pregnancy and decided to be involved, maybe behind the scenes—checks in the post, that sort of thing? He's a nice guy, isn't he? If something went horribly wrong that night at the Montague Club, perhaps because of a misinterpretation or accident of some kind, he'd have tried his best to make it good… wouldn't he?

The search results appear. Priyanka Lawley isn't an easy find. There are several LinkedIn entries, which I can't get into, and a YouTube page for someone in North Carolina. I doubt that's her.

I try Stephanie Brooke instead.

There's so many of them, she could be anyone. I explore the top entries, but none of them are Bath-based.

I tap my teeth together, thinking. And then I type: *Nicola Waite, Bath, UK.*

Her name's popular, especially on Facebook. I check out a few of the searches but they're too young for it to be the Nicola Waite from the letter, who must have been at least in her forties when she died.

I delete the history, close the laptop, hide the letter in my bag again and sit all hunched, taut, just the way you're not supposed to sit if you don't want to become a stiff old lady.

There's not much to go on. The only thing I can really do is show up at the addresses given in the letter. Do I have the guts to do that? There's only one way to find out.

When Max gets up, I'll ask him to drop the girls to school. I'll make up something about being needed at work extra early. He's good like that—always willing to put himself out to give a helping hand.

Ironically, it's exactly this kind of supportiveness I'll be counting on to help me determine whether he's a rapist with a skill for concealment that enabled him to keep his past hidden for the past sixteen years of our otherwise happy marriage.

———

It's a nice house, I'll give them that. *Priyanka Lawley. 32 Walden Way, High Lane, Bath.*

The letter is in my coat. I know where it is at all times. Not like my car keys or phone or specs. This letter is like carrying a burning coal in my pocket. You'll never forget it's there.

I think about memory a lot, since my mum became ill. Just seeing her, so vague and lost, makes me wonder whether it matters who or what we remember. Living in the now is supposed to be more important, although Mum doesn't really have that going for her either.

Turning off the car engine, I swivel in my seat to look at 32 Walden Way.

It's a typical Victorian row house, with no front garden to speak of, nor back. I know so because Poppy's friend lives on the parallel road. The street is steep and narrow, with cars parked on both sides. Once you get started on that uphill run, you have to really put your foot down to avoid meeting another car. The place must be full of speeders, like balls on a bowling alley.

There's bunting in the garden and those solar light bulb fairy lights that everyone has, plus a blanket box with a puddle on top and a silver birch tree with jam jars hanging from it.

And then I spot the straw yule goat in the window. It's unmistakable, even though it's a mess of straw and red ribbon. Eva and Poppy made the same mess, except that theirs didn't stand the test of time. Maybe this one won't either. Maybe it's not even a year old, made only last Christmas by someone small.

Something about that makes me very sad. It's not just the fact that there's a child indoors, maybe more than one. It's the fact that our children have passed the same way before. And now because of the letter in my pocket, our lives are crossing again.

Suddenly, the front door opens and I slope down in my seat. Someone's coming out: a woman and child. I sink lower.

They're getting into the car outside the house. Out of the corner of my eye, I watch as the woman bends to fasten the child's seat belt, her back to me. I take in the green parka coat, the pink hair, the Doc Marten boots, and then she's facing my way and fear squeezes my chest.

They take off down the hill. I follow them, allowing a car to come between us. I don't need to tailgate them. I know where they're going.

————

I almost cry out at the sight of Tadpoles, an old church turned community center at the end of a road I have no need to go to anymore, but that was part of my life for six years. The car park's always full of leaves and acorns, squirrels bounding along the walls. I pull in tentatively, hoping no one recognizes me; or worse, doesn't. I don't want anyone to ask me what I'm doing hanging around here. I'm not sure I can answer that myself.

The woman in the parka with the pink hair is over by the wooden fence, saying goodbye to her little boy. She squats down to talk to him—unconcerned about her coat getting wet or dirty—and hugs him, his face disappearing. Then she jumps up, ruffles his hair, and off he goes. She's chatting to someone much taller than her. And then she's laughing with another mum. I don't remember it being that sociable here, or my being sociable, for that matter.

She doesn't hang around. She's already on her way back to the car, checking her phone, waving her keys, still laughing about something.

She doesn't look like someone who got the same letter as me. I can't laugh like that since reading it. I think my face would crack.

Do I have the wrong person?

I wait for another car to pull away and then I jump out, following her across the car park to the Audi by the wall. The roof is already covered in leaves and she's only been there five minutes.

"Excuse me," I call out.

She's opening the car door, but turns, smile at the ready. Her hair is short, tucked behind her ear on one side and longer on the other. Dusky pink, her roots are black and gray. "All right, me duck?"

The Midlands accent throws me, and the overfamiliarity. I could be anyone.

I can't think straight. I'm distracted by her eyes; they're indigo. "Hi. I…"

"Sorry. Gotta shoot or I'll be late. Catch you later." She's turning away, getting into her car. There's a heap of exercise books on the passenger seat. Teacher.

I knock on the window, wait for her to lower it. "Are you Priyanka Lawley?"

"Yep, that's right." The gears crunch as she finds reverse. She has a butterfly tattoo on her wrist and a nose stud that gleams as the light hits it.

I don't know what I'm doing—what to say. My phone's ringing in my bag. I should answer, but I can't let her go. That's all I know.

"I need to talk to you." I glance over my shoulder as a dad

comes up behind me, getting into the next car. I lower my voice. "It's important."

Her expression darkens. "What do you want?" she says, turning off the ignition.

My heart's pounding so hard, so fast. My phone stops ringing. For a moment, everything's silent. No cars moving. No parents hurrying. Just us.

I force myself to focus. "I'm Jess Jackson. I got a letter about my husband. I think you got one too." This sounds like a question, but it isn't. I know she got the letter because she can't even look at me. She's clamping her hands between her knees, staring ahead. She's wearing a flowery dress and leggings. The laces in her boots are neon. All around her, on the seats, the floor, the side pockets, are sweet wrappers, coffee cartons, plastic toys. The detritus of an ordinary life with ordinary concerns—like I used to have.

"I need to go," she says quickly and starts the engine again, the cluster of key charms jangling in her haste.

"Please. Wait!" I call after her, but she's pulling away.

As she leaves, I feel something troubling shifting inside me, slowly surfacing, a buried relic rising. It was so deep, I didn't even know it was there.

I don't know what it means. I'm too busy watching her car turning the corner. I remember then that I'm on my way to meet with a new investor. I have to get going too.

Following in her wake, I'm clamping my teeth so hard as I drive, my jaw aches.

The traffic's heavy through town, and the sun is harsh on the fancy golden tarmac as I pull into Moon & Co.'s courtyard car park. Going into the office, I take off my puffer jacket, wondering what Priyanka Lawley must have thought of me in my boyish clothes, stalking her. She didn't ask me how I knew she'd be there. That would have been the first thing I'd have wanted to know, especially outside a day care.

It doesn't really matter what she thinks. The most important thing is finding out what Max did or didn't do. If she wants to pretend nothing's wrong or has changed, that's her choice. Everyone's going to respond differently, in their own way. I appreciate that. But she's lucky I didn't break the door down at her house and push the letter into her husband's face and ask him about it right there and then.

Max is lucky I haven't done that to him too. I'd do it, you know. The way I feel right now, I'm capable of that and more.

Sitting down at my desk, I glare at the picture of Max and our girls. I've not even thought about that—about his relationship with them, about what that means. How can I think about that yet?

Oh, perfect. My colleague—bland, kind old Mary—is on her way over. She's going to ask me if I'm okay, and I'm going to have to lie and fake it because that's what civilized people do at work.

Max has done this. *He's* put me in this awful situation... But Mary doesn't say that at all. She's going to the potted rubber plant in the corner to water it.

I click through my emails. They're a blur. I can't concentrate with the family photo beside me. Checking that no one's watching, I open my top drawer and slide the picture inside, facedown.

I don't want to look at him until I know how I'm supposed to feel, and the truth is the only thing that's going to help me decide that. Seems clear to me what I have to do, then: find it.

PRIYANKA

I don't let myself think about her until late in the afternoon. I have learned over time to put on different hats, compartmentalize. When you teach, lines and boundaries are the most important things. You can look attractive, but you can't flirt. You can be friendly, but can't be friends. You can comfort, but can't touch. You keep what's in here very much apart from what's out there.

During afternoon break, I have a pile of books to mark, so instead of going to the staffroom in search of caffeine and someone to chat to, I find a quiet classroom and sit in a pool of sunshine, closing my eyes for a moment. And that's when I allow myself to think of her.

Pale, thin-lipped. I guessed who she was the minute she appeared—knew that her energy was out of place in the Tadpoles car park. She was there because of the letter, a real flesh-and-blood person manifesting from the ink of those dreadful words. I should have known that an accusation like that wasn't going to die in the shredder.

I didn't like leaving her there, as though she were a wounded bird about to be crushed by tires. She looked distraught, unhinged even, and I was worried that she might follow me to school. So I was relieved to get to St. Saviour's without glimpsing her in my rearview mirror.

I didn't sleep last night, but couldn't let her know that. She wanted an acknowledgment—a small nod, or a huge breakdown—that we were both feeling the same thing: shock, fear. And I'd have liked to have given her what she needed; a moment of my time, the promise of a text message, at least. Yet I sensed that even eye contact would have sparked something I wouldn't have been able to handle.

I'm sorry if something traumatic or catastrophic may or may not have happened thirty years ago, but I care more about what's happening now, about what I could lose.

We're complete strangers. I saw her glance at my butterfly tattoo, trying to get my measure. She doesn't know who I am. She doesn't know that I will do anything to protect Andy. I don't believe he's capable of doing what the letter said he did, but I know that allegations like this ruin lives. I did the right thing by destroying it.

Great. Now the bell's ringing and I haven't marked a single book.

I gather my things and go along to C4, where I'm teaching next. It's PSHE for the last period of the day, always a challenge. And it's only as I sit down and open my desk planner that I realize that today—of all days—the lesson is on consent.

––––––––

The boys don't want to take lessons in Personal, Social, Health and Economic education. Well, not the academic ones or those with pushy parents. There's no exam, for a start. We don't even get a table at parents' evening. Even with RPE, which does have an exam, no one wants to visit my table, unless they feel sorry for me or there's a queue for math. We don't prioritize ethics, values or personal well-being as a society. I'd say it was a

Western thing, but my parents—Sikh Indians, originating from
Punjab—are just as bad. My mother wept when I chose flaky
philosophy for my degree.

There's always a group of boys who enjoy my lessons, though,
bundling in, shouting whassup. These are the boys who aren't
going to be doing exams and see my lessons as a space to be
themselves. They like that the format is mostly discussion-based,
with videos too, and they light up when we talk about violence,
drugs, gangs, anything controversial, bloody. These are the boys
who watch murder documentaries in their spare time, play *Doom
Eternal* on Xbox, fill their heads with the dark stuff. It's part of
my job to try to make them less lit by gore.

I have to lower the blinds because the sun's streaming in and
I need to show them a video. I've seen it so many times, it's not
funny. But the boys will think it is. They always do.

"Miss, what happened to Saffron?"

I'm finding the YouTube file on the laptop. It was made by
the police and talks about wanting a cup of tea as a euphemism
for sex. It's lighthearted. Maybe too much so. It doesn't take
much to make fourteen-year-olds laugh at sex. But then I have
to trust the system, trust that the police and the Department for
Education know what they're doing.

So much of teaching is about toeing the line, trying not to
create ripples. Perhaps that's what being a grown-up is, though,
no matter the profession: having the maturity to accept con-
ditions and infrastructures without complaint. It's what we're
primed to do from an early age, especially women: get on with
it, be quiet.

It's so hard doing anything else. Who has the energy?

"Did Saffron get expelled, Miss?"

"Yes." I've found the video. I stand in my usual spot, perch-
ing on the desk, facing them. "He got enough warnings, and
now he's gone."

There's a cackle of laughter at the back and someone says something that I don't catch and there's more laughter, louder.

I can guess what it's about. Saffron pulled down a girl's bra at a party, took a photo and circulated it among his friends. The girl—St. Saviour's admits girls aged sixteen—was drunk at the time and is the head of geography's daughter.

I see it all here. Perhaps I should say that I hear it all, especially because the boys let down their guards with me. I have to stay impartial but alert.

It was me who reported Saffron. I knew about the photo, knew that he was on his third and final warning and that if I went to the Head, it would result in permanent expulsion. But I had to protect the girl, as well as the school.

The sad thing is that he comes from a good home. Both his parents are solicitors and always make a point of visiting me at the RPE table on parents' evening. Sometimes it amazes me that the people you'd most expect to talk to their kids about accountability and acceptable behavior are the last to do so. I'm not going to judge them, though. Saffron was a complicated character; it takes one to know one. I feel bad for reporting him, but I had no choice.

The boys don't know it was me. I'd like to keep it that way.

"So, listen up. Today, we're going to watch a short video, and then we're going to discuss it. Try to take it seriously, please. Even though it's supposed to be a little bit funny."

"That don't make sense, Miss," one of the boys shouts.

"Just watch it." I'm snippy, irritable. Maybe they notice; maybe they don't. As the video plays, I go to the window and watch as a small boy crosses the yard, late for class. From this angle, he looks like Beau, and I feel too warm suddenly, the sunshine on my face.

I turn back to the class. The boys are sprawled over the desks, elbows out, legs splayed. Some of them are laughing. Most of them are. But there are a few who look overwhelmed, Adam's apples wobbling.

I wonder, not for the first time, what the best age is to talk to boys about sex—about how no means no, no matter the context. Beyond the humor, the light touch, the video makes that very clear. You can be dating someone and no means no. You can be in the middle of having sex and no means no. You can be doing it the night before and no means no.

It always means no. You'd think it would be universally understood, but somehow, it's not.

I think of Saffron, my stomach churning. I reported him, yet I shredded that letter last night.

"Miss, you ever been raped?"

The video is over. I perch on the edge of the desk again and look this particular boy in the eye. He always likes to push the boundaries. "No."

"Sometimes I think that girls want it, but don't wanna look like they want it because they don't wanna be called sluts. Do you think that, Miss?"

"That's an interesting question, and I think you're right in that that's what boys can think. But it's quite clear from the video you've just watched, Ethan, that girls will tell you in lots of ways when they mean no. They'll either verbalize it or they'll show you with their body language."

"What's that look like, then, Miss?" There's some laughter. Ethan is staring at me seriously, fronting it out.

"It looks like someone saying no, Ethan."

I get into the car slowly, all of my energy drained from me. The boys will do that if you let them. I usually don't. But today, they've got to me and I feel as though I can't even drive home.

Yet it's not them. I know it's not. It's the letter.

I'm about to start the engine when I see something on the

windscreen, underneath the wipers. Undoing my seat belt, I grab it, getting back behind the wheel with a sinking feeling.

I stare at the business card, its corners sharp, pricking my fingers.

Jessica Jackson.

Senior Account Handler.

Moon & Co.

I look about the car park, leaves scuttling across the concrete, a French teacher carrying a rucksack packed full of books and Tupperware. I smile at him, pressing the card until it hurts.

She knows where I live; the letter would have told her that. And somehow, she knows where Beau goes to day care, and now where I work. That's what she wants this little white card to tell me.

Pushing it into the pocket of my dress, I drive to Tadpoles, feeling as though someone's sitting on my chest.

Beau is waiting for me by the wooden gate, his cheeks bitten by the cold air. I grab my coat and put it on as I walk toward him, my boots feeling heavier than usual. I look downward, avoiding conversation with the other mums. I'm worried they'll see straight through me—will know that I'm barely keeping it together.

In the car, I try to make an effort for Beau's sake, but the sensation in my chest is getting worse and my breathing feels tight. We sit in silence and he doesn't ask why. Why would he? He's three. He's too busy looking up at the trees and peeling glue from his fingers.

At home, I won't have to face Andy yet. He's in the office today. I can see to Beau, focus on one thing at a time.

Unstrapping Beau from his seat, I carry him up to the house. He plays with my nose stud as I open the door. "Blue eyes today, Mummy," he says, gently touching the spikes of my eyelashes.

I kiss him, my chest feeling lighter. "Yes, my little cherub. Blue eyes today."

"Any more problems with Saffron?" Andy asks, forking his pasta hungrily. He's still wearing his suit, a piece of paper towel tucked into his collar to protect his shirt. He always takes a genuine interest in my day at school, and normally, I enjoy telling him. In return, I know everything about his digital marketing company: his eccentric receptionist, how the ivy threatens to block the light from the windows, the throngs of tourists taking photos of the square, the Turkish deli that delivers his daily pita sandwich.

So many details that we know about each other, insignificant trivia that makes you think you know the person you married.

"Pree?"

"Huh?" I look at him.

"About Saffron."

"Oh. Yes. Well, he's gone and that's it." I nudge Beau's plate away from the edge of the table. He's just upgraded his toddler seat to a proper dining chair. I spend half my life picking up peas from the floor. "End of story."

Andy glances up from his plate. "I just wondered if the parents had got involved. Didn't you say they were solicitors? I thought they might—"

"Nothing they can do. Besides, they should have thought about that before they raised a disgusting boy like him."

I didn't mean to say that. Andy will know something's off.

Sure enough, he lowers his fork, raises an eyebrow. "I thought you liked him?"

I stare at my plate, the farfalle bows seeming huge. "I did. I do. I just don't want to talk about it. What's done is done."

"I'm sorry. It's just that you usually like to chat about these things."

"Well, not this time."

"Okay. Duly noted."

So polite. I don't think I know anyone else who says *duly*. And so considerate. He really will note it too and won't mention Saffron again. It's that easy with him. I tell him what I need and he obliges, not because he's weak or under my thumb, but because he loves me.

How can I think of him as a…a…?

The crushing sensation is back in my chest. I can't eat, can't swallow. Maybe I misread the letter. Maybe he was an innocent bystander, or wasn't even there and it's a case of mistaken identity. Andy's a quiet man with a small social circle. It's very doubtful he was involved. He wears Argyle socks and drinks Earl Grey tea, for goodness' sake.

I gaze at him, guiltily, lovingly. His lips are stained with red wine, another one of those details a wife knows and that I'd try to cover up if we had guests. We look out for each other. That's why I shredded the letter, isn't it? For him? Or was it for me?

He takes another drink of wine, unaware that I'm watching him. His mother once told me that all he ever wanted was to get married and have children. He's so easy to live with, happiest when doing something menial; building a train track with Beau, cooking supper with me. I'm sick with shame for having thought even for a second that he could have been involved in a sexual assault.

I can't even say the *r* word, not even silently. Not in front of Beau, who's trying to compete with Andy as to who can get the most pasta on their fork.

I need some air, some space.

"Excuse me a sec…" I push back my chair.

Out in the hallway, I inhale jerkily, my gaze resting on my phone on the side table. Slipping through to the downstairs bathroom, I rest my back against the cold wall, taking the business card from my pocket.

I key the number into my phone.

18.13 P.M. >
OK. Let's talk.

I listen for the beep of the sent message. Have I done the right thing? I don't know. But I'm used to having people around me to bounce problems off—family at home, colleagues at school. I can't figure this thing out on my own, and she's the only one currently in the frame.

Hiding the card at the bottom of my bag, I wipe my clammy hands on my dress as I return to the dining room.

"Sorry about that." I nudge Beau's plate away from the edge again.

"Everything okay?" Andy has finished eating and is sitting with his hands clasped behind his head, a thoughtful look on his face.

"Yes, everything's fine. It's just been a long day. I'll be glad when it's bedtime."

"Me too," he says, winking cheekily, pouring me another glass of wine. Ordinarily, I'd have found this titillating, but tonight I can barely muster a smile.

It's so temperamental, sexual interplay. One word, one look can alter things dramatically. I've never considered it before, yet it occurs to me then that attraction is just smoke and mirrors.

So fragile, desire can vanish at any moment. And then all you're left with is this dark, empty thing, this doubt.

JESS

"Can't they put themselves to bed?" Max says, as I sit down beside him on the sofa with a heavy sigh. He'll interpret this as my doing too much for the girls, wearing myself out, yet it's him who's weighing me down. I swear I've aged more than the recommended amount today. "They're old enough now." He places his hand on my knee.

"I enjoy tucking them in," I say. "They won't always be here."

"Good. Then it'll be just you and me." He smiles at me flirtatiously.

I can't help it: regardless of the burden I'm bearing, I fancy him. And I like him this way most of all—tracksuit bottoms and sweater, contact lenses removed, glasses in their place. He smells of home.

He's a very active guy, running a business, going to the gym, ferrying the girls about. And then he stops, sheds his suit and settles onto the sofa, becoming someone you'd think never left the house. I've never known a man who watches so much TV. He's a person of extremes: either full-on, or full-off.

I wonder suddenly whether his niceness has a flip side too.

He turns to kiss me, touching my chin to keep me in place.

For all his strength, he's very gentle and his kisses can melt me. After sixteen years of marriage, you're not supposed to still crave your spouse, but he can just look at me and I want to go to bed with him. The fact that he's so dynamic at work, has so much energy as a dad and loves socializing too, only makes me want him more when he's on downtime. I don't see it as getting the leftovers, but the real him, the restful one who no one else sees.

"What's wrong?" he asks, frowning.

"Nothing."

I'm thinking about the other side of him, the busy man. I used to fret that his colleagues—ambitious millennials with discreet tattoos—would fancy him as much as I did. They would notice the muscles, the way he helped them when the photocopier was jammed, so hands-on, amiable. But I never thought for one moment that it was anything other than Max being Max. I never worried that he might cheat, because he's always been such a good guy.

Hasn't he?

And why would that accusation make him a cheater anyway? It's not the same thing.

I pull away from him, straightening my top. "Eva said Charlotte's been getting at her again."

He picks up the remote control, mutes the TV. "Why? What's she done now?"

"Keeps flirting with a boy—the one Eva likes."

"Oh." He turns the volume back on, talks over it. "Tell her to ignore it. They're their own worst enemies, teenage girls."

"Really? How so?" I try not to have a tone in my voice, but it's almost impossible.

He glances at me. "Well, you know, fighting over boys. My sisters were a nightmare. I used to go to the club, just to get away from them."

I stare at him, my cheeks burning, but his eyes are on the TV.

I wasn't prepared for a mention of the club, and my immediate reaction is to jump up and leave the room.

"Where you going?" he calls after me.

"To make a cup of tea. Would you like one?"

"Yeah, go on, then."

Standing with my hands against the counter, I bend my head, looking at the kitchen floor. I don't know how long I can keep this up. It's only been twenty-four hours, and I'm already struggling.

I used to think it was adorable that Max had three older sisters—that it was the reason he was so attentive and helpful. But now I'm wondering if it meant he was outnumbered, forced to live a separate life at the Montague Club, where boys could be boys...

And of course...he's surrounded by females here too.

I've no idea how to face him with all this going around my head. I'm terrible at hiding things. I can't stay here like this, though. I need to make a show of acting normally.

Going to the sink, I run the water, filling the kettle.

There's something else too: that thing deep inside me that Priyanka Lawley unearthed in the day care car park... I've thought about it and it's something I'm ashamed of, even though I can't help it.

I have this weird compulsion to get at the truth in people, watch them squirm. I didn't even know I did it until I met Max, and he introduced me to nice couples at dinner parties where the only requirement was being as fake as you could possibly be.

I'd keep it together during the first few drinks, but by the time dessert arrived, I'd be asking that smug man if his neighbors knew about his marijuana greenhouse. Or expressing sympathy for the breakdown of that uptight woman's marriage who smiled at her husband throughout dinner even though we all knew about his hard-core porn addiction.

I didn't do it to hurt them. It was just my reaction to being put in a situation where people were so artificial. I didn't ask them to say anything I wasn't prepared to say about myself. I have no problem with the truth. Why's it such a big deal? Often, though, we didn't get invited back.

That woman whose marital problems I inquired about...we never heard from her again. And that was when Max told me that I was an embarrassment, demanding the truth from people who didn't want to tell it.

Just because my parents played games, he ventured... And then I blew up at him, outraged. What did my parents have to do with it? But I knew he was right. They had everything to do with it.

As the kettle clicks off, I sneak my phone out of my cardigan pocket and reread the text from Priyanka. It had to be her, although there was no name.

I didn't mean to scare her with my business card, but I had to do something. I was going crazy at work and then it came to me: there was an emblem on the pile of books in her car. St. Saviour's school. So, during lunch I drove there, found her Audi, left her my card.

It was her decision to contact me. She didn't have to, but I'm glad she did. Now I'm going to have to do the same thing with Stephanie Brooke.

"Would you like a biscuit?" I call to Max.

No answer. I hover in the doorway of the living room, repeat the question. "Biscuit, Max?"

"Hmm. Please." He's frowning at the TV, picking the skin around his fingernails, lost in the program.

If he did what that letter says he did, I'm not going to be able to take it. It'll break my heart. So why do this? Why not leave it alone? What's wrong with me?

It's because of my obsession with outing the truth. It's come back to bite me in the worst possible way. It's karma for making all those people squirm through dinner. It's the universe telling me that if you want to play with the big guns—Truth, Integrity—then you're going to have to take it yourself.

I always thought I did know how to take it, but maybe I don't.

Back in the kitchen, I don't want tea anymore. Instead, I take my phone into the bathroom since it's the only room with a lock. Doing a search for *historical rape allegations*, I hold my breath, no idea what I'll find.

The Crown Prosecution Service.

A feature entitled *He Thinks He's Got Away.*

Men accused or on trial.

Denials, false accusations.

It's never-ending. I keep scrolling down—article after article about cases being dropped, prosecution rates falling. It was her word against his; he said he didn't do it. Lack of evidence. One in seventy chance of prosecution.

I'll admit I'm surprised how bad it is. It's not something I know much about because I've never been on the receiving end of any problems, maybe because I look like I can handle myself. Do abusers target a type, or is it just anyone and it's the luck of the draw whether it's you?

And what about the offenders? Are they a type too, or do some men get caught up in something against their better judgment, maybe even without realizing?

I'm hoping that's Max, that he did something by mistake. That could happen, couldn't it?

But could you actually *rape* someone without knowing it?

"Jess?" I freeze; he's come looking for me. "What are you doing? I thought we were going to watch that program, the one with the woman with the hair?"

When you're close, you can give descriptions like this.

"On my way," I call, making a show of running the tap, while deleting the searches on my phone, grateful for the door between us.

"Don't be long," he says, moving away.

I can't be doing this while he's here. It's too much. I'll have to look things up at work, where there's some space between us.

Finally making the tea, I think about the first time I ever saw him. We were in a nightclub that's since shut down, but used to be the place to be. I hadn't lived in Bath long, didn't know many people, so was taking it all in. The dance floor was circular, sunken, with railings all around that men leaned over, ogling the women as they danced. Cattle market with chandeliers.

I was having a break from dancing, when I spotted him on the opposite side of the railings. He was wearing a white shirt glowing in the UV lights, and even then, he had big arms—well before *Love Island*. He was with a group of lads, all of whom he was shorter than, yet I looked only at him.

Our eyes met and that was it. I knew I wanted to be with him for the rest of my life.

I return to the living room, sitting on the sofa again. "You're cold," Max says, rubbing my hands. And then he pulls a blanket over me, carefully tucking it in around me. "There you go, baby."

Baby may sound lame to you. It sounds lame to me too. My dad would laugh his head off. But it's what Max has always called me and I've grown to like it. It makes me feel precious. He's always taken good care of me—knew I wasn't as tough as I seemed.

Trying to watch TV, I think again of the first time we met. Maybe Andrew Lawley and Daniel Brooke were there too that night and I didn't pay attention. Maybe the truth was there for everyone to see right from the start, but no one looked for it.

"Warmed up yet?" he asks.

I lean my head against his shoulder. "Yes," I lie.

I'm so cold. This is what fear feels like. Your blood creeps about slowly, sloshing, as though full of ice, dulling your mind.

One thing I'm sure about: I'm not going to be able to keep this up for long.

STEPHANIE

I wake to the sound of grunting, a headache crushing my temples. Dan is on the floor, exercising, teeth gritted, hair glowing in the early sunlight. He knows I'm awake, watching him, but makes no acknowledgment of it. If the house were on fire, he'd complete his sit-ups.

The letter in the cocoa tin flashes through my mind, and I know it's the cause of my headache. I couldn't concentrate at work yesterday, even though I'm certain the girl is making it up. Maybe she's after money; Dan does very well for himself.

Yet then I recall that she was on her deathbed, allegedly.

The whole thing is in very bad taste, and I resent the space it's taking up inside my head. It's difficult enough to focus as it is. My doctor says I have menopausal brain fog, but doesn't advise HRT because my mother died of breast cancer aged thirty-nine.

So, I'm learning to live with the fog. And the letter is going to have to stay in the tin, out of harm's way. I could destroy it, but I feel that would be worse, taking it out of my hands. This way, I have a measure of control, however small.

I can imagine Dan's reaction to an accusation like that. His eyes would bulge, the pressure building like a saucepan of boiling water rattling its lid. I've only seen him like that a few times, but always in response to his character being questioned. His brother accusing him of trying to influence their parents' will. A neighbor challenging him on the boundaries of our laurel hedges. Once, a customer keyed his car because they thought he'd cheated them on a Mercedes deal. I thought he was going to have a heart attack with moral outrage, understandably so. There's nothing worse than being wrongly accused.

"You okay?" He pauses, panting, sweat gleaming on his forehead.

"Just a bit stiff." I make a show of circling my neck but stop when I see stars.

"Well, you know what'll fix that..." He's grunting again, wincing.

I make my way through to the en suite to run a bath. Dan thinks I'm in a vicious circle of not doing enough exercise, which in turn makes me tired. When we met fifteen years ago, I gave it a go, bought a tracksuit and ran along the canal with him. I hated every minute of it, and as soon as I fell pregnant with Georgia, the tracksuit went to charity.

"Seriously," he calls after me, "you're not moving enough. It's bad for you."

I'm sure he means well, but no one my side of fifty wants to hear this first thing in the morning. I flash him a compliant smile, a look I've perfected, and then close the door.

I leave it unlocked, just in case. Dan won't come in—he'll be off for a run shortly—but Rosie likes to join me once he's left, sitting on the edge of the bath, dipping her hands in the bubbles. Sometimes I wonder why I live in a house where people come to see me individually, like a strange one-man show with a single actor playing all the parts, but the answer always escapes me.

I'm gazing listlessly at the fluffy mat, waiting for the bath to fill, when Dan surprises me, poking his head around the door. "I'm off out," he says, strapping on his phone armband.

"Okay." I nod.

"You shouldn't let her…" he says so quietly, I can barely hear him above the running water.

"Pardon?"

He raises his voice a smidgen. "You shouldn't let her come in here."

"Who?" I ask, playing dumb. This isn't the first time we've had this conversation.

"Rosie." He can't say her name without looking vexed. She's been acting out a lot lately and is seeing a counselor for her anger, at his suggestion. "This is your precious me time. She shouldn't be in here with you."

I'd like to tell him that I disagree, that it doesn't bother me, but instead I smile. "I'll lock the door. Don't worry."

He returns my smile. "Good." And then leaves, his footsteps thumping the floorboards, the bedroom door closing.

I relax my shoulders, exhaling.

Poor Rosie. I'm not going to lock her out. Dan doesn't see the side of her that I see. In all honesty, she doesn't show her sweet side to me much either. Yet of my three girls, she's the one I can still picture as a child, even though she's twenty-one. I can see her pigtails, and the way her eyes used to disappear when she laughed. She was only two when her dad left, leaving a hole in her world.

I test the temperature of the bath, adding more hot water. We don't hear from her father anymore, aside from sporadic Christmas cards. He cheated on me—on us—so it's best that he's not in our lives. I've found it hard to forgive him, but I keep that to myself. Bitter looks ugly when unwrapped.

Vivian is my eldest girl; twenty-three and very like me; she doesn't speak her thoughts out loud. But Rosie is emotional, temperamental. I'm hoping the counselor will help, yet I suspect that to a certain extent she's going to have to work things out for herself.

Dan's always nice to her, face-to-face, saving his worst comments for our private discussions. She can't really complain; he's been good to her and Vivian. I've never noticed any difference between the way he treats them and their younger sister. If anything, he's harder on his own flesh and blood. He and Georgia are going through a tricky patch, but every teenager pushes the boundaries. They just need to give it time.

My body aches as I lower myself into the hot water. It's not easy, having a split home. What is it they call it now? *Blended.* It makes us sound like a soup or one of Dan's smoothies.

I soak for fifteen minutes and am thinking about getting out, when the door handle turns and Rosie stumbles in. Rubbing her eyes, she perches on the edge of the bath, running a hand through her tangled hair. She's not what you'd call immaculate, at any time of the day. "No bubbles?"

I shake my head. "I've run out."

She gazes at my body, normally submerged by foam. It probably appears large and pink, under water. Dan likes me to be plucked, trimmed, and I'm suddenly embarrassed. I pick up the loofah, holding it vaguely between my legs as though this is a natural place to put it.

"For fuck's sake, M."

She and Vivian have always called me this; when they were little, I used to wear a sweater with a large *M* on it, working as a waitress to make ends meet. Apparently, it's also ironic, the name of James Bond's boss, who I'm the least likely person to be, in their opinion.

I sit up, drawing my knees to my chest. "Rosie, please. *Language.*"

She shrugs. "Just saying… There's no need to be all coy. I've seen a vagina before."

I stare at her. "Did you have a bad night's sleep?"

"Au contraire. I had an amazing sleep, thank you."

"So, why are you being tetchy?" I reach for my towel. She helps me—hands it to me.

She does that: gives and takes in one breath. It's a skill of hers. "No reason."

I glance at her warily. "Have you been swearing in front of Georgia?"

"No. Why?"

"Because she said the *f* word last night."

"Surprised it took her so long," she says, smirking.

Some people enjoy friction, but I avoid it, having had enough for one lifetime. I'd do anything to lie with my head under the water and not listen to this, but I've already pulled the plug.

"Not everything's about me, M. Sometimes, it's about you."

I pin the towel to me, rubbing the mist from the mirror over the sink, waiting for her to elaborate. I know she's going to.

She folds her arms, watching as I dab toner over my face. "You don't have to do everything he says, you know. You're allowed your own thoughts, your own choices. You don't have to have the perfect bush, the perfect face." She leans against the shower door. "I know it was him who suggested the counseling."

"No, it wasn't. You're wrong."

She laughs. "Yeah, that's right. I'm wrong. It's not him. It's me. Keep telling yourself that. Sounds like a really great plan." And she walks out, slamming the door.

I sigh, reaching for my moisturizer. Dan buys me a divine black rose cream and a face oil, with the combined cost of over three hundred pounds. He looks after us so well. I don't know what Rosie's complaining about. She's got a lot to learn about life.

———

Georgia is the first one to spot her. I wouldn't have noticed. "Who's that?" She points over her shoulder, then looks down at her phone again.

I stop at the traffic lights before answering. "Who?"

"That woman."

My heart wobbles as I look in the rearview mirror. I can just make out a thin face at the wheel behind us. "What are you talking about?"

Georgia tuts, flicks her hair over her shoulders. "She's been following us since home. She was waiting at the end of our road… Seriously, are you even *awake*?"

"Of course." I fix my gaze ahead, running my tongue over my teeth in case my red lipstick has transferred.

Who would be following us? I try to remember the names in the letter. Two of them are dead, I think. So that leaves…the other wives? How many were there—three?

The lights are changing. I drive forward, turning left for Georgia's school. If she's correct, the VW Golf will follow us. "I'm sure you're mistaken," I say.

She's not. The Golf's still behind.

"Maybe you've got a stalker, Mum."

We're outside the school, or as far as we can go without getting wedged. It's very congested. Georgia jumps out. "Ta, Ma."

"Wait," I call, lowering the window.

She turns, frowns in annoyance. "What?"

Don't go. Stay…just in case.

"Nothing. Have a good day, darling."

"Yep." And she's gone.

The VW Golf seems to have disappeared. Back on the main road, I feel calmer, turning up the radio.

Yet as I descend the hill toward the city center, she's suddenly there again in my rearview mirror.

Is she going to follow me to work and make a scene, perhaps in front of my boss? Leonardo is very invested in keeping a calm, professional front at all times, and rightly so.

Would she do that? I don't even know who she is, what she wants.

She stays with me all the way to the car park, where several vehicles come between us. I use the busyness to my advantage, keeping low as I slip from the car and along the sandy path to the exit. There are trees all around. I'm wearing somber colors. She won't see me.

I keep my head down all the way, but just as I'm about to go inside Chappell and Black, I glance back involuntarily, my attention pulled that way. And there she is, on the other side of the Circus, wearing a puffer jacket: a slim middle-aged woman.

I hurry into the building, along the warm corridor, telling myself that if she was going to follow me inside, she wouldn't have stood there, rooted to the spot like that.

———

I'm right. She stays away. My heart bounces every time the reception door opens, but she doesn't appear.

By the afternoon, my headache has gone and I'm feeling better. Leonardo is just showing a client out, when the phone rings. "Good afternoon, Chappell and Black. How can I help?"

"Stephanie Brooke?"

"Yes, speaking." Leonardo is handing me a file. I nod at him.

"My name's Jess Jackson. I got a letter…about our husbands."

Leonardo is waiting to have a word with me, hovering at the counter. I swallow awkwardly. "Do you have an appointment?"

"Oh, you can't talk at the moment?" she says quietly. "That's okay. I understand."

"We should be able to sort something for you next week," I say, pretending to consult the system on my screen.

"Has my number come up?" she asks.

I glance at the monitor. "Yes… How about Wednesday?"

"Good. You've got it, then. Please call me back as soon as you're free. If I don't hear from you in an hour, I'll ring again." And she hangs up.

"Okay. That's lovely. We'll wait to hear from you," I say to the dead ringing tone.

Leonardo draws closer to talk. As might be expected, he has beautiful teeth and is well educated. I was very much in awe of him when I first came here. He was willing to overlook my lack of qualifications—I left school without any—and gave me a chance.

"Could you schedule Mrs. McKenzie for a repeat treatment next Tuesday?" he asks. "And make sure she's the first one in of the day?"

"Of course."

As he retreats, I make a note of the phone number on my monitor, then gaze at the fish tank, wondering what to do. There's no one in reception. I could ring now. If I don't, she'll call back and it could be in front of Leonardo again.

I dial the number. She answers immediately. "That was quick," she says. "Thank you." She has a faint London accent and is talking quietly, maybe for my sake as well as hers.

"What do you want?" I ask.

"Just to talk. Can you meet us?"

"Us?" The reception door is opening. I lower my voice. "I have to go."

"How about Saturday? There's—"

"I can't talk." Thankfully, the client is elderly and is taking his time closing the door, undoing his coat, wiping his nose.

"Meet us on Saturday. Give me your number and I'll text you the details. I know you're frightened. I am too. But it's best we sit down and figure this out together, don't you think?"

I don't know what to think. The client is coming toward me.

This wasn't supposed to happen. My mother's cocoa tin wasn't supposed to let me down—was supposed to make things disappear.

"You'll have more control by showing up, I promise," she adds.

I say my number in a rush, hanging up just as the old man touches the desk.

PRIYANKA

I opt for sterling gray eyes. I don't want to express anything other than my ability to listen, and gray gives nothing away.

"Are you sure you'll be all right?" I crouch down, lacing up my Doc Martens.

"Yep. Got the football pumped and ready," Andy says, like the nonsportsman he is. "We'll be fine, won't we, buddy?" He ruffles Beau's hair, who's going cross-eyed trying to look at a cookie while eating it.

I've told them I'm doing the Christmas shopping, even though it's only the tenth of October. Andy won't question it, though, because he leaves gift buying to me.

"Call me if you need anything." I grab my parka coat and squat to kiss Beau. "Enjoy the park, cutie pie." I go on tiptoes to kiss Andy. "Don't forget to defrost the chicken."

"Will do." Andy's wearing a new hoodie with a line in the middle where it was folded in the packaging. It makes me so sad, that line.

"'Bye, Mummy," Beau says, crumbs cascading.

I hope they don't watch me from the door, but they do. I make a show of being cheerful and waving as I drive away, even though my tummy's doing loop the loops and I can't smile without my mouth wobbling.

I can't believe I'm doing this.

———————

By the time I arrive at Carol's, my mouth is so dry, it makes a clicking sound whenever I open it. This feels like a sign that I should keep it shut.

The café is dingy, down a back alley near the main street. It's the only one of its kind in the city that I know of. Bath isn't known for its greasy spoons. Jess Jackson has chosen well. No one can see inside; the windows are steamed up.

As the door jingles open and the smell of fried onions hits me, I'm more worried about slipping than finding the others. There are dripping coats and brollies everywhere, water dripping on the floor. Staff are shouting orders; fluorescent stars advertising sausage rolls flutter under fans.

It doesn't seem conducive to discreet conversation, and then I notice one of those old-fashioned pointing finger signs and realize there's another floor.

Climbing the narrow stairs, I feel panicky. Near the top, I take a moment. No one can see me. I rest my back against the banister, placing my hand on my racing heart, which I can feel even through my coat.

I can't go in there like this. I must remember what I'm doing, who I am.

I'm neutral. I'm gray.

Jess is sitting alone in the corner, wearing the puffer jacket she wore when she accosted me at Tadpoles. She's not aware of me yet, so I catch her unguarded. She has her arms wrapped around her as though cold; her face is pinched with worry. She looks like she's just lost someone. Maybe she has.

I consider backing away. Then she looks at me and I have

no choice but to approach, wondering whether I'm making the biggest mistake of my life.

She stands to greet me, clutching my wrist in a fumbling way that reminds me of the elderly when they're about to fall. "Priyanka. Thanks for coming."

She smells of fabric conditioner; a comforting scent. I imagine her doing the laundry, getting the shopping, deciding whether frangipani and red fruits will smell nice on their clothes. All these little things that make up a person's life—things that don't matter in the long run.

Taking off my coat, I sit down opposite her, pulling my sleeves over my hands so that she can't see the butterfly tattoo.

She picks up her mug, scrutinizes me. "You've changed your eyes."

"Well done for noticing." I smile broadly, as though she hasn't gone straight for the jugular.

She's still assessing me—doesn't try to disguise it. "I like your nose stud. Is it an emerald?"

"Yes. It's my birthstone."

"Me too! Taurus?"

I shake my head. "Gemini."

"Great." She laughs dryly. "So, I'm stubborn. And you're, what, divided in two? We haven't a hope."

Of doing what?

She takes a sip from the mug. Her nails are bitten so short, the skin looks tender, puffy. "Do you change your hair color too?" she asks.

"Nope. Always pink." I glance nervously around the room. We're the only ones here. There are PVC covers on the tables and spindly mahogany chairs. On the walls are tin pictures of the Roman Baths and the Royal Crescent, and historic photos of people standing outside the front of the café's original building, wearing long aprons. I gaze at one of the women, and she stares back at me in the unblinking way that dead people do.

"Have you been here before?" I ask, for something to say.

"Once. With a client... Don't ask." She smiles, picks at her bun, extracting a currant. I watch as though she's doing brain surgery. "Sorry about the other day, by the way—following you to work. I didn't know what else to do."

"That's okay. I get it."

She gazes at me anxiously just like she did in the car park, as though expecting something from me.

"Is the other person coming?"

"Stephanie..." she replies. "Yes... Hope so, anyway." She picks at the bun again, her shoulders taut, high.

Thankfully, the waitress arrives to break the tension, a teenage girl with a thick plait of hair. I order a cappuccino, then change to a filter coffee and back to a cappuccino, all of which Jess appears to find highly interesting.

And then from behind the waitress, there's a ruffle of movement, the sound of high heels on floorboards. I lean back in my chair to see who's coming.

"Whoops! Sorry!" The waitress turns too quickly, right into the newcomer's path, who looks none too pleased.

Jess stands up to greet her. "Hi, Stephanie. Thanks so much for coming."

Stephanie nods formally. She's not classically beautiful; her nose is turned up and her teeth slightly bucked, yet she has amazing posture and her blond hair is piled into a fussy updo, her lipstick the same shade of red as her coat. I doubt Carol's has seen the like before.

"Hi. I'm Priyanka." I remain seated, unable to stop staring at her.

"Hello." Her eyes brush over me as she sits down, checking the seat for crumbs, touching her hair into place as she settles.

"Would you like a drink?" Jess asks politely.

She seems to consider this a difficult question and takes so long thinking about it that Jess moves on.

"So, obviously this is a very strange situation and none of us want to be here, but I'd just like to get something straight— we've never heard of each other before. Is that right?"

"Yes," I say.

Stephanie's sitting very still and upright. You'd have thought she was here just to take the committee minutes.

"That's what I thought. And that's odd, isn't it? Bath's a small place and our husbands all belong to the Montague Club... Correct?" She looks at us in turn.

We emit sounds of agreement, Stephanie barely moving her lips.

"And what about Holly Waite? Had you heard of her?"

"No." I glance at Stephanie, who shakes her head.

"Well, there we go, then. Our husbands must know each other, yet our paths have never crossed. So that's weird, isn't it?"

No one replies because the waitress has returned with my cappuccino, slopping it everywhere. "Can I get you anything else, ladies?"

We look at Stephanie. "No, thank you," she says quietly.

As the waitress withdraws, Jess takes off her puffer. Her clothes—sporty, colorless—remind me of my students on dress-down day at school.

"So, I don't know about you," she says, "but I've been racking my brains about why this person would have written to us unless there was some truth in it. I mean, why bother?"

"Money?" I suggest.

"But she was dying."

"As far as we know," Stephanie says. "Why would we trust anything she says? How do we even know who she is? She might not be Holly Waite, but someone else entirely."

Her voice is very soft, with a prominent *s* sound that hisses, lingers. Perhaps she's self-conscious about it, so keeps her voice down. Or maybe she's just demure. Could her back be any straighter?

"But why lie about something like that?" Jess asks.

"For all kinds of reasons."

"Really?" Jess folds her arms. "Name one."

Stephanie hesitates. It strikes me that she's not a confident speaker—that her vocabulary might be limited. I see this at school day in, day out. Some people love being put on the spot, challenged; others recoil from it. She doesn't seem articulate, educated, but I wouldn't want to bet on it. People can surprise you.

"Attention… Revenge…" she ventures.

"For what?" Jess sits forward, her cheeks coloring. "Why would she want revenge, unless there were some truth in this?"

Somehow Stephanie manages to sit up even straighter. "Girls lie all the time. I have three daughters. I should know."

I can't comment on that, not having daughters. But Beau lies. It's not exclusive to girls.

"It's almost as though you want this to be true," Stephanie says, gazing into space.

"Of course I don't. But I do think we need to discuss it."

"Do we?" Stephanie touches her hair, runs her tongue over her front teeth.

I watch them both, unable to decide which of them is the more fascinating. I can't help feeling that Jess has some kind of an agenda, and that Stephanie has too, for all her appearance of indifference.

"Don't tell me you're seriously suggesting we should let this go," Jess says. "Pretend we didn't get the letter?"

I keep my eyes downcast. I haven't touched my cappuccino yet. It's sitting in a pool of foam on the saucer.

"Yes, I think that's exactly what we should do," Stephanie says to no one in particular.

Jess is looking at me now. I can feel her eyes boring into me. She wants me to say something, yet I can't. I came here to listen. I'd like to help; my instincts are to take her side, but that could be fatal.

Already, in the space of ten minutes, it's become about sides. I'm always awful at choosing one and tend to see both arguments. You'd think it would be a skill, but it's often a hindrance. My big brother, Jagvir, always says that not having an opinion is a sign of weakness.

"I promise I'm not trying to make trouble," Jess says, putting her hands on her knees, elbows wide. "But I have to be honest with you. I'm not going to be able to look the other way on this. That's not who I am."

I glance at her in admiration. It's not easy to walk into a room and tell everyone who you are—that's if you know the answer to the question in the first place. Yet she's just done it, and I have to applaud her transparency. But I'm still not going to say anything.

I reach for my cappuccino, drawing it quietly closer, hoping no one looks at me.

"So, I think we should find out who Holly Waite was and what she wanted."

"But why?" Stephanie asks.

Jess shifts impatiently in her seat. "So we can decide whether or not the allegation's real."

"And how are you intending to do that?"

"By going to the storage unit. She left us the contents. I'm guessing that's relevant in some way, don't you think?"

Storage unit. I remember something about that in the letter. Suddenly, I wish I hadn't shredded it. Without it, I'm reliant on them for all the information.

"I'm sorry." Stephanie lifts her bag, stands up. "I don't know whether you're a saint or just very naive, but I don't want any part of this. I'm happily married, and what you're suggesting could ruin our lives."

"Don't go!" Jess jumps up, her chair almost toppling. "I'm not trying to ruin anything. I'm just getting the conversation started so we can decide what to do. You're a part of this, Stephanie. Your name was in the letter too. We're a…a team."

"A team? You can't be serious?" Her *s* practically sizzles.

I'm holding my mug so tightly my knuckle is burning against the hot ceramic. Stephanie is standing right next to me. If she moves suddenly, she'll knock me in the head with her boob.

"Think about it. She could have singled one of us out, especially if she was running low on time. But she didn't. And why do you suppose that was?" She doesn't wait for a reply. "Because this affects all of us. She wanted us to figure it out together."

"You don't know that," Stephanie says. "We've no idea what she wanted."

"Then let's find out. *Please.*"

"I'm sorry. I can't."

Jess stands very still, inhaling sharply. "Then you're going to force me to do something I don't want to do. If you're not prepared to get involved, then I'll have to go to the police."

I let go of the mug, staring at the red mark on my finger.

What the actual hell?

Stephanie is looking at Jess in dread, holding her bag in midair. "What? Why on earth would you say a thing like that?"

"Because I can't do this alone."

"I don't believe you. No one would do that to their own husband."

"With all due respect, you don't know me or what I'm capable of."

Stephanie purses her lips. "What is it that you want from me?"

"Your help." Jess's face softens, her eyes glimmering with emotion.

"How?"

"We could go to the storage unit, start there, see what we can find out? Unless you've got any other ideas?" She looks at me then.

"I don't have the address," I say feebly.

"It's all there in the letter."

"I...uh..."

"You destroyed it?" she says. "Well, that figures... How about you, Stephanie? Did the dog eat it?"

I appreciate the attempt at humor, as it's gone very tense.

"I still have the letter," Stephanie says. "Just tell me what time you'd like me to be there."

"Thank you." She smiles, relieved. "How about two o'clock?" Stephanie turns away.

"So, does that mean you're coming?" Jess calls after her. But she's already gone, her heels clunking on the wooden stairs.

We don't say much after that. Jess puts on her puffer and a black tuque that makes her look even more like a boy. "See you tomorrow, then. I'll text you the address."

"Thanks." Our eyes meet momentarily and I wonder whether she's disappointed in me, but then I never gave her any sign of being an ally.

I watch her leave. She has a fast walk, her feet light on the stairs as she descends. And then it's quiet, just me.

I look at her chipped mug and pecked bun. Stephanie left no trace: didn't take off her coat, didn't order anything, had no intention of staying long. Holding my head in my hands, I try to go over what was said, but the words are jumbling together. All I can think of is Jess calling us a team.

Pushing away my cold coffee, I stand up, my legs weak. If I thought this was going to disappear, I couldn't have been more wrong. This isn't going anywhere. Jess Jackson couldn't have made that any clearer. And now I'm on a team I didn't sign up for, with a goal that no one in their right mind would ever aim for.

JESS

I'm not proud of yesterday. I didn't mean to use that cheap line about going to the police. It came out of nowhere, but I don't regret it. I've always been good at reading a room and knew as soon as Stephanie manifested as the most reserved woman in the world, with a straighter back than my kitchen chairs, that I wasn't going to get anywhere by being subtle. They were going to bail; it was written all over their faces. And I can't allow that to happen. This is too big for me to deal with alone. It's all of our problem.

I get where they're coming from; honestly. If I could set fire to the letter and never think of it again, I would. Maybe I'd do that if I didn't love Max so much because I'd be able to set a cheap price for our marriage, valuing it so low that whether or not he had a criminal past was neither here nor there. But that's not me. I'm going to find the truth, and Priyanka and Stephanie are going to help me.

I'm sitting outside Beechcroft Residential Home, my mother's care facility, summoning the will to go inside. I'm freezing, the car heater on full blast. My mouth developed wrinkles recently and I'm examining them in the mirror, pulling the skin taut, checking they've not got worse. Smoker's lines, so they're called—even though I've never smoked. Something else to make me look mean and tense.

I wonder if that's what they thought of me yesterday, especially Stephanie. I don't know how I didn't laugh out loud when she sashayed into the room as though it were the Ritz. It's like someone's playing a trick on us, putting us together to deal with this. We couldn't be more different, but then it takes all sorts to make a team. I learned that in netball at school. I was always Center, boundary-less, making everyone's business my own. Stephanie would be Goal Shooter, not having to run much or break a sweat. And Priyanka... I dunno. Probably on the bench. I don't mean to be funny but she barely said a word.

I gaze at Beechcroft, a flat cheese-colored building, adorned with hanging baskets of flowers, posters for bingo nights. They make an effort here and everyone's kind, but still, it's hard to go inside. I need the human touch, an acknowledgment to make it worthwhile, but Mum never knows whether I'm here or not. That's what makes it difficult. I can't help the way I'm wired. Ultimately, I'm a selfish being, just like everyone else.

In that respect, I'm not so different from Stephanie or Priyanka. To them, pursuing this is self-destructive. I'm going to have a hell of a time trying to convince them otherwise. So, why not drop it?

Because I can't. I've always been the same. I was the kid who went through the door marked DO NOT ENTER.

Not only that...it's rape. You can't ignore that. The others may think they can, but they can't, not ultimately.

I pick up the two bouquets of flowers, glitter dusting the passenger seat, and make my way across the car park. I tend to encounter the same faces, and we always do the same thing: ignore each other.

It's not rudeness. It's just that no one wants to put down roots here. It's easier to pretend you're passing through, even though it's the fourth time this week I've seen that man with the leather Aussie Outback hat.

As I go along the corridor, I think of all the times we walk along in straight lines, carrying flowers: weddings, funerals, hospital wards. You'd have thought by now we'd have come up with other ways to express love and guilt, but the buckets of flowers outside every petrol station up and down the country say otherwise.

I don't know why I feel guilty about Mum. She doesn't know she's in a care home, and it's the best place I could find. Dad died eight years ago, but if he were here now, he'd approve of my choice.

Yet still, I feel horrible about coming here and especially about leaving. Every Sunday I bring fresh flowers and take away the old ones, throwing them over the wall in the car park. It's not litter; there's a convenient compost heap there. Maybe a kindly neighbor knows about the guilt flowers.

"There you go, my lovely," I say, handing one of the bouquets to Olivia.

She dips her nose inside the cellophane, inhaling. "You don't have to do this, you know."

"Yeah, but I want to." It was slim pickings today at the garage. I had to get garish ones. I'll have glitter all over my face for the rest of the day; so will Olivia.

She's a sweet girl, too young to be dealing with the sick and elderly, in my opinion. But maybe that's the best age. She doesn't take it too much to heart—doesn't see herself in them.

"How is she today?" I ask.

"Not so good. I don't think you'll get much out of her." She smiles consolingly. "Probably just an off day."

"Probably." I glance at the clock above the desk. Normally I like to chat, but today I'm using part of my Mum time to go to Stone's Storage, so I can't hang about.

Her room is way warmer than usual; I'm not surprised she's

unconscious. I go to the radiator, touch it, recoiling. Sitting down in the bedside chair, the cushion making its customary sighing noise, I set my bag on the floor and gaze at Mum.

Her hair is wispy, balding, her scalp pink and flaky. I think her hair makes me the saddest; that and the green cardigan—the one she bought half-price. As she snores faintly, her chest shifts rhythmically, her hands crossed over her torso in a way that I don't like. No one needs to have their hands crossed over them while still breathing. I sort that out right away, then sit back down, cushion sighing.

I do a lot of thinking here. I never bring anything to do. It doesn't seem right, getting out the newspaper as though in a waiting room. The man with the Outback hat will be doing the same thing, somewhere along the corridor. The whole place is full of middle-aged people like me, on their own, sitting there, pretending not to be waiting.

Today, I'm thinking about my parents' marriage, as I often do here. I don't compare it to my own—that would be stupid—but I do think about how it made me the way I am. You don't want to acknowledge that you're a product of your childhood because everyone likes to think they're their own person, forging their own path. But we all know deep down that's rubbish, and you're molded for life by ten years old.

I loved my parents very much, had a happy childhood—ordinary. I never went hungry, had friends, boyfriends. It was just that my parents hated each other's guts. Unofficially. In front of everyone else, you'd have thought they were auditioning for a Hallmark TV special. But behind closed doors, they went at each other like snakes.

To give me my due, I played along for seventeen years and you can imagine that wasn't easy for someone like me.

I shift position in my seat, looking at Mum, whose snoring has stopped suddenly. Drawing closer, I listen, watching.

The snoring resumes, and I feel so miserable that I go to the window to watch the elderly and their carers outside. It's sunny today, and I wish I could show Mum the sensory garden and lead her along the path. There's row upon row of lavender, still in flower, and the smell must be beautiful. But she doesn't go outside anymore, not since the last stroke.

Dementia and stroke. One would have been enough, surely.

Max was right when he said my parents were to blame for my behavior at those dinner parties, back when I used to try to peck the truth out of people like a greedy seagull. Yet I can't blame them entirely. In a funny way, they cared for each other. Dad would have told me to put Mum in Beechcroft, no matter the cost. And Mum used to worry herself sick about Dad's asthma, with good reason so it turned out.

But this just made it all the more confusing for me. None of it ever made any sense. "I bet it never made sense to you either, Mum," I say, returning to my chair.

I hold Mum's hand for a while, telling her I love her, hoping she'll forgive me for leaving her here.

My phone beeps and I pull away to read the message. It's from Priyanka.

13.48 P.M. >
You haven't sent me the address?

I meant to, forgot. I'm pleased she's chasing me—that she wants to show up today.

I reply, and then take my leave of Mum, Beechcroft, Olivia, the man with the Outback hat, and it's only when I'm out in the car park that I realize I forgot to put Mum's flowers in water and to chuck the old ones over the wall.

STEPHANIE

It's not difficult to get away. I often have Sunday afternoons to myself. The girls see friends; Dan plays golf. It's fairly clockwork and I can be assured of peace to the extent that I often fall asleep. It's golden time. It's what gets me through the week ahead. So, I'm not happy about giving it up.

Jess Jackson just texted me the address, but I already know where the storage facility is. Rosie dated a boy last year who lived nearby, and I used to drop her there to meet him. I wasn't going to let on to Jess that I knew the place, however. I won't be her puppet.

People often make that mistake with me. They see blond, lipstick, heels and think I'm stupid, and maybe they're right in that I left school without passing any exams. Perhaps I dress this way to compensate for the fact that I'm not the sharpest tool in the box, as Dan puts it.

Women with limited earning potential have to work extra hard if they want to marry well; everyone knows that. My options always were and always will be limited. Not one qualification to my name and I don't even own a passport—am petrified of flying and crossing water. Yet no one would ever wonder why Dan is with me, not when I look like this. Naturally, I keep my mouth closed as much as possible, especially in Bath, where everyone has a PhD.

But it would be a mistake to think of me as a walkover.

I've no idea whether Jess meant what she said about going to the police. Yet I can see that I'm going to have to turn up because I don't know her well enough to be sure she won't follow through. I can't afford to take any chances.

On my way to Stone's Storage, I listen to Otis Redding singing "These Arms of Mine," thinking of my mum. She's the reason I like soul; she loved all the old classics too, except that they weren't old for her but current. Growing up, I hated being out of sync with her, longed to be the same age, sisters.

I do have a sister, Fiona, but we don't see each other very often. That happens, as people age and have families of their own.

Even so, I always felt a stronger connection to my mother than Fiona—adored her, wanted to walk in her shoes. She started a hope chest for me when I turned eleven—linen, baby blankets—in preparation for marriage. I used to open it secretly at night, daring to touch the laundered cotton.

I don't know what happened to my hope chest. When Mum died, our flat was thrown into disarray. Fiona handled it all. I was too distraught to be of much use, but I did make a point of salvaging the cocoa tin.

I arrive at the storage facility sooner than intended, so wait in the car until Otis has finished singing. My hands are damp, and I've a nasty metallic taste in my mouth.

Stone's is a large glass-fronted building. As I reapply my lipstick, Jess and Priyanka appear on the other side of the glass, inside the reception, waiting for me.

My stomach turns over. This could be bigger than anything I've ever faced before, bigger than losing my mum.

I don't care what we find inside this place. I'm not giving up everything I've worked so hard for. I'm not losing my hope chest and my brighter future for a second time.

We gather in the wide corridor. I imagine this is what a police station looks and feels like, with harsh lighting, spongy floor-ing, door after door. The metallic taste is back and I clear my throat, telling myself I'm never going to know what a police station feels like, nor will anyone in my family.

Jess seems just as purposeful today, yet something about her is softer. As she grapples with the door, rattling the key in the lock, there is glitter on her cheek—tiny stars gleaming. I wonder whether she has children, whether she works. Yet at the same time, I don't want to know. My job is to get in here and out again unscathed, and back before Dan finishes golf.

I check my watch as Jess continues to tussle with the door, cursing. Her puffer jacket is oversize, like a man's, and makes her legs look doubly skinny in jeans. She's wearing scuffed sneak-ers and her hair is light brown, straight, fine. I've never known anyone to look so old and young at the same time. I couldn't put an age on her if I tried.

Beside me, Priyanka is leaning against the wall, playing with her phone. It hurts my neck looking down at her, she's so small. I would never dye my hair pink, but I'll admit that on her it looks sensual, exotic, if that's the look she's going for.

And then she drops her phone into her tunic and smiles up at me, and I look elsewhere—at the door, which is unlocked at last.

Jess gives it a kick and an elbow, since something seems to be obstructing it on the other side. I make no move to help, but rock on my heels to keep warm, adjusting my tote on my shoulder.

I'm peering into the sleeve of my glove to check my watch again, when Jess hurtles forward, the door suddenly giving way.

So, I don't see what it is that she's gasping about until I move forward, following them inside.

"Oh my God!" she says, feeling for the light switch.

The smell is putrid. Sour mildew, paint, pizza. I pinch the tip of my nose, backing away, but Jess clutches the sleeve of my coat. The light flickers, blinks, clicks on.

"Not so fast," she says. "We're doing this together, remember?"

How could we forget? Must she be so obsessed?

"Ready?" She's still holding my sleeve. I'm too busy staring around me at the contents of the room to shake her off.

PRIYANKA

No one speaks. We're too shocked. I've never seen anything like it before, and I have met a lot of unique types over the years. When you hit the party circuit as hard as I did, you encountered these sorts of people all the time.

"Well, this confirms what I thought, to be honest," Stephanie says, the *s* in *honest* whistling sharply.

One of the language teachers at school has the same slight impediment, her *s*'s making distracting whistle sounds, much to the boys' amusement. It never seems to get to her, though. I guess when you can speak five languages, including Cantonese and Russian, you don't care about a hissing *s*.

"And what's that?" Jess asks.

"That this is a waste of time."

Jess doesn't respond, is moving a sheet of cardboard out of the way—the reason she couldn't get the door open. There's paint-splattered cardboard all over the floor, maybe as insulation.

"Is she some kind of artist?" I gaze at the canvases leaning against the walls like drunken bystanders: semiclad women with droopy breasts, messy mouths. Why would anyone want to create art like that? Yet at the same time... I can't look away.

Maybe it's the same hollow-eyed woman in each painting, although it's hard to tell.

"Was," Jess says.

"Sorry?"

She pushes her hands rigidly into her coat pockets. Under these lights, her features look feline. "You said *is* she some kind of artist. But it's *was*... She's dead."

"And you know that for sure?" Stephanie asks, holding her gloved hands in front of her as though scared she might fall knee-deep into the mess. It would be hard to cross the floor without stepping in a paint pot or rotting takeout. It's that disgusting.

"Yes. I checked with the front desk before you arrived. They said someone on reception called Lewis knew her quite well... She was still young, only twenty-nine, poor girl, but had a drink problem. So tragic."

I gaze at a Pot Noodle container and an empty bottle of vodka, wondering whether that constituted supper, my stomach churning guiltily.

It's possible that everything in sight belonged to the unclaimed daughter of one of our husbands. The others are contemplating the same thing, I can tell. Stephanie's face looks pinched. Jess is chewing her lip; she has marionette lines on both sides of her mouth—puppet lines, as my big sister, Meena, calls them.

At the thought of my sister and family and Leicester, my guilt increases. No matter how bad things seemed at times, my only real issue was that their grip was too tight. Yet imagine if it had been the other way around, with no one holding me, no safety net beneath me.

How could Holly Waite have lived here? How had she kept herself clean, safe?

I gaze at the portraits in turn, wondering whether one of them is her—whether I might see Andy's likeness in one of them, but the faces are too distorted, ghoulish.

"Looks like she slept here," I say, pointing at the bony mat-

tress along the back wall, strewn with tampon boxes, bras, paint-
brushes and congealed palettes. It reminds me of that famous
work by Tracey Emin; the disheveled bed.

I remember then that Holly left all of this to us.

"You work for a gallery, don't you, Jess? Presumably this is
her work? Is it any good?"

"I wouldn't know," she says dispassionately. "I look after the
relationship side of things." She runs a finger along the nearest canvas, wiping the dust on her jeans. "I could have it evaluated, but what would be the point? Hardly seems fair, making
a profit off her."

"Oh, I didn't mean that. I just thought maybe the money
could go to Rape Crisis or something."

"Nice idea." Jess nods. "We'll circle back to it later." She steps
forward, accidentally kicking over a tower of Styrofoam cups,
black coffee streaming across the cardboard flooring. "I wonder how long she lived like this." Bending down, she opens a
box, pulling out a teapot.

"You're not going through all of that, are you?" I glance at
my watch.

"No. I'm thinking of coming back tomorrow to talk to Lewis.
He works Mondays…if you're around?"

I consider this. Mondays are a bad night for me: marking
books.

Stephanie is examining her gloves, pretending not to have
heard. She really is the strangest person. I can't make up my
mind whether I pity her or want to be like her. Somehow she
can just stand there, not feeling the need to say or do anything.
Alongside her, I feel needy, immature.

"What do you do for a living?" I ask her.

She looks at me, blinks rapidly. "I'm a dental receptionist. At
Chappell and Black, in the Circus."

Never heard of it. Must be private.

She doesn't like talking about herself, is shifting her weight. "Are you looking for something in particular?" she asks Jess.

"Not really. Just anything that helps us find out whether she was telling the truth." She pushes away the box with a disappointed expression.

"The artwork *is* hers, look…" I point at the nearest painting. "Her initials—HW."

"Oh, yeah. Well done." She laughs wryly. "You'd think I'd have spotted that in my line of work… They're actually quite beautiful, aren't they, in a disturbing kind of way."

"I agree." I glance at Stephanie for her opinion, but she's looking up at the ceiling.

I want to give Jess something, some sort of support, without signing up for too much. "Have you tried the local council?" I offer.

"Yeah. They gave me the date of death, 4th October. But couldn't tell me anything else because of the risk of fraud."

"Ironic," Stephanie mutters.

"I'm sorry?" Jess says.

She hesitates. "It just seems ironic, given that she was the one committing fraud."

"Oh? How so?"

"Well, obviously she needed money. And I'm assuming your husbands do well for themselves if they're members of the Montague Club?"

Jess seems as fascinated by her as I am, staring at her as though she's stood there naked. "Where are you going with this?"

She hesitates again and I confirm my original opinion of her: she's not a confident speaker. "I…"

"Because Max and I don't earn all that much. Our kids are at state school." Jess folds her arms, making them look huge in her puffer. "And I don't suppose Priyanka makes much as a teacher."

At this point the boys at school would be chanting, *digging a hole, digging a hole…*

She should stop now.

"But her husband…" Stephanie begins.

"Oh, so it's about our *husbands* earning the money? *We* can't?" Jess isn't being aggressive—even smiles; but Stephanie is floundering and doesn't notice.

"That's not what I'm saying…" She looks tearful and I feel sorry for her. I would put my arm around her and call her me duck if I knew her better. But even if we were sisters, I sense that she wouldn't want me to.

Jess kicks an empty can of lager, the ring pull tinkling inside. "Let's drop it. I was only messing with you." She glances at me and I shrug, not wanting to get involved.

I can tell that this trick of mine is going to wear thin. So, I try to offer her something again, anything.

"I don't think this is about money," I say. "She only had a few days to live."

"Exactly." Her face brightens. "Maybe it was revenge, or closure."

"Then why tell us right before dying?" I ask. "How could she get closure if she was dead?"

"Dunno." She casts her eye around the room. "But I reckon there's something here we're supposed to find. She left us that key for a reason, right?"

I smile, even though there's nothing to smile about. "I'll help," I say impulsively.

I can feel Stephanie staring at me.

"Great. Thanks," Jess says. "I've paid three months up front to keep the place going. So we don't have to worry about that." Her phone beeps; she peers at it, then drops it into her pocket. "I've gotta go. Can you make six o'clock tomorrow night?"

I nod uncertainly. "I'll do my best."

"I'm afraid I can't," Stephanie says.

"Well, that's disappointing." Jess picks her way across the floor toward the door.

"I think you should come," I say, daring to touch Stephanie's elbow. "We might be able to disprove this and forget it ever happened."

"That's the least likely scenario. But yeah, why not?" Jess says sarcastically. "Hey, I wonder what this is." Crouching down, she pulls a large book from underneath a crate.

"What is it?" I ask. "Sketches?"

She opens the pad delicately, looking at the loose pages. "Yep. Lots of them… All of doors. Do you reckon these are real places? Look at all the details, and in charcoal too. They're amazing. I couldn't do that, could you?"

I know full well I couldn't do that. I'm useless with my hands, unless I'm eating. "Why draw so many doors? Isn't that a bit odd?"

"Maybe she was making some kind of point." She examines another sketch, holding it up to the light. "Wait…this is my front door! We've got a special door plaque—number five, look." Kneeling down, she fans the sketches on the floor. "Are any of these yours?"

I peer down, immediately spotting number thirty-two. There are even jam jars hanging from the silver birch tree in the foreground. "Stephanie?" I prompt her, sensing that she wouldn't have spoken otherwise.

"Number seven," she says, pointing at a shiny black door with twin bay trees.

"So, what are all the other doors, then?" Jess gazes up at us, hands on knees.

"It's anyone's guess," Stephanie replies, not that helpfully. "Didn't you say you had to leave now?"

"Oh. Yes. Right." Reluctantly, Jess gathers the sketches, slotting them back inside the book, placing it back down with reverence. "Do we care about whose she was, by the way?"

"What do you mean?" I ask stupidly.

"Whose *daughter.*"

Behind us, Stephanie gives a derisive sigh.

"No." I look down at my boots. "I don't want to know. Not yet, anyway. Maybe never."

"Okay. We'll play it by ear."

I follow her to the door. "How would we even find out?"

"There are ways, surely?" She roots in her pocket for the key. "Aren't DNA tests a big thing now? I think you can get them online."

"But she's dead." I have a knack for stating the obvious.

"I don't think that matters. I bet there's a brush in here with her hair on it."

The idea seems macabre. And I'm picturing a morbid DNA test, when Stephanie says something that astounds me.

"Why not just show your husband the letter?" She's asking Jess, but I feel the weight of the question as though it's directed at me.

Jess blushes, frowns. "I...uh..."

"You seem hell-bent on finding the truth. I'm surprised you're not going straight to the source."

"The source?" Jess says, playing for time. But there's more to this. She seems very uneasy.

"Stephanie has a point," I say, jumping in. "I think there's a strong possibility that my husband's innocent, and I'd like to give him the chance to tell me his version of events."

"*His* version of events?" She smiles, shakes her head.

I turn to Stephanie. "Do you want to tell your husband?"

She stares at me, her eyes hardening. "Of course not! I've no intention of doing that. He'd absolutely explode."

"Really?" Jess says, glancing at me. But Stephanie is already facing the door, waiting to be let out, probably having said more than she intended to.

I don't need their permission. The idea of talking to Andy fills me with hope and relief. And yet... I want Jess to approve it.

"Would you be okay if I spoke to him about this?" I ask, touching her arm.

She avoids eye contact. "It's your choice, not mine."

I press her arm more firmly, making her look at me. "But I'd value a steer from you."

"I can't do that. Only you know what's best for you." And she opens the door, Stephanie leaving quickly as though running low on oxygen. "For what it's worth, though, if he's innocent, then you still won't know for sure. And if he's guilty... then he'll lie."

I flinch at this, following her puffer jacket down the corridor, no one speaking.

We must have missed a heavy downpour of rain. The trees overhanging the car park are dripping, and there are black puddles like craters in the gravel. Jess pecks a kiss onto my cheek, which surprises me. "Good luck. Let me know what he says."

That's it? That's my blessing? I don't have time to respond—she's already getting into her car.

Stephanie is lingering, fiddling with her bag. "Are you really going to tell him?"

"I don't know."

"I think it's a good idea. It could save us from rummaging through all that lot." She gestures loosely to the storage building.

"I care more about the fact that I share everything with him, and keeping this from him is killing me."

"Of course," she says. "I'm in the same position."

Somehow, I don't buy it. "Are you coming tomorrow?"

"I don't know. Perhaps you'll give us some good news and the whole thing will be called off." She smiles.

Driving home, I wonder what that smile meant, and why Jess was so uneasy.

Maybe they know something I don't. Maybe they're holding back because the first person to speak up is the one most at risk of marital damage. I'd be letting Andy know that I believed—no matter how hypothetically—that he was capable of sexual assault. The other two wives could play none the wiser if they so wished.

Pulling up outside our house, I dial Jess's number.

"Hi?" she whispers. "I can't really talk."

"I'll be quick." I wonder where she is. It's very quiet. "I just wanted to ask—why haven't you told your husband?"

"Because if he lies, I'll know."

"And you're worried he might?"

She hesitates. "Maybe."

"So do you think I should wait?"

"Totally up to you. It all depends on whether you can handle the answer."

My stomach lurches. I gaze at our house, the table lamp in the front room casting a blissful glow. "Do you think they'd tell each other? Is that what you're worried about, that your husband would find out that way?"

"Not really. If it's all a lie, then why would they even bring it up?"

They probably wouldn't.

"So, really this boils down to whether or not I have faith in him?" I ask.

"I think so, yes."

"Then I'm going to do it."

"Okay," she says.

For all her apparent transparency, it feels as though there's something she isn't telling me, and Stephanie too. Maybe it's simply that their marriages aren't as strong as mine.

I end the call, going up the path to the front door. Andy and Beau are sitting by the bay window in the armchair, poring over a book together.

No one's making me do this. Yet I can't bear the thought of another night with this secret hanging over me. I must talk to him.

———

We take our cups of Earl Grey through to the living room, sitting on opposite sofas. It feels like an interview or staff appraisal. In the room above, Beau is asleep, oblivious. I tell myself again that I'm doing this to restore peace and harmony in our home.

I won't mention Jess and Stephanie, or the storage unit. That would only complicate things, make him feel cornered. I'm going to keep it simple, just between us, husband and wife.

"Andy…" I take in his tufty hair, the way he crinkles his lips to drink the tea. He's wearing houndstooth slippers, the ones I bought him for Christmas. Does he have to look so homely, so mine?

"Yes, my love?" He isn't even listening, his thoughts elsewhere.

How to word it in a way that's not utterly offensive? I press my feet together, bracing myself. "I got this letter…"

"Hmmm."

"It wasn't very nice. In fact, it was shocking."

He's looking at me now. "What? When?"

"Doesn't matter… The point is that it was about…well…you."

"Me?" He looks perplexed. I'm watching him carefully, trying to catch any signs of realization—small ripples of panic. Yet there's nothing.

"It was from someone called Holly Waite."

I'm scared to blink in case I miss something.

He scratches his head pensively. "I don't think I know anyone called that."

"Her mother was Nicola Waite." As I say her name, I sit forward, waiting.

"Nope." He shakes his head. "Don't know her either."

"Think about it. Are you absolutely sure?"

He looks at me then, right in the eye, and I know he's made the connection. "Oh," he says softly, swallowing.

I feel nauseous. I set my tea down on the table. "Andy... Do you know what I'm talking about?"

"Yes. I'm afraid I do." He rubs his face. Is he erasing his expression, hiding it?

"Okay..." I sit on my hands to stop them from shaking. "So do you want to tell me about it?"

He smiles without humor. "Not really."

"Is it true?" I ask.

"Is what true?"

I've no idea whether he's being honest. Somehow, I've lost the ability to tell. I'm going to have to say the words. He's going to make me say them.

"Did you sexually assault her?"

He looks horrified. "What? God, no! Whatever made you think that?"

"Well, what did you think I was talking about?"

"I don't know." He runs his hand through his hair in agitation. "I remember her making some such accusation, but it didn't bear any weight. We all knew the truth."

"We?"

"The chaps I was with. Jackson someone and someone Brooke."

I cross my arms tightly. "I'm supposed to believe you're not friends with them, even though you all belong to the Montague Club?"

"Hey?" he says, his forehead creasing in surprise. "It's the truth! I've not seen or heard from them in years! I barely go to the club anymore, you know that. What is this, Pree? Surely you don't think that I..."

"I don't know what to think."

He's over by my side in an instant then and I don't stop him, even though I don't want him crowding me. He kneels before me, his hand on my lap, trying to look me in the eye, but I'm staring down at the carpet.

"Please, my love. This is me we're talking about. You know I'd never do something like that."

"Then why would her daughter say you did?" My voice sounds small, childish, as though navigating a playground hurt. I look at him then, feeling myself being drawn toward him. I so want to believe him, to make it all go away.

"I've no idea. Probably because her mother lied about it in the first place."

"And why would she have done that?"

He seems to take strength from this question, exhaling. "I don't know. Why does anyone ever lie about this sort of thing? Attention, sympathy? Or maybe because she was embarrassed about what happened?"

"What *did* happen?"

He puffs out his cheeks, looks up at the ceiling. "Crikey, we're going back, what, thirty years or more? I can't remember all the details."

"Try," I say firmly.

"Okay..." He scratches the stubble on his chin. "Well, I remember that she came to the club one night. It was Christmas and everyone was plastered, as tended to be the case back then. From what I recall, she came on to us rather heavily. She was an attractive girl, seemed to know what she wanted."

"What do you mean?"

"Well, she slept with the other two chaps."

"Willingly?"

"Yes!"

I gaze at him. "You weren't involved?"

He clasps my hand impassionedly, looking into my eyes. "Of course not. You do believe me, don't you?"

"I want to."

More than anything, I want to.

But I just don't know.

"What can I do to convince you?" he asks. "Isn't my word enough?"

It is when we marry. A simple *I do* suffices, seals the deal. Yet now words don't seem enough—not nearly enough.

"Are we okay?" He looks desperate, his body teetering as he rests on his gangly haunches. I want to put him out of his misery, like setting a daddy longlegs free from a spiderweb.

So, I lie. "Yes."

"Okay." He relaxes his grip on my hand, then sits down on the floor, head in his hands. "Christ, what a shock…for you, I mean," he says, gazing at me. "Where's that damned letter now?"

"In the shredder," I say, picking up a cushion, hugging it.

"Best place for it." He nods slowly, gathering his thoughts. "Do you think it would help if we spoke to her discreetly, straightened it out?"

I'm surprised. "Who?"

"The girl who wrote the letter. Her daughter?"

"Yes, but…" I stop.

Would he really do that? Momentarily, I'm reassured. Yet surely he knows this is impossible. Is it an empty offer, designed to trick me?

"We can't, Andy. She died recently. She was an alcoholic."

I watch him closely. If he already knew so, he's a very good actor. He seems suitably surprised, then appropriately sorry. The look of someone at a funeral when you barely know the deceased.

"So there's nothing more we can do?" he asks.

"No."

Neither of us says anything after that. We withdraw to separate sofas, not acknowledging that normally we would never sit on opposite sides of the room.

I pretend to watch the TV when he turns it on. He seems settled enough, even laughs once or twice. But when he thinks I'm preoccupied, I notice him watching me, a look of speculation on his face.

————————

As Andy cleans his teeth, I text Jess.

22.23 P.M. >
He said N made it up.

I wait for her response, tapping my foot, hoping she'll be quick.

22.24 P.M. >
Does he know Max & Daniel?

22.24 P.M. >
Barely. Couldn't remember their names. Wish I hadn't said anything. Have I made it worse?

22.25 P.M. >
No. Are you still coming 2moro? x

22.25 P.M. >
Yes x

As I climb the stairs, I realize she was right. He was never going to say that he did it, was only ever going to say that he didn't.

Tiptoeing into Beau's room, I kneel on the carpet beside him, inching his cover from his face, blowing him a kiss, whispering a frightened prayer.

I feel as though I'm at a crossroads, but maybe that's just an illusion and not the case at all. Maybe I already made the choice, set things in motion the moment I agreed to meet Jess. There's a hideous inevitability about where we're headed that I can't bring myself to acknowledge, yet I'll probably fight it nonetheless, like aging or death.

I shouldn't have said anything to Andy. I did it to protect my family, yet all I've done is invite mistrust into our marriage, the most destructive ingredient of all. I walked right into it, volunteering to be the messenger. And we all know what happens to them.

JESS

I can't seem to get myself warm anymore. My shoulders ache where I'm holding them so tightly, my nose is permanently damp, my lips have taken on a lilac hue. Somewhere in the house I've some lipstick. If I can't find it before work, I'll take Eva's. I know she has some stronger colors that she hides from me, called things like Tramp or Sassy Bitch. Poppy snitches on her quite a lot.

The girls are upstairs getting dressed for school, so it's just me and Max at the breakfast table. I'm still cold, even though I've just eaten a bowl of porridge. Max hasn't touched his yet. It's steaming in front of him, but he's too caught up in WhatsApp.

I've been thinking about him and his phone a lot over the past few days, especially since last night when Stephanie confronted me about why I haven't shown him the letter.

That question bounced around in my head all night. I hated my evasive answer. Normally I'd have nailed it, had it been about anything but Max. But he's my weak spot, always has been—my *blind* spot.

Am I blind? Have I been misled, fooled? As I drink my coffee, I look at Max in his fitted shirt, still absorbed with his phone.

It's always in his hand first thing in the morning: sport updates, messages from colleagues, WhatsApp notifications. Drives me mad, but it comes with the job, apparently. I've never run a company so wouldn't know.

Two years ago, he got a message on WhatsApp that made me question him for the first time, except that I didn't, not really. I let it go, for all the many reasons that we let a lot of things go as women. You can't fight everything, everyone. You pick your battles because it's a long life.

It was a photo of a woman's genitalia, which I happened to see accidentally.

I voiced my shock, and he completely agreed with me, saying it was a different world out there now, that young people were less inhibited. The girl had sent the picture to her boyfriend, for his eyes only, not knowing that he would share it with his workmates on WhatsApp.

When I suggested that maybe he could ask not to be included, he said that would alienate him from his colleagues who he went to the gym with, but in future he'd delete them without looking.

I accepted it. I knew these sorts of things went on, especially in financial services. Maybe I was out of touch, working in a bubble at aesthetically pleasing Moon & Co.

Still, I can't help thinking now that if he was unable to draw the line in his own company, in a position of seniority, then how would he have handled a situation thirty years ago, probably involving alcohol and peer pressure?

I'm staring at him, my heart pounding so hard, I'm sure he can hear it.

And then he looks up with those heavy-lidded eyes and I feel ashamed of my thoughts. "All right, baby?" He puts down his phone, stirs the porridge. "You look like you've seen a ghost."

He's not wrong. It feels as though there are ghosts everywhere, all around us. They followed me home from the storage unit, those women in the paintings, and now they're tracking me with their scooped-out eyes, waiting to see what I'm going to do next.

"Just tired," I say.

"Well, maybe you should think about cutting down on your trips to your mum. It's exhausting you, and it's not like she knows you're there."

I tap my teeth silently. I'm not going to erupt. In his own clumsy way, he thinks he's helping.

"But *I* know, Max."

This feels incredibly meaningful. But a pinging sound announces the arrival of another message and he's gone again, turning into work Max, gym lad; someone who lets things slide to fit in and save face.

―――――

The office is very quiet today. The photocopier is humming and a seagull cries plaintively as it circles the sky. It couldn't be stiller out there either. It's like the whole world is waiting for me to do something.

Mary normally makes a beeline for me or the potted rubber plant first thing. Today, the plant's won again and I'm pleased about that. But on her way back, she stops at my desk and offers to make me an instant cappuccino. She always seems disappointed if I decline, so I tell her yes and give her a smile that makes my ears creak.

"Righty oh," she says, beaming, straightening her cardigan.

She's sweet, Mary, but I do wonder. She lives alone and probably should have retired by now. Maybe she doesn't want to be lonely. I think she buys the coffee sachets especially. There's only six of us at Moon & Co., including my boss, Gavin, so it's quite intimate, family-like.

I've never admitted to him how little I know about art, although I'm sure he knows. When I need information, I tap Elliott, my cultured colleague. He's so nice, with his waistcoats and French cinema blog—one of those men who women adore, while never actually picturing them naked.

"What can you tell me about doors, art-wise?" I lean against Elliott's desk, blowing my cappuccino to cool it.

"Open or closed?"

"Good question... Closed."

He nudges his specs into place, blushing slightly. It's occurred to me before that he has a little crush on me, but this is probably arrogance on my part.

Besides, he's not my type. Max is, I think...

"Aside from the obvious?" he says. "Dead end, confinement, no way out?"

Those things weren't that obvious to me, but I nod as though they were. "Anything else?"

"Not that I know of."

"Okay. Thanks." I'll admit, I'm disappointed, even though I didn't really think those sketches were going to tell me anything.

I flit through my emails, unable to make anything stick. If I keep going like this, my work will slide, I'll miss something big with the girls or Mum and will never forgive myself. I've already got far too much on my plate. The sandwich generation, they call us. I'd say it's more like a kebab—lots of chunks skewered together. And we're the thin wiry bit, holding it all together.

Max will notice soon that I'm giving him the runaround. He'll get restless, skittish, and will flick through the diary, working out when we last slept together. Then he'll notice I'm avoiding eye contact and that my lips are blue.

Priyanka's attempt to clear things up didn't work, not that I thought it would. If it were that easy, I'd have done it myself. It's too *he said, she said*, making your head spin with doubt. I would have preferred her not to have said anything, in case it got back to Max. Yet I suspect that if a secret that big really *had* been buried for that long, they wouldn't be in a rush to talk about it. All she's done is create an urgency that wasn't there before.

I need to know the truth before Max finds out about the letter and starts inventing alternative realities.

I'll have to come up with something to propel this forward. I can use Mum as an excuse for my absences from home. Max never presses me for details. If I were to test him, he'd guess that Beechcroft was the name of the country house hotel we stayed at in Sussex, 2015.

———

The idea comes to me over lunch, while Hannah Greene talks art. One of my favorite kookiest clients, she always has paint under her nails as though she clawed her way across a wet canvas to the restaurant.

"The aim," she says, flicking her hair over her shoulders, "is to, like, paint as close as you can to the shape without actually touching it. Do you see what I mean, Jessie?"

"Yes. Hmm."

I don't always listen to the artists' pitter-patter about technique and process. But something she said resonates with me and I replay it.

As close as you can…without actually touching it.

I smile at her. She's a genius. I know just what to do.

"Your kids could have a go. It's, like, so easy. And it's an awesome way to get into the watercolor groove."

Watercolor groove?

"That's great, Hannah. I'll remember that."

I probably won't.

As we part company outside the restaurant, rain is spotting the air. The Montague Club is only two streets away, in a Georgian square. I barely notice the journey, my mind crowded with thoughts.

I rarely have cause to go to this square, mostly a cut through for walkers en route to a car park. It's deathly quiet, even at lunchtime. I've no idea what the buildings are for; they have such subtle markings, you're none the wiser until you get really close, which is doubtless their intention. If you don't know what's there, it probably doesn't concern you.

I know which one of the doors leads to the club, having dropped Max off here before. Like its neighbors, it doesn't give much away. There's a small coat of arms above the door and a faint *M* for *Montague* on the brass knocker, which I lift and rattle, cringing as the sound clatters around the rooftops.

Once inside, I'll be as close to the past as I can possibly be, without actually touching it. Just like Hannah said.

Smoothing my hair, I take a deep breath.

Wait, this is nuts. What am I doing?

The door opens and a woman with lead-gray teeth smiles at me. She's wearing a cleaning tunic and holding a feather duster. "Can I help you?"

"Hi. I was wondering if I could take a quick look around?"

"Oh, I'm sorry." She frowns, waggling the duster as she speaks. "I'm just the housekeeper. We're closed Mondays."

I knew that; Max told me at some point.

I lower my voice confessionally. "I didn't want to look around with everyone staring at me. You know what it's like."

She doesn't appear to. "Are you local?"

"Yes. I just moved down from the City."

This doesn't seem to mean a lot.

"Of London," I add.

She looks me up and down, opening the door wider. "I don't see the harm. But you won't have long, I'm afraid. I'm locking up in twenty minutes."

"No problem. Thank you so much," I say, gushing. "I just want to get a quick feel for the place before I commit."

Commit? To here? I gaze around the hallway, which is lit by brass sconces giving off a woozy amber light. The wallpaper is palm leaf, the fronds gargantuan, eerie. On the nearby console, a vase of stargazer lilies wafts soapy perfume.

Max likes this place? Why?

It's nothing like home. We're Ikea, light, minimalist.

"Do I go through there?" I ask, pointing to my right.

"Yes. That's the Green Room. And over here..." She gestures in the opposite direction. "...That's the meeting room, where they have talks and that."

I point at the staircase. "And up there?"

"Nothing much. There's a games room, but no one uses it. I barely have to go up there anymore."

"Have you worked here long?" I try to sound offhand, but my heart feels as though it's based in my ears.

"Twenty years or so."

Not long enough to have been here in 1990, then.

"Well, I'd better be getting on," she says, "but give me a shout if you need anything." And she withdraws into the meeting room. Within seconds, there comes the sound of the vacuum cleaner.

I go through to the Green Room and stand at the edge of an Oriental rug, inhaling the smell of lemon furniture polish. The room isn't green anymore. Maybe there used to be green bankers' lamps, dark oak wall panels, a few mounted animal heads. But now it's eclectic, bohemian. Rose gold wallpaper. Jewel blue velvet chairs. A stupid toucan lamp.

I hate the idea of Max being here, in his tight shirts, with his attentiveness. He likes to really look at a person when they're talking. Does he sit on that bar stool and order Grey Goose for some gorgeous self-starter whose mortgage he's arranging?

Or maybe he sits in a corner with Andrew Lawley and Daniel Brooke, drinking scotch through gritted teeth, the cloud of conspiracy hanging over them.

The vacuum cleaner has stopped. I listen, gripping my rucksack, hoping the housekeeper doesn't come in and find me standing here in a sweaty stupor. But it starts up again, farther away.

Relieved, I return to the lobby, sneaking to the foot of the stairs, wondering why I'm drawn to that area. If I were a metal detector, I'd be beeping.

I touch the smooth banister, my eye running up the faded seashell-patterned carpet. The light reaches only part of the staircase, stopping halfway—a definite line, not to be crossed.

I try to imagine what it might have been like here in December 1990, just three days before Christmas. The warmth, laughter, mistletoe. Sneaking up creaking stairs, peeling off hats and gloves, static crackling through their hair. Max would be twenty years old, new to the club, there purely because of his father. Immature, excitable, everything to play for, everything to prove.

I gaze up into the darkness, my throat tightening.

Who was Nicola Waite? Was she a nice person, a good girl? Why does that matter? It shouldn't. It doesn't.

I need to know why she was here that night, though. How old was she? Was she a club member? Did she know Max and the others?

The vacuuming has stopped. I swing around, expecting to see the housekeeper looking at me suspiciously for creeping about, but the hallway's empty.

I don't want to be here anymore. I hate everything about this place.

Heading for the front door, I wonder whether to simply let myself out. "Hello?"

Nothing.

I glance at a portrait of the club's founder, Sir Graves, in a fancy necktie and waistcoat. Max mentioned once that Sir Graves was from a family of merchant traders whose fortune was amassed by exploiting Chinese labor.

Suddenly, this feels like a much bigger deal than he made it out to be and I start to walk along the long line of paintings, spawned by their founder, generations of males wearing the same proud expressions.

I stop, stare at a framed photograph, my reflection gaping at me in shock.

It's definitely, unmistakably, Max.

Checking the housekeeper isn't in sight, I move closer to study the picture. He has a terrible perm and is standing with his arms draped around two men in the easy way of close friends. I estimate that it was taken round about the time I just imagined: the early nineties.

I recognize the others from the pictures I found of them online; they haven't changed very much. Daniel has a military hairstyle, just like now; Andrew has skull-head eyes, even then, and a prominent vein on his temples as though his blood pressure's high.

I can hear footsteps approaching. I have about two seconds to take a photo, dropping my phone into my pocket just in time.

"Seen enough?" the housekeeper asks.

"Absolutely. Thank you."

"I think you can inquire online if you're interested."

"Perfect. Will do. Thanks again."

A waft of damp air hits us as she opens the door. It's still raining, but I'm happy to be outside. Smiling goodbye, I dart across the square as the door closes behind me, taking shelter underneath a large sycamore tree.

Trembling, I look at the image on my phone, zooming in on Max, taking in his green eyes, his handsome face.

The pain I feel is immense. It sears through me as I stand underneath that tree. I know this isn't evidence. Of course it isn't. But it may as well be, to me.

He knows these men. They're inside the club, framed, a moment in time captured. Yet I'd never heard of them until Holly Waite wrote to me. They've crept around, keeping their distance from us and maybe from each other.

I know then that it's true. I just know it.

"Oh, fuck, Max… What did you do?" I start to cry, my arms

wrapped around my waist, chilled from my nose to my toes. My teeth chattering uncontrollably, I text Priyanka and Stephanie, sending them the picture.

13.59 P.M. >
They DO know each other. You'd better be there tonight, both of you. Or

That's not going to work. I look up at the branches of the sycamore tree, thinking, and then try again.

14.00 P.M. >
I found the attached pic. Please come to Stone's tonight, 6pm. I need you, Jess xxx

Three kisses are too much. I delete two, press send.

Making my way back to work, I cry into my scarf, wishing I'd never opened Holly's letter. My life is changing right in front of me, as though I'm not the one in control of it anymore. I can kid myself that I'm calling the shots, but in truth they were called years ago, the echo fading to a faint whisper, so faint that they thought we'd never hear it.

But we did.

STEPHANIE

Dan is waiting for me outside work. I can see him through the glass door, scowling, checking his watch. I'm ten minutes late, but it couldn't be helped.

His face changes to a smile. "Hi, darling." He kisses me lightly on the cheek, avoiding my mouth since I've just applied lipstick. "What's the matter?" He glances over his shoulder to see what I'm looking at.

A woman wearing a black coat is standing in the exact same place as before. My heart misses a beat, but it's not her—not Jess. It's a tourist, taking a photo of the Circus.

"It's nothing." I force a smile. "I thought I'd left something at—"

"I don't have long." It's starting to rain, so he puts up his golf umbrella, holds it over me. "Time's tight today as it is."

"Sorry. Mrs. Edgell was in for a checkup. She—"

"Shall we cut through behind the bank?"

"Yes. Good idea."

He often interrupts me when I'm speaking, doesn't ask what it was that I was going to say. He doesn't mean it nastily. He's just an impatient sort of person and I've learned to keep my sentences short.

We make our way down the steep hill to the main street, going a little fast for my liking.

"Should you be wearing that?" He touches my elbow to lead me across the road. We're crossing recklessly on the corner; I normally walk along farther to the lights. It's busy and we dodge between cars. I pull my scarf to my nose, trying not to breathe in exhaust fumes.

"Wearing what?" I glance at my reflection in a shop window. I'm wearing my red wool coat, a cashmere scarf and—

"That dress. Isn't it the revealing one?"

It is, yes. A wrap dress that's slightly low-cut, but I'm wearing a scarf over it. No one wants to see cleavage when booking root canal work. "Not sure."

"Well, you need to be sure. I'd hate you to be taken advantage of. You know what men are like."

If anyone knows, it's Dan. He's always been surrounded by men, with two brothers, an army career and now a car business, which he inherited from his father. Mr. Brooke Senior was a notorious character about town at one point, brash, yet granted access and even a key to the Montague Club by merit of his money. Dan says he could tell me things about his dad that would make my hair curl, without actually ever telling me those stories, not that I want to know. He can keep his dirty anecdotes for the club.

I didn't mean to think about the club. I've been purposefully not thinking about it, or about that silly girl, Holly Waite. It's not *her* life she's trying to destroy. She was already dying. Why ruin our lives too for something that happened thirty years ago? Only a vindictive person would do that, and only an idiot would let her.

"Everything okay?" Dan asks, steering me out of the way of a lady walking two Dalmatian dogs. I'm not a fan of dogs, or animals in general. "You seem tense."

I'm gripping his arm too tightly. I relax my hold. "Just work. It's busy."

"Well, make sure they don't pile too much on you. Tight wads. They don't pay you enough for that."

I think they pay me very well. Leonardo is always kind to me. And the new specialist endodontist is turning out to be quite the charmer with the older clientele. He's from Miami and finds England chilly at this time of year. One of the elderly ladies is knitting him a scarf.

I keep these thoughts to myself. Dan would misread them. He can be slightly possessive.

Slightly possessive? Are you *serious*?

This is one of Rosie's favorite rants. I don't know why it bothers her, if it doesn't bother me. Her father was a far worse husband—couldn't keep his hands to himself. After he slept with half the town and abandoned us, my life in Midsomer Norton was never the same. I died many times over, just pushing the pram along the main street, trying to avoid the gossip and sniggers.

"Maybe you shouldn't wear that dress to work," Dan says, as we go along the corridor of shops, underneath the hanging baskets of flowers.

It's pretty, the corridor; chic. I used to dream of shopping here as a child, but we were always on our way to the indoor market near the abbey, to the secondhand books, food counters and cheap haberdashery. My mother used to make our clothes out of itchy material scraps, haggled for, but I never complained. Nor did Fiona.

"Hmm?" Dan is waiting for a response. We're standing outside a designer jewelry shop. I'm still thinking about my mum, about how much she went through. Holly Waite isn't the only person to have suffered, to have known hunger and deprivation.

"The *dress*." He frowns, leans toward me, picking a blond hair from the lapel of my coat, flicking it away. I watch it drifting to the pavement, landing in a puddle. "I know you, Stephanie. You think you're being friendly and polite, but other people will take advantage of that. I'd hate to think of someone ogling your breasts. Especially that slimy Leonardo."

Leonardo is slimy in Dan's view because he drives a Jaguar XJ, and didn't buy it from him.

I smile, tug his hand. "Forget about that. You don't have much time, remember? Let's go inside."

We're picking out a sixteenth-birthday present for his niece. I don't like the girl. She's sullen, pampered and recently blocked Georgia on social media just because she could, but I said I'd help.

As Dan speaks to the shop assistant, I lean against the glass counter, looking at the rows of lit gems. I would have died for something like this as a teenager—something sophisticated for my hope chest. Welling up, I glance at Dan, but he's busy asking for a cabinet to be unlocked.

I think of Rosie again, how she would call this shopping trip *total bull*. She doesn't like anything about Dan, nor his family, which is an awful shame. She thinks everything about him is *suspect*, including the fact that he's allowed to be called Dan, whereas I'm not allowed to be Stef or Steffie anymore, but have to be Stephanie in full.

Her constant griping gets me down, as though I've failed once more to find her a happy home. After all, Vivian accepts Dan. Why can't she?

"Why aren't you helping?" Dan hisses, even though we're alone. The assistant has gone to the back room for keys.

"I am." I take his arm. "Show me which one you like."

He taps the glass with his fingernail. "That one."

I stare at it. "The sapphire?"

"Yes. Why not?"

Because it's £375?

I swallow, blush. "It seems…"

"I'm her godfather." He lowers his voice. "I want to do this."

"Yes, of course." I glance about, wondering whether I can find an alternative. But he'll see straight through me.

"Happy?" He bends his knees to look in my eyes. Sometimes, his breath smells a little sharpish. It's the smoothies.

I give my best impression of a smile and Dan grins, rubbing his hands together. As the assistant returns with the key, I stand by the window, looking at the bunting flapping in the breeze and the rain dripping from the baskets of flowers.

His niece won't give that necklace a second thought. She'll rip off the ribbon and toss the box aside, to the bottom of her wardrobe. It's a complete waste of money, but he wants to show off in front of his brothers—show them that he's *got this*.

There's a beep as a text message arrives. Dan will be annoyed—thinks phones should be turned off in public spaces. Yet he's not paying any attention to me, is talking to the girl as she wraps the sapphire necklace painstakingly.

I read Jess's begging text, my heart beginning to race, my finger hovering over the image. I can just about make out three men, but daren't click on it, not here.

What is she doing, taking chances, sending this to me? Pressing delete, I drop my phone back inside my bag.

I watch Dan as he reaches into his back pocket for his wallet, feeling a surge of loyalty and sympathy for him. He's just trying to get by, like we all are—fighting middle-age, boosting his thinning hair with volume gel.

The shop assistant is polite, but wary. He's too masculine for some women, especially young ones, which is why Rosie hasn't taken to him. It takes maturity to appreciate a man like him, whose feminine side isn't evident. His hair is soldier-short; his friends have nicknames like Captain and Sniffer; they organize boys' tours where they're sworn to secrecy.

It's all rather immature. Yet I understand there's a line between us that he doesn't want crossed. I don't want it crossed either. As far as he's concerned, I'm a natural blonde. He doesn't want the details, doesn't want to ruin the mystique, as he puts it. And nor do I. It's not necessary or appropriate.

But now… I think of those tours, those secrets, and feel a niggle of doubt as he smiles paternally at the shop assistant.

His footsteps are heavy as he comes toward me. He's a bit of a stomper, heavy-handed. And I wonder at the power in his sinewy body; the fanatical sit-ups, running, strength building. He could easily overpower someone. He could—

"Okay?" He takes my arm and we leave. It's stopped raining. The sun is shining, causing a glare on the wet pavement. "That's a job well done. Thanks, Stephanie." He pats my hand. I can smell his breath again and I turn away, looking at the appealing shop fronts—a jade lamp glowing within, a string of fairy lights, a log fire—wishing I could have brought my mum here once, just once, to treat her to something.

I'm welling up again, so I root in my bag for my sunglasses. I never leave home without them. Squinting is very aging.

Outside my office building, Dan kisses me goodbye before thudding off to work, his footsteps sounding loud in the quiet Circus.

Back at the reception desk, I fix my cashmere scarf over my chest, ensuring there are no peepholes. Dan is just looking out for me. He's right: there are a lot of perverts around.

I gaze at the fish tank, watching an angelfish fluttering along the glass. I don't want to go back to that ghastly storage unit tonight. I don't have the energy. I want the whole thing to crawl away to a dark place and die. But if I leave Jess to sort this out without my input, she could ruin my life.

It takes me the rest of the afternoon to reply. I save the text, mull it over. It's only three words, but still... I'm not sure.

On my way.

Just as I step outside into the fading light, I press send.

JESS

I've been practicing what to say all afternoon, but now the time's come I'm going to have to wing it. It's so cold in here, I've got brain freeze. I know my lips are lilac again. I bite them as we approach the reception desk so that I don't startle the lad too much by looking dead.

Beside me, Priyanka is rocking on her feet as though we're on a boat. It's not exactly stabilizing, yet I'm glad she showed up. Stephanie hasn't appeared, but I have faith that she will. She's on our side; she just doesn't know it yet.

I glance at his name badge, checking I've got the right person. "Hi, Lewis? I'm Jess and this is Priyanka. We were wondering if we could talk to you about Holly Waite. Apparently, you knew her fairly well?"

Lewis, who has beautiful brown eyes, framed by a Superdry tuque, looks at me cautiously. "Yeah, I knew Holly."

It's not the best conversation opener. His tone is flat, mistrustful. He begins to crack his knuckles, one by one, staring at his computer screen.

I'm not sure what to say next.

I'm relieved when Priyanka jumps in. "We were friends of

hers too," she says warmly, her Midlands accent more marked. Maybe she switches it on when needed. "We're trying to find out what happened to her."

"Friends?" Lewis turns down his mouth. "Where were you last week, then?"

Priyanka looks up at me. It's a decent enough question. We'd never even heard of Holly last week.

"Thought so." He looks back at his screen.

Damn it.

I nudge Priyanka subtly, trying to prompt her to do something. She deals with young males like him every day; he can't be much older than twenty.

"How long had you known her for, Lewis? And just to be clear..." She raises her hand as though swearing an oath. "...You don't have to talk about her if you don't want to. Only if you're comfortable."

We wait to see if he is.

"Not long." He adjusts his tuque, scratching his forehead. "About a year. Just after I started working here. She'd already been here a while, I think."

"And how did you get to know her?"

"She kinda stood out."

"Oh. Why was that?"

He blushes, nudging his tuque again.

"She was pretty?" Priyanka offers.

"Yeah." His blush deepens. Then he stares at her. "But why don't you already know that, if you were friends?" He does air quotes around the word *friends* and everything goes quiet.

She opens her mouth, then stalls.

I attempt to sidestep the issue by appealing to his hormones. "Did you date her, Lewis?"

"Nah." Thankfully, he smiles, swiveling back and forth in his revolving chair. "I didn't get the feeling she was, like, available. I asked her once if she was with anyone, and she said she couldn't see herself being in a relationship because of her lifestyle. I mean, she was an artist and that."

He says this as though it's completely out there—the wackiest job known to man.

"Artists, eh?" I say, trying to bond. But it comes out clumsy, forced, and I fall silent again.

"So, did you, what, just hang out here, chatting?" Priyanka says, tucking her pink hair behind her ears. She's wearing her usual parka, the ashen fur of the hood mingling with her hair like strange extensions.

There's a noise behind us, and I glance over my shoulder as Stephanie appears. She's twenty minutes late and looks pleased about it—probably waited in a turnout down the road.

"Yeah, mostly," Lewis replies. "She wasn't always here when I was. Sometimes she stayed in her unit overnight." He lowers his voice. "I didn't tell the boss. They'd have kicked her out. It's against policy."

"Did she sleep here often?" Priyanka's voice changes direction as she turns to look at Stephanie, smiling at her in welcome.

"I reckon."

"So, she was homeless?"

"Think so, yeah… I did try to help. I didn't know what to do, though."

"Of course." She manages somehow, in those two words, to sound compassionate, maternal.

Lewis looks at her uncertainly, tapping a pen on his palm. "I knew she was an alcoholic. She didn't talk about it, but it was obvious. I could always smell, like, booze on her and she was up and down, depending on whether she was sober or not."

"Did she work? How did she afford the rent here?"

He shrugs. "Dunno. It's not expensive, though, is it, compared to a flat. She never mentioned it, but I got the feeling she did odd jobs—painting, cleaning and that. And she scrounged and probably nicked stuff too. She never fell behind on payments, so management let her get on with it."

"Did she…well, did she have any friends?" Priyanka asks.

"Other than you?" He smiles wonkily. "Don't think so. She didn't have any support, from what I could see." He tosses the pen aside, sits up straight, folding his arms. "But then people like her don't, do they? No one wants to know them."

I shuffle my feet awkwardly. Priyanka is looking up at me for help, appealing to me to say something. She's wearing hazel contact lenses today.

"She collapsed right there, where you are," he says, pointing, and we turn to look at Stephanie, who gazes at the ceiling, tote on wrist.

"If it hadn't happened here, I wouldn't have known anything about it. Even then, it was impossible to find out anything. I had to lie to the hospital about being related, so I could, like, see her. But I was too late. By the time I'd got there, she was already dead."

He looks at me with an expression I can't read. Is he angry with us?

"She died all alone. There were nurses and that, but no friends or family. She didn't have a single soul in the world to comfort her. No one should die like that. Not even a dog."

I stare at him numbly. He's right, yet I don't seem to be able to tell him so.

"What did she die of?" Priyanka asks softly.

"Heart failure. Dilated cardio something. The doctor said she was the right age group for it—late twenties—and that it was alcohol that had done the damage." He pushes his hands into his pockets, swivels back and forth again in the chair. "I wish I could've done more for her. She was a good person."

There's a swishing noise as the double doors open and a woman about my age leaves the units, eyes straight ahead, grim-faced. Makes you wonder what goes on here—what people store, and why.

I wait for her to pass through the main entrance before speaking. "Do you have a photo of her, by any chance?"

"What?" he says, as though miles away. "Uh. No. She wasn't like that. Didn't even have a phone that I knew of."

I try to look at him sympathetically, gratefully, but I'm not sure I pull it off. I'm too dismayed. "Well, we won't take up any more of—"

"There's a self-portrait of her in there." He gestures with his thumb in the direction of the units. "It's a good likeness. She did it a few months ago, showed me when it was done. I think she was pretty proud of it."

"In her storage space?" I ask, my face flushing. "There's a—"

"Yep." He nods.

"How will we...well, how will we know which one is her?"

I wait for his response, filling in the gaps.

She had green eyes.

She looked like Eva.

She was Max's daughter.

"She always wore white," he says. "Said it made her invisible."

I don't know how I manage to move my legs away from that desk, away from that boy with his accusing looks, but somehow, I do.

Priyanka's breath is fast, shallow, as I fiddle with the keys, kicking the base of the door to open it. I'm not aware of Stephanie, until suddenly she's there, inside the unit. I close the space between us, touching her hand, and to my surprise, she doesn't wriggle free.

And that's what we're doing when we find her—forming a straggly line, scared to move.

"There, look," Priyanka says.

She's hanging above the mattress where she slept, a canvas of a young woman in white. The painting is so pale, transparent, it's almost vanishing into the background like a water mark or damp stain. Maybe that's significant. It's the portrait of someone who scrounged, lived off the grid, died alone.

She was pretty; somehow you can tell that, even with the distorted features. And now that we know it's her, it seems obvious that the other paintings are of her mother, Nicola.

I lean against the wall, pressing a finger to my temple, which is throbbing. I've looked into what would have happened to Holly. The town council would be organizing a pauper's funeral; still called that, so Victorian-sounding, and not as rare as you might think. Our local council alone handles about four thousand a year. It's more than likely that she would have an unmarked grave or resting place. We would never be able to find her. A fitting outcome for someone who lived life as a shadow.

I wish I could have done something to help her. Yet even now, it's impossible. I can't contact the council and offer to pay for a personalized grave, claiming a biological link, when nothing about any of that is certain. Nor can I implicate Max.

I may be standing here, sickened, ashamed, but I'm not ready to turn my husband in. Not without proof.

"This is horrible." I kick an empty paint can. "This was no way to live."

Priyanka is making her way across the cardboard floor to the canvas, tiptoeing as though scared she'll disturb rats. "I can't see Andy in her. Can you? I mean…can you see a likeness to either of your husbands?"

I can't see Max, no. And from what I know of their husbands, I can't see them either. But how can you tell from such a strange painting?

My gaze settles on the nearest canvas, taking in Nicola's melancholy features. She was probably a beauty, but Holly didn't want to depict her like that. Instead, she wanted us to see, what—squalor, anonymity?

Behind me, Stephanie gives a little cough before speaking. "Did you talk to your husband, Priyanka?"

"Yes, I did."

"Oh. Didn't it help?"

"No." She's squatting underneath the trestle table, pulling a cardboard box toward her. "He said it was a lie."

"And do you believe him?"

"I don't know, which is why I'm doing this." I watch as she tries to unpick the brown tape on the box lid. "This is very tightly sealed. If I was going to hide something, it would be in here."

I catch sight of two paintings then that I hadn't noticed before, in the shadows of a mini-fridge. "I wonder who they are?" I say, pointing. "I don't think that's Nicola or Holly, is it?"

Priyanka glances up. "No, it's not. Look at the eyes."

One of them has dark hair and a big gap between her teeth, with angry black holes for eyes. The other one is blond, pasty, and again, the eye color's not right. The blue is piercing.

"Creeps me out." I lower my chin into the funnel neck of my puffer jacket, shrinking.

"Me too, especially when you consider that she must have known we'd be here like this, looking at her stuff."

"So maybe it's an act—performance art?" I suggest. "One of my artists is into that, making himself part of the art, a sort of living painting. Maybe everything was placed intentionally for us to find, and the chaos is a ruse."

"It all sounds highly unlikely," Stephanie says, killing the idea.

Priyanka looks about her for something to cut the tape, finding a plastic knife on the floor. Then she turns to look at us somberly. "So, ladies, are we ready for this?"

I'm making my way across the mess to join her, when Stephanie says, "No. Please don't."

I stop, straddling an electric sandwich maker that's missing a plug. "You don't want us to open it?"

She shakes her head, adjusting her tote on her shoulder. "It's like Pandora's box. Whatever we find, it'll do us no good."

"But you agree that we need to know what happened?"

Her nostrils flare ever so slightly. "No. I still think we should leave it alone."

"But you saw the photo that I sent you, right?"

"Yes. Why?"

"Because it looks as though they were close friends after all."

"You don't know that." She stares at me, her pupils shrinking.

"We don't know *anything*. Which is why we're here." I place my hands on my hips. "We can't keep having this same conversation, Stephanie. At some point, we're going to have to agree."

"I'll never agree."

Something gives way inside me then—the feeble thread that was holding my emotions in check. "For God's sake!" I snap. "Stop being such a bloody housewife!"

I don't know why I said that. It was the first thing that came to mind.

"Housewife? I'll have you know I've worked my whole life." She blinks, offended, pulling her gloves from her pockets. "I knew I shouldn't have come here."

She's heading for the door. I sense that I should apologize. I can feel Priyanka looking at me with her teacher face.

"Look, I didn't mean to say that. It was rude, ignorant. Please stay, Stephanie. We need you. We can't—"

"Oh my!" Priyanka cries out.

We both turn to look at her. She's kneeling on that dirty floor in front of the open box, holding a book. "I don't believe it…"

"What is it?"

She looks at me and it seems in that moment that she's a little girl, with her furry hood framing her face, her Doc Martens tucked beneath her. "A diary."

I have to ask.

"Which year?"

"You know which year—1990."

"Put it back," Stephanie says hastily. "We've no right to be snooping."

Priyanka complies, dropping the book back into the cardboard box, where it lies tantalizingly on top in plain view.

"Snooping?" I retort. "She gave us the key!"

"But the box was sealed for a reason," Stephanie says. "Maybe she didn't want us to pry."

"So why write to us, then? Why grant us free access to her belongings? I'll tell you why—because she wanted us to do this, that's why!"

"You don't know that."

"No, we don't know anything, remember? I told you that two minutes ago. That's why we're here!"

"I can't do this right now. It's too much." Priyanka is scrabbling to her feet, knocking over a broken lamp in her hurry to get away. "I'm sorry." She puts her head down and her hood up as she makes for the door.

"Priyanka! What are you doing? Wait!" I try to reach her, but she's already through the door and gone. I frown at Stephanie. "This is because you keep arguing! She doesn't know which way to turn. You've driven her away."

"Me? You're the one calling me names!"

I look away from her in irritation, my gaze falling on the cardboard box. There's something up with that. Something's missing. I can't think what.

And then I realize: the diary is gone.

PART TWO: THE DIARY

PRIYANKA

"Pree, it's time to get up."

Andy is shaking my shoulder gently. I was dreaming about Beau. We were in the neonatal unit with the yellow elephant curtains and the green padded chairs, listening to mechanical beeps, navigating the wires.

"Are you all right?" The mattress dips as Andy sits down, smoothing my hair.

My face is wet. I was crying in my sleep. And I remember then: Beau didn't make it and I was devastated. Except that it wasn't him in my dream but a baby with an indistinct face.

I prop myself up on my elbows, wiping my eyes. "I dreamed about Beau again."

He reaches for my hand. "That's all behind us now."

But the letter isn't. And maybe he's thinking the same thing, because a look of uncertainty passes over his face.

This is exactly what I didn't want to happen. I didn't want anything coming between us, spoiling our marriage.

I look away, out of the window. The trees are almost bare. Somehow the leaves have fallen and I haven't noticed—haven't kicked through the autumn leaves with Beau, simple pleasures evading me.

"Are we okay?" he says, fiddling with my fingers.

After years of teaching Ethics, my word used to mean something to me. I believed that you made choices throughout the day—great and small—as to how much truth your words contained.

Now honesty feels perfunctory, optional. "Of course."

Andy's still wearing his pajamas, his hair stuck on end. I've tried all kinds of gels for him, but he's not a product guy. It looks wrong on him. Somehow, bushy, startled, suits him. And I find this unbearably sad at that moment.

He's fifty-one, his whole life wrapped up in me and Beau. Where would he go from here? What would happen to him, if falsely or rightly accused? Would anyone even care which way around it was? Wouldn't being accused in itself be enough to ruin him? Graying, skin loosening, bones weakening, all the little injustices that life deals as you age...only to have your reputation and self-respect taken too.

"You're not still upset about the dream, are you?" he asks gently.

Yes, it's the dream. That's what's breaking my heart, Andy...

I've decided what I'm going to do today. I thought about it all night. I don't like letting down my pupils, but Tuesdays are my lightest timetable day, mostly lesson planning that I can catch up with from home. I don't feel I have a choice; I'm desperate.

Trying to get up, I sit back down heavily, holding my head. "Oh..."

"What's wrong?" He looks at me in concern, still entwining his fingers with mine. I sense that he doesn't want to let go, is lingering.

"It's my head," I whimper. "I've never had a migraine like this." That's because I've only ever had one, a dozen years ago, tequila-induced.

"Maybe it's…" He doesn't finish the sentence. He doesn't have to.

Stress, anxiety, fear. Pick one. They all work.

"Maybe I should stay in bed." I sink onto the pillow, lying still.

He touches my forehead, as though a doctor. "You do feel a little warm."

"My tummy's hurting too. I don't think I can go into school."

"You definitely shouldn't… Do you want me to call them for you?"

"No. It's better coming from me. But could you drop Beau to Tadpoles on your way to work and get him later?"

"Of course."

He's been extra kind to me lately, since our talk Sunday night. It pains me to see. I want to reassure him that he doesn't have to try so hard, that he already has my unwavering love and support. Yet even with my new ability to lie, I can't bring myself to say that.

Stooping, he kisses me lightly on the cheek. "You just rest, my love. Would you like some ibuprofen?"

"No, thanks. I'll sort myself out when I'm up."

"Well, I'd best get a move on, then." He claps his hands against his legs. "Anything in particular Beau needs to wear?"

I manage a smile. "Use your imagination."

"That'll be interesting."

Staring up at the ceiling, my eyes grainy, I think about my dream: about Beau as a baby with pneumonia. You'd think I'd be focusing on the positives; the fact that he's here now and so healthy. Yet the wallowing isn't intentional. My subconscious likes to dredge it up from time to time, aided and abetted by my very conscious fear that his bad start was my punishment.

I did try to talk to a counselor about it, but she kept telling me I was being far too hard on myself—that my past had nothing to do with Beau's illness. I didn't even get around to telling her about the butterfly tattoo.

I watch Andy as he puts on his blazer with elbow patches and his corduroy trousers, looking like a college professor. He was wearing something similar the first time we met, and it was what warmed me to him: the idea of a genteel man who was devoted, tender. We were married within a year, something that didn't feel rushed or reckless at the time.

He had been married before, but I didn't see this as a negative. I thought it meant he embraced responsibility, in contrast to the succession of commitment-phobes I'd dated over the years.

Katie; that's what his first wife was called. That's almost as much as I know about her. He hardly ever mentions her, aside to say that it was as a complete disaster.

But *why* was that?

I squirm farther down beneath the sheets. There could be a host of reasons, none of which seem all that pleasant. I'd love to ask him about her, but how can I?

Ironically, if I hadn't confided in him, I could have asked him anything I liked—could have initiated a completely open conversation. As it stands, everything will seem suspicious, as though I don't believe a word he said.

He's about to leave the room, but again I sense that he's reluctant to go, glancing at me circumspectly. "Aside from you being poorly…everything else is all right, isn't it?"

"Yes." I nod.

"It'll get better…everything…" he says vaguely. Yet I know what he's trying to say: given time, we'll forget and move on. He smiles sadly. "It's just that I'm happy the way things are. I was, well, you know…"

I know.

I was happy the way things were too.

———

I light the gas fire. It's nine thirty in the morning, but still dark out. I watch the blue flames leaping from the artificial coals, the diary on my lap. The gold embossed date on the front is faded yet legible. I run my finger across it, feeling the grooves. On the table beside me, steam curls upward from my coffee cup. Beau's clunky Lego bricks are lying all over the floor. I haven't got the energy to clear up; I like them being there anyway. While the bricks are there, life is normal.

Tugging up my sleeve, I examine my tattoo. I've thought many times about having it removed, but I've heard it can be painful in areas where there's little skin. And besides, sometimes it's a helpful word of warning.

I wasn't exactly an angel, growing up. At university I was known as Party Pree, drinking too much, sleeping with too many men.

Going to teacher's training in Bath was just another way of running away from all that—from the dislocation between who I thought I was and who my family wanted me to be.

I outmaneuvered them, winning my freedom. Good times. Until one morning in my late twenties, after a heavy night out, I woke up with blood all over my arm.

Tattooists aren't supposed to accept drunk clients. Alcohol thins the blood and causes excess bleeding. My tattoo, when I'd washed away the blood, turned out to be a patchy butterfly. I had no idea why it was there.

And then I bumped into a man with a gold tooth in a bar in town, who asked me how the *tat* was. Turned out, he'd taken me to an unlicensed backstreet shop, the sort where they don't sterilize equipment or worry about blood poisoning. He said he'd asked them to give me a butterfly because he'd never known anyone to open and close their legs as fast as I did.

I met Andy not long after. I told him about Party Pree and Priyanka Bandyopadhyay; two very different people. And he offered me a fresh start as Priyanka Lawley.

Reaching for my coffee, I take a sip, welling up. Whatever I find in this diary, I can't lose Andy. I can't lose him.

———————

Nicola Waite wasn't much of a diarist. Some of my least dili-
gent pupils could have done a better job. In all fairness, though,
it wasn't her idea in the first place. According to her half-hearted
entry on New Year's Day, her mother had pressed the diary on
her for Christmas because she'd heard that writing a journal was
good for anxiety. Her mum, so Nicky divulged, was a long-
term agoraphobic. Her dad had abandoned them years ago and
was *a total prick face*. Her words, not mine (February 4th 1990).

On the second day of the New Year, she wrote simply: *113 lbs* ☹
On the third: *114 lbs* ☹ ☹

Aside from the brief mention of her dad in February, she
wrote fondly about everyone back in her hometown of Leeds.
She preferred it to Bath, but maybe was just homesick. Her two
flatmates, Kim and Lucy, didn't help matters. Both from the
counties surrounding London, they were wealthy, into horses.

The three girls were at Bath university, in their first year,
studying for a business degree. Most of Nicky's worries were
about trying to find a work placement for her third year, at a
time of mass unemployment. They didn't need to secure the
placement until spring 1991, yet Nicky was beginning to panic.

Kim's father, an entrepreneur, had made a few calls on his
daughter's behalf; Lucy was equally well taken care of. They
had personal contacts. Whereas Nicky, with her armchair mum
and absent father, seemed to have none.

A straight A's student, she had thought that going to university and getting a first class honors would be enough to set her
up in life.

How stupid and naive can you be? (May 11th 1990).

Weeks would go by without anything in the diary, aside from
her weight, which she logged religiously. If she lost a pound,
she earned a smiley face.

The summer passed with a riot of blank pages. Back in Leeds, she hung out with her mum in their small row house. There were a few lines about boys whom she went out with, even though she didn't seem to really want to. Maybe it was boredom. Maybe she was flattered. She liked to record not what she wore or where they went, but the compliments they gave her.

You're beautiful, you know that?

I can't stop thinking about you.

She'd go out, have a few drinks, kiss them and then return home, where she'd end up in the kitchen, eating toast, chocolate, cake, anything in the tins.

The next day there'd be several sad faces.

———

Laying the diary aside, I look at the fire, listening to it softly buffeting. One hundred and thirteen pounds doesn't sound a lot to me, no matter what height she was. She must have been starving.

My coffee's gone cold. I go through to the kitchen to make a fresh one, thinking about Nicky and her neat handwriting and love of record-making, trying to marry this to the distorted canvases in her daughter's chaotic storage unit.

I don't want to read on. I know what's coming and it's all the worse for knowing who she was and seeing her words, so raw, immediate.

Picking up the diary, I slowly make my way forward through the empty pages until at last I meet an intense sea of black ink, signaling the beginning of the end.

———

Saturday, December 15

It's midnight but I had to write, even though I'm so tired. I wasn't going out, but Lucy begged me—fancies a guy in marketing class. So I went along to help her out.

It was so busy. Soon as we got to the White Hart, Lucy went off to find her man, leaving me with Kim. She always waits for me to get my purse out first, even though she owns half of Kent, so I gave her the slip and went to the jukebox. And that's where I met the boys, just as a party popper landed in my hair and the whole pub started singing along to Slade. This guy appeared—short, but handsome!—and helped me untangle the string from my hair. He was with 2 friends. It was too loud to talk so we went outside.

The short one's Jack, a student home for Christmas. Lee, also a student, is so tall and a real gent. (He lent me his jacket 'cos I was cold.) And Brooke's a soldier, on leave, the first one I'd ever met. We talked as though we'd known each other all our lives. But then when time at the bar was called, they suddenly downed their drinks and left. I didn't know whether I'd see them again, so I ran after them.

Turns out, they were going to the Montague Club! (Lucy and Kim are always plotting how to get in there.) I told them, casually, that I'd always fancied seeing inside the club and they said we could talk about it tomorrow, if I fancied joining them at the White Hart for lunch?

Lucy & Kim will be dead jealous. I could be about to get into the most exclusive hot spot in town! Who knows—it could even help me to secure a work placement, if I meet the right people. That could actually happen. Is my luck changing?

Sunday, December 16

112 lbs ☺

I was supposed to be going home on the snail coach to Leeds this morning, but knew that wasn't going to happen. I rang Mum to explain and she sounded disappointed, but she'll come around. I'm only postponing by a week—will be there next Sunday.

Then I spent an hour panicking about what to wear. Turns out, I don't have an outfit for lunch with rich people. In the end, I decided on my black shirtdress. I asked Lucy to come because I didn't want to go on my own, but she was meeting her parents. I even asked Kim, but she made up an excuse about writing an essay. Her loss.

I needn't have worried. Lunch was perfect. Jack was so attentive, looking into my eyes when I spoke. I felt like the most fascinating girl in the world. Brooke was dressed in a smart polo shirt with his collar up. He wasn't so chatty but seemed to listen well. And Lee had to stoop to avoid the ceiling beams and again, such a gent—pulling out my chair for me to sit down. No one's ever done that for me before.

They told me about the club, how their fathers are members, how it's just had a makeover. There are giant lilies that leave pollen on their clothes if brushed against, and they serve champagne piña coladas and something called a Flying Grasshopper, which has to be tried at least once.

The dress code is business smart and the boys keep their suits in a special dressing room to change into. The fire in the Green Room's always lit, even in summer. The women—only permitted to join 2 years ago—wear diamonds and sequined cocktail dresses. My heart sank at that and then I thought of Lucy. If I could get her into the club too, she'd definitely lend me a dress. That's how it works isn't it? At least, it seems so in Bath.

By the time we left the pub, the day was already losing light and the city felt magical, lights glowing inside windows. As we said goodbye, they invited me to join them on Saturday night at the Hart again. I pretended to think about it before saying yes...

Tuesday, December 18

112 lbs ☺

I told Lucy and Kim about the Montague tonight. Lucy was excited, but Kim didn't say a word. I asked if they fancied joining me Saturday night, to see if maybe we might end up at the club. Lucy started squealing and dragged me through to her room, emptying her wardrobe onto the bed. I didn't even have to ask. Kim stood in the doorway, looking like she was sucking a lemon. I bet she'll come on Saturday though. She's just not going to admit that she needs anything from someone like me.

Mum rang tonight and got all funny about me missing the coach and wasting money, even though the ticket was cheap as chips. I tried to explain that it's a great opportunity, but she wouldn't listen. She said I don't know these boys from Adam and rang off in a huff. I was upset, but can't let it get to me. Mum doesn't know how these things work—that business is all about who you know. You just need to be moving in the right circles. I love her but she has her life to lead, staying home all the time, and I've got mine. And maybe I want something a little different for myself. I'll see her on Sunday anyway and it'll all be forgotten by the time we're sitting down by the Christmas tree.

Thursday, December 20

111 lbs 😊 😊

Jack rang tonight to ask if I'd like a quick drink at the Hart. I hadn't been in long from lectures and was in the middle of warming up a tin of soup. I burned my mouth where I ate it so fast, putting on some makeup before dashing out. Going up the main street, I told myself to slow down so I wouldn't arrive all disheveled.

Jack was sitting near the window and jumped up when he saw me, kissing me on the cheek. When he went to the bar, I secretly checked him out, eyeing his muscly arms. We'd only just started talking, Jack telling me that he's not all that rich and I was thinking how his eyes are like toy marbles—green with swirls of blue and brown—when there was a rap on the window and Brooke and Lee were there, wagging their fingers.

They joined us, accusing Jack of trying to pull a fast one. I laughed, but then realized they had some kind of bet or competition about who was going to date me. It seemed jokey, but still, I didn't want any friction. So I decided to go ahead and ask whether my friends could join us Saturday night.

They seemed to like the idea. They were allowed to sign in one guest each, they said.

I took from that that we definitely are going to the club and somehow managed to keep my face completely blank, as though it wasn't a big deal.

I stayed for one more drink, Jack telling me about his economics course, and Lee his IT studies. Brooke was very quiet again, probably because he's not a student so couldn't comment, but I noticed that he looked at me a lot.

When I got up to leave, Jack reminded me to wear a little black dress Saturday night. Brooke didn't take his eyes off me, but it was Lee who walked me to the door, stooping to ask whether I'd like him to walk me home. I said no, but on my way home I decided that if he asks me out, I'll say yes.

Girls like me always go for guys like Lee. It's just that no one ever seems to realize why and always acts surprised about it.

I break off reading. The next entry is Christmas Eve, two days after that Saturday night.

I can't understand how things changed, how they went from congenial drinks in the White Hart to a…sexual assault allegation. A little bit of friendly rivalry between young males seemed about the worst of the tensions in the run-up to that night.

What on earth happened?

Looking about me, I'm surprised to see such banal details as the flames of the gas fire and Beau's Lego bricks on the carpet. I'm barely aware of the present, still in 1990.

Turning the page, I read on.

JESS

Priyanka is waiting for me on the forecourt, her arms wrapped around her. She looks so small standing there, with the imposing facade of St. Saviour's behind her, teenagers everywhere. I've no idea how she does it.

"Come on," she says. "Let's get out of here."

We head across the field, the sun warm on our backs. The school is set on the brow of a hill, adjacent to a park that tourists huff and puff up to admire the views. On a day like today, the city seems to have a halo, a circle of golden trees above it. "So, autumn happened?" I ask.

"I thought the exact same thing yesterday."

That's all we say. I know what this is about. It's obvious: she's read the diary. On her shoulder, there's an off-white canvas tote—the sort you get free at eco fairs—and I can see the sharp outline of a book within.

"Let's go in here." We've arrived at a cricket pavilion. She turns the key and we enter. The place must be new, smells of wood and varnish. It's deathly silent as we shuffle to a bench beside the window, setting down our bags as we sit.

She doesn't say anything for a few minutes. I let her do what she needs to do, which is have a little cry. I'm not very good at consoling talks, other than with my girls. I look at the puffy spider sacs in the eaves above us, the particles of dust floating in a beam of sunshine near our feet.

She doesn't have any tissues. I can help with that. Locating a packet of pocket tissues in my bag, I hand it to her, this single act of kindness setting her off even more.

I look at the tote, spying a glimpse of red leather, the corner of a book, and feel so nauseous I can't swallow. I won't be able to eat all day, or ever. This will kill me. I'll be too frail to function and I'll—

"Jess..." She turns to me, a tear trickling down her cheek. "...I think they did it."

So do I.

I guessed it the moment I saw the photo of Max with those two men in the Montague Club. Two friends whose names had never been mentioned; the same names in Holly Waite's letter. It was too much of a coincidence.

I don't know what to say, though: that I suspected as much— that I don't know what the hell we're going to do?

I try to think practically. "Don't cry, Priyanka. You have to go back to class."

"Call me Pree. Everyone calls me Pree," she says, looking at me with her big brown eyes, and I wonder whether I'm seeing their true color for the first time.

"Okay, Pree." I smile, but fudge it, mouth trembling. Pressing my hands on my knees, I watch as four boys roll about on the lawn across the way, jostling, laughing.

She glances at them warily, then bends down, reaching for the tote. "The bell's going to ring in a sec. But here, take this."

Our hands touch as I take the bag from her. I want to hug her, but she's already heading for the door.

Outside the school, on the forecourt, she's tiny again, her pink hair catching the lunchtime sun, exposing gray and black roots.

"Look after yourself," I tell her. "And remember, we're in this together, okay? You're not alone."

Her eyes widen and she bites her lip as another wave of upset hits her. And then she turns and goes, passing through the large wooden doors, out of sight.

I look up at the building, picturing her hurrying up the stairs, taking a class in a stuffy room, trying to keep order and concentrate, trying to deliver her best to a constant stream of boys looking to her for guidance and support and a clue.

Of the three of us, she has by far the hardest task, and I wish it weren't so, that it were me instead. But I can't change that, or anything.

Going to the car, I hide the tote at the bottom of my rucksack, slamming the door behind me so hard it hurts my hand.

———

It's another two days before I read the diary or even attempt to get it out from the bottom of my bag. And even then, it's with Mum at Beechcroft Home.

The place is deserted. No one wants to come here on Friday night, not after a week's work. Just the guilty ones like me and the guy with the leather Outback hat. I saw him earlier in the car park and we ignored each other.

Olivia isn't here tonight, doesn't work Fridays. The glittery flowers are starting to wilt and smell. But I have a system, and the flowers remain until the new ones arrive. Sometimes, Mum notices that her vase is empty and it upsets her. She's smashed a few. So, now they stay until replaced, rotten or not.

"Have you come to give me my bath?" Mum says, vaguely in my direction.

"No. It's me, Mum, Jess. Your daughter."

I can't tell you how many times I've said this. But tonight, they feel like the saddest words imaginable.

"Don't run it too hot, will you? I don't like it too hot."

"No, Mum." I touch her hand tenderly. Her skin's so soft, barely there, the veins bulbous.

I don't want to be sitting beside her as I read the diary, even though she has no idea who I am or what day of the week it is, so I move over to the window. The door is closed, which they don't really like, but they won't bother me about it. They know me by now.

I face away from Mum, the book propped on the window ledge. To anyone outside, in that black abyss, I'll be on full view. Yet no one will notice me. No one looks at Beechcroft. They're in too much of a hurry to get in and out.

Turning the pages, I search for writing. There's not a lot, not until the 15th December 1990, and then there's such a sudden onslaught of ink that it's like looking at a car crash. You don't want to. You know it's going to hurt. But still…you look.

Monday, December 24

I don't know what to think or feel. It feels unbelievable as though I imagined the whole thing. But I know I didn't. Everything feels disturbing, dark, heavy. I haven't moved all day. Where would I go? It's Christmas Eve and my world has no sides or floor or ceiling. I'm all alone and I want to die. I can't think of one good thing.

I need to try to put the events in the order that they happened.

On Saturday, I woke up with a bad cold, but was determined to ignore it. Lucy and I spent the morning sorting out outfits. She even lent me a beautiful gold necklace with a topaz pendant. I don't know what happened to it.

Then I rang Mum to tell her I'd be on the 9.15 a.m. coach in the morning and for her to get the fire lit and the kettle on.

By early evening, my cold was worse. Kim got out her cough medicine, telling me to swig it, tilting the bottle. She said it

*wouldn't work unless you took a really decent dose, and I was
desperate to feel better.*

*The Hart was so busy, there was a blast of heat and noise as we
walked in. Do They Know It's Christmas? was playing. The
boys were waiting by the jukebox and then we all went outside.*

*It was loud, even in the street, and cold too. Lee and Jack ar-
gued over who was going to give me their coat, and Kim tutted.
I don't think she smiled all night. I drank a bit too much. Peach
Schnapps was on promo and I'd never had it before, couldn't gauge
its strength.*

*When last orders were called, Jack said shall we, ladies? And
we followed them, wobbling in our heels across the cobblestones.*

*The club was tucked away in a Georgian square. It was so
quiet, the moon hiding behind racing clouds. I felt giddy for a moment, looking up. I remember checking my watch for the last time:
11.15 p.m.*

*Brooke was trying to light his cigarette, but it was too windy.
The boys huddled around him and I heard whispering, but was
too busy smoothing my hair to worry about what they were doing.*

*Kim was waiting by the front door, but they walked right past
her, around the side of the building.*

Where are you going? I called after them.

We're using this entrance tonight, Brooke said.

I didn't think anything of it. Why would I?

*We went in through the tradesman's entrance. Maybe this was
where the members entered, or the young ones, at least.*

*Inside, they steered us along a dark corridor. I could smell cigar
smoke, hear the rumble of voices and tinkling of glasses behind
closed doors. And then we were going up a staircase.*

*Halfway up, Lucy stopped, pulled on my arm. Why are we
going up here?*

Come on, it'll be fun, I said.

*But why aren't we staying on the ground floor? Kim asked.
We're moving away from the party, not toward it.*

I hesitated. Maybe the cool kids meet up here?

At the top of the stairs, Jack whispered are you coming or what?

Why's he whispering? Kim said.

I waited for him to move away before reaching for Lucy's hand. I didn't bother with Kim—didn't care what she said or did. But I wanted Lucy with me.

Come on, Lucy. Let's just go with the flow. We're inside the club aren't we?

She smiled. Okay.

We continued upstairs, following the boys into a room with a pool table. I understood the secrecy then: they were raiding the bar, pouring spirits into crystal tumblers. Everyone was whispering, cheeks glowing, aside from Kim who sat with her arms folded.

Why aren't we down there? she said every time a swell of laughter rose beneath us.

Because this is more fun, Lee said, filling her glass.

We sat around on leather sofas, chatting, and it was as comfortable as it always was with them. At some point, Kim said she was going in search of the bathroom and took Lucy with her.

Brooke announced we were all out of scotch. That was when I asked if he was American, because of his name, plus I'd noticed he was wearing a US-style military neck tag. I was so surprised when he said his real name was Daniel Brooke. Jack was Maximilian Jackson. And Lee said Andrew Lawley at your service, ma'am.

I only needed to hear the names once. I'm good at retaining information. I remember feeling disappointed that they hadn't told me sooner though.

It was around about then that I noticed my stomach was burning. I wasn't used to drinking spirits and had a fuzzy recollection of taking cough medicine too.

And then I realized that I was all alone. I had no idea where everyone had gone—hadn't even noticed them leave.

I went along the corridor in search of the boys, to ask whether we could go downstairs now. It was so dark, but I could see light ahead, underneath a door. I felt wobbly, rested my hand against the wall. Then I opened the door, squinting at the bare light bulb. It was a storeroom full of stacked boxes. Jack was straddling a crate, eating a packet of crisps. Lee was smoking. Brooke was ripping open a box, bottles tinkling. It was the club's bar supplies, a grown-up tuck shop.

Lee said they'd just been discussing which one of them I was going to choose. He said they thought it was probably Jack, that the ladies tended to go for him.

I was about to hint that not every woman went for muscles and that some preferred gentle souls like Lee, but to my embarrassment my speech was slurry. I could barely understand myself.

Jack leaned past me then to shut the door and before I knew what was happening he was kissing me, lowering the straps on my dress. I wriggled, looking at Lee to say something. But he was just standing there, watching, a strange look on his face. Brooke was drawing closer, military tag gleaming.

The room was spinning. I couldn't move or speak. I couldn't stop them, couldn't do anything about it.

I'm sorry. I can't write this yet. I'll leave a space and will come back, when I'm ready.

On Sunday morning, in the early hours, I realized I was on the move.

Driving Home for Christmas was playing, barely audible. I could smell coconut. A crucifix was swaying. For one moment, I thought I was in Leeds, in the back of a mini-cab—had made it home on the coach. But then someone spoke and I remembered Lee, Jack and Brooke—something happening with them, something bad.

Around here is it? a man said.

My hair was everywhere, in my eyes. I peered out of the window at the dark, empty streets, my stomach lurching. Can I get some fresh air? I asked.

A pair of eyes fixed on me in the rearview mirror. Not gonna be sick, are you? he said.

The window opened, cold air blasting. Closing my eyes, I held my face to the wind, trying to recall details. Where was I?

He turned the radio down even lower, to a crackle. They said to take you somewhere studenty, but that's a bit vague, innit. At some point, you're gonna have to tell me where to go. We've been circling the uni for the past fifteen minutes.

I tried to recognize something, but nothing seemed familiar. I lived nowhere near here, but couldn't remember the name of my street. And if I didn't look straight ahead, I'd be sick.

Panic clouded my eyes. My nose was running, my forehead felt hot. I remembered then that I had a cold.

You all right? The eyes were looking at me in the mirror again.

I don't know, I said. Shifting position, I noticed that the strap on my dress was broken and that Lucy's necklace was missing. I began to cry.

I live near the petrol station, I told him. And it came to me: Maple Street.

When I got home, Lucy and Kim were asleep, their travel bags packed and ready. They didn't wake me in the morning— went home for Christmas without a word. I woke up later that day to an empty flat, knowing that nothing was ever going to be the same again.

This is a faithful record of that night, exactly as I remember it, as much as I can manage for now.

Signed,
Nicola Waite

———

Wednesday, December 26

I stayed in bed for 24 hours yesterday, all through Christmas Day. The phone rang and rang, but I was too tired to move. I guessed it was Mum. I didn't know what to say to her.

There was a hammering on the door half an hour ago. I dragged the duvet with me—thought I'd better answer in case it was the landlord.

It was the police. Mum reported me missing, adamant that I'd taken the coach to Leeds on Sunday. The policemen took one look at me, muttered something about drugs and bloody students and then left.

There was a split second when I thought about telling them. But I wasn't ready, wasn't prepared.

Thursday, December 27

Today was the same as yesterday. We don't have an answering machine so the phone just rings and rings. I'm not going to answer it. Mum won't come in search of me, can't make it to the end of the road without panicking. Eventually, she'll give up.

I don't want to write any more today.

Saturday, December 29

Things felt different today. I didn't want to lie around. I tidied up and unplugged the phone to stop it ringing.

As it got dark, I realized a week had already passed by, a week of my life lost in oblivion. An anger came over me and I started to pace the floor. I began to see how clever they'd been—how they hadn't given me their phone numbers, any details, not even their real names until the last minute and maybe only then because they thought I'd be too drunk to remember. They were the ones with all the control and I hadn't even noticed.

Scraping back my hair, I found a pair of jeans, shocked by how baggy they were. I don't own a belt and didn't want to take anything else of Lucy's so tucked my sweater in to keep them up.

When I entered the Hart, my heart began to pound so much I thought about giving up and going home. There was still tinsel fluttering above radiators, mistletoe withering on ribbons. It was quiet—easy to see in one sweep of the room that they weren't there.

I could have gone home, but something made me keep going, along the cobblestones to the square. Being there again made my ears ring with panic. In the shadows of an old sycamore tree, I squatted and waited for them.

———

A sudden noise—a door slamming out in the corridor—makes me jump. I exhale heavily, as though I'd been holding my breath. Going over to Mum, I check on her, touching her hand, listening to her breathing, before returning to the window. Propping the diary on the sill, I continue reading, Beechcroft falling ever quieter around me as night thickens and stills.

STEPHANIE

Weekends at Chappell and Black are busy, so we run a rotation on reception. I work Saturday mornings only, something I negotiated several years ago with Leonardo. He said I didn't have to explain—that my work spoke for itself. I can't say how much that meant to me.

Saturday afternoons are the highlight of my week. After work, I walk down through town, buy magazines, pick up treats for the girls—lip glosses, accessories—and pastries from the deli. Dan works till late; Saturday's his busiest day. So, in the winter, the girls and I light the fire and chat, the magazines fanned out on the carpet. In the summer, we drink prosecco on the patio and give ourselves pedicures.

That said, they aren't always available now, especially Vivian. And Georgia is beginning to drag her feet. Rosie will always be there, especially if there's food and wine. My biggest critic, yet the least likely to leave my side.

This morning, work is typically hectic. I've noticed that one of my colleagues has booked Shelley Fricker in for deep cleaning at one o'clock, but I'll be gone by then.

My phone buzzes the arrival of a text, which I read on my lap underneath the counter.

10.03 A.M. >
Hi, hope you're OK. Need to see you ASAP, only for 5 mins. When's a good time? J xx

There isn't a good time. I'm still feeling offended because of the housewife comment. It will take more than a kissy text from her to make me forget it.

10.05 A.M. >
Sorry, but work's too busy today. It'll have to wait.

I press send, slip the phone into my bag and turn to the booking screen just as a client arrives. And I'm looking at him, at his protruding teeth, which he's showing me, when I realize that I made a mistake. I shouldn't have told her where I was.

I spend the rest of the morning worried she's going to show up, watching the door, my heart skipping each time I hear footsteps ascending the stairs.

By the time twelve thirty arrives, my nerves are so bad I'm jumping whenever the phone rings.

"Are you okay, Stephanie?" My colleague Ali goes to touch me on the arm before thinking better of it. I'm not tactile and most people know that.

"I'm fine, thanks." I'm trying to leave and making a mess of it, the strap of my bag caught in the wheels of my chair. Bending over, I'm untangling myself when I hear a familiar voice.

"Steffie, that you down there?"

Freeing my bag, I stand up, straightening my blouse, looking straight at Shelley Fricker. She's hitching up her leggings, grinning at me.

I glance around the crowded waiting room. It's as though she does it deliberately, waiting until the finest selection of coats is seated, with the best-cut suits and lowest voices, so she can ring out loud and clear exactly who I am and how she knows me.

"How you getting on? All *right*?"

She couldn't sound any coarser. And to top it all, Leonardo is heading this way.

I give her a tight smile. I can't be rude to a client, not in front of him. "Hello, Shelley. I was just leaving..."

She cocks her head at me. "Bit early, innit? Hope you're not slacking off." She laughs, flapping her hand. "Not that I'm saying you ever did that at school, mind!"

I'm making my way out from behind the desk, but Leonardo has caught the tail end of the conversation. "Do you two know each other?" he asks, leaning against the counter, a faint look of amusement on his face. I think he finds me a little uptight; he's enjoying this.

"No, not really."

"Oh, we go *way* back, don't we, our Steffie?" Shelley nudges me. "We were at school together, down Nor'on."

Leonardo frowns. Then his expression clears. "Midsomer Norton?"

"That's right," she says proudly.

Why stop there, Shelley? Why not tell him about the sanitary pad in the school bathroom? Why not tell everyone how my ex-husband used to grope women while waiting for the number 173 bus to Bath?

"I didn't know you were from there, Stephanie?" Leonardo lifts an eyebrow.

Picking up my coat, I busy myself with putting it on. But to my relief, Leonardo's too busy to linger and is returning to the treatment room. I mutter goodbye and leave Shelley for Ali to see to.

Outside, it's refreshingly cold. I'm checking my messages, so I don't see Jess right away, not until she's standing in the middle of the pavement, blocking my path.

"Hi, Stephanie."

I press my lips together in frustration. "Why are you here?" I whisper, glancing over my shoulder. "I said I was busy."

"Sorry, but I really do just need five minutes. Please?"

There's not a lot I can do about it. I can scarcely say no and cause a scene right outside work. "What is it?" I ask resignedly.

Directing me to the railings at the side of the pavement, she glances around her before pulling a tote bag from her rucksack. "I need you to do something for me. I need you to take this."

"No."

She laughs as though I'm outrageous. "You can't just say no! It doesn't work like that."

I don't reply.

Touching my hand, she looks at me earnestly. "Look, I know we're different, Stephanie. Chalk and cheese. But we're in each other's lives now and have to try to figure this out."

Two tourists are approaching—a young couple, the boy's hand in the back of the girl's jeans pocket. I stand aside for them, giving Jess a look of caution. She waits for them to pass by.

"Please. Take this." She presses the tote into my hand.

There's a giant tea-colored stain on the bag. "What is it?"

"The diary."

I look at her in surprise. "And you're trusting me with it? What if I destroy it?"

"I don't think you'll do that. Besides, I'm willing to take that risk because you need to read it. We won't move on unless you do. And I'm hoping it'll change the way you feel."

"Then I definitely don't want it." I try to return the tote, but she steps back, hands in pockets.

"It's yours now. Let me know when you're done. And then we can meet and discuss a way forward."

The couple are on their way back again, the girl pausing for a photograph of the Circus, fluffing her hair, giving a toothy smile, the dental practice aptly in the background.

"You don't seem to understand," I say, still holding the tote out for her. "Nothing in here is going to change anything for me. So, if you don't take this bag, I'll hang it on the railing."

She smiles pleasantly as though I've just agreed to water her houseplants. "Thanks, Stephanie. Call me when you've read it, okay? See you soon." And she turns on her heel, walks away. I have no choice but to take the bag, concealing it within mine.

———

"Sorry, Mum, I thought you'd be cool with it." Georgia isn't even looking at me, is playing on her phone. "I can cancel… But Daisy will be here in five to pick me up."

I'm setting the wineglasses on the living room table, dusting the crystal, holding it to the light. "I see."

She glances at me. "I don't think you should bother with any of that. You might wanna check with the sibs, but I think they're out too."

I examine the inside of a glass, wiping away a fleck of dust. The girls could have told me sooner, before I bought pastries and nail polishes. But I won't show how upset I am. They have their own lives to lead. It's just disappointing, that's all.

Upstairs, Rosie's booming music stops and then a door slams shut.

A few moments later, she enters the room wearing a skull and crossbones sweater, and camouflage miniskirt as though off to a protest rally. She doesn't get her dress sense from me.

"Right, I'm off to—" She gazes at the pastries, claps her hand to her head—an affectation. We've been doing this every Saturday for years; she couldn't have forgotten. "Shit! Will you be all right if I go out, M? Only Scarlett's asked me over to her place…"

"That's fine." I smile, but it's an effort.

In truth, I'm not feeling wonderful today. I get good days and bad days, depending on how I've slept: night sweats, palpitations. Dan keeps urging me to seek different medical opinions, but I find it too upsetting. They always ask how my mother's menopause was, and I have to explain all over again that she never made it that far—not by a long stretch.

"Are you sure, M?" Rosie's going through her purse, counting notes, mumbling to herself.

"Yes. It's fine. Vivian will be here to keep me company."

"Uh. Yeah, about that…"

I set the glass down on the table. "She's not staying either?"

Rosie smiles sympathetically, closing her purse, setting her bag on her shoulder. She carries a satchel like the one our milkman used to use in the seventies. Ugly, leather.

"Sorry," Rosie says, hitching down her skirt. "But Viv's at Tom's. Didn't she text you?"

"No. I don't think so." I pick up my phone, drumming my nails on the counter. Sure enough, there's an apologetic message from Vivian, full of emojis. "Well, I'll just have to drink this on my own, then," I say, picking up the bottle of Rioja.

Outside, there's a car horn. "Oh, that'll be Daisy." Georgia kisses me hurriedly on the cheek, barely touching my skin, before darting to the hallway. "Her mum's bringing me home at six," she calls over her shoulder. "Save me a pastry, won't you?"

I follow her in my fluffy slippers, wondering what I'll do with myself, with the sudden free time. "Look after yourself, won't you, darling?" I tell her. "Don't talk to any strangers in town."

Rosie's looking for her boots in her usual agitated style, kicking the shoe rack. "Where the hell *are* they?"

At the door, I tuck Georgia's hair behind her ears, who shakes her head to put it back the way it was. She looks sweet, like a peppermint, in a green-and-white sweater, faded jeans. "Be safe, darling. There are a lot of—"

"Weirdos, pedos and pervs?" Rosie says, wrinkling her nose,

sitting on the floor to put on her boots. "You're even starting to sound like him now."

"Like who?" I ask, watching Georgia go down the driveway, giving a little skip in her excitement. She's half-girl, half-woman; the hardest age.

"Like the arsehole we call Dad now."

"Don't call him that!" I hiss at Rosie. "Have some respect for him when you're living under his roof. You owe him that much while he's paying the bills." I close the door slightly, worried that Daisy's mother can hear this conversation. She's outside in the car, window down, waving at me. "I mean it."

"God, you're so conditioned. You don't even hear it anymore."

I turn to point at her. "I'm not arguing with you, young lady. These are the things you should be discussing with your counselor—trying to manage your anger." I open the door again to wave at the car, smiling.

Rosie is skulking off, wheeling her bike down the driveway. "Where's your helmet?" I call after her.

"Fuck's sake. It's, like, a five-minute journey." And she's off, up the road, long hair flailing behind her.

Closing the door, I inhale, listening to the silence.

In the living room, I look at the empty glasses, the pastries, the new nail polishes. Pouring a glass of Rioja, I sit down on the sofa, my eye falling on my work bag.

I'm halfway through the glass of wine before I move. Even then, I sit with the grubby tote beside me for a long while before reaching into it.

Saturday, December 29

A church bell was ringing somewhere in the city as they appeared, jovial, eager for their next drink. I was struck by how much they were the same, how nothing had changed for them.

I caught them just as they were about to knock on the door. They didn't recognize me without my makeup. We need to talk about what happened, I said.

Jack touched my shoulder in concern. Everything okay, Nicky?

I yanked my arm away. Don't touch me! I shouted.

Shush! Lee glanced around the square. What's wrong? Are you ill?

You know full well what's wrong! You raped me!

Wooahh! Jack held up his hands. Now wait a minute... He led me to the side alley, near the tradesman's entrance. I stared into the gloom between the buildings, my heart racing. This wasn't the cool entrance at all, the one they normally used. It was the one for me—for people like me.

What's this all about? he asked, as though he really didn't know.

Inside my coat, my hands formed fists. You raped me, I repeated.

Raped you? That's not how I remember it.

Are you kidding me? I shouted.

Hush now. Lee lit a cigarette. Obviously, there's been a misunderstanding. We had too much to drink and things got...interesting. Maybe you regret it and feel ashamed, but that doesn't mean you can change the facts.

Not to mention that you were using us to get into the club, Brooke said, looking me up and down. I mean, come on! How else would you have ever got in?

That's a bit harsh, Jack said. I don't think we need to be chucking accusations around.

Why not? She is.

That's because you did it! I said. You know you did!

Look... Lee's voice was kindly, sympathetic... I think you think you're telling the truth, Nicky, but we know differently. And it wasn't rape.

My anger left me then, my eyes filling with tears. You really believe that?

Jack nodded. It's the truth.

How can you treat me like this? I asked Lee, searching his face for a glimpse of regret, shame. If anyone was going to break, give way, it would be him, I felt sure.

I'm sorry, he said. Truly. But I can't admit to something I haven't done.

All hope left me then and I felt airless, weightless.

I guess there's no more to say then, I said.

Guess not, Brooke said.

———

Wednesday, January 23

Lucy and Kim come and go, the only sign that days are beginning and ending. Kim says if I don't go to classes soon, they'll throw me out of the course. Like she's the faculty dean. What does she know? Lucy comes in to see me, brings me messages saying that Mum's phoned again. Other than that, nothing happens.

———

Saturday, March 16

Something strange happened. When I woke up, I had to run to the bathroom to retch. I haven't been eating much lately, can't think what's upset my stomach.

———

Sunday, March 17

Same again.

———

Thursday, March 21

Just realized that I haven't had a period since December.

Saturday, March 23

I waited for them underneath the sycamore tree tonight, freezing to death. There was snow on the ground and I didn't have enough on—wasn't thinking straight, wearing a pair of tracksuit bottoms and sneakers. I haven't left the flat in so long, I hadn't realized how cold it was. Lucy and Kim have gone home for Easter so I knew that two of the boys would be home from university too.

It took them even longer to recognize me this time. Jack looked shocked. What are you doing here?

You're shivering. Lee went to take off his coat for me, like he did the first time I met them. It stunned me, the act of chivalry. Even now.

I dropped his coat into the snow. I need to talk to you.

Brooke rolled his eyes. The subtlest of movements, but I caught it.

I'm pregnant.

Jack ruffled his hair. Really?

For God's sake... Brooke muttered.

Lee rubbed my arm. Poor thing. Do you know who the father is?

I opened my mouth, speechless.

Could be anyone, let's face it, Brooke said, looking up at the sky as though bored.

Anger ripped through me. I prodded him in the chest. How dare you? It's yours! I pointed at Jack. Or yours! Then Lee. Or yours! I know your real names, where to find you. You have to help me. I'm miles from home. I don't know what to do. It's your problem too, not just mine. If you don't take some responsibility, I'll... I'll...

You'll what? Brooke stood with his legs astride, teeth bared viciously. If you've got any sense, you'll leave us alone, he said. Christ, I wish I'd never laid eyes on you. Come on. Let's go. I've had enough of this crap.

He thudded toward the club, rattling the knocker, the sound
splitting the air. Jack joined him. Lee hesitated. I looked at him
pleadingly. I'm sorry, he said. He seemed to mean it.

I lingered, hoping he might do something, anything, but he was
turning away.

The door opened, warm light spilling onto the square, the swell
of voices, laughter, and I thought of the giant lilies they'd described
during that perfect lunch at the White Hart and the champagne
piña coladas, the fire that was always lit in the Green Room, the
women wearing diamonds, and then it closed and I knew that I
was never going to see any of them ever again.

———

I don't know how long I sit like that, with the empty glass
of Rioja on the sofa beside me, the diary on my lap. When the
mantelpiece clock chimes, I look at it in surprise. The room is
so dark, it's a wonder I could see to read.

Returning the diary to the bottom of my bag, I turn on the
lights, drawing the curtains, making my way upstairs to run a
bath so I can forget all about Nicola Waite.

Naive child. What did she expect? Going into a private club,
sneaking upstairs with three men she didn't know from Adam,
as her mother put it. There's a line, invisible, but we all know
it's there, and there are always consequences if you're foolish
enough to cross it.

She knew they were attracted to her, all three of them. Yet she
didn't clarify which of them she was interested in, didn't want to
burn her bridges before gaining entry into the club. Setting foot
inside there was all she really cared about. She said so herself.

Instead of creating boundaries, she drank too much, put herself in danger, kept all her options open. She captured so many
details about that night, yet when it came to the deed itself was
unable to describe anything concrete. And why was that? Probably because she was ashamed.

Running the bath, I dip my fingers in the water, testing it.

She was using them just as much as they were using her. It's just that with things being as they are these days, you're not allowed to say that anymore. Everyone's a victim. Common sense has gone out of the window.

She wasn't a victim; she was ambitious. She felt owed, was bitter about her lack of connections, desperate for a passport into the world of Bath's elite. What was it she called her father? Prick face?

My father was no good too, but I'd never have called him that. He gambled everything away, left my mother destitute. I often saw her crying in desperation, frightened she couldn't feed us, which was why she taught me to value financial security above all else—to find a reliable life partner who could support me and any future children. She set up my hope chest and told me to be graceful, courteous, and to pay attention to my looks.

It's hard work doing it that way. I didn't just get drunk and have sex in a storeroom in the hope of advancing myself socially.

It sounds as though she didn't put up a fight or tell them to stop. She allowed the situation to be so ambiguous that the boys didn't even see it as rape. And I believe them too. After all, women like me don't get caught out like that. Because we keep things clear, on the level. She was playing a game, trying to get what she wanted, using her sexuality to influence them.

You can't have it both ways. She knew what she was doing, what she was risking.

Taking the glass plunger out of a blue bottle, I pour geranium oil into the water, the scent of lavender and mint meeting my nose. I add more, sitting on the side of the bath, watching bubbles form, then disperse.

I refuse to ruin my life for this silly girl. I've come too far, have been through too much.

If Jess thinks the diary changes things for me, she couldn't be more wrong. I was expecting, I don't know—something horrific, blatant.

But not this. Not this vague murky account.

The boys were drunk, boisterous, out for a good time, as males that age tend to be. She knew that when she threw herself at them. Even her friends didn't want to go up those stairs, creeping around in the dark.

I'm adding cold water to the bath, about to step in, when something occurs to me. Going through to the bedroom, I step over Dan's exercise mat as I approach his bedside cabinet. At the back of the drawer, there's a small leather box. I flip open the lid, removing the contents.

It's his military tag. I watch it twirling, catching the light. He's so proud of it, keeps it by the bedside, a memento of heroism. I've always rather liked it.

Suddenly, the hairs stand up on the back of my neck and I put it away again, pushing it to the back of the drawer, slamming it shut.

PRIYANKA

Andy is sitting at the kitchen table, reading the weekend papers, picking at a chocolate muffin, when I tell him that I'm going out for milk.

He looks up quizzingly and there's something else there too: a look not of mistrust exactly but of doubt. I know what he's thinking. He's been thinking it ever since I told him about the letter.

Does she believe me?

Beside him, Beau is eating a muffin also, dragging chunky crayons across his drawing pad, creating a colorful sketch of cows and pigs. I always know what it is once he tells me.

I wonder about taking him with me, just for company. Lately, I hate being alone. But on this occasion, there's no way I can risk it. I'm not just going for milk; I'm going to see Stephanie.

"Don't be long, my love," Andy says, and it's as if he knows.

Our eyes lock. I'm the first to look away.

Out in the car, I pull up all the recent searches on my phone, deleting them. Whenever I have a spare private moment—in the bath, in the car before going into school, in the staffroom if no one's around—I'm doing research into rape.

I can say the word now. Something changed after I read Nicky's diary. It made me braver, more willing to fight in her corner, and yet more confused. Which is why I'm going to Stephanie's. I want the diary back.

The streets are quiet as I drive. It's a nothing day, a poorly defined Sunday with a gunpowder-gray sky. There are no obvious signs that it's mid-October, no autumn leaves in sight, and I try to imagine which season I'd guess at if I didn't know. But as I've come to learn, you can't unknow things, no matter how hard you try.

I want to read again what Nicky wrote about Andy. I was relieved that he came across as the nicest character, but her description of him was so accurate, it seemed to validate everything else she said.

Yet there's something else happening here too... I haven't been focusing on historic offenses and prosecution statistics, like Jess has. I appreciate that we need to know the context, so I've delved a little and I know prosecution rates are at an all-time low; if alcohol was involved, the victim's word was less likely to be taken seriously; consent is everything. It had to be proved that the victim didn't give consent, verbally or otherwise, and that the defendant *knew* she didn't.

I know also that the amount of lapsed time is a factor: maybe the justice system had changed since the crime was committed, or the offender had been a model citizen ever since. Maybe he was elderly now, deemed little or no threat to society.

All of that is important, yet there's something bigger coming into play—something that I can't stop thinking about or looking up online.

Nearly all of my searches relate to one thing.

Do nice men rape?

I felt foolish typing the question, expecting the oracle of the internet to answer it for me. Yet, in a fairly direct way, it did.

I discovered that whenever a nice man was accused publicly

of rape, women rushed forward to defend his character. In one such high-profile case, *sixty-five* women testified.

Journalists described the difficulty in accepting that someone close to you might have offended. They talked about how tough it was to imagine that someone who was so kind and considerate to you could have sexually assaulted someone else—the false logic in basing what he *might* have done purely on how he was with *you*.

I haven't just read these articles once, but several times, over and over, each time the words proving harder to swallow, my discomfort growing.

Not only did those close to the accused struggle to believe him guilty, but society as a whole found it hard to accept. We thought of rapists as monsters, frightening deviants, and that was how it had to stay. If we started looking at the Earl Grey drinkers and Argyle sock wearers, everything we knew and believed would unravel.

Defenders of accused young men were quick to point out that juvenile drunken *horseplay* wasn't to be confused with rape or cross-examined, certainly not in a way that would ruin their excellent prospects.

There didn't seem to be a lot of consideration for the young woman whose life probably hadn't held as much promise in the first place, and certainly didn't now. Maybe that was the whole point, the imbalance at the root of this.

Yet here's the conundrum: I can't see Andy doing that depraved act. Does that make me part of the problem, or right? What if he's innocent? I've never seen any glimpse of that other person—his alter ego, Lee—during our marriage. Doesn't that stand for something?

A week ago, I thought it did. Now I'm not so sure.

Lost in thought, I notice with surprise that I've arrived in a smart part of town where the properties have crested *keep out* gates and security cameras. Stephanie texted me her address, and I'm trying to find the message on my phone when I realize that I'm right outside her house, the gates slowly opening with eerie anticipation.

It's very quiet as I get out of the car. The Edwardian house, flanked by baby oaks in coats of autumn red, is standing there expectantly, glistening as though it's just taken a shower.

I had no idea she lived somewhere like this, but then I never asked. It strikes me that I know nothing about her, nor Jess. We've been thrown together by the most intimate of circumstances, yet the questions we're asking each other are nothing like the usual ones—families, careers, holiday plans.

Instead, it's: What is rape? And: Would you report your husband to the police? I know the answer to that one. I looked it up. It's yes.

In a recent government survey, 77 percent of Britons said they would report a loved one for murder; 76 for rape. So, there it is. Our moral compass.

Ringing the doorbell, I run my fingers through my hair, hoping I don't look in too much of a state. My personal appearance was the least of my concerns when I set out.

Of course, it's easy to say you'd do the right thing. Everyone's a saint when surveyed, just like no one ever smokes or drinks according to medical forms. It still means that 24 percent wouldn't report the rape.

The shiny black door opens and Stephanie is standing there looking as fresh as ice cream in a vanilla cardigan and velour tracksuit pants. She makes dressing down look like something I'd wear to work, if I could be bothered to make that amount of effort, that is.

We smile at each other and I look inquiringly at her empty hands, expecting her to have brought me the diary. She opens the door wider. "Would you like to come in?"

"Oh… Okay. Why not?"

There's lots of reasons why not. Yet I want the diary, so I follow her.

She leads me through to the living room, which is sumptuously furnished, all praline and pale pink. A generous burst of sunshine is spilling through the French doors, making a crisscross pattern of light on the carpet. I feel a pang of envy at the peace and space, thinking of Beau's Lego bricks all over the floor, the marks from his toy car wheels on our walls. "You have a beautiful home." I gesture to the sofa. "Shall I sit here?"

"Please do... Can I get you something to drink?"

"No, thank you. I'm not stopping long." I sink onto the soft cushions. "Wow! This is cozy. I'd never want to leave the house."

She smiles cordially.

"How do you keep everything so perfect?" I ask. "Do you have a cleaner?"

Of course she does. Her nails are beautiful, her hands are unwrinkled. There's no way she mops.

"No, I do it all myself."

"Really?" I stare at her, impressed.

She perches on the opposite sofa, hands clasped on lap. "Although the girls help me, I'll admit."

I nod.

The girls.

She has kids. I look at the photographs on the mantelpiece, counting the faces. Three daughters. And then my heart falters as I catch sight of something.

Writhing to get up from the deep sofa, I approach a gilt-framed photo on the wall above the fireplace.

It's Brooke. The military hair. The proud dots for eyes. The suggestion that somehow, for some reason, he's laughing at you. Beside him, Stephanie is a comparative fluff ball, her hair piled high, her makeup flawless, feature-blurring.

"How long have you been married?" I ask.

"Fourteen years."

The girls' pictures are arranged in chronological order: sun hats, swimming armbands, gappy teeth. And then bridesmaids, body-con dresses. "They look older than that. Are they…his?"

"Only my youngest, Georgia—the one in the school uniform. Vivian and Rosie are from my first marriage."

I touch the glass on the frame, the schoolgirl's eyes boring into mine. She looks like her father. "Don't you…well, doesn't it upset you that Holly might have been his too?"

"No." She frowns at me as though I've said something deeply offensive. "I haven't given it any thought."

"It's just that… I mean, don't get me wrong. My family are a complete pain in the arse, but I love them to bits. Family's everything to me. And my son, Beau, well, he…" I trail off.

She doesn't seem all that interested in what I have to say about Beau. And I realize then that she's not interested in any of us: me, Jess, Nicky, Holly. Nor does she want to tell me anything about herself. She's saying as little as possible, as usual.

Yet we're going to have to be personal. We're going to have to ask questions of ourselves and of each other. That much is becoming clearer every day.

I try to look as friendly as possible. "Can I ask you something?" I sit back down, the sofa embracing me.

She nods almost imperceptibly.

"Is he good to you, your husband? Has he ever given you any cause to doubt him?"

She looks surprised, which annoys me slightly. It's not as if this question has come out of nowhere. "No. Not at all."

"Okay. It's just that…he didn't exactly get a glowing review in the diary, did he? In fact, I think he came off the worst of the three men."

"I didn't pick up on that." She touches her hair defensively, cheeks coloring.

"Really? I thought it was quite apparent. I think she even used the word *vicious* at one point."

It's so quiet, the ticking of the mantelpiece clock seems blaring. Perhaps I shouldn't have got into this, here and now.

So much for intimacy.

"Do you have it, then? The diary?" I ask.

"Yes. Follow me." She seems glad, hurries through to the hallway, removing my tote from her bag.

I take it from her, holding it to my chest, glad to have it back again. She watches me, a strange look on her face. Perhaps she's wondering why I'd want something so destructive near me.

On my way to the door, something in me—the teacher, perhaps—makes me try one last time to reach her. I've no idea how she would have been at school, but imagine she was unobtrusive, barely leaving a mark. Some pupils carve their names on every surface they can find, while there are others who no one even remembers were there.

"Didn't you feel anything for her?" I stand on the doorstep, cradling the diary.

"Who?"

"Nicky," I whisper, just in case.

She said her husband was out, but even so... Something about him scares me.

"It's not about what I feel," she says, one hand on the door.

"Isn't it? Because I think that's *all* this is about."

She frowns at me in incomprehension. "I'm not going to let this destroy my life. It was too long ago."

"But we found out now."

"So?" She shivers, tightening the belt on her cardigan.

"So, it's about what we do now—what we're prepared to live with."

"And what do you think the answer is?"

She watches me anxiously and at that moment I feel sorry for her, for each of us. Why should she give up this beautiful home, risk losing everything? It wasn't her fault. None of us deserve this. What about our children? What about those innocent girls in there, in their bridesmaids' dresses? What about Beau?

"What do you want to do, Priyanka?" she asks more insistently.

"I don't know." A sudden wind gusts up the garden behind me, lifting my coat, making the twin bay trees quiver on her porch. I pull up my hood. "I don't think I can bare losing my husband, though."

"Then talk to Jess. Make her see reason."

Reason? I don't even know what that means anymore.

"I'm sorry," I say, shaking my head. "I can't promise I'll do that. Besides, I'm not sure I want to."

"Then how do you intend to keep your husband?"

"No idea. But we do need to stick together. Jess is spot-on about that. It makes more sense every day."

"What does?" she says suspiciously.

I smile, knowing she'll hate what I'm going to say next.

"What she said about us being a team." Tapping the pockets of my parka, I find my car keys. "Well, I'd better go. I said I was only popping out for milk… Take care, okay?" And I set off down the driveway.

"If you don't rein her in," she calls after me, "she'll run away with this and it'll be out of our control."

She's right. Jess will run away with it. Maybe she already has.

I drive home, feeling worse for having seen Stephanie. It's hard to feel like a team when you're all pulling in different directions. But at least I have the diary.

At the bottom of my road, I'm struck by the sudden urge to look at it again. Pulling over, I check around me and then open the book at the back where the ink is thickest, feeling the familiar sense of guilt and regret as the spine creaks.

If she'd been my friend, I would never have let it happen to her. Where were Lucy and Kim? Why didn't they help her?

Why did she end up coming around in a cab, alone, abandoned, in shock?

I'm about to hide the diary and head up the hill to home, when I notice an extra thick page at the back. Inspecting it more closely, I realize that two pages are stuck together.

I always keep a stash of school supplies in the glove compartment. Rooting through the mess, I find a ruler, prying it carefully between the pages.

They give, separate, fall open.

"Oh my God," I say. Grabbing my phone, I ring Jess.

JESS

I'm outside Beechcroft Home, tossing last week's flowers over the wall onto the compost heap, when Priyanka rings. It's a windy day, the sort that won't leave your hair and clothes alone, and I'm miserable as sin. Mum was asleep, so I just sat there stewing about Max. I've been in a state of turmoil since reading the diary and am close to the edge, but I don't know what of.

"Slow down. I can't hear you. You're gabbling." I get into my car, gazing at the stone wall, picturing the flowers rotting on the other side.

"Sorry… It's about the diary. I got it back from Stephanie."

"When?"

"Just now. I went to her house…"

They got together, without me? I'm not insecure—at least, I didn't use to be. But I don't trust anyone now, not even Mary. On Friday afternoon in the office, I was looking up rape online—convictions, false allegations—and she kept hovering. Was she spying on me?

"…And she's rich, by the way."

"Doesn't surprise me." The woman's fighting for something, and it doesn't look much like love to me. But then what do I know?

"Anyway, I just found something in the diary. You wouldn't believe it—contact details for Lucy and Kim, her friends, the ones who were there on the night."

"Okay…"

Do I sound flat? I mean, those details are thirty years old.

"I know what you're thinking," she continues. "But guess what? It's not Nicky's handwriting. I think it's Holly's—the same as in the letter. Phone numbers and addresses in Bath. Which means we could talk to *real living people*, instead of relying on dead ones." She catches her breath, the line crackling. "What if these women know something? What if they saw what happened?"

"What does Stephanie say?"

Her voice drops. "What do you mean?"

"Well, what did she say about the phone numbers?"

"Oh. She doesn't know. I only just found them, after I left her."

There's more to this than she's saying. I can feel it.

"So, what did she say about the diary in general—about what Nicky wrote?" I ask. "Has she read it?"

"Yes, she has."

"And?"

She pauses. "She seemed even more determined to bury it… I'm sorry, Jess. I wasn't going to say anything…"

I sit forward, placing the key in the ignition. "We need to get her on board before we do anything else."

"What? Why?"

I stare at the stone wall again, looking at the ivy growing in the cracks. I don't know why I feel like this. If it were the other way around, she probably wouldn't spare me the same consideration. Yet there's something very vulnerable about her, something she's keeping from us.

Regardless of that, she deserves a say. We may be opposites, yet maybe that's why it's even more important that I listen to her. She's yin to my yang, but what she doesn't appreciate is that if you take a proper look at that Chinese symbol, you'll see that the opposite forces are actually interconnected, interdependent—complementary, even.

"Jess?"

I sigh. "Oh, I dunno. It just feels like the right thing to do."

"So we, what, let her have her own way?"

"No. I think she needs more time, that's all."

I tap my teeth together, wondering whether that's true. Would time change anything? We could give her the rest of her life and she could take her viewpoint to the grave with her, the way some people are buried with their pearls.

Something occurs to me then, and I feel a stab of mistrust. "Why are you being so proactive all of a sudden? I thought you wanted to forget all about it too?"

"I don't think I ever actually said that, did I...? It's just that I thought this might give us something concrete instead of all this guesswork and worrying. It's so draining."

"I agree. So, if we could prove it, you'd go to the police?"

It's a horrible question. I can feel her squirming.

"God, I don't know, Jess. I'd just like to know either way for sure so we can make an informed choice, instead of shooting in the dark."

"Yeah, me too," I say, but this isn't true.

I have no problem with shooting in the dark. In fact, I'd welcome it.

"Can you send me a photo of the contact details?" I start the car engine. "And in the meantime, I'll speak to Stephanie."

"What about?"

"Whether to contact those women. I'm hoping the three of us can sit down and work something out."

"Well, good luck with that," she says.

I don't think it sounds very realistic either. But one thing to be positive about: Stephanie didn't destroy Nicky's journal when she had the chance. "Pree?"

"Yes?"

"Look after the diary."

"Will do."

———————

As I kiss Poppy good-night, she frowns. "You okay, Mummy?"

No, not really. My world's falling apart, and I'm trying to stop yours from doing that too.

"Course, munchkin. Why'd you ask?"

"Dunno. You seem sad."

"Do I?" May as well stick to the same excuse I'm giving everyone. "It's just Grandma."

"Thought so… Do you think I should go with you more often, keep you company?"

"No, my love, although I appreciate the offer. But I think you should remember her how she was. She's not the same anymore."

She thinks about this, lifts her sharp little chin. "Want me to have a word?"

This makes me laugh. I tap her nose lightly, smoothing her hair. "If only it were that simple."

"Sometimes it is." She twists beneath the sheets, closing her eyes.

"Night, Pops." I turn out the light. "Sweet dreams."

Downstairs, Max is flicking through the calendar with a look on his face I've been dreading: the niggling feeling he's being shortchanged in some way. Wearing a T-shirt and pajama bottoms, he scratches his belly button absently.

On the counter, there are two glasses of wine. My stomach churning, I open the dishwasher, even though there's nothing to go in or out.

"When did we last…you know?" he asks.

What is it about sex? You can be married for years and still there's a delicacy around it. He doesn't want to appear vulgar, and would hate it if I was. Yet why act like the perfect gentlemen in front of us, while secretly sending each other pictures of genitalia? I've been thinking about that WhatsApp photo almost incessantly. I can't help but think it wasn't the first or the last—that he didn't stick to his promise not to look at them in future.

It's the insincerity that gets me. Leading two lives. Is that Max? Is he two-faced? And if so, which one's the real him?

How would I know a thing like that? They don't even give you a fighting chance.

"Hmm?" Max closes the diary, picks up his wine. "When was it, do you think?"

"It?" I ask innocently.

"You know…rumpy-pumpy."

I absolutely loathe that expression. He means it as a joke, but it's lost on me.

"I dunno," I say, trying to control the snap in my voice. "It's difficult at the moment…what with Mum…"

"I know. But she could be like that for a long time, and besides, I miss you." He tries to touch me, but I'm too quick for him, contorting away and into the living room.

He pads after me, bare feet slapping the tiles. It feels mean doing this to someone in their own home—picking them apart, reducing them to a question mark. But that's the way it has to be.

Settling in a slim armchair where there's no danger of him joining me, I toss him the remote control and he picks it up happily. "Are we still watching that show with the woman with the hair?"

"Yes. Two more episodes to go."

"Perfect." He drinks his wine, eyes on screen.

The credits are still appearing, in that drawn-out way they sometimes do, surprising you ten minutes into the program, when he presses pause. "Jess…"

The way he says this makes me go colder than I already was.

He gets up, approaches, crouching before me. "Don't you miss me, baby?" Tenderly, he starts to kiss me.

Yes, I miss you. More than you could possibly know.

I kiss him back.

Then I think of him with Nicky in the storeroom at the club. He may not have masterminded it or even premeditated it, but he kissed her first, made the first move. And my sorrow on learning that firsthand in her diary was palpable.

There were parts of him that I recognized from her description: attentiveness, bonhomie. And parts that were alien: denial, manipulation.

Two sides to Max, good and bad. It's just that I only ever saw the good.

And I know then that I'm never going to be able to kiss him again—the same lips that kissed Nicky Waite.

He did it. I'm certain of it. He raped her, married me.

I stiffen, clamping my mouth shut, nearly biting his tongue, the whites of his eyes enlarging in alarm. Jumping out of the chair, I scramble to the bathroom down the hall.

Moments later, he knocks on the door. "Jess? Unlock the door."

"It's open."

The handle turns and as he appears I start to cry, sitting on the closed toilet seat, rocking back and forth.

"What's going on?" he says, squatting, knees clicking. His arms seem gigantic at this angle, and I wonder why I haven't considered before how vain this is. He's fifty. Who's he kidding? We're old. Our bodies are falling apart. Everything's falling apart.

But I can see now that the arms were part of an act that I wasn't granted access to because it was male-only. There I was, thinking I was lucky enough to have a husband who made an effort for me. And all along, it was to fit in to somewhere I couldn't go.

"Max, is there anything you've ever kept from me?" I blurt.

He stares at me. "Like what?"

"Like anything—anything whatsoever?" It's vague, but I'm building up to saying it.

"No! Of course not! Where's this coming from?"

He seems so genuine. It's confusing.

I have to ask him outright. I swore I'd never be like my parents—playing games. Of all the things he could have done to me, turning out to be full of fake has to be the worst.

"There's something I have to tell you."

"What is it...? Jess?" His eyes widen—beautiful green eyes. I hate that he looks so vulnerable. "You're scaring me."

I know what to say. I've practiced it dozens of times. Two words: her name, and watch his reaction.

I open my mouth. He holds his breath. And in that second, I fold.

I can't do it. The moment I say her name, everything will change. He won't be able to hide it in time. And I'm not ready to see that look yet, the one signaling the end of our marriage.

"It's Mum," I say.

I'm pathetic.

"Oh, baby. I'm sorry. Why didn't you say something earlier? What happened?"

"She fell, really badly." I'm howling now, huge tears, partly in despair, partly in shame.

"I'm so sorry." He rubs my back. "I know how hard this must be. What can I do to help?"

Where do I start? I'm going to lose him and the girls are going to lose their dad and no one's going to win, least of all Nicky and Holly Waite.

This isn't about protecting him. It's about protecting me. This is my unhappy ending. So, I get to choose how and when it happens. And if I say I'm not ready, I'm not ready.

"Come on." He strokes my hair. "Let's watch telly and finish the wine. We don't have to do it tonight."

We're back to that again? Even though I'm crying, exhausted, telling him my mum's fallen, he gets to tell me whether or not we have sex, like it's his decision, not mine.

And that's the real problem, isn't it, underneath everything that's going on. After all these years—over fifty years since the introduction of the pill and the abortion act—and they still think it's their choice, not ours.

STEPHANIE

No one I know would go to Carol's café, which is why Jess suggested it again; it's safe to talk. She wanted to meet sooner than Saturday, but I couldn't fit it in and needed time to think.

I've barely slept the past few nights, and work has been such an effort. It's not that I don't know what to do about this or what I want. It's a case of expressing myself well enough to make them listen. They're seriously considering contacting Nicola Waite's friends, unless I can come up with something solid to persuade them otherwise.

Carol's is overflowing with Bath rugby hats and the smell of fried food. There's a big game on today that Dan is taking Georgia to. She hates rugby, but hasn't found a way to break it to him yet.

The ground is near the leisure center where I'm parked, so I'm having to be extra careful. Thankfully, it's sunny out, so I'm wearing large sunglasses and a ski jacket that no one would associate with me. I feel bulky and self-conscious, even though the idea is that no one will notice me.

Making my way upstairs, I leave the noise behind but not the greasy smell that lingers underneath the dingy tables. It's so gloomy, I can see the light below through the cracks in the floorboards as I make my way over to the others in the corner, the only ones here again.

On seeing me, Jess smiles warmly. "Thanks for coming, Stephanie. How you doing?"

"Not too bad, thanks." I nod hello to Priyanka, who looks at me uncertainly. She's wearing a knitted dress, her eyes dark brown today.

"Well, I've had a bloody awful week," Jess says, puffing out her cheeks. "It's a nightmare trying to cover up why I'm being off with him."

"What have you said?" Priyanka asks, folding her parka coat and dropping it carelessly on the condiments table behind her.

"Oh, I've been blaming everything on my mum."

"Is she...?"

"In a care home. Dementia, two strokes."

"Gosh. I'm sorry," Priyanka says. "That must be really difficult."

"It's just one of those things..." Jess turns to me. "Are your parents still alive?" Maybe she's hoping we might have something in common.

"No." I leave it at that.

"How do you manage to juggle it all?" Priyanka asks. "Do you work full-time?"

"Yeah... I dunno, to be honest." She rubs her face brusquely, settling the question in my mind as to whether or not she wears foundation. "I guess you just do what you have to do, you know?"

Is that a dig at me—at our situation? I've no idea. I don't know how to read her.

"What are you two doing about sex?" she asks bluntly. "I mean, it's tricky, isn't it, in the circumstances?"

She must know I'm not going to answer that. I pretend I haven't heard.

But to my surprise, Priyanka takes it seriously, tucking her hair behind her ears. "Well, it's easier for me. I've got a toddler—a ready-made excuse. We're always too exhausted to do anything, although I do miss it."

I look sideways at her in wonder and with some envy, the same way I used to look at girls at school who swapped makeup or shared a toilet cubicle. That wasn't how I was raised to be. I don't know how to do that.

"Me too," Jess agrees. "What about you, Stephanie?"

"What about me?"

Something about the way I say this makes her laugh, but it's short-lived. She seems very tired, and her face falls serious again as she picks at a chip of paint on the table, digging it with her thumbnail.

"So..." She pulls a long strip of paint off the table. "Whoops." Tries to put it back the way it was. "We need to talk about Nicky's friends, about whether we want to try to contact them."

My pulse quickens as I reach into my bag for my notebook and reading glasses, summoning the nerve to speak. "If you don't mind... I made a list."

She looks intrigued. "What sort of list?"

I falter, embarrassed. "Of questions, if that's all right?"

"Impressive." She nods in approval. "Go on, then."

I glance around the room even though I know it's empty, aside from the faces in the wall photos: archaic people who seem to share my fear of the spotlight. These days, children practice public speaking at school, encouraged from an early age not to be frightened to speak up. Yet I went through twelve years of education barely saying a word.

"I should explain... I'm not very..."

They look at me with curiosity.

They don't need to know that. Just read the list.

I look at my first question, my eyes blurring. "You said... you would take Holly's letter to the police and perhaps now the diary too. But do you think they'd take it seriously? Isn't it just someone's opinion? Creative writing?"

Jess opens her mouth to reply, just as the waitress bounds up the stairs, floorboards creaking. I'm relieved at the interruption, even though I've only just started. I hide the list on my lap.

"What can I getcha, ladies?" The waitress has a nose ring, which she fiddles with as she waits. I hope she washes her hands before handling the food. I glance at Priyanka, who wears a nose stud, if I remember rightly. But there's nothing there today, merely a dot on the side of her nose that could be a hole or a mole. I don't like to stare.

The waitress stomps off again. No one's hungry, aside from Jess, who ordered a currant bun. The waitress said she liked her Snoopy sweatshirt; the sort of thing my Rosie would wear ironically. No one ever says things like that to me and I'm in cashmere.

Now that we're alone again, Jess is looking at me, thinking about how to answer my question, picking the skin on her thumbnail. I'd like to ask why she's wearing a tuque indoors. It's not very flattering, making the grooves around her mouth even more distinct.

"I wondered the same thing, so looked it up online," she says, sucking her thumb. She seems to have no qualms about biting and picking things in front of us. "I think it would be considered documentary evidence, but it's hard to tell. You're right. Nicky could have been writing creatively. That's what makes it so difficult. And if there was no way of telling for sure, then it would be classed as hearsay, making it inadmissible."

"In court?" Priyanka asks, wriggling fretfully.

"Yep... Even if it *was* hearsay, that doesn't mean it would be automatically ruled out. It's more complicated than that, from what I can gather." She removes her tuque at last, running her hand through her hair. "But going back to what you asked, yes, I'd hand it in, if it came to it... Okay?"

"Um. Yes." Well, she answered the question, at least.

Satisfied, Jess sits back in her seat, pressing her hat between her hands, waiting for the next one.

I look at my list.

Question two is whether she still intends to go to the police in any event, but I don't want to ask that now that I'm in front of her, in case I don't like the response.

"I…uh… How do we know that Nicola wrote the diary and not someone else?"

"Well, I don't see why anyone else would have," Priyanka replies. "Surely there are ways of testing it, though? Can't they do that?"

Jess tosses her hat onto the condiments table with Priyanka's coat. "I expect so. But I think we should assume she wrote it because that's the most logical answer, or we'll just start going around in circles… What else is on your list?"

I skip number four, sensing danger. *Don't you think she brought it on herself?* And head straight to number five.

"Why do you believe her?"

Jess fiddles with her wedding ring, twisting it around, a look of apprehension on her face. "I dunno. I just do."

"But her mother was a…" I look at my notes. I wrote it down somewhere. I can't remember the word.

"Agoraphobic?" Priyanka offers.

"Yes."

"So?" Jess says. "That doesn't make Nicky a liar, though, does it?"

I curl my toes inside my shoes, pressing them against the leather, trying to find the right words. "I… I meant that her mother had mental health problems and wondered if Nicola was the same way."

"And what are you basing that on?"

"I…" There was something in the diary that made me think

the girl was unstable. But what? This is what always happens. It's why I'm supposed to stick to the list, to my notes.

"Don't worry." She pats my hand, smiles. "This isn't about putting you on the spot. It's about us having a conversation… Let's move on. Anything else you want to ask?" But the waitress is back again, bringing a tray.

My shoulders subside as a large mug of tea is set down before me. This hasn't gone very well. Despite her assurances, I can tell that Jess doesn't like my questions; I'm asking the wrong ones. Yet they were always going to be the wrong ones for her because they're the right ones for me. I think we've already established that we're incompatible.

I pick up my tea gratefully, my mouth horribly dry. Thankfully, I've only one question left. There were others, but I've lost my momentum, not that I had any to start with.

They're both looking at me expectantly now that the waitress has gone, and I can see that bringing my notebook was unwise. I know what they must be thinking. The list has shown them that I need a script, a prop, and without meaning to, I've made myself look weak. I'm not as clever as them. They're educated, well-informed, whereas I've been living in the past for too long to know how modern women think.

"I… I just wanted to ask one last thing—she didn't write very much about what actually happened, but the one thing she did say was that she didn't tell them to stop. Why was that?"

A silence falls. Downstairs goes quiet at the same time, with uncanny timing. Jess picks at her currant bun. "Good question."

She doesn't have an answer?

My heart skips and I hope that, somehow, despite being out of my depth, I've stumped them.

But then Priyanka sits forward, one hand flat on the table. "That was bothering me too, so I did some research and it's a known phenomenon. It's the body's way of dealing with trauma, going numb to survive the ordeal. It's a myth that everyone fights back. That's just not the case. Everyone deals with it differently, and you don't know until you're in that situation how you'd react."

"Oh… I see." I try not to show my disappointment, busying myself with returning the notebook to my bag, taking off my glasses.

"Talking of myths…" Jess says. "I thought you were going to ask whether she was asking for it because she was drunk. Or whether she meant yes because she didn't say no out loud."

I know she's outsmarting me in some way. But to me, these are valid questions. And I wonder whether she read my list somehow when I wasn't looking.

I don't feel so good. My mouth is still dry, despite the tea, and I'm too warm.

"You all right?" Priyanka asks. I well up, tapping my pockets for a tissue, but there are no pockets in my cashmere sweater, so I look even more stupid.

"I didn't upset you, did I?" Jess says. "I was only joking…" And then she peers at me. "Wait, you didn't actually have those questions on your list, did you?"

Priyanka frowns at her, before pulling a handful of napkins from the dispenser and handing them to me as though expecting me to break down. "There you go, hon," she says gently.

I've managed to pull myself together. Straightening my back, I focus on the wall, my eye trailing the dried brushstrokes of paint.

"I almost don't want to have to bring this up now," Jess says, her eyes on me. "But I'm conscious of the time and the fact that we've probably all lied about where we are… So I think we should decide here and now—are we going to contact Lucy and Kim?"

I look at Priyanka, hoping the warning I gave her on my front porch last Sunday had some effect. "Is that what you want?" I ask her.

She drops a sugar cube into her coffee, stirs it pensively. "Yes, if it helps bring clarity."

"But what about your husband?"

"What about him? If he did this, it changes everything. Which is why I need to know one way or the other."

"Then what about your children?"

"Child," she replies. "Only one."

"That's enough, surely? How many people's lives need to be destroyed before you'll put the brakes on? Both the Waite women are dead. This isn't going to help them. All it's going to do is tear our families apart."

This is more than I'd normally say and they look at me, not inspired exactly, but with new hesitance.

I hope it's enough. It has to be. I don't have anything left to add.

"Look," Jess says, touching my hand. Her skin feels so cold. "I know this goes against your instincts, but we need you on board, Steffie."

No one's called me that in a long time, except Shelley Fricker. My mum always used to call me Steffie too.

"Why?" I ask. "Why do you care what I think?"

When you've made it perfectly clear that you think I'm out of touch.

"Of course I care what you think. Pree does too. I can't keep stressing how much we're in this together. Our opinions carry equal weight. And when you say no, it casts doubt over the whole thing."

So, I have more power, more sway than I thought? If I continue to say no, I could stop her?

If that's the case, it seems like a foolish thing to have admitted.

"Is it a yes to contacting Lucy and Kim, then?" she asks.

"No."

"Wow." She laughs lightly. "That never grows old, does it?

The way you say no like that... Gets me every time." She shakes her head, glances at Priyanka.

"Jess, I..."

I'm trying to apologize; I don't like being difficult, obstructive. I'm not sure how to phrase it, though. It's taking me a little while to summon the right words.

She's looking at me hopefully.

"I... It's just that I can't do this. I can't agree with you. I'm very sorry."

And just like that, her hopes are dashed.

"Then I think we're going to have to go ahead without your blessing, Stephanie."

I gaze at her in surprise. Beside her, Priyanka remains quiet, still stirring her coffee, eyes cast downward.

"I see. So that was a lie about our opinions carrying equal weight," I say.

The air thickens around us as no one speaks. I look once again at Priyanka, but she's unreachable. Perhaps she agrees with me; perhaps she doesn't. She's not going to say either way.

There seems little point in my staying any longer. "It's probably best if you don't contact me again," I say quietly, leaving some money on the table for my tea.

"As you wish," Jess replies.

I withdraw shakily, hoping one of them will call after me, but they don't. They let me go.

As I descend the stairs, becoming engulfed in the heat and the noise of the crowded room, I imagine what they'll be saying about me now that they're free to speak—whether they'll say I'm a disgrace to the women's movement.

Outside, I'm gulping in the fresh air, trying not to cry, fiddling with the unfamiliar togs and zips on my ski jacket, when I bump into Vivian.

"Mum!" She glances at Carol's in surprise. "What are you doing here? Aren't you supposed to be at Pilates?"

"I…"

She points at the window, at the crowd of blue rugby hats. "Are Dan and Georgia in that dump?"

"Yes." That was stupid. What if she mentions it later? "No."

She laughs in confusion, her mouth wonky with the cold. I feel awful for lying to her—the undisputed kindest of my girls. "Are you all right, M?" she asks.

I want to tell her everything. Instead, I put on my sunglasses. There's no need for my daughters to get caught up in any of this; I'm doing all this so that they don't have to.

"Is that the ski jacket Dan bought you, the one you've never worn because you hate travel, heights, snow and sport?" she says teasingly.

"Yes. That's the one. It's chilly out."

"O…kay…" She doesn't sound convinced. "So, are you walking my way? I'm going to Tom's."

"No. I'm going home, darling."

"See you later, then, M." She kisses me on the cheek, pressing my hand. "You take care now." She says this as though *she's* the parent. Well, she is a little taller than me.

I don't look back as I walk away. I'm too upset. Behind my shades I cry, tears running into the fur trim on my hood. I've let Dan down and I lied to my beautiful daughter and all for nothing. Because they're going to do it anyway. Those silly, silly women. They're going to destroy our lives and there's nothing I can do to stop them.

PRIYANKA

"So, we hear a lot about the polarization of views in society today. But who can tell me what it means?" I go over to the blinds to adjust them, the sun shining on my face. When I return to my desk, only one boy has his hand up. "Yes, Ruben."

"It's when people are opposed, normally politically, but not necessarily."

His father's a social science lecturer.

"Correct. Yes. Well done." I smile, leaning back against the desk. In the front row, a boy is doodling a penis. I try not to look. "And why do you think that's cause for concern? What's the problem? Surely it's good to encourage people to have opposing views...? Yes, Ruben."

"It's dangerous for democracy, Miss."

"And why is that?"

"Because people aren't listening to each other. They're hanging out with friends who have the same opinions and are hating on people who don't agree. It's them and us, and you have to pick a side. You're not actually hearing people's views as part of a democratic process."

"Very good, Ruben. And there's growing concern about this

trend, not just here in the UK, but globally. You might be surprised to hear that many democratic countries, such as the US, Kenya, Bangladesh, Poland, India and Colombia, are experiencing a similar problem. To make matters worse, political leaders are inflaming the situation, demonizing the opposition as a political tactic." I turn to the whiteboard, the pen squeaking as I write.

Them...................... *Us*.

"But from our point of view—the general public, the individual—when you over-identify with a side, you narrow your own perspective and worldview. There's a danger we'll lose not only our ability to listen and tolerate others, but to debate also because we're so entrenched in the idea that our side is right. And when societies become divided, it's hard to move forward, reaching what's known as an impasse. Who can tell me what that is?"

"Brexit, Miss," a boy at the back shouts.

I point the pen at him. "Yes, Jake. Just like Brexit... Yet the truth of the matter is that it can be very uncomfortable hearing someone else's views. Especially if you're morally opposed to them on religious grounds, for example, with issues such as abortion or gay marriage."

"Yeah, Ruben knows a lot about that too, Miss," Jake shouts. There's a titter of laughter.

I tap the space on the whiteboard between *Them* and *Us*. "In order to cohabit peacefully and move forward, we need to inhabit more of the space here, where opinions meet, so we can debate meaningfully and respectfully... So, why do we think this is happening on such a wide scale? Why now, in this day and age?" I look at the boys. "Anyone, other than Ruben?"

He puts down his hand, but no one else moves. The boy in the front row is spurting liquid out of the doodle penis.

"Okay, Ruben."

He looks pleased. "Social media, Miss?"

"Yes. Good. Can you expand?"

"Social media is about speed and volume. If you base your opinion on what you've read online, there's a danger you're not getting all the facts. Which leads to people thinking in broad terms, like them and us."

"Absolutely." Turning to the board, I think of Jess and Stephanie, my stomach churning as I write the word: *impasse.*

I'm about to talk about the polarization of views in Nazi Germany as a propaganda tactic, when someone shouts, "Look, Miss!"

Scraping back their chairs, the boys gather at the window. "Isn't that Saffron?"

———

It's bitter outside, a nasty wind scraping the leaves along the concrete. Saffron has been waiting by the school gates all afternoon. It's not clear what he's doing there, so I haven't reported him—can't see that he's doing anything wrong. But as I make my way across the car park, he heads toward me, gathering speed.

I could pretend I haven't seen him—get into my car and lock the doors—but that seems cowardly. He was expelled because of a decision I made. Only a few weeks ago, I was sad that I didn't get to say goodbye, and now I'm running away from him? What's changed?

I know exactly what's changed.

"Hello, Saffron." I'm about to add *nice to see you*, before stopping myself, knowing this would sound insincere.

He seems taller out of school uniform, his hair cut extremely short. It makes him look plucked, raw. "Do you know what you've done, Miss?"

"What do you mean?" I glance around me, wondering whether I should call for help. I have an alarm in my bag somewhere. Yet it's daylight and my colleagues are waving goodbye, getting into their cars. I tried to stick up for Saffron on countless occasions, so they won't think anything of my being here with him.

"I know it was you." He points at me, stopping short of actually poking me. "You told on me."

"No, I didn't."

"You're full of shit! My parents are sending me away to military school." He slaps his forehead harshly. "That's why I've got this haircut... See what you've done?" His eyes tear up, his voice breaking. "You didn't have to tell on me, Miss. I thought you liked me."

Reaching for his arm, I dare to touch it. "I'm so sorry, Saffron."

He yanks himself away from me. "Piss off, Paki."

I stare at him in shock. And then he takes off toward the gates, jumping over puddles, jacket flailing.

"Priyanka, are you all right?"

I turn to see one of the science teachers hurrying toward me, bike lock dangling on his wrist.

"No. Not really," I say croakily, going to my car.

"I heard what he said to you. We should report him to the police."

"I don't want to do that." I unlock the door. "I want to forget all about it."

"What? But you can't let him get away with it!"

Yes, I can.

"Sorry. I have to go."

Starting the car, I drive away. As I get onto the main road, I pass Saffron sitting at the bus stop, his back turned to the traffic, head in hands.

———————

Outside Tadpoles, Beau is waiting in his usual spot by the gate with his teacher. He doesn't look at me, and when I reach them, I can see why. There's a distinct red circle on his cheek.

"Oh. He's poorly?" I hold out my hand. He approaches lethargically, dragging his day bag along the floor.

"There's a sickness bug doing the rounds. If he vomits, you'll need to keep him home for forty-eight hours."

"Sure thing." I smile, trying to look as though the childcare isn't an issue. Andy often steps in to help. But I wouldn't mind taking some time out this week. "Come on, then, Master Beau. Let's get you home in the warm."

He's very quiet on the drive home, not answering my questions, so I let him be.

As we park outside the house and I unstrap him, he looks at me intently, touching my eyelashes. "Your eyes, Mummy."

I can't think what he means. And then I realize: they're brown, natural, for the third day in a row.

"Don't you want to change them anymore?" he asks, as I carry him up the front path. He breathes on me, smelling of stale milk.

"Not at the moment, cutie pie."

He nods, kisses me, subject over.

Beau is sick in the night. I rock him back to sleep, loosening his bedcovers, bringing his temperature down. And when I climb back into bed, it's almost dawn.

Andy is asleep, and I sense the pit of dark space between us where our bodies no longer touch. For the past few nights, I've waited for his breathing to become rhythmic and deep before I inch away, the edge of the bed precariously close.

Piss off, Paki.

I flinch, tensing. Why am I doing this to myself? He's just a nasty boy and is getting what he deserves. He had enough warnings. What he did to that girl was inexcusable, and there's no excuse for what he called me either. I don't care how scared or angry he was.

"Mummy?" Beau calls for me across the landing.

Forcing myself out of bed, I tiptoe from the room, Andy shifting position, mumbling.

I turn on Beau's carousel night-light, pastel horses dancing slowly around the room. "It's okay. Mummy's here." Crouching beside him, I feel his forehead, his cheeks pallid. I hate seeing him so pale, listless.

I think of what a rock Andy was when Beau was in intensive care. Everyone said he was incredible, even my sister, Meena, who calls him The Anorak.

How could I spoil that for Beau, taking his daddy from him, and all for what—to settle a historic long-forgotten score? After the countless hours that Andy sat vigil by his side?

Is Stephanie right? Are we sacrificing the living for the dead?

Drawing up a chair, I take Beau's hand and watch him as he tumbles into sleep, the night-light flashing on my butterfly tattoo before plunging it into darkness again.

———

Meena FaceTimes me at lunchtime. Beau is sitting on his beanbag, watching CBeebies. I'm lolling on the floor, propped up against the sofa, sipping a Cup-a-Soup.

"Where are you?" she says, spotting that the background isn't my classroom.

"At home. Beau's not well."

Her eyes narrow. "What's wrong?" She's a GP—can't help herself.

I sigh. "Just a sickness bug. It's nothing. He's fine."

"Does he have a temperature?"

"Little bit, yeah."

"You should be monitoring it. Have you given him acetaminophen?"

"Duh…didn't think of that."

She pulls a face. "No need to be sarcastic."

"So…did you want something?" I ask, yawning.

"Yes. Just to warn you. Mum's on the warpath. She wants you home for her birthday."

"Well, that's not gonna happen. Besides, I *am* home."

"You know what I mean." She peers at me, looming closer, nose growing. "You look different."

"Just tired." I yawn again. "I was up all night with Beau."

Realization dawns. "No contact lenses! Crikey. Can the real Priyanka Bandyopadhyay please stand up?"

This is a very tedious old joke of hers. Today, it doesn't warrant even an eye roll from me.

"Why the sudden change? Thought you loved your lenses?"

I shrug, my mouth trembling.

She doesn't miss a trick. "Are you okay?"

"Course."

"You'd tell me if something was wrong, wouldn't you?"

"Absolutely."

She peers at me again. "Is it The Anorak?"

"Don't be silly. Everything's fine."

"Honest?"

"Honest."

"Well, I'd better get back to surgery. Speak soon."

"'Bye, big sis." I manage a smile.

"'Bye, little Pree."

I watch Beau swaying happily to a song on TV. I miss Meena, my brothers, my parents. I wish they could tell me what to do.

I'm stuck bang in the middle between Jess and Stephanie. I knew all along that I'd end up there. I've never been able to see what it is precisely that's best for me until long after the event, aided by hindsight. At which point it's always much too late.

JESS

I wait for Gavin, my boss, to be out for lunch and Mary to be safely installed inside the filing room before picking up the phone. I'd have preferred to have talked it through with Priyanka first, but she's got her little boy home sick and I remember what those days were like. I'll have to get on with this without her because if I put it off any longer, I'll lose my nerve.

Kim Turner lives in a posh area on the east side of Bath, the right side of the city for London. As Priyanka said, the phone numbers were written by Holly. I've compared the handwriting to her letter and it's the same. She must have tracked them down, just like she did with us.

I dial Kim's number, chewing my thumbnail. She doesn't answer. Hanging up, I pace the carpet.

I can't give up that easily. So, I try again. And this time she picks up. "Good afternoon, K&L. Kim speaking?"

I've done my research. Originally, I was hoping K&L stood for Kim and Lucy, but that would have been too good to be true, as well as a bit girlie and way too easy. Nothing about this is easy. You'd have thought I'd know that by now.

K&L is Kim's business management consultancy. It looks like

her father and his contacts came through for her after all, just like Nicky knew they would. She's been in business since 1995, making her about twenty-five when she started her own company. Nicky would have needed twenty more years of hard work to have achieved the same.

"Hello, this is Jess Jackson." I wipe my sweaty palms on my trousers. "I'm sorry to ring out of the blue, but I was hoping I could meet with you about a private matter?"

"What's it in connection with?"

"Nicola Waite."

She inhales abruptly. "That's a name I haven't heard in a very long time."

How long? But I don't want to get into that yet, not over the phone. I want to look her in the eye. If she'll let me.

"Could we meet please, by any chance?" I ask as gently as possible. I can be gentle sometimes.

She takes her time responding. I wonder for a moment if she's still there. And then she speaks, more slowly, guardedly. "How do you know her, exactly?"

I've prepared two options: truth and lie.

I go for the lie. "We were at school together."

"You don't sound Northern."

Shit.

Flustered, I reach for the truth. "My husband was at the Montague Club that night." I wince, close my eyes.

"I'm sorry. I can't get into this."

"I understand," I say quickly, "but can I just ask—are you aware that she died?"

Her voice sounds very far away when she replies. "Yes."

"How did you know?"

"Lucy told me. Lucy O'Neill."

"Oh, so you're still in touch?"

"Not really. We fell out a long time ago."

"Over Nicky?" I wait.

The filing room door opens and Mary appears. Her timing couldn't be worse. I stare down at the floor, pressing the phone to my ear.

"Look, I don't know who you are, or what you want," Kim is saying. "But whatever you *think* happened, you're wrong. You can't believe a word she ever said… Please don't contact me again."

And before I can do anything about it, she hangs up.

I continue to speak into the phone to prevent Mary from approaching. It doesn't work, though. "Phew, I'm glad that's all done. I hate filing!" She claps her hands, rubs them together. "Cappuccino?"

I'm busy for the rest of the day and the next, so there's no chance to call Lucy. But this is a pitiful excuse. There's always time to make a phone call. No one's that busy.

It's just that I can't get Kim's words out of my head—the way she said it, like it was fact.

You can't believe a word she ever said.

What if Lucy says the same thing? If she does, I may have to give up. What grounds would I have to carry on? Stephanie's been clear all along about what she wants, and although Priyanka seems to want to help, it's all a bit yada yada. She hasn't been in touch all week. Granted, her lad's poorly, but even so, I reckon she'd be happy never to hear from me again.

Friday is Gavin's birthday, so he takes the six of us from work to an Italian restaurant for lunch. It's a beautiful day, the sort that Bath was made for, sunshine lighting the honey limestone of the luxurious Georgian buildings, designed in lines and circles with the geometrical precision of honeycomb itself.

I don't often see it this way, as a local resident, but today—after two glasses of wine—I'm full of awe. On our way back from the restaurant, we pass a shop front adorned with fake roses and I know it'll only be a matter of time before the council takes it down. There are strict rules here. New-builds must be in keeping with the city's architectural heritage. Residents in listed buildings have to file a request if they want a nonstandard color for their front door. I know a woman who fought a yearlong battle for a green door, and lost.

There's a price to pay for this kind of beauty and civility. It doesn't just happen.

We take a shortcut through the square, everyone talking loudly, pigeons scattering. As we pass the Montague Club, I glance at the unmarked door, thinking of the portrait of Sir Graves and the long line of males made in his image, and realize I'm ready to call Lucy.

While the others go inside the office, I make an excuse about needing to call Beechcroft Home and walk a little way along the pavement. I don't want anyone to hear, so I scan the building's face for open windows.

Lucy O'Neill is CEO and cofounder—with her father, over twenty years ago—of LRC Ltd., providing employee training packages throughout Europe on a whole range of subjects, including harassment prevention, so I noticed.

She answers right away and seems nicer than Kim, if you can tell that sort of thing over the phone.

"Hi there! This is Lucy." Bubbly, positive. Still horsey, though, like Kim.

"Hi, this is Jess J—"

"I'm afraid I'm going to have to stop you right there. I'm at the airport, going to Geneva, and they're calling my gate." There's an announcement behind her—loud, echoey. "I can't hear you very well. Did you say it's Jess from R&P? Phone Stacey. She'll sort you out."

"I... When will you be back?"

"Two weeks, sweetie."

Sweetie? Two weeks? My heart sinks. I try to think of a way to speed things up, but can't. I need to speak to her face-to-face, in person. She's my only hope.

Of what? What am I even doing? It's cold out here. I should be indoors in the warm, doing my job, flirting with Elliott, drinking Mary's cappuccinos, keeping my family together and prioritizing them like Priyanka and Stephanie are doing.

At the window above, an elderly resident is watching me, her pale face close to the window. She reminds me of my mum and I feel ashamed.

Do I actually care about Nicky and Holly, or am I just angry, wanting someone—Max—to pay for what he's putting me through?

I don't think this is what Mum would tell me to do. She'd put the girls first.

I'm about to hang up, when I realize Lucy's beaten me to it. I guess they really were calling her gate.

———

An hour later, I'm deep into sulking, the way I do when I know I'm right and everyone else is wrong, when something unexpected happens.

Lucy calls me back.

"Hi, Jess, have you changed your number? This isn't the one I've got for you. *Anyhoo*, I felt bad cutting you off. I know you've been having some issues. Can you chat now? I'm on the plane."

She doesn't sound as though she's on the plane. It's very quiet. But then she'll be flying first class, not in a cramped cabin surrounded by screaming kids.

"Jess…? Are you there?"

I have to put her straight. If I were so inclined, I'd use this case of mistaken identity as a way in. But I'm sick of lies, plus I've been drinking and don't trust myself to carry it off.

"I'm not who you think I am," I murmur, walking the phone

out of the office, down the corridor to the front door. Stepping outside, I hug myself on the top step, wishing I'd brought my coat. "I'm Jess Jackson, a friend of Nicky Waite's."

Silence.

I gaze up at the blue sky, watching a seagull riding the current, wings gleaming. "Hello?"

"I'm here," she says. "You just caught me by surprise, that's all. I've not heard that name in a very long while."

"That's what Kim said."

"Kim Turner? You've spoken to her?"

"Yes."

I'd like her to make the next move. It shouldn't be me all the time. It feels like it's always me.

"God, I haven't spoken to Kim in years." She sighs and then swallows something. I picture a glamorous woman, legs curled underneath her, sipping champagne among the clouds. "Not since we graduated. We fell out big-time. And now it's just a round-robin email every few years and Christmas cards... Doesn't that sound complete nonsense?" She laughs.

Yes, it does, but I don't say anything. I sense that I've found a talker. At last.

I remember seeing butterflies in the garden as a child, creeping up to them as they rested on the wall, wings spread. Closer I'd creep. If I stepped on a twig or kicked a stone, they'd be off in a puff of dust.

"Nicky died, didn't she? I think that's the last time Kim and I swapped personal emails, when I contacted her to tell her... *Oh, yes, please. Thank you...*" Her voice is muffled, changes direction. Bottle and glass clinking. "I didn't know a thing about it at the time. The first I knew was when her daughter wrote to tell me, about a year after it happened. What was her name? Hannah, Helen?"

"Holly."

"Yes, that was it. It was a bit odd, really. She didn't give me any way to contact her in return, so it felt one-sided, like a hit-and-run. She just wanted to tell me that her mother had died of an overdose and she didn't believe it was accidental—she'd been deteriorating for years. Well, obviously I was upset to hear this, especially when she said it was because of what had happened to her in—" She stops.

There's a long pause.

"Kim told me that you couldn't trust a word Nicky ever said," I say. "Is that true?"

"No, it isn't!" She laughs scornfully. "That's *so* Kim. Now you see why we fell out. She used to have it in for Nicky. I always thought she was jealous of her, quite frankly."

Jealous...of Nicky?

"So, she was an honest person, in your opinion?" I ask. "You could trust her?"

"Absolutely! She just didn't have the easiest start in life, that's all. I don't think Kim had ever met anyone like her before and didn't know how to take her. But Nicky was fine—more than fine. I liked her a lot. I was very sad to hear she'd died."

How sad? Sad enough to help us?

"I need to talk to you in person, Lucy. It's important. Do you think we could meet when you return?"

"I could probably sort something out, yes. Where are you based?"

"Bath."

"Oh, well, that's easy, then. Why not...? I always felt I could have done more for her. I think about her sometimes, you know?"

Yes. I think I'd have done more for Nicky too, had I been in her shoes.

But then who's to say? People in their early twenties aren't known for their excellent choices. At that age, I was too busy holding a grudge against my parents to have a care about anyone else.

"I'll have my PA, Stacey, set something up," she says.

"Okay."

We're about to end the call, when she adds something. "Sorry, how did you say you knew Nicky, again?"

If she's who I think she is—not exactly a social activist, but not at peace about Nicky either—she'll set up the meeting, no matter what I say. And I won't be cornering her, doing it under false pretenses. I'm tired of forcing people to do the right thing. Was this how Holly felt, rounding up the key players, trying to persuade them to have a conscience?

People aren't butterflies. And I'm not five frigging years old anymore.

As I speak, I kick a pine cone from the step, shuttling it across the road, knowing I've nothing left to lose. "I think my husband raped her."

"Oh my *God*! I wasn't expecting you to say *that*..." She's pausing to have a long drink, by the sounds of things. I don't blame her.

Does she remember the men? Is she bringing their faces to mind, wondering which one I was stupid enough to marry?

"Okay, *now* I get it... Don't worry. Stacey will be in touch. We'll talk."

There's hope in that voice, in our conversation. It feels like a small victory, one that I can't celebrate because nothing about it spells good news.

I return indoors, heading straight for the bathroom, where I hold my hands underneath the hot air dryer, warming myself up so that I can be of use this afternoon and type.

———

Ten minutes later, I receive a text from her. I read it under my desk, my heart thumping.

14.58 P.M. >
You didn't say what you wanted? If it's the truth, I can help. I never doubted what Nicky said. But if it's proof, there isn't any. Kim's the only one who saw and she swore Nicky was lying. I'll tell you more when we meet. Lucy x P.S. you can email me if you like. LucyONeill1970@image.com

STEPHANIE

I think I prefer it when Jess pesters me. The silence this week has been unbearable and I've had a constant headache and palpitations, worrying what she's up to. I've thought several times about contacting her but don't want to seem as though I'm giving way, because I'm not.

By Saturday, I'm so tense I don't react well when the girls tell me they're not spending the afternoon with me, again.

"Well, I'm staying. Or don't I count?" Rosie says.

"Of course you do." She does come out with some silly things.

Vivian and Georgia are hovering near the living room door. "Are you sure you'll be all right?" Vivian asks.

"Yes, darling." I adjust the neck on my sweater, which feels too tight, restrictive. "It's just that it's been ages since we were all together. And Saturday's our special time."

We follow them out to the hallway, Rosie propping her foot behind her against the wall, examining her nails. "You know, M, you wouldn't take this so badly if you had some friends of your own, instead of relying on us."

"Hey!" Vivian flashes her a warning look.

"What?" She shrugs. "It's only what you were saying the other day. Except you haven't the balls to say it to her face."

Sometimes they talk as though I'm not there. Vivian goes red, zipping up her coat.

"I have plenty of friends," I say.

"Yeah, *right*." Georgia steps into her wellies. "Let me see… that's Miss No One, Ms. No One and Mrs. No One."

I look at her in surprise. I expect this sort of thing from Rosie, who went through a lot as a child, but not Georgia. Doesn't she have everything she could possibly want, or am I missing something?

"Shut up, Georgia." Vivian rubs my arm consolingly. "Sorry, M. They don't know what they're talking about. Rosie's—"

"No, *you* shut up. You're such a suck-up." Rosie scowls, marching from the hallway.

I take a moment to calm myself, looking at the wallpaper, a delicate floral pattern called Amelie that I chose purely because I loved the name. When Georgia was born, I couldn't settle on a name for her so went with Dan's choice—didn't even consider Amelie until years later. Only I could do that.

Vivian smiles at me. "We'll see you later, M. I'll give Georgia a lift back from the stables."

"Thanks, darling." I kiss her goodbye, but can't bring myself to do the same for Georgia, not after what she just said.

Back in the living room, Rosie is skulking by the window, watching her sisters as they unlock the garage. Her dungarees are very baggy, unflattering. "You know, you could always go out too, M, instead of moping around here."

I'm very tired today. Sitting down on the sofa, I wonder whether it's too early for a G&T.

She swings around to face me, hands in pockets. "You could phone Auntie Fiona. We never see her now…"

We've had this conversation so many times, I can't be bothered to argue anymore. I've told her before that I wasn't ever close to my sister. Rosie's memories of her are from when I was a sin-gle parent and she helped out. She used to babysit, that was all.

"…She's lovely, Auntie Fiona."

I press my fingers to my temples, circling them, wishing she would stop. "You don't even know her," I say.

"And whose fault is that?" Her mouth twists sourly—a look I'm far more used to seeing on her face than a smile. "I don't say this stuff because I like the sound of my voice or because I was born angry. It's because it's true. You need to take a long hard look at yourself!"

"Please just leave me alone, Rosie. I'm not in the mood for this. You've no idea."

"About what?" She looks at me as though I'm speaking a for-eign language. "Fuck this. I'm going out." And she sets off to the hallway, clambering for her boots, thrashing around.

I cross the room to the window, watching her run after Viv-ian's car. I've no idea where she's going, and for the first time since becoming a parent, I don't care.

I decide to make that G&T. Going through to the kitchen, I check my mother's cocoa tin, just to see if the letter is still there. It's strange I haven't destroyed it yet. I don't want to think about why that might be.

Sitting at the table, I think about what Rosie said about Fiona. I sit there for some time—until half my glass of gin is gone—before reaching for my phone.

Fiona answers to a chorus of dogs. She's a veterinary assis-tant. Always crazy about animals, she never wanted children. It was one of the many things that set us apart from an early age, given my aversion to pets.

"Hey, Stef!" She's always cheerful, I'll allow her that. She's not a bad person. It's a shame we're not close, but some people are just too different.

"Hello, Fiona. How are you?"

"Good, ta. And you?" Unlike me, she never lost her Midsomer Norton accent. Over the phone, she sounds like Shelley Fricker.

"Not too bad, thank you."

She laughs, although I'm not sure why. Maybe she thinks I'm too starchy. "So, what can I do you for?" She always says this—her little joke.

"Oh, nothing. I was just ringing to see how you are."

"Really? Oh… Right."

It goes quiet, aside from the dogs.

"So, how have you been—I mean, *really*?"

"You been drinking, Stef?"

"No, of course not." I push away the glass. "Can't I call my sister?"

"Course you can. Whenever you want, you know that. It's just that normally it's never. Only Christmas and funerals."

"Well, maybe we could change that… Why don't you come over sometime?"

She laughs again, her voice high-pitched. "Uh…because I don't think Dan would like that."

"What? Why? Besides, you could come over when he's out."

She pauses. "Listen to yourself, Stef. Do you hear it…?" She sighs. "Sorry, I've gotta go. See you at Christmas, if no one dies before then." And she rings off.

———

I'm not in the mood for lovemaking tonight, but several years ago decided there were times when I had to get on with it. That's not to say I don't draw pleasure from it; naturally, I do. It's just that it would have been my personal preference to read a book or run a bath instead. Yet when I agreed to marry Dan, I agreed to allow him certain rights. Left to my own devices, I'd probably never do it again. And I'm sure millions of wives feel the same way, not that they would admit it. We're all supposed to be highly sexual beings now, or at least declining it without apology. No doubt if Jess were a fly on my wall, she'd call it nonconsensual because I didn't sign a form.

She'd also have something to say about what's happening now, I would imagine. To the uninitiated, it might seem strange, over-rehearsed, but I'm quite used to it now. It begins with me standing at the foot of the bed, undressing for Dan while he lies there, watching me.

As I start my approach, the room feels crowded as Jess and Priyanka join me suddenly, distracting me. Crawling seductively across the bed toward him, just as he likes, I feel animal-like on all fours, something that's never occurred to me before. I know it's Jess, judging me. And now Fiona's here too, with her barking dogs.

Our lips meet, just as things become even more crowded, with the Waite women on the bed too. They look like their paintings—droopy, ghostlike—and for a moment I contemplate calling the whole thing off, but Dan absolutely hates that. I tried it not long after Georgia was born and never attempted it again. We had a huge row and he didn't speak to me for a week.

"God, Stephanie, you're gorgeous, you know that?" I make myself smile as he pulls me on top of him. It's a smooth operation, never any fumbling because we both know the routine, and I don't see what's wrong with that.

My head feels a little achy. I drank too much gin this afternoon after my run-in with Rosie and then the conversation with Fiona, which threw me. I didn't know she felt like that.

How does she feel, exactly? She didn't say for sure.

I feel damp breath on the back of my neck, my palpitations returning. Nicola and Holly are leering from their canvases, smearing oily paint over me, telling me I'm letting them down, that I'm complicit in my silence. Jess is begging me, *please, Steffie*, and Priyanka is looking at me doubtfully with deep brown eyes.

My body is soaked with perspiration, but Dan reads this as excitement, flipping me onto my back, clenching his teeth. And

I find it then: my off button. I'm no longer with him. I can't see his face, can't hear him above me.

I'm walking along the corridor, holding my mum's hand. There's a little pocket of blue sky above us, a gentle breeze flapping the bunting. I'm so happy. I'm taking her into a jewelry shop, buying her a beautiful sapphire.

PRIYANKA

"Why didn't you call me?" Jess asks, kneeling on the cardboard floor of the storage unit, looking into the same box that we found the diary in. She asked me to help search the rest of Holly's things, and I couldn't come up with a good enough reason not to. "I thought maybe I wasn't going to hear from you again."

"Sorry. I caught a bug from Beau. It totally knocked me out."

That's partially true, but I overplayed my symptoms so I could lie low. I couldn't face school, not after what happened with Saffron. I was worried that the science teacher would report the incident and things would escalate; yet when I returned yesterday, nothing was said.

Jess doesn't look convinced. After all, I could have texted, yet saying what? Begging her not to contact Nicky's friends? Nothing I said would have changed that. She was always going to contact them, despite what she said about being a team and needing Stephanie's approval. She needs the truth more—can't help herself. And maybe I wanted her to go ahead. I don't know. It doesn't appear to have led anywhere anyhow, after all that fuss.

It's Tuesday the third of November; exactly one month since Holly's letter arrived, and we're still no closer to knowing what to do. At least, I'm not. All I can think about is what Stephanie said at the café about destroying lives and tearing our families apart. Every time I think about her—her eyes filling with tears, her sad little list of questions—I feel terrible. We shouldn't have let her walk away like that. But Jess is a strange mix of compassion and determination; and I think that's what worries me the most.

"I thought maybe you had cold feet," she says, removing a large envelope from the box. "Wonder what's in here...?"

"I don't think I'll ever have warm feet about this. You know that." I perch on the edge of an upturned tea crate, watching as she opens the envelope, pulls out a newspaper cutting.

She reads it, then shakes the envelope, others fluttering to the floor. "What are they about?" I ask.

"Come and take a look."

Crouching beside her, I pick up one with the headline Young Grad Opens for Business, dated 4th April 1994. It's about Kim Turner and her father, who helped her set up a business management consultancy. With long dark hair and a pronounced gap between her front teeth, I recognize her. "Isn't that her there?" I point to the paintings by the mini-fridge. "The one on the left?"

"Looks like it." She takes the cutting from me. "Nasty piece of work."

"Why?"

"I told you—she wasn't very nice on the phone. And Lucy said she was jealous of Nicky."

"Really? I'm surprised to hear that. Look at everything she achieved..."

"Yeah, must have taken a lot of hard work and talent, asking Daddy for the money." She picks up another cutting, holding it at arm's length to read it. "Trust me, she was jealous."

Most of the articles are about Kim. Cutting the ribbon for a hospital ward; business success; employment growth. "Do you think Nicky collected these?"

"I'm guessing so," Jess says.

"But why?"

"To torture herself?" She hands me an article about a different woman. "That's Lucy."

She has full lips, bobbed hair, a friendly expression. Local Businesswoman Wins Award for Best Newcomer. I compare her photo to the face in the painting beside Kim's. "The hair's different, but it's definitely her. Look at the mouth."

"I agree." She spreads out the cuttings, then places her hands on her knees.

I watch her, wondering what she's thinking. She's so invested in this, in a way that I could never be. There are too many things I'm scared of. I don't know how she copes with all the worry, the fake alibis.

I told Andy I'm at a cheese-and-wine function, but I've not been to one of those in years. When I first joined St. Saviour's, I decided that the best way to be a woman in a boys' school was to keep a professional front at all times. No cheese on cocktail sticks, no wine.

"This must have killed her, seeing these," Jess says. "Just think...year after year, clipping articles about her peers—her own life unraveling by the day...wondering where she went wrong, why it wasn't her in place of them. Knowing all along that it was never going to be her."

Looking dejected, she collects the scraps of paper, putting them back into the envelope.

"Is that why you're doing this, Jess—for her?" I ask. "Or Holly?"

She chews her lip pensively. "I think it's for both of them. I mean, I was raised to care about this kind of thing, to look out for the people around me." Frowning, she glances about the room. "And all along there were two women living right under our noses without us even knowing. That has to matter, doesn't it? There has to be some kind of justice, doesn't there?"

I nod. I feel for them too, especially Nicky. I could have written something similar to her diary myself. Not about assault, but how it feels not to be able to say no, to want to be loved, handpicked.

But *justice* is still a word that terrifies me.

It's that that I'm frightened of, not Jess's determination. That's just an excuse.

"Do you want to carry on?" she asks.

I check the time on my phone. "Okay."

She digs deep inside the box without looking, as though it's a lucky random draw—the worst one in the world. She removes a photo album. It rustles as she opens it, the plastic pages stiff.

Together, we survey the pictures—faded Polaroids of a time long gone when homemade haircuts were uneven and trousers flared. "Is that Nicky?"

Aged five or six, hair in pigtails, Nicky is wearing a sundress with a pineapple motif. I think of her mother buying the dress, setting it out for a special day, brushing her hair, making her stand still for the photo.

Jess turns the pages, unsticking them. Nicky at primary school, senior school; with two friends in little black dresses: Lucy and Kim. "She was beautiful, poor girl."

She's the prettiest by far, standing between them, her hands draped on their shoulders. It reminds me of the photo that Jess found of the men in the Montague Club. Three friends, yet not friends. Friends who let each other down when it came to it.

Right at the back, there's a photo of Nicky holding a baby girl. Reaching underneath the plastic film, Jess prys out the picture, reading the writing on the reverse. "'Holly, Victoria Park, Bath.'"

The photo isn't great quality. Whoever took it didn't know about shooting into the sun, and no one's smiling. Nicky looks completely different—straggly, emaciated. Holly has a daunted expression that toddlers don't often have.

At the thought of Beau, I don't want to be here any longer. Getting up, I fasten my parka, stamping my feet, which are numb from squatting.

"You okay?" Jess asks.

"Not really. I'd like to call it a night, if that's all right. Don't you have to get to your mum's?"

"I'm fine for another five minutes." Opening her rucksack, she places the press cuttings and photo album inside. She's taking them and I want to ask why, but daren't. I've a feeling all of this is building to something I'm not going to like. But what? Hasn't she explored all avenues already?

"Can you help me check out the rest of the box?" She looks up at me appealingly.

Somehow, I can't deny her. I know her heart's in the right place.

Sighing, I crouch again. "Quickly, then. I don't know how much more of this I can take."

"I'm sorry." She squeezes my hand. "Thanks, Pree."

"Gosh, you're freezing."

"I know."

The bottom of the box is filled with library books—battered hardbacks with catalog numbers on the spines. She selects one at random. *Empowerment for Women.*

I flick through another, the smell of old paper meeting my nose. *Six Steps to Success.* "Do you think these were Nicky's?"

"Dunno." She turns to the front page to examine the date of the last stamp. "No, I don't think so. It says 2012." She checks another. "This one is 2013. I think she was dead by then."

"So, they were Holly's, then. She was ambitious?"

"Seems so, yes." She stacks the books into leaning towers, then hugs her legs ponderingly, chin on knees. "I reckon she must have stolen them. Can't see her having a library card, can you?... God, it's all so tragic."

I think of the sketches then, glancing over my shoulder at the book, still lying near the door where we left it. "What about the drawings of the doors? Where do they fit into all this?"

"Not sure." She scratches her nose.

"Do you think maybe she wanted to be part of us?"

"What, like, family?"

I nod, even though that's not precisely what I meant.

I try again. "Do you think she was hoping one of our husbands would claim her as their daughter—give her a lucky break? She must have stood outside our houses to sketch them—must have seen Stephanie's beautiful home. Why not knock on the door and introduce herself?"

She shrugs loosely. "Maybe she was too scared to do that."

"So why not be underhand instead, blackmail them? If she wanted success so badly, she could have got a decent sum from the three men combined. That's what I'd have done."

"Would you, though?" She narrows her eyes at me skeptically. "It's one thing to say it, but would you really blackmail someone? It would take some balls, when you think about it."

"I suppose it would depend how desperate I was."

"Besides…" She shifts position, sitting cross-legged. "…You're equating success with money, but maybe that's not what she was after. And she couldn't have wanted a lucky break either, because she was about to die."

"Then what? Why bother writing to us?" I say despondently. "Why put us through this? What did we ever do to her?"

She doesn't reply. She's too busy fishing something out of the bottom of the box.

"What is it?"

"Just this." She holds up a tatty twine bracelet. "It's nothing." She's about to put it back and then changes her mind, dropping it into the pocket of her puffer.

We pack away the books, putting everything back the way it was.

"Well, I think we're done." She motions to the door, sweeping her hands dramatically. "Shall we?"

At last. I smile, relieved.

But then, just as she's about to turn off the light, she looks at me with that hard-to-deny expression again. "Pree…can I ask you something?"

I feel weightless, as though I'm levitating.

What now? *What?*

She touches my coat sleeve, leaves her hand there. It's like a thin little bird claw, pinning me in place. "Would you do something for me?" My face must be a picture, because she adds, "I promise I won't ask for anything else."

Oh, God. No.

"What is it, Jess?"

"I want to get some legal advice and need you to come with me."

"Legal advice?" It comes out as a croak.

"Yes. I've found a great lawyer who'll give us a free consultation. She's brilliant, Pree, part of a women in law organization. If anyone can help us, it's her. And she's based in Bath." Her grip tightens. "What do you think?"

What do I think?

The cardboard underneath me seems to wobble as though it's all that's holding me up and I'm about to crash through the floorboards to my death. "I…"

"I know it's a lot to ask, but it'll give us some clarity. That's what you want, isn't it?" She bends her knees to look in my eyes; Andy often does the same thing. "You told Stephanie you wanted clarity, right?"

I don't know what I said or why. Clarity doesn't sound all that appealing anymore.

"Oh, Jess. This is really hard… I mean, Andy knows about the letter. If he was to find out I'd consulted a lawyer, well, you can imagine…" I trail off, unable to imagine it myself.

"But it would be completely confidential and we'd be very

discreet… Please… I can't do this alone." She presses her palms together. "Say yes, Pree. I need you."

"No, you don't. You're the strongest person I've ever met."

She gazes at me and then blinks, looks away. "You know what? Forget I asked." She doesn't sound angry, more disappointed. "I can't keep begging people to do the right thing. It's exhausting. No wonder Holly was an alcoholic… Let's go."

I stay where I am, reeling with indecision. "Wait, Jess…"

She looks over her shoulder expectantly.

I can't believe I'm about to say this. "Okay."

She exhales, shoulders sinking. "Thanks, Pree. You're a star. I can't tell you how much I appreciate it." Then she frowns, looms closer. "You look exhausted. I'm sorry. I shouldn't have kept you so long. Come on—let's go." And she turns out the light.

"So, when are you meeting this woman?" I say, following her out of the door.

"We, Pree. *We.*"

"Okay…when are we meeting her?"

"Saturday afternoon. I'll text you the details."

"What about Stephanie?" I ask. "Are you going to include her?"

She knits her lips as we go along the corridor. "No. I think we should give her a little time to come around. Because she will."

Really? Nothing about Steffie's attitude so far has hinted at acquiescence, but if Jess wants to believe we're all going to hold hands and do this together, then I'm not going to be the one to point out the obvious defects.

We say brief goodbyes, Jess not hanging around, perhaps in case I change my mind.

Inside the car, I take Andy's hip flask from the glove compartment and swallow a mouthful of whiskey, shuddering. I hate the stuff, but if I've been to a cheese-and-wine night, then I should smell of something other than Holly's storage unit.

I drive home, praying the world will end on Saturday and I won't have to show up.

JESS

This might come as a surprise, but it was Stephanie who inspired me to set up the meeting with the lawyer. The idea came to me after hearing her list of questions at Carol's. I knew she was withholding something and guessed what it was, the question she couldn't ask.

Wasn't she asking for trouble?

It hadn't occurred to me to unpick Nicky's diary, second-guess it. I didn't wonder how much she had drunk, or whether her signals were clear enough or her dress too tight. Focused on Max, ashamed of him, I was more concerned with the men: too much testosterone, alcohol, privilege.

Yet Steffie's questions—the way she went about it—made me realize there was a completely different way to view things, like looking through the other end of a telescope. Without her, I wouldn't have known what we were up against.

After meeting her, I had the longest bath of my life, doing research on my phone until I was wrinkled like walnuts. Steffie was on to something and by no means alone in her thinking.

I was wrong. It wasn't a case of Nicky's allegation having merit simply by nature of its existence. In fact, that was so far from being the case, it wasn't even in the same solar system.

It seemed shocking to me, but Steffie's question wouldn't only be raised in court but *discussed*. And that's when I realized we couldn't do this alone, but needed professional advice, someone with agency and knowledge and extra iron and adrenaline running through their veins. Because trying to get any kind of justice for Nicky would be the biggest uphill battle you could possibly imagine.

Thanks to Steffie, I discovered things I might never have known: that juries pulled a face, and people—the folk at home—watched the news or logged on to social media, wondering with a perplexed expression just how much that young woman who was knocked unconscious, brutally raped and left for dead was asking for it to happen.

That was the way it worked.

As a woman, it would be impossible to feel anything but the absolute fear of God when you heard what he did to her. Your next thought would be to wonder whether it could happen to you or your daughter or sister. So, then you'd look for further details because there *had* to be something this woman did wrong—something you wouldn't do, something to distinguish you from her.

It wouldn't be long before you found it. In fact, it would be prominently displayed so you couldn't miss it. If you were lucky, there would be several to choose from. They couldn't make it any easier for you.

Intoxicated.

Flirting.

Promiscuous past.

Provocative language.

Inappropriate attire.

Length of skirt.

Heavy makeup.

Five-inch heels.

Ambitious.

Insecure.

Attention-seeking.

Unreliable.

Prone to storytelling.

Mentally unstable.

History of substance abuse.

All you'd have to do is pick one and hang on to it. Even if you thought you were the most liberal-minded person on the planet, chances are you'd store it somewhere and get it out when you needed it. How else could you walk about freely, knowing it wasn't going to happen to you? How could you right swipe on Tinder, date, fall in love, meet your future husband, raise daughters?

By hanging on to the thing that distinguished you from her, that's how. There's no other way.

And now here comes the judge and the barristers and the jury and each of them are hanging on to their own word secretly.

None of them has any personal experience of rape, aside from what they've seen on TV. They're expecting violence, a dark alley, a stranger pouncing, holding her at knifepoint. So, when this young woman tells a different story, a murky one in which she was coerced against her will, they don't buy it.

When the jury learns that she was in a relationship with the accused, a quarter of them shake their heads. Consent wasn't needed in that case, they believe.

On hearing that she was drunk when the accused had sex with her, a tenth of them think it wasn't rape.

When it's divulged that she flirted with the accused over dinner, a third of the male members of the jury believe this discounts rape. And when the same men hear that she consented at first, but changed her mind halfway through the act, she has lost. The whole case collapses.

I know the facts, have gathered as many as I can in preparation. The more I've learned, the more I've come to realize that this isn't about me. It's not even about Nicky Waite. It's bigger than that. It's about all of us.

Like Holly said, you can't draw a line where one life starts and another begins.

Maybe I'm delusional, but as I hurry to meet Priyanka on Saturday afternoon, I've picked a word of my own to hang on to.

Hopeful.

Deborah Scott is one impressive lady. I can't help staring at her. She has red hair in a swishy updo, plum fingernails and is wearing a trouser suit. She's the kind of woman who makes me wish I'd tried harder at school. I didn't go to university and it's never been a regret, until now.

Watching her sitting at her desk, reading our file, I wonder what it must be like to look men in the eye and say, yeah, I'm doing what you do, buddy, only better. Watch and learn.

Beside me, Priyanka is fiddling with her nose stud, which has changed color. I'm sure it wasn't pink before. Her eyes have changed too: gray. I look away from her, at the walls. I've never seen so many awards, certificates and books.

"So," Deborah Scott says, taking off her reading glasses. "Let me get this straight—you're the wives of the accused?"

"Yes, that's correct," I say.

Confusion clouds her face. "And you want a legal practitioner's perspective on how to bring this out into the open…? Why?"

Priyanka looks at me to answer.

"That's a question I've been asking myself a lot lately. And all I can say is that I want them to take responsibility for what they did. It's the right thing to do."

She raises her eyebrows, looking at us steadily in turn, and then looks back down at the file.

I've made copies of everything, but she's got the diary, with key pages bookmarked for convenience, plus the original of Holly's letter. I've told her everything we know, and it feels like a lot.

"Is this everything you have?" she asks.

I get an itchy feeling around my neck, down my spine. "Yes. But it's all there—Nicky's record of events. It's crystal clear, isn't it, that it was rape?"

She gathers the items, placing them painstakingly into the leather conference file I purchased specially to give Nicky the best chance of being taken seriously.

"It would appear that the account—if true—is of rape, the absence of consent being the determining factor. But in this case, it's impossible to prove. And without proof..." She holds up her hands. "...There's no case."

"Surely there's something you can do?" I say, trying to sound measured. "I read about an assault that happened forty years ago and it only just went to court."

She smiles regrettably, doing up the clasp on my folder. "The justice system isn't in great shape when it comes to rape. Believe you me, I'm doing all I can. But there's been a big drop in charges, despite an increase in reports to the police. Prosecutors are being urged to drop weak cases. And I'm afraid this case wouldn't get very far at all—not even beyond my door."

"But they did it! I know they did! And I think they'd confess, if it was handled professionally—by someone like you."

"It doesn't work like that, I'm afraid."

"Why doesn't it?"

Priyanka reaches for my hand, but I pull away. I don't want to be comforted. I want to fight. But who am I fighting? Deborah Scott? She's already standing up, handing me the file, the diary bulging through the leather.

"Please," I say. "This isn't fair. Two lives were ruined because of what they did."

She's standing right in front of me, a few inches taller. Her skin is flawless. I'm thinking so many things: how graceful she is, how educated, how powerful. And even she can't help us.

She's fading, her voice becoming muffled.

"I'm so sorry. I really am. You don't know how much I wish things were different. I see cases like this all the time and it's so disheartening. So many of them will never see daylight, and I know how unfair it is. But the crux of the matter is that the victim is deceased, as is the person who made the allegation, plus the offense took place thirty years ago, all of which are stacked against you. I'm sure you can see that, given the challenges facing the justice system, there's nothing I can do. But thank you for coming in and I hope you find the closure you're looking for... Did you know the complainant?"

I notice that her lips have stopped moving. She's looking at me kindly, waiting.

Priyanka jumps in. "No, not personally." She tugs my arm, gets me to stand up. "Come on, Jess. Let's not take up any more of this lady's time."

"You were more than welcome," Deborah Scott says. "All the best."

She shakes our hands: a light powdery touch. And then we're making our way along the creaky hallway and pulling open the doorway, going down the steps to the courtyard below.

"Jess?"

I'm looking up at the sky, thinking that it's the same sky Nicky and Holly saw—the same earth, the same city. And yet too much time has passed and now it's standing between us and justice.

"Say something." Priyanka's gazing up at me like a child, waiting for my next instruction. She seems like a good person, a good parent and teacher. I'm sure she cares. But she wasn't cut out for this.

And as for Stephanie...

"I'll see you later, Pree. Thanks for coming." Setting off, I feel wobbly, depleted. I dressed up too, in my best trousers and boots. What was the point?

"Jess!" Priyanka hurries after me. "Where are you going?"

"Home. And we probably shouldn't walk together. Someone might see us. We're not supposed to know each other, remember?"

"Since when do you care about that?"

A mum and three little children in colorful knit hats are coming along the alley toward us. I lower my voice. "Since I realized that we haven't got a leg to stand on... Well, at least you're happy now."

"Happy? This isn't what I wanted!"

"Yes, it is. You just can't admit it, that's all." I stare up at the solicitor's office, wondering what Deborah Scott's doing now—discarding allegations that don't involve blood, bruising, date rape drugs, dark alleys or that do involve flirting, alcohol, skimpy clothes or the passage of time. Basically, only keeping the no-brainers, if there are any.

What a job.

"Look, it's fine...it's over." I hold up my hands. "You were right all along. It happened too long ago to matter anymore."

She looks confused. "So...?"

"So it's probably best we forget it now." And I start to walk away.

"Jess, wait." She runs after me, pulling on my arm. "You don't mean that."

"Yes, I do. You heard her in there."

"So, what now?"

I'm not even going the right way home—am heading in totally the wrong direction. Town's manic; there are people everywhere and I didn't expect to be left reeling.

But why didn't I expect it? Everything I read online warned me how impossible this would be.

"Jess, *please*, talk to me! What's the plan?"

"The plan?" I stop abruptly, stare at her. "*I don't know!* I don't have all the answers! Why don't you decide something for once, instead of leaving it all to me?"

We're standing in the middle of the pavement, forcing shoppers to go around us. The road is noisy, crowded. A tour bus is passing by, a man on the top deck speaking through a microphone.

She bites her lip forlornly, smaller than ever.

"Oh, God, Pree. I'm sorry." I look up at the top deck of the bus, the woolly hats, indistinguishable faces. "We're just gonna have to figure out what's best for each of us…on our own."

"But what about what you said about us being in this together?"

"That was yesterday. Before…" I trail off.

"It's okay," she says, nodding, tears brimming in her eyes. "I understand."

I want to tell her that I didn't mean what I said about going it alone and that I'll call her…but my legs are thinking differently and I'm already walking away. Before turning the corner of the street, I look back, intending to wave, but she's not there.

———

As I pull into the driveway, there's a magenta glow on the horizon, the trees outlined in black like one of Holly's charcoal sketches, and I wonder where her talent came from—whether Jack, Lee or Brooke were artistic. There are so many things we don't know, sides to our husbands we weren't aware of when we married them.

I gaze at the house, the porch light casting a welcoming glow. I can't go back to how things were before. I'm convinced they did what Nicky said they did, but would never be able to prove it. The girls wouldn't forgive me for bringing something so dangerous and unfounded to light. I'd risk losing them and probably my home too.

If only there were a way to extract him subtly, with minimal effort, just like they got rid of Nicky.

Checking that the leather file is concealed inside my rucksack, I make my way inside the house, the smell of pizza greeting me. The TV's on very loud. And then I remember: it's the big fireworks display tonight. That's why town was so crazy. I'm going to have to stand there and look happy.

I step warily into the living room. Eva and Poppy are sitting either side of Max on the sofa, his arms around them. Noticing me, he smiles and I smile back.

———————

I rub my eyes in disbelief at the kitchen clock. Nine fifteen?

"Morning, baby," Max says, turning back to Poppy. "So, what does that do?" She's sitting on his knee, showing him a game on her phone.

"It kills that one, Daddy. See?"

The radio's playing Spandau Ballet's "True." Opposite them at the table, Eva's tapping on her iPad. It occurs to me that I haven't asked her in ages how her mean friend, Charlotte, is—whether she's still getting at her. But now doesn't seem the right time.

"Why didn't you wake me?" I flick on the kettle.

"Because you were out for the count," Max replies. "It's no biggie… What time are you going to see your mum?"

I go to lie as usual, before realizing that I don't have to anymore; there's nowhere else I need to be today. "Around two."

"Only, I thought I'd take the girls swimming." He taps his stomach. "Don't want to get saggy."

"Okay." There's not an inch of fat on him.

"Thought we'd go for coffee afterward, drag it out—give you some me time."

"I don't need me time," I say emotionlessly.

"Well, it couldn't hurt. I know you've got a lot going on."

"Is Grandma getting worse?" Eva looks up from her screen.

"Yes, she is." I take my mug of tea over to the window, sur-
veying the icy lawn. The sun is trying to break through the fog.
When it does, the red berries on the firethorn hedge will look
spectacular. It's the first frost I've noticed this autumn. There
may have been others, but I wouldn't have had a clue—have
been elsewhere, preoccupied.

As I look at the trees, the roots, the soil, I feel envious. Everything around me seems solid, grounded. I'm the only one
that's adrift.

———

I'm locking the car door, two bunches of carnations and winter jasmine in my arms, when someone calls to me. "Do they
help?"

I look about the car park, but can't see anyone. I begin to
walk toward the building, when the voice calls out again. "Do
they help...the flowers?" This time I turn to see an elderly lady
on the other side of the wall, near the compost heap. She nods
at the bouquets I'm holding.

"Oh, I see..." I take a step toward her, embarrassed by my
mistreatment of her garden. "I'm not sure. I buy them for my
mum."

"Who are the other ones for? Yourself? I'm sure you need
them just as much." She touches her hair into place, adjusting
her cardigan in the way that elderly people do when speaking
to strangers.

"No. But that's a nice thought... They're for Mum's carer."

"Well, I expect she appreciates them. I know you bring them
every Sunday."

My cheeks flush. "I'm so sorry. I've been tossing them over
the wall. I really should have...well, not done that."

"Oh, don't you worry." She flaps her hand. "If we can't help
each other out in times of need, then it's a poor state of affairs.
What's a few dead flowers on a pile of eggshells and whatnot?"

"Well, that's very kind of you." I smile, turning to go. "I'd better be getting on."

"You take care now."

As I walk away, I can feel her watching me. I've never noticed her before. I'm not attentive to old Mary in the office either. I haven't noticed the frosts. I haven't considered my girls' needs. I haven't asked Eva whether Charlotte's still giving her a hard time; I haven't spoken to Poppy one-to-one in ages.

I'm a hypocrite for being angry about Holly. I'm no better than anyone else, caught up in myself and my own concerns, not paying enough attention to what's going on around me.

I scowl, muttering to myself as I enter Beechcroft, the doors whooshing open. Olivia isn't at the desk, so I leave her flowers there, heading through to Mum's room with such a sense of routine that I'm barely conscious of my actions.

She's asleep, so I continue on around the side of the bed, heading for the vase, when I catch sight of her face and gasp, dropping the flowers.

There's a nasty swollen bruise on Mum's cheek.

"Damn!" I'm picking up the smattering of carnation petals from the floor, when Olivia appears, smiling. "What happened?" I ask.

She takes a moment to realize what I mean. "Oh. She had a fall. I did think about ringing you, but it was in the middle of the night."

"Well, you should have," I say gruffly.

She looks taken aback. "I'm sorry, Jess... I'll keep you updated in the future."

What's wrong with me? Now I'm making Olivia apologize?

I drop the petals into the wastepaper basket. "It was just a shock, that's all."

"I understand. It won't happen again."

I try to smile. "It's fine. Don't take any notice of me. I'm just having a bad day." I approach Mum tentatively, peering at the bruise. "Is she all right?"

"Yes. It looks worse than it is. And we'll put crash mats down in case it happens again." Somewhere down the corridor an alarm is beeping. She points in its direction. "I have to…"

"That's okay. Go. And please forget what I said."

Sinking onto the bedside chair, I hold my head in my hands, looking at the petals underneath the bed that I missed when cleaning up.

I knew this would happen. Mum never falls. And now—because I kept using that as an excuse—she fell.

Taking off my coat, I sling it onto the floor in frustration, something falling from the pocket. I pick it up, baffled, before remembering that I took Holly's bracelet from the storage unit.

I examine it over by the window. The cheap metal is tarnished, the black twine threadbare in parts. There's a tiny charm that I can barely see without my glasses. I hold it up to the light to inspect it. I think it's a key.

PART THREE:
THE KEY

PRIYANKA

Yesterday, after Jess said we had to work things out on our own, I told myself that at least now I would have more room to think.

How wrong I was. Since then, Nicky hasn't stopped plaguing me, getting inside my head, saying I'm just like her and that if I'm not careful, I'll end up the same way: alone, unloved.

This morning, I looked up tattoo removal online. I've decided that I don't want the butterfly on my wrist any longer. I hate it, hate that Beau has a mum with a past like mine.

"Are you sure you don't want to come with?" Andy says, zipping up his jacket.

I look up at him in annoyance. Why does he have to say *come with*? And what's he done to his hair—all bushy, inane? No wonder Meena calls him The Anorak. And as for his brown corduroys, for God's sake. Who wears those anymore?

He bends down, hands on my shoulders. "Can I help with the shopping list? What have you got so far?"

I hold up the notepad for him.

"Bread… Okay. Well, it's a start." He stands up straight. "Can't it wait, though? It's a beautiful day. Seems a shame to spend it in the supermarket."

"Yes, Mummy, come with us," Beau chimes in.

See? Even Beau knows it's *come with us*.

"I can't, cherub, I'm afraid. I'd love to, but we have to eat this week, don't we? We can't have you going hungry." I tickle his tummy and he giggles.

"Go get your wellies on, Beau," Andy says, then turns to me. "Everything all right? You don't seem your usual self."

My usual self? So this is how we're playing it? Almost a month after our discussion of a rape allegation, followed by a few weeks of tiptoeing around and extra nice behavior, and now we're pretending it never happened.

He seems surprised by the look of anger on my face. "What's up, my love?"

That does it.

Snatching up the notepad, I storm from the room. Beau is peeling muddy leaves from his wellies, lining them up along the hallway floor. "Stop making a mess!" I yell. "It's difficult enough, trying to keep this place clean!" And I stomp through to the kitchen, where I start pacing.

Don't touch the vodka.

I head for the freezer, Nicky following me.

That's right. Go for the vodka. That's what I'd do too.

Slamming the freezer door, I'm wringing my hands in exasperation when the door opens. "Do you want to talk about it?" Andy asks cordially.

"No, I don't! Leave me alone!" I shout, pushing past him. In the hallway, I plow through Beau's leaves, hating myself, and he starts to wail. Grabbing my parka and bag, I slam the front door behind me and run to the car, barely knowing what I'm doing.

Instinct is telling me to get as far away as possible from everyone, including Nicky. I still have to do the shopping, though— have used that excuse so many times under false pretenses, we've no food left in the house. The farthest supermarket I can think of is on the outskirts of Bristol. That'll do.

Taking off, I speed down the hill, joining the main road out of the city. But the more distance I put between myself and home, the closer Nicky seems to come, as though she's stronger when I'm alone.

It was she who made me start a fight with Andy and made Beau cry, because that's what the Waite women do. They brought everything on themselves, every bit of rotten luck in their miserable lives. They had the reverse of the Midas touch: the Sadim touch, ruining everything and everyone they came into contact with. Death hasn't made them less unlucky to be around.

Jess did the right thing by walking away. No one could accuse her of not having tried. Only a masochist would continue.

But by removing herself, she's left a big hole in the middle of my life and my marriage that I've no idea how to fill. Without her, decision-maker and leader, I'm lost.

I'm at the supermarket already, not having even noticed the journey. It's so crowded, I can't find anywhere to park. Around and around I drive, close to giving up, until finally I spot a tight space near the trolleys.

A sensible person would try to compose themselves before going into a megastore on the weekend, but I'm way past that. It takes all of my strength not to whack the car alongside mine as I open my door and squirm out, sucking in my chest.

There's a queue for trolleys. Searching through my purse, I realize that I don't have a pound coin to release the trolley lock. I'm about to start crying pathetically, when someone touches my arm and I turn to see a familiar face that I can't place right away.

And then I've got it, because no one ever forgets what their husband's first wife looks like. And she recognizes me because no one ever forgets his second one either.

"Priyanka? Hi!"

We don't hug or kiss—barely know each other. So, there's that awkward moment when we don't know what to do instead.

"Katie!" I'm about to launch into my familiar comedic routine, when I stop myself. I don't want to be that person anymore. "What are you doing out this way?"

We step aside from the queue. "I live here. Well, not actually here at the supermarket." She laughs. "But nearby."

"Oh, yes. Of course!"

"What are *you* doing here?" she asks.

Now, that's a good question, with a very long answer. I gaze up at her wistfully, wishing I could tell her everything. They say strangers make good listeners when you're desperate, but she's not a stranger. She's Andy's ex-wife, making her one of the worst people to confide in. Plus I'm in awe of her. She's prettier than I realized and is wearing a red leather jacket with puff shoulders, which I instantly covet.

Still, the timing of this is very strange. She's been on my mind for weeks. You don't teach RPE without believing in fate, divine intervention. Call it what you will, I think something bigger than us has caused this encounter and I'd like to know why.

"I don't suppose you fancy a coffee, do you?" I point at the café at the front of the store.

She looks at her watch, but it's not just the time that's bothering her; she's considering what we could possibly find to talk about. I'm not about to let her get out of it that easily, though.

"Okay," she says.

"Great."

We walk in silence, but it's not noticeable because of the announcements inciting shoppers' frenzy. I feel like her parole officer, walking her to the café, making sure she doesn't give me the slip. "I'll get the drinks. What would you like?"

She shrugs. "You choose."

I hate it when people say that. I haven't a clue what she'd like. "Tea? Coffee? Gin?"

She laughs, flicks her hair over her shoulders. "Skinny latte, please."

"Got it," I say, pointing both index fingers at her, then regretting it. I thought I was going to drop that. I don't have to play the fool.

As she takes a seat by the window, I gesture to the iced buns. She nods enthusiastically.

Waiting for the coffees, I practice what to say. I won't mention the universe or mystical connections because few people like to hear that, in my experience. But somehow, I have to probe into her past—specifically with Andy—all without her knowing why. How am I going to do that?

I pay the cashier, then concentrate on carrying the tray, not spilling anything, not knocking into anyone. I want to seem mature, in control. Perhaps things went wrong with Jess because I didn't come across like that, but the very opposite, in fact.

There's a bit of awkwardness as we settle, getting teaspoons—which I forgot—and napkins—those too—and sugar—I haven't done a great job—both of us laughing and bumping hands. And then there's nothing else to arrange and it's time to speak.

"So, Katie…it's so funny running into you because I was thinking about you only the other day."

"Really?" Her lips pucker as she tests the latte.

"Yes. You pop into my thoughts from time to time. You know… I never really knew what happened between you and Andy."

I watch her expression change. Something's there, but I don't know what. It's gone too quickly.

"Oh?" she says. "Well, there's not much to know. It was a bit of a disaster. We were young, didn't think it through."

"He said something similar."

"Well, that's because it's true." She frowns, her voice slightly edgy, vexed.

I pop a piece of bun into my mouth, just to have something to do. It's busy in here, yet the tables are well spaced. No one can hear us.

"Would you mind if I asked what the problem was?" Picking up my coffee, I sip it, wincing; no sugar.

"You can ask, but I probably won't tell."

"Why not?" I take in the details of her face, watching as she tries to decide how to reply. There's a fine thread of red above her mouth where her lipstick has run into a wrinkle. It's her only flaw, to my mind—a tiny dropped stitch.

"How much do you know about him, exactly?"

I glance around the room, my heart racing. "A fair amount, I believe."

"So, when you said you'd been thinking about me lately, was there a reason for that?"

"Um, yes."

"Do you know what I do for a living?" Her voice has lowered for discretion, but has also taken on a weight of meaning.

Crossing my boots one over the other, I shake my head dumbly.

"I'm a crisis counselor. Part of my role involves being based at a rape crisis center in Bristol." She waits for my reaction.

I can't speak. My eyes are stinging where I'm unable to blink or move any part of my body.

I don't know what my face is doing, what she reads there. But she reaches for my hand, leather jacket creaking. "I'm so sorry, Priyanka. I wasn't sure if you knew."

This feels like the biggest confirmation I could have had.

I feel tiny, alone, even with this stranger holding my hand.

"How did you find out?" she asks.

"I... I got a letter, from the daughter of the woman he raped."

She stares at me uneasily. "That must have been very difficult. I know how that feels."

I realize then what she's saying: she knew—went through the same thing.

"Oh my goodness. How could you have let me marry him?"

"It was…complicated." Her face tenses as she looks away, out of the window.

"Then please try to explain."

"I… Okay," she says, shoulders sinking. "Well, we were on our honeymoon in Santorini, and on the second night, he told me there was an incident in his past involving him, a young woman and two other men."

She looks at me then, but it's as though I'm not there—as though she's looking straight through me. I wait, hands pressed together underneath the table.

"He said the woman accused them of rape and that they were shocked. He wanted to know my thoughts—to pick my brains, was the phrase he used, I think—on whether it was possible to rape someone without realizing… We were in a floating res-taurant at the time. You can imagine how I felt."

"What did you do? What did you say?"

"What *could* I say?" Her brow furrows. "I was stunned, hor-rified."

"And what else did he tell you?" I pick up my coffee, hav-ing forgotten it was there. Reaching for a sachet of sugar, I rip it shakily, tapping it messily over the mug.

"Nothing. I couldn't face sitting through the rest of the meal. I caught the next flight home, and as soon as we'd met the legal requirements, I filed for divorce."

"Just like that?"

"Yes. I didn't tell anyone the real reason. We just cited irrec-oncilable differences and parted ways."

"But what about your job?"

Her cheeks redden. "What about it?"

"As a rape counselor," I whisper. "Surely—"

"I should have reported him?"

"Well, yes."

"I wanted to. I thought about it a lot, but I knew how the system worked. Six years had already passed since the incident.

And when it came down to it, I didn't have any facts, didn't even know the victim's name or who the other men were."

"Couldn't you have pushed him to tell you—to confess?"

"Really? You think he'd have done that?" She looks at me with a stony expression. "He didn't even think it was rape." She glances about her, then leans toward me. "I don't think he even realized why he was drawn to me in the first place."

"What do you mean?"

"Well, I was already specializing in domestic violence and rape by that point. I think that must have played at least some part in his interest in me, whether he knew it or not." She grips the handle of her coffee cup, knuckles whitening. "Once I knew what had happened in his past, I couldn't shake the thought that he was looking for some kind of absolution from me. I think he actually thought we were going to sit there on our honeymoon in that restaurant and discuss how easy it is to misread a situation and commit gang rape completely innocently."

"When you put it like that, it sounds insane."

"Yes." She sighs, propping her head on her hand as though suddenly tired. "I think that's what shocked me the most—the thing I've thought about most over the years—his total lack of perception."

"But he must have known on some level that he was guilty, otherwise why even bring it up in the first place?"

"Exactly." She leans forward, animated. "He knew what he did, deep down. I'm sure of it. Which is why the last time I saw him, shortly before getting divorced, I urged him to go forward to the police and to convince the others to do the same."

"Well, they didn't," I say bitterly.

"Of course not." She finishes her latte, the iced bun untouched. I haven't eaten much of mine either, my appetite diminished.

"Are you still with him?" she asks.

"Yes. Unfortunately."

"You have a child together, don't you...? I'm a bit of a Face-book addict." She smiles.

"Beau." I brighten at the mention of him. "He's only three. He needs his dad, but he also needs a good man, and I'm not sure that's Andy anymore."

"I'm sorry I didn't try to warn you," she says softly. "But in all honesty, I didn't know he was remarrying. And by the time I'd heard the news, it was too late for me to say anything... Was it quite quick?"

I nod. "Just under a year."

Maybe he rushed it before I changed my mind—before I found out anything about him or bumped into Katie.

I feel hopeless, desolate. Looking down at my wrist, I gaze at my patchy butterfly tattoo.

She reaches for my hand again and this time clasps it tightly. Our eyes meet, two women who both made the same mistake. "What are you going to do, Priyanka?"

———————

By the time we leave, the sky is an inflamed red and there's a frost shimmering on the car roofs. Katie waves goodbye before moving out of sight.

I didn't do the shopping, ran out of time. I didn't even buy a loaf of bread.

Getting into the car, I sense a subtle shift of some kind. I sit for a while thinking about what it might be, replaying the conversation with Katie, thinking about how much she must have suffered in silence—yet another woman bearing a load that wasn't hers.

I didn't want to say goodbye, could have carried on sitting there for hours, sharing a secret that's painful and overwhelming.

And I realize then what's different: Nicky's gone and it's just me now.

JESS

On Monday 9 Nov, at 09.42 a.m., Jess Jackson <*jess_jackson@ firestar.com*> wrote:

Dear Lucy,
I hope this email finds you well and that you're having a nice time in Geneva. I appreciated you taking the time to talk to me on Friday, but wanted to let you know that I've decided not to take things any further. I'll spare you the details, but suffice to say it's in everyone's best interests to leave the past alone. So, I won't be meeting you after all.

I'm sorry for this change in plans. Thank you again for your time. I wish you the best of luck for the future. It's a far nicer place, so I've heard.
Best wishes,
Jess

———

On Monday 9 Nov, at 11.58 a.m., Lucy O'Neill <*lucyo-neill1970@image.com*> wrote:

Dear Jess,
I can't tell you how disappointed I am to hear this. I really wanted

to meet and talk things through. Are you sure you don't want to? Maybe I should make it clear that we'd be meeting more for my sake than for yours. Obviously, this might make you less inclined to do so! But you'd be doing me a favor, is what I'm saying. So please think about it.
Best wishes,
Lucy x

———————

On Monday 9 Nov, at 16.07 p.m., Jess Jackson <*jess_jackson@ firestar.com*> wrote:

Dear Lucy,
I really think it's best we don't meet. I know you mean well and probably want to put things right, but nothing's going to bring Nicky back and I realize that now. Holly's life was always going to be tragic too, being conceived the way she was, and we can't change that either. Please, let's all move on.
All best,
Jess x

———————

On Monday 9 Nov, at 16.22 p.m., Lucy O'Neill <*lucyoneill1970@ image.com*> wrote:

Jess,
What do you mean—the way she was conceived?
L xx

———————

On Monday 9 Nov, at 16.24 p.m., Jess Jackson <*jess_jackson@ firestar.com*> wrote:

Well, what do you think...? As a result of that night at the Montague Club.
J xx

_____

On Monday 9 Nov, at 17.51 p.m., Lucy O'Neill <*lucyo-neill1970@image.com*> wrote:

Jess, we need to talk. Please let me set up the meeting. I won't take up much of your time, I promise. And afterward, you can still let the matter drop. But there's something I have to tell you. L xx

_____

On Monday 9 Nov, at 20.33 p.m., Lucy O'Neill <*lucyo-neill1970@image.com*> wrote:

Jess, please reply. I'm serious.

STEPHANIE

"I've told you before, Georgia. You can't let people walk all over you. Isn't that right, Stephanie?" Dan looks at me.

I wasn't listening, but will try to from here on so I can nod and smile in the right places. "Yes, darling."

Opposite me, Rosie rolls her eyes.

Dan is wrestling with a pork loin steak, cutting it vigorously. "It's like when your uncle Kev used to call me 'ginge' when we were kids. He knew I hated it, but he kept saying it. So, guess how I sorted it out?"

"How?" Georgia lays down her fork, intrigued.

He places a large piece of pork in his mouth, making us wait while he chews. Again, Rosie rolls her eyes, sighing. She calls this holding court, when Dan dominates the conversation, mansplaining. Is that the right word? She comes out with so many things—words I've never heard before.

Manspreading, that's another one. Apparently, he does that too. The poor man daren't move an inch or open his mouth.

Last winter, Rosie walked out of a wedding reception because Dan was holding court in front of the fire. I found her cold to the bone and ranting out in the car park, swigging a bottle of wine as though homeless. After I'd calmed her down, we went for a walk around the grounds and she told me that only the most important person should stand in front of the fire because it's the focal point of the room. By standing there, he was claiming seniority over everyone else, including his wife. Why couldn't I see that?

I've never been able to see it. I don't understand why it matters, why she was so upset about it. I'm sure Jess would, though; she and Rosie would get along very well.

"Well, I bided my time, Georgia," Dan says, cutting another slice of pork. "I waited for the right opportunity to present itself. And then, finally, I saw my chance."

I hold myself tight, flinching as his steak knife scrapes on chinaware. I've been like this all week, on edge, tetchy. If it continues, I'll have to go back to the doctor again to discuss hormone therapy.

"What happened?" Georgia asks, hooked.

Dan is pleased by her interest. He smiles at me and I smile back distractedly. "Well, Kev had his heart set on being a commercial pilot. So, he applied for a place on a training program, and when the letter arrived offering him an interview, I intercepted it and destroyed it. Course, he thought they hadn't bothered to contact him and he hadn't made the grade. Ha! You should've seen him cry. Wept like a baby!" He takes another mouthful of pork, talking out of the side of his mouth. "And *that*, Georgia, is how you handle bullies. Knocked him right down to size. He never called me 'ginge' again after that, I can assure you. And he never flew a plane either! Ha!"

A silence falls. Georgia is mortified, blinking at her plate. Vivian is the only one still eating; like me, she's good at carrying on. Yet I'm too busy watching Rosie, who is holding her knife and fork upright in her fists. I wait for her to say something derisive. Yet to my surprise…she doesn't.

"Maybe if your mother stood up for herself a bit more, then you wouldn't struggle with it so much, Georgia, hey?" Dan says.

I glance at him. He seems perfectly reasonable, just chatting.

"I'm not struggling, Dad. It's never happened before. It—"

"She's worn ragged, running after those dentists for little to no pay." He turns to me. "Perhaps you might think about being more of a role model for your girls, Stephanie?" His voice is so pleasant, I'm not sure of his meaning.

I'm thinking of a response, when Rosie drops her cutlery with a clatter and gets up from the table. "I can't listen to this bullshit anymore. What's wrong with you all?"

I don't know where to look. In desperation, I eat a baby potato.

"Looks like that expensive anger management therapy is really paying off," Dan mutters, shaking his head.

I continue to chew, even though my throat feels as though it's constricting.

"Do you need your eyes tested or something?" Rosie says. "Why can't any of you see what's going on? Why's it just me?"

No one utters a word. If Georgia was mortified before, she looks as though she's swallowed her plate now. Dan is staring at me, chin raised. He's always left it to me to discipline Vivian and Rosie because they're not his. It's the only distinction he's ever made between the girls that I'm aware of, but suddenly it feels like a large one.

"You're such a fucking doormat, Mum, and you can't even—"

"That's ENOUGH!" Dan's fist hits the table so hard, everything vibrates with a terrible clash. He points at Rosie, his chair toppling over as he jumps up. "How dare you talk to your mother like that? Who the hell do you think you are, you ungrateful little bitch?"

I stare up at him, my heart galloping. "Dan…please…"

Georgia clutches her napkin, holding it to her mouth.

"I won't stand for this!" he shouts down at me. "I've held my tongue long enough." He turns back to Rosie, fists clenched. "Apologize, *now*! Or I'll really lose my temper!"

Rosie blanches. "Mum?" she says quietly.

My mind is blank. Vivian gazes at me fearfully and then says, "Do it, Rosie."

I echo this. "Yes, Rosie. Please apologize."

She seems to take this as a betrayal and looks devastated, about three years old again. I have to go to her.

"Stephanie!" Dan hisses, but I ignore him. Rounding the table, I try to take her hand, to lead her back to us, but she pushes me away.

"Leave me alone!" she wails, running from the room, slamming the door behind her.

Humiliated, I look at Dan, but he gives me a *told you so* glare, his eyes bulging in anger. There's a morsel of food on his chin, a smear of grease around his lips. Gulping his wine, he finishes it in one go, before smoothing his hair.

No one speaks for several minutes. I want to check on Rosie, but daren't. Georgia is looking at me as though it's all my fault. Vivian's the only one eating.

Pouring himself another glass of wine, Dan shakes his head. "About time someone did something about her. She had that coming. Rude little brat."

The next day at work, it's only acetaminophen standing between me and mental collapse. I can barely see, the pressure in my temples is so strong. I can't remember a time when I felt so weak, without actually being ill. I'm ill with life. I'm ill with being me. I've no idea what to do about it.

I could blame Jess for stirring up the past; or the Waite women. But Priyanka texted me yesterday to say that Jess is dropping it. We can forget all about it, pretend we never set eyes on the letter.

You'd have thought I'd have been relieved to hear this. Yet I felt fearful, as though I was being abandoned. How is that possible? My old life was being handed back to me, intact, unspoiled, just the way I wanted it. This was a triumph. So why did I feel the most awful dread the moment I woke up?

To calm myself, I'm doing filing during a lull between appointments. It's such a dreary task, almost meditation, from what I've read. Some of my colleagues talk about mindfulness and mantras and it sounds very pretentious to me.

I'm barely awake, leaning over the filing cabinet when Leonardo approaches, asking for a word in private. He rarely does this and instantly I feel anxious, my pulse quickening.

"Let's go in here," he says, opening the door to the conference room. I follow him, inhaling the stuffy sealed-in air. "Take a seat." He pulls out a chair for me and one for himself. "No need to look so alarmed." He smiles.

I return the smile as best I can. "Sorry. I…" I trail off, unsure where I was going with it.

He crosses his legs, an inch of flesh appearing above his socks. "So, Stephanie, I just wanted to touch base with you. We haven't had a chance to catch up lately. How are you?"

"Wonderful."

That sounded idiotic. I think about correcting it, but he's pressing on and it's taking all my energy to listen, to concentrate.

"Do you remember my asking you to book a repeat for Mrs. McKenzie?"

"Yes. I do."

Do I? I'm not so sure.

"Well, she rang me in person to say she didn't hear anything. Not only that, but after chasing it and booking an appointment, when she rang back to double-check that the appointment had been made, well…it hadn't."

"Oh."

"Look…" He uncrosses his legs, sits up straight. "I want to be frank with you. You know how valued you are, but this isn't the first complaint I've received recently." His voice softens, slows. "Even with long-standing clients, it doesn't take much for people to move their business elsewhere."

"Of course. I understand."

"Which is why I wanted to ask you, in complete confidence, whether there's anything I can do? Because I'm here if you need anything."

I stare at my legs through the glass table, feeling the shame of his words. My calves look dumpy, bulbous, and my skirt sausage-skin tight. I can't believe I've jeopardized my position here. Without this job, I'd be—

"Please don't cry, Stephanie. This isn't a telling off in any shape or form. It's an offer of help."

His kindness is only making it worse. I bow my head, thinking that I don't have my tissues to hand. Taking his handkerchief out of his pocket, he hands it to me—a neat square of laundered cotton. It feels like the single nicest thing a person has ever done for me.

"Why don't you take a week's holiday, off the record? It's the least I can do after all your years of service."

"I… You can't do that. It's too much."

"No, it's not. Go on. Take a break. Come back refreshed, rested."

"I don't know what to say."

"How about 'yes'? But let's keep this between ourselves, or they'll all want a free holiday."

"Okay." I don't appear to have much choice. "Thank you, Leonardo."

He holds open the door for me and we return to the desk. The reception is freakishly empty; sometimes, that happens.

"What are you doing?" he asks, as I resume filing. "The break starts now."

"Oh. Yes. Of course." I gather my things, log off.

He waits, watching me with a look of curiosity, concern. "I meant what I said about helping. If there's anything I can do…"

"Yes. Thank you."

"I'll give you a call at the end of the week, see how you are."

"Thank you." I feel stiff, my limbs mechanical as I walk away, almost crashing into the door frame. I hope he doesn't think I'm an alcoholic.

Outside, I stare at the Circus as though I've never seen it before. It looks completely different: whiter, sharper, taller. There are fragments of rain in the air that feel like splinters hitting my face.

What am I going to tell Dan? I'm supposed to be meeting him for lunch in an hour. What am I going to say about why I'm suddenly home from work for a week?

As I walk the length of the Circus, I realize I'm going around in circles and have just passed the entrance to work for the second time. Something is very wrong with me, and if I don't do something about it soon, it's going to get worse.

Pulling out my phone, I call the only person I can think of who can help me: a menopause health care specialist, as recommended by Dan.

JESS

Things have got better—or worse, depending on how you look at it. Since the weekend, the sense of being adrift has intensified and I don't seem to be able to make any decisions. It might be a kind of paralysis because I don't know what to do about Max. Whatever it is, I feel numb, incapable of carrying out the smallest of tasks.

I've even altered my morning routine to make things more manageable. Previously, on my way to work, if I saw a full bin—chip cartons hanging out of the top, wrappers fluttering down the road, littering the hedgerows—I used to stop and text the council the bin number so they knew to send someone to empty it.

Then I would pass this poor guy lying on the footbridge, rigid with the cold. The local papers are always running campaigns, telling us not to give the homeless money. So, I'd buy him a coffee and hot dog from the sausage van underneath the arches.

Well, I can't face that now. It feels overwhelming—the bins, the homeless, the idea that I can't make things better, no matter what I do. I'm just one person, and there are too many people in need of help. There was a story in the news a couple of years ago about an elderly lady who took her own life because of all the donation requests she received in the mail from charities. I never really understood that, until now.

"Everything all right, Jess?" I look up to see my boss, Gavin, standing there, frowning at me. I'm about to ask why, when I realize that I'm holding the receiver of my desk phone and it's starting to make that high-pitched noise when it's been off the hook too long.

"Sorry," I mumble, hanging up.

"Are you meeting with Cole & Co. today?" he asks, rocking on his heels.

"Uh, yeah, that's right."

"Want me to tag along?"

I cast a double take at him. "Why?"

He plucks up the ball of elastic bands from my desk that I've been building for years and tosses it into the air. "No reason. Just a bit of moral support." He catches it. "They can be tough."

"That's no problem. I can handle it."

He gazes at me for longer than necessary, as though trying to suss something out. "Okay. Hope it goes well. Let me know how you get on." And then he goes to talk to Mary.

Quick as a fly, I go to Elliott, whisper in his ear. "What was all that about?"

He's wearing a colorful waistcoat today—is that Betty Boop? His Adam's apple bulges as he looks at me, adjusting his specs. "I…uh… I'm not sure."

He *is* sure. I can see it on his face.

"What's going on?" I ask.

And then I think: wait, I don't want to know. If it's something bad, I'm not going to be able to handle it.

Going back to my desk, I sit down and start prepping for the Cole & Co. meeting.

I'm going to need all the help I can get.

———

When I get back from Cole & Co., which went as well as could be expected in the circumstances, meaning it didn't go very well, the office is empty.

I sit chewing on a tasteless panini, wishing I hadn't gone for melted cheese. Everything feels flat, hopeless. I wasn't my usual self in the meeting and could tell they thought I was off my game. They'll probably filter this back to Gavin.

And I'm starting to worry about that, about what that could mean, when my phone rings inside my bag.

I don't recognize the number. "Hello?" I'm still eating, trying to do so quietly.

"Is that Jess?"

"Speaking."

"This is Kim Turner. We spoke the other day."

"Oh."

I set down the panini, wondering what she could possibly want.

"I know I told you not to contact me again, but I've been thinking about what you said and I'd like to talk to you... Hello?" she says impatiently.

"I'm here."

"I know you'll have spoken to Lucy by now, and I'd like you to hear my side of the story. Is now a good time?"

I gaze at the congealed panini, before dropping it in the bin. "Okay." Taking the phone to the window, I lean against the sill, watching a pigeon hopping up the wrought-iron fire exit.

"You said your husband was involved that night at the Montague Club. So, I thought it was important for you to know what really happened...because I can assure you, it wasn't rape."

Her voice is echoey and it strikes me that she's somewhere confined, maybe in the ladies' loos.

"Go on..."

"Well, I'd always wanted to go to the Montague. I mean, who didn't back then? But it was clear as soon as we got there that something was off. They were sneaking around as though we were breaking the rules, and I kept thinking that if the faculty found out, we'd—"

"The faculty?" I ask.

"At *university*," she says, as though this were obvious. "I've never broken the rules in my life and there were a lot of distinguished people in that club, people in my father's network… I wanted to get out of there as soon as possible, so Lucy and I went to find a bathroom, to talk about what to do."

"You left Nicky?"

"It wasn't like that. She was perfectly happy—didn't seem to care whether we were there or not."

"I see. So, what then?"

"Well, when we got back to the games room, no one was there. I told Lucy to stay put, while I went to look for them. I couldn't see a thing, it was so dark. And then I saw a light at the end of the corridor, so I crept forward and opened the door, took a peek. I don't think anyone knew I was there. They were too engrossed in what they were doing."

"Which was?"

"Having sex. Nicky and— I don't remember any of their names…"

"One of them was my husband."

She hesitates. "Oh… Yes, well, it looked to me as though she was enjoying herself. Not that I hung around to spectate."

"Were all three of the men there?"

"Yes. I was disgusted! I'd never have shared a flat with her, had I known what she was like."

I absorb her words, still watching the pigeon. It looks straight back at me and then takes off, ascending to a chimney pot.

"Didn't you feel guilty?" I ask.

"No!" She laughs. "Why? She put us in that position, no one

else. She could have got us into real trouble if the club had found out we'd entered against policy. I wasn't convinced that the boys were members. They didn't even sign us in."

"But you gave her a lot of cough medicine, though, didn't you? It must have been a potent cocktail, along with all the alcohol. I mean, she didn't have a lot of weight on her. Don't you think it must have contributed to what happened?"

"What?" She sounds flabbergasted. "You're blaming *me*? You weren't even there! How do you know all this, anyway? Who cares what she weighed? What's that got to do with anything? She was a grown woman. She could have said no!"

"But why give it to her in the first place, when you were going out drinking?"

"Why are you so fixated on that?" Her voice is louder now. She drops it again, whispering into the phone. "Forget about the cough medicine. She—"

"Lucy said you were jealous of Nicky. Did you do it out of spite?"

"Do what? This is ridiculous! Of course not! I was trying to help... God, I can tell Lucy's got to you, and Nicky too. She had a way of twisting everything, when it was clear as day that she was manipulating things for her own gain. That was what she did. Men flocked around her on campus and the lecturers all wanted to get inside her pants. Drove me mad. And—"

"Yeah, jealousy will do that to a person," I say, turning away from the window, sitting down at my desk.

"I wasn't jealous! I felt sorry for her! She was pathetic, throwing herself at men. But Lucy wouldn't hear a word against her, especially after what happened. She took Nicky's side against me and wouldn't listen, even though *we* were friends first. She said she was going to help Nicky press charges against those men. I couldn't believe it... In the end, we fell out and I lost my best friend *and* I had to look for a new apartment."

"Must have been a real bind," I say.

She pauses, and when she next speaks her voice is low, controlled. "I know what you're thinking. That I'm a bitch, and now she's dead, so that makes her untouchable, an angel. But let me tell you something—she'd have done anything to get what she wanted. She was out for herself. There's a girl just like her in my sales department, and as CEO, I have to try to police it and it's impossible. Because there are Nicky Waites everywhere, using sexuality as leverage. And there's always a soft touch like you or Lucy waiting in the wings to mop up their tears and turn them into a victim. If she were alive now, you'd see what I mean. I assume you never met her? Well, I can tell you that whatever you *think* she was, you're wrong. Very wrong."

I wait. Then I ask, just to make sure. "Are you done?"

"Yes. I think so."

"Good. Don't ever call me again." And I hang up.

———

I go home the wrong way, the old way, without thinking. Force of habit. I don't realize until it's too late and I'm passing a bin that's spilling out over the top, milkshake cartons leaking over sulfur-yellow chips. Seagulls squawk at me aggressively for disturbing their feast. But I don't take my phone out to text the council. I keep on walking, tapping my teeth together.

Under the arches I go, ignoring the smell of urine. It got dark quickly tonight. There's ice underfoot as I go up the incline to the footbridge.

He's there, where he always is—the triangle of his legs in his sleeping bag, his head against the railings, cardboard underneath him as insulation against the cold. The sausage cart has packed up for the day. I've nothing to give him. Besides, I don't do that anymore.

I'm trying to step past without knocking him, when he speaks. He's never spoken to me before. All he ever did was smile up at me with that broken face—rotten teeth, cloudy eyes. "Missed you the past couple days, sweetheart."

I'm amazed he knows who I am. He always seemed so out of it. "I go a different way now," I say.

He nods peacefully in response.

I point into the shadows of the arches. "The sausage cart's gone. Or I'd have…"

"S'okay." He closes his eyes. There's a full moon tonight, the branches of the trees stark in contrast against it. At least he has light. I start to walk off, and then stop, wavering, looking back at him, the frost sparkling on the bridge.

Taking off my puffer, I empty the pockets as I return. He doesn't open his eyes. His skin is withered with cold, his mouth sunken over missing teeth. Bending down, I lay my coat over him. "Hope this keeps you warm," I say, and go on my way.

PRIYANKA

"But why now? What's brought this on?" Andy chews a piece of fried chicken, dipping into the take-out carton for a duck roll. It's amazing, his appetite, yet why shouldn't he be hungry? As far as he's concerned, I've moved on. If I hadn't, I'd be discussing it with him; that's how his logic goes—how their logic goes.

If they're not saying it aloud, then it's not there, right?

I'm having mental conversations like this all the time now. Just me, myself and I, going around on a loop.

He doesn't really think I've forgotten. It's just wishful thinking, denial.

"No reason," I reply. "I've been considering it for a while." I'm nibbling the end of a spring roll, otherwise my plate is empty.

Does he accept this explanation?

Seems to.

"Why aren't you eating?" He picks up another duck roll, lifts it toward me with the chopsticks. "These are really good. Try one."

"No, you're all right. I'm not that hungry."

"Go on." He pushes it closer to my lips.

"No, thanks."

Shrugging, he puts the roll into his own mouth, crunching it gustily. Then he pours me another glass of wine. I gaze up at the ceiling, wishing I were snuggled up in bed with Beau and not sitting here as though on an awkward date, where sex is a subtext every time you shift position or remove an article of clothing.

The candlelight, takeout and sauvignon blanc are his way of making things right after my meltdown last weekend. He's been tiptoeing around me all week, his hair growing bushier as he scratches his head, looking at me askance.

Yet, still…no mention of the letter.

"Are you going somewhere reputable to have it done?"

I wish I hadn't told him about the tattoo removal. He probably wouldn't have even noticed it was gone. "Course I am. You don't have to patronize me, you know."

"I'm not." He smiles. "I love you, that's all. I don't want you to get hurt."

Well, it's a little late for that.

"Do you want me to come with?" he asks.

Frowning, I wrap an arm around my waist, trying to imagine him telling his new bride about the rape while in a floating restaurant on honeymoon. I've not been able to get it out of my mind all week.

How could he have got it so wrong? Is it possible he believed he was innocent and that Katie would agree? He must have thought there was a strong chance of that, or he wouldn't have risked telling her.

Yet why wait until after the wedding day? Didn't that show a large element of hesitation on his part?

It's all such a horrible mess. I could ask him outright, but I've already done that and his word is valueless.

I sip the chilled wine, feeling it cool my empty tummy, thinking of the early days of my relationship with him. There I was, with a real man for the first time—a grown-up who knew how to treat women—and I wasn't in the least bit prepared. All I'd done romantically speaking was get a seedy tattoo, party too hard, sleep around. I thought that maybe there was no hope for me, for us.

I needn't have worried, though. He listened as I told him my life story and accepted it wholeheartedly. And in doing so, freed me.

Yet what if he wasn't accepting me at all, but himself? What if by being so tolerant and understanding he was trying to get from me what he'd hoped to get from Katie, before it backfired so drastically: exoneration?

"You didn't answer my question, Pree."

He's still eating. Despite everything, I feel a quell of pity as a piece of chicken misses his mouth, tumbling from his chopsticks. So tall, he has to stoop to eat. As he ages, he'll get a stiff neck and back. I don't know whether I'll be there for that.

"About…?"

"Coming with you in the morning."

"Oh. No, it's fine. But could you look after Beau?"

"Okay… Actually, I've been thinking about taking him to Bristol Zoo. We could go tomorrow? That's if you don't mind us going without you?"

"Be my guest."

He lays down his chopsticks, frowns. "Is it about Saffron?"

Saffron?

"Is what about him?"

"Well, it's just that since he left, you don't seem the same." He peers into the carton, turns it upside down, shaking out the last roll. "I know you were fond of him, but you mustn't blame yourself."

"I don't." It's impossible to miss the edge in my voice.

He glances at me apprehensively. "Sorry if I've said the wrong thing. I seem to be doing that a lot lately."

We eat—he eats—the rest of the meal in silence. I'm worried

that I've been too transparent. He'll know what I'm thinking and things could quickly unravel and I'm not sure I'm ready for that.

In the bathroom, as we clean our teeth, I reach for his hand. He smiles at me, a trail of toothpaste escaping from his mouth, trickling down his chin. Getting his towel, I go on tiptoes to wipe his face. "Thank you, my love," he says.

He's only ever been kind to me. My father used to tell me to judge people on how they treated me and nothing else—not on hearsay, gossip. But isn't that precisely what I'm doing?

Andy was the first man in my life, other than Papa, to make me feel truly loved. Which is why I allow him to cuddle me as we fall asleep; a thank-you for his empathy when we first met— regardless of motives—and for all he did when Beau was in intensive care. I'll never forget any of that.

Yet nothing can stop the repulsion I feel at being close to him, his heartbeat against my back, his hands curled around my breasts. I wait, as usual, for his breathing to settle, before slipping away to the edge of the bed.

My wrist feels as though it's burning. The technician, Dave, warned me about this. We're both wearing goggles because the laser beam is so strong. I'm wearing pain-numbing cream, yet still it feels as though someone's holding a cigarette lighter to my skin.

I wonder where the man is now who risked my health by taking me to a dodgy tattooist against my will. And it *was* against my will. I don't remember a thing about it; therefore, I didn't give consent. If someone isn't capable of making a decision, don't make it for them. Even my youngest students can grasp this concept.

I suppose to his mind, someone like me didn't care about my health or safety, else I wouldn't have been acting the way I was.

The only good thing is that because the tattoo was done so unprofessionally and is so patchy, I'll only need two sessions to get rid of it. I don't think I could face more than that.

Dave said that the tattoo will feel hot afterward and will be red and swollen for a day or two. And then, over the next few weeks, it will start to fade.

Laser treatment on brown skin isn't without risk. Sometimes you can experience a loss of color temporarily; sometimes, it can be permanent, leaving you with a ghost tattoo.

Please don't let that be me.

I tear up in pain. "All right, love?" Dave asks. I nod, close my eyes.

Leaving the tattoo parlor, I daren't put on my coat, don't want anything to touch my arm, which is on fire. Dave covered my wrist painstakingly with a dressing, gave me antibiotic ointment, told me to phone with any problems, otherwise he'd see me in a month for the final session. He was very helpful, patient; I couldn't fault him. But still, the discomfort is immense and I'm petrified someone will knock into me.

Walking along the edge of the road—a backstreet of gaming shops and fast-food restaurants—I pass a sandwich board outside a hair salon that says, *Half price colors today. No need to book!* I think about sitting there, reading magazines, allowing my wrist to cool down. And then I go inside.

At home, the house is cold, gloomy. I turn on the table lamp and stand looking at myself in the mirror. I saw it in the salon, but here it's more startling, as though it's not me.

I dial Meena, waiting for her face to appear on my phone.

"Oh my God!" she screeches. "Pree! Is that *you?*" Clapping her hand to her mouth, she laughs, jumping up and down. "I barely recognized you!"

"It's only hair," I say quietly.

Her laugh instantly disappears, her face stiffening. "What's wrong?"

"Nothing."

"What happened to your pink hair?"

"I wanted it natural."

"But it was your thing."

"Well, this is my thing now."

She peers at me suspiciously, looking just like our mother. "Where's your nose stud? And your colored lenses...? What's going on?"

"I thought you'd be pleased. You're the one always saying 'Can the real Priyanka Bandyopadhyay please stand up?'"

She frowns. "That was just a joke."

"Well, maybe I want to be taken seriously."

Silence.

"Pree, there's something wrong, isn't there? Don't make me come down there and see for myself. You know I hate the south."

"Everything's fine." I give a half smile. "I just fancied a change. Honestly... Anyhow, I'd better get on. Just wanted you to see my hair. I'll phone you during the week. 'Bye, big sis."

We've been ending our calls this way for years. She always replies: *'Bye, little Pree.* But today she stalls, as though she doesn't know what to call me now.

I go through to the kitchen. The aroma of vanilla and butter fills the air. On the table there's a plate of wonky butterfly cakes and a note in Andy's handwriting:

I made these for you, Mummy. Butterflies to replace the one that's going.
Don't eat them all.
Beau xx

I stare at the cakes, my eyes filling with tears, my wrist throbbing. Going to the freezer, I extract the bottle of vodka from its nesting place between bags of frozen vegetables. I pour a generous splash into a mug and sit down at the table, licking the icing from the top of a cake.

I play with my phone for a while before summoning the courage to phone her. I know she's trying to move on. But still, I need to hear her voice. I can't cope with having only myself to talk to about this.

To my disappointment, she doesn't pick up. I leave a message, my voice sounding small. "Hi, Jess. It's me. I've been doing a lot of thinking and…we need to talk. So, please, when you get this message, call me back. Thanks."

Hanging up, I look at the window, a neat reflection of the room, a strange dark-haired woman looking back at me.

STEPHANIE

"I wouldn't recommend it for you. I think you'll find whoever you consult, they'll say the same thing."

The doctor is talking to me very slowly as though I'm not of sound mind or am hard of hearing. But he's the deaf one. He's barely listened to a word I've said. Every time I mention brain fog, he smiles as though I'm exaggerating. He's making me feel as though I don't have any real problems—not important medical problems. Just trivial middle-aged female ones that barely warrant his attention.

"I… Is this because there's a shortage of hormonal drugs—they're running out of stock?" It's all I can think to ask, yet I did read that in the paper recently.

He smiles again, throws down his pen. "It's nothing to do with that. As I've already explained, because of your family history of breast cancer, the risks would outweigh the benefits. But I'd be happy to prescribe you a course of antidepressants or refer you for cognitive behavioral therapy to help alleviate some of your symptoms."

I don't want to take antidepressants; I'm not depressed. And therapy isn't going to lift my brain fog. I'm going to have to tell Dan that his menopause expert was useless. In fact, I don't like dealing with men in these matters. I want a female doctor, I realize—someone who understands firsthand what I'm going through.

Standing up, I dab the perspiration above my mouth discreetly with a tissue. "Thank you, but this was a complete waste of time. How can you possibly be of help if you don't take women's symptoms seriously?"

He looks at me in surprise. I'm a little surprised at myself too. I'd never have dreamed of talking like that to someone in his position before...before...meeting Jess.

Outside, I take a moment to gather myself. It's Monday already; I'm due back at work tomorrow and don't feel any better for my week off. If anything, I'm in a worse state than when I left.

Just now in the waiting room, I read an article about the body's reaction to being attacked: fight, flight...or freeze. I wonder whether that's part of my problem in some way. I know I've heard about this somewhere else recently, but where? My thoughts are so disjointed, it's a wonder I can remember where I parked the car.

I look at my watch, wondering what to do. Originally, I was intending to go to town for a stroll around the shops. But in light of the doctor's appointment being such a flop, I decide that the best place for me is home; peace and quiet before tomorrow.

To my disappointment when I pull into our driveway, Rosie's bike is leaning against the garage door. I consider getting back inside the car and driving off, anywhere... But I can't, shouldn't. Rosie's not a monster; it just feels like that sometimes.

I'm tiptoeing down the hallway, hoping to make it upstairs without disturbing her, when she calls out. "M?"

I set my face at pleasant. "Yes, darling?"

"Can you come here?"

Her voice is labored, monotone. Is she bored?

"Mum!"

No, she's angry.

I know from experience there's only one thing to do: hear what she has to say. If I don't, it'll escalate to a full-blown rant.

Hanging up my coat, I go through to the kitchen, my feet leaving damp trails on the wooden flooring. It's a frosty day, yet I'm too warm. I'd like to take a shower and get out of these clothes. I hope she isn't going to—

She's sitting with her arms folded. In front of her, on the table, is my mother's cocoa tin.

I drop my tote in shock, my compact mirror falling out with a tinkle of broken glass as it hits the floor.

"When did you get this?" Grim-faced, she holds up the letter.

"I…" I busy myself with the broken mirror, bending to pick it up, blood rushing to my head.

"I can tell you exactly when you got it," she says, scraping back her chair. "The postmark was six weeks ago today. Six weeks! What the actual *fuck*?"

"Please, Rosie," I say, setting my tote on the counter. "Don't do this. Not today."

"Don't do what? Don't make a fuss? Are you for real?" She comes toward me, seeming taller than usual, or maybe I'm shrinking. I can't feel my feet. Are my feet on the floor? "I don't believe it! You get this letter and your response is, what, to put it inside a fucking cocoa tin?"

I grip the counter edge. "Stop swearing. I can't think when you get like this." She's standing too close. I'd move away but daren't let go of the counter.

"When *I* get like this? You think this is about how *I* get? Oh, that's priceless!"

I look beyond her at the tin, feeling violated, as though it held my mother's ashes. But it held more than that. Her spirit was in there, her struggles against a man who let her down repeatedly, at a time when men had all the power. She couldn't even purchase a washing machine without his say-so. He left her destitute and I grew up in the shadows of that.

What does Rosie know? She's twenty-one and spoiled rotten.

I straighten my back, letting go of the counter. I'm not going to be intimidated in my own home. She's just a child. "How dare you go through my things? Who else knows about this?"

"What, the tin…or the dirty little secret?"

My face reddens. "I meant the tin."

"Just me. I've known about it for years. I check it from time to time to find out what's going on, because *you* never tell me anything… But this?" She flaps the letter. "This doesn't belong in here. This isn't one of Georgia's shite school reports or a till receipt for Marc Jacobs… So why's it there?"

"I don't know what you mean."

"Really?" She's got a nasty smirk on her face. "Because I think you wanted it to be found."

I laugh, tucking my trembling hands inside my cardigan pockets. "That's ridiculous! That makes absolutely no sense."

"Yes, it does. You wanted someone to rescue you."

"Rescue me?" I laugh again, up at the ceiling, but it makes me feel dizzy. "From what?"

"Don't you mean *who*?" She looks at me as though I'm an idiot. "Dan, for God's sake. *Dan!*"

"What? How is—"

"He's a bully, Mum! He manipulates you. He's a master at it—controlling your every move and making it seem like he's looking out for you."

"That's because he is!"

"No, he isn't!" she yells, hands flailing. "That's how he does it! He makes it seem like he has your back, like he's the nicest guy in the world. But he isn't. He's a controlling bastard. And you can't even see it!" She takes a step toward me, stabbing the air between us with her index finger. "Look at you! He's made you afraid to be yourself and interact with people and have a life of your own. You're all perfect and stylized and scared to have an eyelash out of place."

I smile reassuringly. *That's* what she's basing this on?

"But I was always like that, Rosie. You can't blame Dan, just because I like wearing nice clothes and doing my hair. If anything, my mother—"

"God, it's not about the hair."

"You were the one who mentioned how I look."

"Okay, then," she says triumphantly, one hand on her hip. "What about Auntie Fiona? She's scared to visit because of him."

"Oh, that's rubbish and you know it. That's not why she doesn't visit. She's busy with her puppies and—"

"Oh my God, you're doing it again!" She stamps her foot. "It's not about the fucking puppies! Stop getting off track. You've got him by the balls with this!" She waves the letter at me. "I've prayed for something like this to come along and prove I'm right—to show you what I mean. And now we've got him, M. It's all here, in this letter, everything we need… So, what are we going to do about it?"

I look at her standing there with her hair in plaits, wearing a miniskirt with stripy tights and a revolting sweater that says SHIT across the chest: militant, furious, determined. And I know this is my fault, that I've let her get away with this for too long.

"We're not doing anything, Rosie. You're going to calm down and you're going to stop swearing at me and being abusive… Obviously, the anger therapy isn't working, which Dan very kindly pays for."

"*I'm* abusive? What the hell's wrong with you? What about the way he spoke to me the other night? He threatened me with violence, called me a bitch."

"That's because you swore at me. He was defending me."

"Oh my God, Mum! Look at yourself, look what you've become. Stop being so docile. Wake up!"

I can't take any more of it then. Closing my eyes, my hands in fists, I scream, the only way I can think to silence her. *"STOP IT!"*

It was so loud, so shrill, I think I've broken my throat.

When I bring myself to look at her, she's wearing a different expression. Her hood is up and the anger and height are gone.

"I'm sorry I lose my shit with you all the time, but it's hard when you love someone." She folds the letter back up, dropping it into the tin, putting on the lid, sliding it across the table toward me. "Do what you want with it. I honestly thought you finally had a way out, that I'd get you to see what I've been able to see all along. But obviously that's never gonna happen."

She walks from the room, head bent.

"Where are you going?" I ask hoarsely.

"Anywhere that's not here." At the door, she turns to look at me. "You'll never find a way out. And I can't stay and watch it anymore."

For a moment, she seems older. She looks like a woman who has been through life and has suffered its disappointments. Maybe she has. Maybe she knows more about what I experienced growing up than I realize. Maybe she's been going through her own version of it right here.

I don't want her to end up like me, somewhere like this. I want her to be happy.

So, I let her go.

The garden's very still, drops of ice on the tips of the grass and leaves. As I walk across the crispy lawn in my socks, without my coat or scarf, I don't feel the chill underfoot.

Sitting on the swing seat near the summerhouse, I swing back and forth, the wood squeaking, metal chinking.

I'm still holding my mother's cocoa tin, the folded letter rattling around inside.

I'm not thinking about Mum or Fiona or Dan or the letter. I'm thinking about Rosie, who is somewhere out there, cycling around, distressed, alone.

I shouldn't have let her go.

Some people, like her and Jess, can't stand by and watch things happen; nor should we ask them to. I know that now.

———

It takes me half an hour to find her, driving around the neighborhood, my wet socks slipping on the pedals. Finally, I spot her bike leaning against a bus shelter. She's sitting on the bench with her knees drawn to her chin, rocking herself as the electronic display announces the next bus. She doesn't notice me because she has her hood up and is wearing headphones. But even when she does see me, she makes no sign of recognition.

She approaches the car, though, lets me put her bike in the boot. And although we drive in silence, she puts her hand on my knee and I feel a connection between us that I haven't felt in a very long time. "You're not wearing any shoes" is all she says.

"I know."

Back at home, the cocoa tin sits between us at the kitchen table. "I'm sorry," I tell her.

"No, *I'm* sorry," she replies.

"You must think I'm pathetic."

"Not at all. I love you."

"I love you too, Rosie."

She hesitates before speaking again, dunking a biscuit in her tea. "Is it about the money?"

"Only partly."

"Then what?"

"It's difficult to explain."

She smiles sadly. "It's okay. You don't have to."

———

I wait for Rosie to go upstairs to run a bath before phoning.

"Hello?" I wrap my fingers around my mother's cocoa tin, feeling the soft metal buckle. "Jess?"

"Yep?"

"It's me."

"I know it's you."

"Oh. I'm sorry if this is a bad time to talk…?"

"It's not. You're fine."

I close my eyes to concentrate. "I… I'm sorry this has taken me so long. I hope you can forgive me for being so…so difficult. But my situation is complicated and I…" I pinch the bridge of my nose.

"It's all right."

"Is it?" I start to cry very quietly, but I think she can hear me—can tell.

"Yes. Tell me what you wanted to say."

"Can't you guess?" I ask.

"Just say it."

I hold the tin a little tighter. "I want to do something about the letter."

JESS

It took six weeks, but we're in agreement. That's not so bad. Maybe with a different combination of people it might have taken less time. Some women might have shown their husbands the letters right away. Some might not have met and consulted with each other—might have gone their own ways from the start.

But I had to do it like this, couldn't have done it any other way. I told you before that I'm ordinary, community-minded. I read once about a South African tribe where every single person had to be in agreement before a decision was made. They'd stay up all night, sometimes for days, weeks, debating, listening, until everyone was on board.

I think there's something pure and honorable in that. After all, you need 100 percent commitment from a jury to condemn a person. Majority rule as a form of democracy isn't all it's cracked up to be.

I'm saying all this like it was some master plan, like I knew what I was doing. But I didn't. Until Stephanie rang yesterday, I didn't even know how I felt. I'd managed to convince myself that being in a permanent state of numbness and indecision was the best I could hope for.

I've no idea what we're going to do now.

We need to talk.

I meet her at lunchtime, just the two of us. I can tell right away that she's changed, yet can't put my finger on how. Priyanka couldn't make it, couldn't get away from school, but that's fine. Because I want it to be just Stephanie and me, face-to-face, opposites united.

"You seem different," I say, as we take our coffees to a table by the window. We're at an overpriced deli around the corner from her workplace. I thought we deserved an upgrade from Carol's, plus I'm tired of tiptoeing around.

"So do you," she replies. "I like your coat."

I don't think anyone's ever said that to me before. I glance down at myself. "Oh. Thanks. It's new." I pre-spent my Christmas bonus on a winter coat with lapels and everything in an effort to smarten myself up.

"What happened to your puffer jacket?"

"Gave it to some homeless guy."

"Course you did," she says.

I've ordered her a selection of pastries because she looks like she could do with them. And I certainly could. I've been eating like a hound lately.

"What made you change your mind?" I take a bite into a horn-shaped cake, cream spurting out, flakes of pastry showering down.

"My daughter."

I pause before taking another bite. "What? So, she knows?"

"Yes. She found the letter."

"Bloody hell. How did that go?" I dab my mouth, pick up my coffee, trying to absorb this information without looking horrified.

"Badly, as you can imagine… But it's done now and she'll keep it secret. Dan's her stepfather, so she wasn't as upset as she might have been. And she's left it to me to handle. She's a good girl, really. She cares an awful lot. In fact, she reminds me of you."

"Oh. So is that a compliment?"

"Yes. I meant it as one."

I nod and we exchange smiles. It feels like we've come a long way, the two of us.

"Steffie," I venture gently, "if we do this…what is it that you're expecting to happen, exactly? What do you want?"

She gazes out of the window, the sunshine lighting the downy hair on the side of her face. It makes me sad to see. Maybe because it's proof that she's fallible, after so much effort on her part to appear otherwise.

"I don't know, Jess."

"Okay. Let me put it another way, then. Is your marriage over?"

Around us, the clientele is classy, unobtrusive. A businessman is typing on a laptop. Two Italian-looking girls with dark kohl eyes and scarlet lips are laughing quietly over antipasto. Behind them, the counter is stocked with tins of panettones and amaretti in preparation for Christmas, just five weeks away.

"I'm not sure," Stephanie says.

"Because I think mine is. I knew it as soon as I read Holly's letter, but it's taken me this long to admit it. No one can decide something like that overnight—not even someone like me."

This is my way of making a small joke, but she's playing with her coffee cup, lost in thought.

"But the fact that you want to do something, Steffie… Surely you can see it's going to have consequences? I mean, if we do this, then we're basically telling them we know what they did and that we want some kind of payback."

"Of course."

"And you're prepared for that?"

"I…"

She doesn't look it.

"Deciding to do something was only half the battle," I continue delicately, trying not to startle her. "Now we have to work out what that means. And unless you share your thoughts with me, I can't work out a solution that'll suit everyone."

She looks at me, her eyes tired-looking yet painstakingly made-up. "I don't want to lose my home."

"Okay. Go on..."

She looks down at the tablecloth, running her nail along the thread. "I can't struggle financially. It's nothing to do with being money-grabbing, but being secure—not having to scrimp and save and panic about where the next meal's coming from... Not crying whenever a bill arrives..." She breaks off, glances around her. "I can't do that."

"No, and you shouldn't have to. And you won't, I promise. I've no intention of struggling either." I lean forward, tapping my finger on the table. "Why should we? This isn't about punishing us. We've done nothing wrong. We're not splitting anything fifty-fifty. If we do this, it's happening our way, on our terms."

"Does Priyanka agree with that?"

"Yes."

I've not spoken to her about it yet. But she wants out of her marriage—told me to do whatever it takes to make this right.

I'm interpreting that as: tell them we know, make them pay. In no shape or form does it mean make *us* pay.

There's a pause in the conversation as Stephanie selects a pastry, taking a dainty bite, icing sugar sprinkling over her plate. I'm not really watching her, though. I'm thinking about how we can do this with minimal damage to ourselves.

At that moment, one of the Italian girls with the dark kohl eyes turns to look at the wall clock, her eye drifting over to me, meeting my gaze.

And then something occurs to me.

"Steffie." I rap the table in front of her to get her attention. "I've got an idea... I'm not sure if you're aware, but we met with a solicitor and there's nothing we can do about this legally speaking."

She nods, holding a manicured hand in front of her mouth as she chews. "Priyanka told me."

"But we do have a secret weapon."

"We do?"

"Yes. Lucy O'Neill, Nicky's friend who was there on the night at the club. She's been emailing me, saying she has something to tell us and wants to meet. I think she feels guilty about what happened to Nicky."

"Why?" Stephanie asks.

"Why?"

Sometimes, she really is slow to catch on.

"Because of the *rape*," I whisper.

"But she didn't do it."

"No, but she was there."

It goes so quiet that I can hear the businessman's hands clicking softly on his keyboard.

"What does she want to talk to us about?" Stephanie's reapplying her lipstick after eating the pastry, even though she's about to drink her coffee. Sure enough, she leaves a red mark on the cup, which she wipes off with her napkin.

"I dunno. I've not replied to her emails."

"So, what does your idea have to do with her?"

"Well, I spoke to Nicky's other friend, Kim, and I use the term *friend* in the loosest possible way. She..." I'm about to say she sounded like Stephanie, the way she blamed women for everything, but I stop myself just in time.

"And?"

"Well, it turns out that Kim was the only one who saw anything and she swears..." I lower my voice. "...That it wasn't rape. But what if we asked Lucy to say that she saw what happened? Then we'd have a witness."

She blinks at me, mouth open. "Isn't that illegal?"

"Only if we were going through the legal system, but we wouldn't be. This would be personal, just between us and our husbands, so we could tell them what we liked." I hold out my hands, shrug. "How would they know?"

She doesn't look sure. I give her a minute.

"So…we use it as a bargaining tool…to get what we want?"

"Exactly!" I say too enthusiastically. The businessman glances over, eyes full of logistics, not even seeing me. I lower my voice again. "We'd have to stick to our story, mind you—work it all out beforehand."

She looks worried, a frown trying to crack the makeup on her forehead.

"But it needn't be complicated," I add. "In fact, the simpler the better. We just need to work out what we want and then go for it."

"Okay…" she says uncertainly. "But would Lucy do that? Isn't it a lot to ask?"

"Only one way to find out." I pull my phone from my bag, tap it.

"You're not calling her now, are you?"

"No. Just checking I've still got her details. I went on a rampage the other day, clearing my contacts… I'm surprised you're still in here."

"I'm sorry."

I laugh at the look on her face. "Don't be daft. I was kidding." I put away my phone, smile at her. "You're here now, aren't you? You're part of this now, right?"

To my dismay, she wells up. And I realize then what's different about her now: she likes me.

———

All afternoon, I'm agitated, huffing and puffing in my seat, being too heavy with the hole punch. I expect Gavin notices. Mary definitely does; she hovers, offering cappuccinos, and I try to be nice, I really do, especially since my encounter with the old lady and the compost heap. But in truth, she's a pain in the backside and I could do with the space to think.

I want to think about how to approach Lucy. I don't know what we'll do if she says no. I don't have a plan B.

I'll never forget the look of relief on Stephanie's face at the idea of getting what she wanted. Women like that—so groomed and unapproachable—always seem like the sort who get everything their own way. But you'd be surprised.

What she said about struggling, crying over bills. That obviously came from personal experience. And it really got to me. In some respects, I'm doing this more for her than for me. That may sound crazy. But at this point, nothing sounds sane anymore.

On Tuesday 17 Nov, at 16.12 p.m., Jess Jackson *<jess_jackson@ firestar.com>* wrote:

Dear Lucy,
I'm sorry I didn't reply to your emails. I needed time to think. This doesn't affect just me, but also the other women whose husbands were involved, plus our children. So please forgive the radio silence.

I've decided I'd like to meet you after all, and I think the others should be there too: Priyanka and Stephanie. If that's OK then please go ahead and have your assistant set it up.

In the meantime, there's something I need to ask you. I'd prefer to talk about it in person, but would rather not wait until we meet. So when you get this message, could you please give me a ring, at a time to suit you.

I hope to hear from you soon.
With love and best wishes,
Jess x

———————

On Tuesday 17 Nov, at 17.33 p.m., Lucy O'Neill <*lucyoneill1970@image.com*> wrote:

Jess,
Just going into a meeting. Will ring later.
L x

JESS

"Are you sure this is what you want, one hundred percent? Because once we press go, there'll be no going back." I rest my elbow on the bucket of cleaning products, my legs stretched out on the cardboard floor, too tired to worry whether I'm sitting in ketchup or paint. I was going to give the place a good scrub tonight, but it turns out I haven't the energy to lift a cloth.

"Yep, one hundred percent." Priyanka picks at her tights, pulling off a dust ball. "As soon as Katie told me what he'd told her, I knew he'd lied to me. He gave me a different story— that he'd had no involvement whatsoever... And to think that I trusted him. What an idiot. I thought we shared everything. I told him everything about *me*." She sighs. "And now I can't stomach being near him. When it's over, it's over, you know?"

"Yeah, I do. I'm sorry."

"What a nightmare." She kicks a shriveled apple, sending it across the floor where it lands with a bump against the mattress. "Do you think she knew what she was doing when she wrote to us—basically destroying our marriages?"

"I'd like to think it wasn't as calculated as that, but how can we know for sure?" I look at the painting of Holly above the mattress. Cryptic, dressed all in white, frustratingly mute. "I doubt we'll ever know whose daughter she was either."

"Does that even matter anymore?"

"No, maybe not." I glance sideways at Priyanka. She sounds so weary and seems older, quieter. Can hair make you quieter? I guess when it was loud pink before then it can. "I still can't get used to your hair."

"In a good or bad way?"

"Good. But it doesn't look like you."

"I can assure you it is me. I've still got the shabby parka and Doc Martens look." She points at her neon-laced boots, wiggling them.

"Maybe you'll go back to pink hair someday."

"Maybe."

We sit in comfortable silence, which is all that's comfortable because the floor is hard underneath us and I won't be able to stay much longer like this.

Priyanka draws her legs toward her, hugging them, a bandage appearing on her wrist as her coat sleeve rises.

"What's that?" I ask.

"Nothing. I'm having a tattoo removed, that's all."

"Oh. Does it hurt?"

"Not as much as breaking up a marriage."

I look at Holly's portrait again, wishing she could tell us what she'd been hoping to achieve. Although it was her mother's story, without her involvement—her letter—we wouldn't have known anything about it and would be happily married still.

"Do you think anyone could have lived with a secret like that?" I ask. "I mean, I know you and Steffie wanted to at the start, but do you think you could have actually spent the rest of your life ignoring it?"

"I dunno. I mean, maybe for a while. But eventually you'd start to wonder what else you'd missed. And it would probably show up in other ways."

"What, like finding out he's a creep—a bit handsy in the office? And everyone knew but you?"

"No, not really," she says. "Just that he was a liar."

I copy her, hugging my knees, resting my chin on them.

When the moment comes, I've no idea how to face Max. How do you go from preparing someone's porridge and packed lunch, to tying a rope around their neck? I always imagined— unrealistically, as it happens—that the law would do it for us, but now it's going to be us, standing there, telling them that we know about Nicky.

Where am I going to do it, exactly: in the kitchen, the back garden? Do I take him for a walk around the block, go for a drive? And what about the girls? When do I tell them? How?

And if I'm going to find it difficult, how is Stephanie going to manage? Or Priyanka? Should we do it together, round them up? Or would that make it worse?

Priyanka moans, rubbing her shoulder. "I can't sit here any longer. I'm seizing up."

"Me too." I get up, offering her my hand, tugging her upward. She laughs as she wobbles to her feet. I can't remember whether I've heard her laugh before, and it feels like a real shame. "I'm sorry this is happening to you, Pree."

"You didn't do it, Jess. This is on them. And besides, it's happening to you too."

"I know, but your lad's just a tot. It's a horrible age for this to happen."

"Oh, and you can think of a better one, can you? Your girls aren't going to fare any better." She means this as a consolation, and I take it as one. That's how twisted things have become.

"I wonder what they'll do…whether they'll talk to each other?" I put my hands in my pockets, leaning against the wall.

"Who?" Priyanka crouches down, tying her laces.

"Our husbands, when they find out."

"Dunno." She straightens, frowns. "I've not really thought that far ahead."

"But do you think they're close?"

"Doubt it."

"They must see each other at the club, though, surely?"

"Andy doesn't go very often. And besides, he doesn't seem to have told them about the letter, does he…? What does it matter anyway?" she asks.

"It doesn't. I was just thinking, that's all."

I don't know why I'm homing in on this. It's just that I keep wondering how well acquainted they are. If the three of us are discussing what to do, will they do the same thing once they know? And if so, will the three of them combined be a stronger force than ours?

I'm paranoid everything will go wrong. It's a simple enough plan: use the threat of a witness to scare them into doing what we want. Yet it feels very unstable. They got away with it once before. What if the same thing happens again?

They're liars, criminals who were happy to live unpunished, becoming family men as though the whole thing never happened. They don't appear to have consciences, so how do we know how they'll act when cornered?

We don't know, and that's what's bothering me. We can plan all we like from our end, but the truth is, we don't even know who they are.

I look at Priyanka, my stomach churning anxiously. "Pree?"

She picks up her bag, rubbing her tired eyes. "Yes?"

I shake my head. "Nothing." I can't put my worries on her. I pushed for this, so it's my responsibility to find a way to make it work. And there's no rush; it's been thirty years. We can take all the time we need. "Come on. Let's get out of here."

Outside in the car park, the pewter moon is hanging languidly in the trees, caught like an abandoned ball. I wonder whether Holly ever stood in this same spot—how she got here in the first place, whether she owned a car or had a driving license, a bank card, a passport. All the humdrum things we take for granted, but that are in fact only given to people whose lives are accounted for.

We stand in front of our cars, shoulders hunched against the cold. "So, what's next?" Priyanka asks.

"Well, Lucy said she'd help us. So now we need to sit down and work out what we want. I promised Steffie she won't suffer financially or in any other way. None of us will."

She nods, the shadow of disbelief on her face. Maybe she thinks it's a hell of a thing to promise, one that I can't keep.

"Also, Pree…we need to think about how to go about breaking it to them."

She looks at me warily. To her credit, she manages a smile, though. "Just let me know when you want to meet and I'll be there."

"Will do."

We hug and there's real warmth, real affection between us.

"Mind how you go," I say, squeezing her hand.

"You too, Jess. Call me."

On my way to Beechcroft, I think about the main points I'd want to get across. We would work things out individually, but from my part I'd be telling Max to leave, with no visitation rights to the girls. It's up to the others what they do on that score, but I wouldn't budge. He's lost the right to be in their lives, as far as I'm concerned.

Financially, we would insist that they continued to support us. If they didn't comply, we'd threaten to post Holly's letter on social media, as well as distributing it around their businesses, friends, families. We would also threaten them with the police. Despite what Deborah Scott said about prosecutors discarding weak cases, they wouldn't take the risk—couldn't be sure how the law would react, especially if they thought there was a witness.

I don't need to drive myself crazy with some elaborate plan.

They'd be insane to try to outsmart us or create a scene, given that we hold all the cards.

And we do, don't we? Unless there's something I've missed.

We'll do it as a group. We won't tackle them alone, but as a united front. We're stronger that way—always were, always will be.

I pull up outside Beechcroft and turn off the engine, thinking about Steffie—how fragile she looked earlier. Getting out my phone, I send her a text.

19.01 P.M. >
Hope you're all right. Everything's going to be OK. J x

As I go along the corridor to Mum's room, my phone beeps.

19.03 P.M. >
OK Jess. Hope you're right. S x

STEPHANIE

It's not so bad being back at work. It's better than I expected. Leonardo said I looked refreshed, and while I wouldn't go as far as to say that, I do feel better for the time off. My brain fog has lifted slightly, and I'm finding that I can absorb more of what's being said. I don't think I realized how serious the problem was—how close I was to losing my job, and maybe my mind.

In my lunch hour, I walk around my favorite department store, looking at shoes, pretending I'm close to happiness. In reality, I'm nowhere near it. My life is in tatters, and it's a wonder that my concentration has returned. I think it's because the disagreements have stopped and a decision has been made. And while I'm frightened about whether it's the right one, and the consequences of making it, a weight has been lifted.

I'm beginning to wonder whether my marriage isn't what I thought it was. I'm not able to go any further than this basic thought. I wouldn't ever—or can't—put it into words. I don't even know whether it's true. I'm only basing it on what Rosie said, and I'm not convinced by her reasoning. She's always been melodramatic. There's every possibility that Dan has my best interests at heart, isn't a bully.

When all's said and done—regardless of what my marriage is, or who Dan is—I'm holding on to the fact that Jess has promised me that, no matter what, I won't end up struggling to get by.

Am I being naive? Perhaps. But there's no one else in my life at the moment who I can depend on. She may be an unlikely ally, but she's my only one. So, I'm putting my faith in her.

———

The afternoon passes quickly, uneventfully. It's cold when I leave work, and I draw my coat around me. Wednesdays are normally my shopping day, but because of my time off, the fridge is well stocked. As I drive home, I'm thinking about what to cook for supper—whether there are any prawns in the freezer.

I'm almost always back before Dan, so I'm surprised to see that the garage door is wide open. The light isn't on, so it takes me a moment to distinguish that his Porsche isn't there.

Perhaps he left it open by mistake this morning, or Rosie's been poking about in there. Sometimes she likes going through his tins and tools, claiming she's doing bike maintenance. He complains to me in private, saying she mixes everything up deliberately to annoy him. He says she's a classic middle child and has split home syndrome.

I'm not sure this is a syndrome. Yet I suspect she feels left out, displaced, and I've always tried to go easy on her, which was perhaps a mistake when it came to allowing her to treat me the way she does.

Georgia has left her school shoes in the middle of the hallway, clumps of mud on the rug. "Georgia? Georgia!"

Upstairs, music is thumping. I'm stooping to pick up the shoes with a sigh, when I glimpse someone in the shadows under the stairs and give a little start in surprise. But it's only Rosie.

"What are you doing, darling?" Really, she does the strangest things.

As she moves into the light, still wearing that horrible SHIT sweater, I notice that her face is streaked with tears. "Rosie?" I step out of my heels. "What's wrong?"

She opens her mouth, shakes her head.

Upstairs, a door opens, music swelling. Georgia appears at the top of the stairs. "All right, Mum? What time's tea?"

"I've done something really bad," Rosie whispers, tugging my sleeve.

The look on her face…the open garage door. My heart skips a beat. I smile up at Georgia. "Soon, darling. About an hour. Can you hang on?"

"I'll see what I can do," she says, withdrawing, shutting her bedroom door.

I turn back to Rosie. "Where's Vivian?"

"Still at work, I think."

"So it's just us, then. You can tell me what's going on." I hold out my hand to her, as though she's a little girl again. "We'll go through to the kitchen."

She doesn't move. "You're gonna kill me, M."

"I doubt it."

"Yes, you are." She starts to cry again.

"Whatever it is, it can't be that bad." Can it? "What is it to do with, work? Did you get fired?"

"No."

"Then what? Come on, darling." Gripping her hand so she can't wriggle away, I tug her through to the kitchen. And then I stop.

The cocoa tin is lying on the table, on its side, lid off. Empty.

I turn to look at her. "Where's the letter?"

"Oh, Mum…" She hides her face, sobbing into the crook of her arm.

Prying her arm away, I raise my voice. "Tell me, Rosie!"

"I… I thought I put it back. I was sure I did. I only wanted to read it. I didn't…"

"Didn't what, Rosie?"

Her face crumples, tears streaming down her face. "I'm sorry, M. He…"

"He what?" I stare at her in horror. "Oh my God, Rosie! What have you done?"

"Please forgive me. I'm sorry. I'm so sorry. I didn't—"

"Stop saying that! I can't think!" I sit down at the table, picking up the empty tin, gripping it until it buckles. "What happened? Where is he?"

"I don't know… He came home early. I wasn't expecting him. I didn't even know he was back. I was just looking at the letter and popped to the loo. And when I came back, he was reading it."

"What do you mean he was reading it? I thought you said you put it away? How could he have been reading it?"

"I don't know. I thought I put it back in the cupboard. But maybe I didn't. I was only gone two seconds…"

"Oh my God!" I slam the tin down on the table. "This is bad! Really bad!"

"I know. I told you it was. I told you you'd kill me."

I jump up, shaking the tin at her. "How could you have been so careless? Have you any idea what you've done?"

"I'm sorry." She wails, the veins in her forehead bulging. I turn away from her, my heart pounding.

I don't know what to do. What do I do?

"Sorry isn't good enough!" I shout, spinning around to look at her again. "Why did you have to touch it? I told you I was handling this. Why couldn't you leave it alone? What is wrong with you?"

"I… I wanted to read it again…to find out something."

"But it was none of your business!" I shout so loudly that she winces. "What could you have possibly wanted to know?"

"Whether I…"

"Whether you what?"

"Whether I had a half sister."

I stare at her.

Before I can stop her, she smacks the side of her head. "I'm an idiot! This is all my fault! I'm—"

"Stop it!" I snatch at her wrist, pull her to me, grasping her firmly by the shoulders. "This is not your fault. None of this is your fault, do you hear me?" In my arms, she's limp, her clothes damp, smelling of stale sweat.

What have I done? It was my letter, my tin, my stupid mistake.

"I'm sorry, darling." I cup her face in my hands, kissing the cold tip of her nose. "I didn't mean to shout at you. You've done nothing wrong. This is more complicated than you realize. There are other people involved."

Jess… I have to tell her.

Hurrying to the hallway, I grab my bag, returning to the kitchen as I dial her number. "Please pick up…"

"Who are you calling?"

I close the door behind me, standing against it for support, looking up at a crack running along the ceiling.

"Hello? Steffie?"

"Oh, thank God, Jess…"

"Who's Jess?" Rosie's watching me fearfully.

"What's going on?" she asks.

I close my eyes, calming myself enough to speak coherently. "Something terrible has happened. It's the letter… Dan's got it."

"What? How?"

I look at Rosie. "I'm so sorry. We've ruined everything. And—"

"Where is he now? Is he with you?"

Rosie seems to be holding her breath, going blue. "Where is he?" I ask her.

"I don't know. He stormed out, slamming the door so hard the windows rattled, and then took off at about ninety miles an hour."

"Did you hear that?" I ask Jess.

"Yes. Was that your daughter?"

"Yes."

"When?"

"What time was that, Rosie?" I ask.

She looks up at the kitchen clock. "About fifteen minutes ago? I'm not sure…"

"Okay, Steffie… I'll call you back. Don't talk to anyone about this and stay where you are. Just wait!" And the line clicks as she hangs up.

"Who was that?" Rosie asks, hiccuping.

"A friend."

"You don't have any."

"Don't start, Rosie. You've done enough."

"I'm so sorry, M." She hiccups again, pulling her sleeves down over her hands. "Where do you reckon he's gone?"

"I don't know."

There wouldn't have been a good way to tell him. But this way…behind his back…in front of Rosie…had to have been the worst.

I look at my phone, wondering when Jess will call back. What will she be doing? I'm still wearing my coat, but I'm shivering. Perhaps a hot drink—

The front door slams and we both give a start, eyes widening.

"Mum…" Rosie whimpers, reaching for me. I grip her hand as the kitchen door opens.

Vivian enters the room in her work suit, hair specked with drizzle. She stops, taking in the scene, looking at us in turn. "What's going on?"

PRIYANKA

I'm at parents' evening in the school hall, yawning silently, when my phone vibrates. No one's looking at me. No one's queuing to talk to me. Math is predictably popular, as is English; French, even. Yet people peer at my sign, see RPE and then pretend to be needed elsewhere.

I read the message on my lap.

17.55 P.M. >
Call me ASAP. Steffie's husband found the letter.

My brain makes a sluggish connection: Andy already knows and is steeped in denial, prepared to playact for the rest of his life; but what about Daniel Brooke? What sort of person is he? Stephanie's barely said a word about him.

I have to get out of here. Leaving the hall, I stumble along the corridor, moving away from people and noise. I push open the double doors to the canteen. It's perfect: dark, empty.

I feel about in the blackness, inching forward until I knock into a chair. Sitting down, I dial Jess, my hand on my heart, feeling it race.

"Pree?" She sounds out of breath, on the move. "Where are you?"

"Parents' evening. Where are you?"

"On my way home from work. You got my text?"

"Yes. What happened?"

"No idea. Steffie just rang to say that Dan found the letter. I don't know what to do. This wasn't supposed to happen!"

"No," I say unhelpfully.

"But then maybe we don't have to do anything? I mean, this makes it easier in some ways, doesn't it? They had to find out somehow. Saves us having to do it… Damn it! I'm going under the subway. If I lose you, I'll—"

My phone remains lit for a moment and then blacks out and I'm sitting in the dark again.

Andy's looking after Beau right now. He'll be getting fish fingers out of the oven, taking baked beans off the stove, buttering toast.

Or maybe none of that's happening. Maybe—

She's ringing again.

"Look, I'm nearly at the car. Steffie doesn't know where he is. But chances are, he's told Max and Andy, so be on your guard… Pree? You there?"

"Yes."

"Good. Thought I'd lost you again… I don't think this changes anything—doesn't give them any power. We're still doing this our way. We just need to wait for things to calm down. So let's stay strong, okay?"

"Okay."

"I'll call you later, soon as I—" In the background, a car honks and she gasps. "Oh my God, that made me jump… Pree?"

"Yes?"

"Good luck."

"Jess?"

She's gone.

Rocking myself, I think about Meena's old joke: Can the real Priyanka Bandyopadhyay please stand up? If ever there were a time when that applied, it's surely now.

But I don't want to go home to more lies and protestations of innocence. Or worse: acting as though nothing's wrong.

Getting up, I smack my bandaged wrist against the edge of the table and stop in shock before the pain hits me and I yelp, dropping my phone. Crying, I grope about in the dark, my nails scratching at the wooden flooring.

Retrieving my phone, I stand up, feeling determined suddenly.

I know exactly what I'm going to do. It's what I should have done right from the start. No one's better equipped than me. I solicit confessions every day of the week, from small misdemeanors to gross infractions resulting in expulsion. It's all the same thing, the same technique.

Tell me what happened.

The trick is not to respond as soon as they reply, but to wait. Because the truth nearly always comes next, filling the silence.

———

Our home looks idyllic from the outside: the silver birch tree twinkling with fairy lights, the stained-glass door panel depicting the sun with rainbow rays, Beau's straw yule goat in the living room window.

As I get out of the car, carrying my books in one hand, my wrist is weeping through the bandage. I'm going to have to soak it off and apply ointment as soon as I can.

Fumbling for my keys, I realize it was the butterfly—that side of my personality and history—that got me into this marriage. Without it, I wouldn't have needed someone like Andy to rescue me and everything would have been different.

But it's no use thinking like that now. I did marry him. And he withheld his past from me. And now we have to face the consequences of those choices.

"Pree?" he calls out, as I close the door behind me. Setting down my keys and bag, I take a moment to compose myself. "How did it go?"

I look at Beau's latest creative endeavor on the console table: painted macaroni glued onto a paper plate. Everything's going to change for him. I tried so hard to avoid this, to stop his world from being devastated. Yet in the end, I couldn't stop it. No one could have.

Andy appears in the doorway, blocking the light. "How was it?"

I can tell by the look on his face that Daniel Brooke hasn't contacted him yet. "Fine."

He doesn't approach for a kiss—has one eye on the TV in the living room.

"Is Beau okay?" I ask, picking up a double-glazing flyer, feigning interest in it, stalling.

"Yep. All fed. Just needs a bath, but I thought you'd like to do that."

I would, yes, ordinarily. Tonight, though, it feels like a mammoth task. I examine my bandage, tentatively lifting it away from the wound. "Where's your phone?" I ask.

"Uh." He taps his pockets, glances around the room. "Maybe I left it in the car. Why? Have you been calling?"

"No."

"Oh." He looks confused, then nods at my wrist. "Is it playing up?"

I go to respond, slipping into domesticity, chitchat. But I have to stop his game...and start mine.

"We need to talk."

"That sounds serious." Incongruously, he smiles. "Shall we go through to the kitchen? I'll just get my cuppa..."

"Leave it," I say.

"Okay…" He glances at me warily. Going to the door, he holds it open for me. "Shall we?" Something about him feels stilted, forced, reminiscent of something, but I can't think what.

The kitchen smells of egg and beans. A frying pan is blocking the sink, and the counter is littered with dirty plates and cutlery. "Sorry about the mess," he says, opening the dishwasher. "I haven't had a chance to—"

"Don't do that now," I say, leaving the door ajar so I can listen for Beau. "It's not important." Sitting down at the table, I find a clean place among the crumbs to rest my sore wrist, *In the Night Garden* music drifting from the living room.

I gaze at the PVC tablecloth that Beau chose especially: lines of toy soldiers with curly mustaches and shiny boots.

That's what he thinks men—heroes—are like. That's what he thinks Daddy's like.

"What's up?" Andy rests his back against the sink, one foot crossed over the other. "Did something happen at parents' evening?" His voice is so pleasant, so considerate. And that's when I realize what his stilted demeanor reminds me of, or *who*.

Lee.

What was the phrase Nicky used? *The act of chivalry…*

"Tell me what happened."

It goes quiet and I can hear *In the Night Garden* again. I focus on one of Beau's day care paintings on the fridge. Trees, block houses, stick people with huge heads.

"What happened…" he says, as though trying to recall an obscure fact. "I'm not sure I follow you."

I help him get there. "The letter, Andy."

"You mean about Nicky Waite?" He looks surprised.

Funny that he struggled to recall her name when I first mentioned the letter. And yet now it's right there, at the surface of his mind, bobbing like a rotten apple.

It's the first sign he's given that the truth is within my grasp. Not as far away as I'd imagined.

"Yes," I reply. "That's right."

"I thought we already discussed this and agreed it was purely attention-seeking."

I nod.

He continues. "I thought we decided to put it behind us? And that's exactly what I've been doing, and I thought you were too."

Again, I nod. He takes this as agreement, his face brightening. "So, what's the use in raking it up? It has absolutely no bearing on our lives."

I nod a third time. "Except that you haven't had a chance to tell me your version of events. And I think you deserve that."

He frowns. "I… Well, I told you. She slept with the two other chaps."

"And somehow that became a rape allegation."

Shifting position, he folds his arms. "But it was nothing to do with me, as I already said."

"Yet your name was in the letter."

"I don't know why that was." He narrows his eyes at me, unsure where I'm going, whose side I'm on.

"Andy… I know everything. I met Katie, your ex-wife."

"You what? Why on earth would you do that?"

"She told me about the floating restaurant and—"

"Floating restaurant?" He laughs unconvincingly. "What does that have to do with anything?"

"She said that you wanted her take on it…as a rape counselor." I let those words linger, watching his face grow taut. "Why would you have done that, if you weren't involved?"

He opens his mouth to reply, hesitating.

"It's okay, Andy. You can tell me. I know you want to lay the burden down."

It was the wrong thing to say—too on the nose. I feel him drawing away from me again, from the truth.

"You're not seriously going to believe a word Katie says, are you? She's a flake, a do-gooder. I should never have married her."

"Actually, I thought she was very nice and utterly convincing."

A noise from the television—raised voices—causes him to stare at the door, in Beau's direction. Getting up, I close the door with a soft click.

I sit back down, my hands sticking to the PVC cloth.

I can do this. We're almost there. I have two more cards to play.

"It's ridiculous how a bit of fooling around gets blown up into something it's not," I begin. "You see it all the time, especially at school. It's so over the top, when really it's just boys being boys."

He looks at me uncertainly.

"It's such a minefield." The fridge hums. I cock my ear, listening for Beau, hearing the murmur of the TV. "I can see how things might be misinterpreted, especially in the heat of the moment."

"Right," he says, fiddling with a plate on the counter beside him, nudging it away.

He's not daft—is more worldly than my students. He's not going to fall for it.

I change tack slightly. "Besides, like you said, it's not as if it matters now anyway. It was thirty years ago. Nicky's not even alive."

He stiffens, eyebrows rising. "What?"

"She died."

"When?"

"Ten years or so ago, of an overdose. Her daughter didn't believe it was accidental."

"That's terrible," he says, rubbing his cheek. "Poor woman." But I catch the relief on his face. He's not quick enough to conceal it. "And how do you know all this?"

My face flushes. Jess told me to be on my guard. I don't want to mess anything up.

I'm going to have to play my last card and fast.

Standing up, I set my hands on the back of my chair. "Why did she think it was rape, Andy? What did they do—restrain her, beat her up? Were you the one keeping lookout, or holding her down? Is that why she included you in the allegation, because—"

"That's not how it went!" he says heatedly. "No one used violence against her or even threatened her with it. I told you before—she seemed very into the whole thing."

I want to take him up on that word *seemed*, but I don't.

He regains his composure, tucking in his shirt, standing taller. "She was drunk. We all were. She followed us into the storeroom of her own free will. No one made her. Brooke thought she was leading *us* on, if anything—a social climber."

"So, you decided to teach her a lesson? Is that why you used the side door, instead of signing her in? Because it was a trap?"

He tries to look outraged, but doesn't succeed. There's something else dominating his expression, an internal conflict. "How do you know about—"

"Why did you use false names?" I ask. "Had you used them before, or was it just that night—part of the plan to make sure she couldn't trace you?"

"Stop it, Pree! There wasn't a plan." He places his hand on his hip, his other hand waggling at me, but it's trembling. He can't hide that. "The nicknames were just a bit of fun. We used them sometimes when we were chatting up the ladies."

His hand drops limply to his side, the conflict there on his face again.

"What is it, Andy? What's bothering you? Did you get caught up in something and couldn't stop it?"

He gazes at me, torn.

I recall a detail from the diary then: the whispering outside the club before they went in. "Was it a last-minute thing—a sudden change of plan?"

"I knew something was up," he says, "but I didn't know what—didn't catch what was said."

I nod sympathetically, taking a step toward him. "Tell me what happened."

He reaches for the plate again, nudging it distractedly. "Everyone had too much…" He searches for the right word, or excuse. "…Too much alcohol."

He's looking at me to say something, anything, but I'm not going to. I'm going to let him fill the spaces now. Instead, I take another step forward.

"Jack… Max…made the first move. He started kissing her. I didn't really know what was going on, but it was…well, she was a very attractive girl."

Again, he looks at me to speak.

I'm thinking about how previously he'd called them Jackson someone, someone Brooke. And yet now how well versed he is.

I wait, keeping my face blank.

"Before I knew what was happening, Jack was…having sex with her, against the wall. She didn't say a word, didn't stop him or put up a fight. I thought she must have been enjoying it."

Must have.

He looks away, at the floor, at his feet.

"Brooke was… Well, Dan…he…he was a bit rougher with her. She didn't say anything. Her face was buried, hidden, so I wasn't sure what was happening."

It's so quiet, I pray for Beau's TV show to remain unobtrusive, no sudden noises.

He shuffles his feet, fiddling with the plate. "Afterward, she stayed still, didn't move an inch. I didn't want any part in it. But Brooke and Jack turned on me, accusing me of being a voyeur, gutless. Brooke said that a real man would just get on with it."

I'm right in front of him now, looking up at him so intently he's morphing into someone else. Faces do that, if you stare too hard. It's just that his face was so familiar, I never thought I'd see anyone else there.

I take in the silver hairs, the jade vein on his temples, wondering how he could be saying this, here, now, after so long. It's so fragile this moment, one wrong move and it would break.

His voice drops to almost a murmur. "Just before I...started... she opened her eyes...and..."

And what? I hold my breath.

Stay quiet, Beau. Please, baby boy.

"...There was no one there. Her eyes were like glass. I didn't... I didn't want to. But I felt railroaded. In the end, it felt like the only way out of there."

I don't move, don't speak.

"Afterward, I realized she was in shock. Her skin was cold. She was breathing quickly, staring around as though lost. Brooke and Jack ran out. I wanted to stay and help her, but Brooke called me a moron and pulled me away."

He breathes in deeply, exhales in a shudder, his face ash gray. And then he looks at me as though he didn't even realize I was there.

"Andy..." I begin, wondering whether to say it.

I have to.

"...It was you who she liked. She was there because of you. She thought you were kind, a real gent."

"What?" His body sways, disorientated.

There's a swell of sound behind us, footsteps approaching. The door handle rattles, and Beau enters looking very pleased with himself.

"I turned the television off, Mummy," he announces, pressing his hands together.

Andy is staring at him, startled. Turning away, he bows his head over the sink. I think for a moment that he's going to be sick, but then I realize he's crying noiselessly, shoulders shaking.

I've never seen him cry before.

Beau looks at him quizzingly and then holds out his hand to me, beaming. Nothing interferes with bath time.

"Come on, then," I say, glancing back at Andy.

Ascending the stairs, I'm aware of him underneath us, the grim silence.

"Does it hurt, Mummy?" Beau points at my bandage.

"Yes." I press a kiss onto his forehead, inhaling the scent of his day care hair. "It does."

As he splashes about in the bath, I sit on the edge of the tub, redressing my bandage as best I can with shaking hands. Then I check my phone. Nothing from Jess yet. I can't remember how we left it, other than her telling me to stay strong.

I watch Beau, my heart barely ticking.

Downstairs, a door closes. Whoever that is down there, it's not Andy, not anymore.

JESS

As soon as I get home, I know that Max knows. His car isn't in the driveway. The girls would normally be upstairs doing homework now, yet the house is in darkness.

The security light clicks on as I approach the front door, checking my phone again. No word from anyone. No explanation for his absence, other than the obvious one.

"Eva? Pops?" I call out in the hallway, putting down my rucksack. The house answers me with silence.

Oh, God. What if he's taken them? Would he do that? Maybe to use them to get what he wants? Why didn't I consider that a possibility?

My heart starts to thump in panic. I don't want to be in the kitchen if he returns, but I don't want to be in the hallway or upstairs either. And I'm trying to work out what that means—which room that leaves me with—when the key turns in the lock and the front door closes and I'm out of options because he's standing right there, in the kitchen doorway.

"Hello, Jess."

I didn't put on the main lights in the kitchen, only the stove light so that I could still see outside. The room is in semidarkness, casting an ominous shadow over his face. "Where are the girls?"

"At Mum's. Just for a couple of hours."

"Why?"

"You know why." He doesn't say this unpleasantly, but my heart shrivels all the same. I glance about me, at the knife block, the cutlery drawer, the saucepan rack.

He puts his hands in his pockets. He's wearing his work suit, has loosened the tie. "How long have you known?" he asks.

"About six weeks."

Hanging his head, he says, "I'm sorry." And then turns on his heel, leaving the room.

What am I supposed to do, follow him?

I listen. He's in the dining room. The click of the drinks' cabinet opening and closing. Liquid pouring. Silence as he drinks. The sound of a glass meeting the table. Now he's going through to the living room.

I think for a moment. I'm still wearing my shoes. The car keys are in my coat pocket. I can make a run for it—collect the girls, take it from there.

I'm tiptoeing down the hallway when he calls to me. "Jess?"

I stop, hesitate. "What do you want?"

I know what he wants. I look at the front door, telling myself to keep moving, to leave before he sucks me in to all his lies and artifice.

"To talk… Please, Jess?"

Beside me on the dresser is a photo of Poppy I've always loved. She's two years old, holding a baby watering can.

He's still their dad. What if he were to say something that might make this good? Is there the slightest chance of that? Probably not. Yet maybe I should hear what he has to say.

Five minutes. I'll give him five minutes.

He's poured me a drink—holds it up for me as I enter the

room. But I don't take it from him. I want to be able to think clearly and to drive.

"How much do you know?" he asks.

"Enough."

"Jesus." He pulls off his tie, tosses it onto the floor. Then he takes a gulp of whiskey, shuddering.

"Should you be drinking on an empty stomach?" I remain close to the door.

"Don't see why not." He looks up at me with those big green eyes. "Did she find you and tell you in person or something?"

"Who?"

"Nicky... I can't remember her surname."

"Nicky Waite." It feels strange saying her name out loud, in front of him.

"Well, did she?"

"No."

He doesn't know what happened to her?

"She's dead, Max. Has been for nearly a decade."

"What?" He stares at me, incredulous. "So, why does this matter, then? Why do you care?"

"Why do I care?" I step toward him and then retreat again, not wanting to get too close. "You raped her, Max! *Raped* her!"

"Stop saying that," he snaps, setting his drink down heavily on the table. "That's not how it was. She turned it all around, lied, but we knew the truth. And it wasn't rape, I can tell you."

"Really? Because we read her diary. And it read like rape to us."

"Us? Who's *us*?"

"Me and the other wives. Priyanka. Stephanie. Surely your friends must have mentioned them at some point over the years when you were hiding this from us, making sure the truth never came out?"

"They're not my friends. I barely know them."

"Liar!" I yell. "I saw your photo in the club—the three of you, thick as thieves."

"Shut up!" he shouts, springing up. "You don't know what the hell you're talking about. You weren't there. *I* was there. *I* know what happened!"

"Yes, and so did Nicky. And it was rape!"

"For fuck's sake! Listen to me! She was a prick tease and she was drunk out of her mind." He squares his jaw, pointing at me. "She didn't say no. She didn't lift a finger to stop us. Sound like rape to you? No, didn't think so."

He sits back down, snatching up his drink, downing it in one, then picking up my full glass.

"She was terrified, Max! It was three against one. What did you expect? She was too frightened to say or do anything. There's no *way* you didn't realize that! Had you paid enough attention—had you cared. Had you stopped to actually *think* about what you were doing to her. She was just a kid!"

"So was I!" he yells, jumping up again, slopping his drink on the carpet. "I didn't know what was going on any more than she did. She used us just as much as we used her. And then afterward she tried to twist everything."

"No!" I scream, waving my arms in frustration. "That's a lie! You're lying! There's a massive difference between doing something against someone's will and getting their consent. And she didn't give you her consent."

"Oh, God, listen to yourself. They've got to you, haven't they? The fucking PC brigade."

"What PC brigade? There is no brigade! This is just basic decency, and abiding by the law. What you did was a crime. And I'll prove it. We have a witness!"

I stop abruptly, turning away.

"What witness?" he says.

I didn't mean to say that. I stare at the mantelpiece. Eva's looking at me; her most recent school photo, her dental brace gleaming. She seems so pleased with herself and her life. I hate that that's about to change.

"She had a daughter, you know... Holly."

"*She* was the witness?"

I spin around. "No, you idiot. Holly was conceived that night. One of you had a daughter. And she had a terrible life from start to finish. She died of alcoholism, and before she passed away, she wanted us to know what you did to her mother. And *that's* how we found out."

Look at him, his eyes bulbous with fear, sweat staining his shirt. I loved him. Six weeks ago, I loved him just as much as anyone's ever loved anyone.

"I didn't know that," he says.

"But she told you she was pregnant, and you did nothing to help her."

"Maybe." He nods. "But I didn't know about...that girl... Holly."

"Sounds like there's a lot you didn't know. Like what constitutes rape."

"Just drop it, Jess!" he shouts, his hand forming a fist. "These are people's lives you're screwing with."

"I'm screwing with?" I shout back. "Well, that's rich! Maybe if you'd done the right thing thirty years ago, we wouldn't be in this mess!"

"What mess? You said she's dead. Nothing's going to change that. So, why are you stirring all this up again? What's the point?"

I watch him as he squirms, undoing another button on his shirt as his conscience chokes him.

He knew exactly what happened that night—knew it then, and now. But he was never going to admit it, not even if Nicky came back from the dead to testify.

"You're right," I say, stepping back into the doorway. "This is a waste of time. I'm not going to argue with you. We're going to sit down when the air's cleared and things have settled, and we're going to discuss this like adults."

"Who is?"

"The six of us. And we're going to work out what's going to happen."

He downs the remainder of the whiskey, wincing. "You're out of your mind. No one's going to be sitting down and discussing anything. You've no idea what you're dealing with."

"And what's that supposed to mean?" I ask, my heart faltering.

"You'll see."

"Tell me what that means now, or I'll phone the police."

"And say what?"

"You know what I'll say."

He looks at me apprehensively. "I don't know anything. I don't even know who you are anymore."

"Well, then now you know how it feels."

Sinking into his chair, he rubs his face, speaking into his hands. "Dan's a control freak, ex-military."

"So?"

"So, he's out there somewhere, stressing about a rape allegation, coming up with some plan."

"I still don't—"

"See? Clueless. You should have left all this well alone."

"Are you saying he's dangerous?"

"No. I'm saying you should have told me first and I could have handled it. He was the worst person to have found this out."

"Have you spoken to him?"

"I tried to. He left me a garbled message. And since then, his phone's been switched off."

I clench my hands inside my coat pockets, thinking about why Stephanie hasn't called.

Max doesn't matter now. I shouldn't be here, babysitting him. I should be ringing the others, checking that they're okay. I should be with my girls.

As I leave, I look over my shoulder, my progress arrested by the sight of him sobbing. "Is that it? Is our marriage over?" he asks.

I don't sugarcoat it for him. "Yes."

"Oh, God, no." He covers his face with his hands. "No, Jess. Please…"

Despite everything, I feel sorry for him. I wrestle with the unwanted emotion, telling myself not to fall for it—to keep walking. This is what they do. This is what they're so good at.

Getting up, he comes toward me. "Please, Jess, I'm begging you. Please don't let the girls find out about this. Don't break up our family. I love you, baby." He reaches for my hand.

I close my eyes briefly as he touches me. I'm remembering the first time I saw him. White shirt glowing, UV lights.

And then the image is gone. I pull my hand away. "Which one was the real you? Who did I marry? Jack or Max?"

"Hey?" He frowns. "I don't get it. What do you mean?"

I shake my head. I already know the answer.

"Do you really believe you didn't do anything wrong?" I ask, looking into his eyes.

He returns my gaze, his eyelashes wet spikes. "I… I've thought about it over the years. And…"

"And what?"

"I don't know."

"Then let me tell you—she was outnumbered. She was in shock. She fell pregnant. She never got over it and died of an overdose. Her daughter was raised in poverty and died a lonely, miserable death too."

"I didn't know about any of that," he says. "I've already told you."

"And as I've already told you, you knew she was pregnant and could have helped her."

"How? I didn't have any money. I was a student."

"Emotional support costs nothing."

"Emotional support? I couldn't have given her that either! I was twenty, for God's sake!"

"Then maybe you should have thought about that before you raped her."

He goes to bite back again, then changes his mind, shuffles his feet—as much of an admission of guilt as I'm ever going to get.

"I've got to go." I do up the buttons on my new coat, pulling it straight.

"Is that what the brigade's wearing these days?" he says spitefully.

I look at him in disappointment. I don't want to remember him for that. I want to remember him for the tears, the quiet remorse.

"I'll let that go, Max, because I know you're scared. But this isn't a manhunt, a conspiracy against you. You committed a serious crime, and I'll never forgive you for it."

And then, finally, I leave.

Outside in the car, my hands are trembling so badly, I can't start the ignition. Smacking the steering wheel, telling myself to get it together, I try again and this time manage to pull out of the driveway.

I go only as far as the end of the road, before stopping to get out my phone. I try calling Stephanie and Priyanka. Neither of them pick up, so I leave messages, asking them to call me back as soon as possible. And then I drive to get the girls, wondering what to tell them, how much to say.

STEPHANIE

I'm running late, barely able to remember the days when I used to walk calmly to work, when Jess rings again. "Still nothing?"

"No." I hold my phone underneath my chin as I do up my coat. It's chilly this morning and dark still, the sun reluctant to rise. "No sign of him whatsoever." I glance behind me at the car park, twisting my neck. I'm aching from being on the couch all night, my eyes puffy with insomnia.

He could be anywhere. I thought about ringing his parents or one of his brothers last night, but what would I have said? Besides, he's too proud to seek help from them. He wouldn't risk them finding out about the letter.

"How are your girls?" Jess asks. It sounds as though she's filling a kettle while speaking.

"Not too bad, all things considered. But I had to tell them—it was obvious something serious was happening. Was that all right?"

"Course." She's moving around, slamming drawers, rattling cutlery. "I had to tell my girls too."

"It's just that you said not to talk to anyone..."

"I meant them—the men."

"Oh. Yes." She always makes me feel stupid. I don't think it's intentional.

I think about the background noise then, realizing she's not on her way to work. "Where are you?"

"At home with the girls."

"Aren't they going to school?"

"No, they're too upset... Why, yours aren't, are they?"

I bow my head as the wind gets up, shaking the trees as I pass underneath them, leaves tumbling. One lands on my shoe, disappears as I move. I feel as frail as a fallen leaf; I'm not sure how long I can hang on.

"Steffie?" She's waiting for me to reply. I try to recall what we were talking about.

School.

"Georgia's the only one who's still at school," I say. "My other two daughters have jobs to show up for. And I can't take any more time off, not after being out last week."

"But don't you think you'd be better off at home, all of you? I mean, obviously, you know what's best for your family, but you're safe, aren't you?"

"Yes. Why?"

"I'm just worried, that's all." She stops what she's doing, her voice sounding closer. "Max said that Dan was the worst person to have found out. Why would he have said that?"

"I've no idea. Perhaps you should ask him yourself."

"There's no need to be defensive. I'm just trying to cover all bases. I made you a promise, remember—to keep you safe. And I meant it."

Do I sound defensive? Perhaps. I haven't slept—am covered in perspiration, having made the wrong choice of a fitted wool turtleneck this morning. And I'm just about managing to walk in a straight line, so I'm bound to go on the defensive if she implies that I'm not protecting my girls. I've looked after them long enough, on my own in the early years too.

"Even if you're right, Jess, and there is something to worry about, I still think we're better off surrounded by people, in our normal routine. Not sat like goldfish in a bowl at home."

"Good. Okay." Her voice brightens and she goes back to shutting drawers, moving around. "I just wanted to know that you'd thought it through."

"Of course I have. I'm not a complete…" I trail off. I'm not far from work now, about to turn into the Circus. I need to end the call, get my mind focused on the day ahead.

"It's just that if you're worried, Steffie, then we should think about phoning the police."

"Well, I'm not. I know Dan. He wouldn't do anything to harm us."

Would he? I can't say for sure, not anymore. But he's still my husband. Resolving things quietly between ourselves was one thing, but I'm not ready to betray him on a larger scale. Right from the start, I was clear about not contacting the police, and I'm not going to back down on that now.

"So, where do you reckon he is?" she asks.

"If I had to guess, I'd say he's gone somewhere to lick his wounds."

"Which is why he could be dangerous."

"No. You—"

"We wouldn't have to tell the police everything, Stef. We could just get you some protection, if you felt you needed it."

"Well, I don't. He's never given me any reason to be afraid of him."

I doubt my words as soon as I say them. Sometimes, I can hear Nicky Waite's narrative above my own, seeing his heroic military tag in a whole new light. *Narrative?* That's not a word I would normally use. It's a Rosie word. I speak Rosie now.

I'm standing outside work, the streetlight casting a sickly yellow glow on the pavement. I rest my hand lightly on the railing spike, testing it through my glove. "I thought we didn't want a scandal."

"We don't. But two women are dead because of them. We have to be careful."

I look up at the first floor of the building to the reception where my colleague Ali is pulling up the blinds. "I really have to go. I'm late."

"Okay. Just promise me you won't take any chances."

"I promise."

———————

I decide to walk to town at lunchtime for the fresh air. On my way back, the wind is icy and forceful, pushing me along faster than I'd like to go. I'm trying not to eat a mouthful of hair, unsticking it from my lipstick, when I catch sight of Dan outside work, his back to me.

You always know your husband's back, or anyone else's whom you love. Do I still love him? I don't know. My first instinct is to hide, though—to duck down the steps beside me, leading to a basement. If I'm quick...

But he has spotted me, and there's nothing for me to do but continue toward him.

He's wearing his work coat, indigo jeans, polished brogues. You would think he was meeting me in his lunch hour like any other day.

My hands feel numb. I left my gloves on my desk, didn't think I'd need them since I was so warm all morning. Yet my index finger has turned a morbid white. And I'm holding it, cocooning it in my other hand, when we meet.

There's a moment, with the sunshine on our faces and the wind tugging our clothes, when I sense regret. He wishes none of it had ever happened, and so do I.

And then it passes and he opens his mouth to speak, the smell of alcohol permeating. Up close, he doesn't look well. He's unshaven, his eyes are bloodshot, and I think of what Jess said about not taking any chances.

"Stephanie." That's all he says. I wait for more, but that's it.

"Hello, Dan. How are you?" This feels wooden, as though I'm a terrible actor, using over-rehearsed lines.

After a long pause, he says, "How do you think I am?"

"Not so good, I would imagine."

"Then you would imagine correctly."

I glance at Chappell and Black's. "Can we…?"

"Walk and talk? Absolutely." He takes my arm. There's no tension there—no tight grip or aggression. If it weren't for the smell of whiskey, I wouldn't think anything was wrong.

We stop outside work. "I'd better get on. We're very busy today."

He nods. "Mustn't keep them waiting, then." I scan him for sarcasm, but there doesn't appear to be any.

"Are you going to be all right?" I ask.

I don't know whether I'm supposed to care about his well-being and be looking out for him, or whether we've gone past that point.

"Course I am."

"You're not working today, are you?"

He smiles in amusement, gazes up at the sky. "Not today, no."

I adjust my bag on my shoulder. "Will I see you at home?"

"That all depends…"

"On what?"

"On whether you believe me."

A shiver runs through me. I shouldn't have got into this now, outside work, of all places. I'm about to retreat inside the building, when he pulls something from his pocket, flapping it in the air.

It's the letter. "You don't believe this, do you, Stephanie?"

"I don't think you should be waving that around." I look

about me and then quickly take it from him, slipping it into my bag before he can object.

But he doesn't seem to care what happens to it. His eyes are locked on me. "How can you believe her—a complete stranger, a no one—over me?"

I glance up at the first-floor window of work and then walk toward the door. Jess would tell me to run, not look back. She would call the police and they would swarm, causing a scene. Everyone in the Circus would see.

Yet this isn't about what people would think. It's about me, him, us. He was there for me and my girls when no one else was.

So, I don't go inside; I stay where I am.

He edges closer until we're both standing right outside the door. A client or colleague could come along at any moment, yet I remain, watching him.

"Who got to you, Stephanie?" he asks, looking at me earnestly, the gray stubble on his face gleaming in the sunshine. "This isn't you. Someone's manipulating you... Who is it, darling? Who?" He sways drunkenly, and I feel myself soften with compassion.

He's right, in part. Where do I start with who's influenced me? Jess? Nicky? Rosie?

Yet no one more so than him.

"It's a lie, Stephanie. You should be taking my word for it. We're husband and wife." He lays his hand flat on his chest. "Haven't I been good to you? Haven't I cared for you and your girls—provided for you? I deserve a little loyalty, surely? You should believe me over anyone else."

I well up, the wind stinging my eyes. "I tried to, Dan. You don't know how much I wanted to believe you. But..."

"But what? Who's doing this? Tell me. Someone's got to you and has driven a wedge between us and—"

"It's not like that. I'm sorry." I turn away. "I have to go."

"Please, Stephanie. Don't go. Please..."

Jess got it wrong. I can hear in his voice that he isn't going to hurt me. He would do it now, were that the case. But he's not capable of that. He's broken. Anyone can see it.

My eyes fill with tears as I pull open the heavy door. The last thing I hear is him calling my name.

I wonder whether it was the right thing to do, cutting him off like that; of course I do. I keep replaying what he said about being husband and wife, and giving him a little loyalty. My mum would have told me to do the exact same thing—stand by your man—but maybe that's not always the best advice, not in situations like this.

It takes all my strength, but when he calls me an hour later, I turn my phone to silent, my heart lurching as I watch the call go to voice mail.

About forty minutes later, my phone rings again, vibrating on the counter. I'm dealing with a rude client, so I let it go to voice mail. I'm tempted to pop to the bathroom to listen to the message, but there's no letup all afternoon, with an emergency abscess messing up the schedule.

It's twenty past four when I'm aware of my phone vibrating again. I'm exhausted, my vision is blurry, my head pounding. I can't take the call, but text Jess quickly under the counter.

16.22 P.M. >
I saw him. He came here & left again. Can't speak now. Will call when I leave work. S x

She replies instantly.

16.22 P.M. >
OK. Be careful. Will wait to hear x

At five o'clock, when my phone buzzes again, my colleague Ali is telling me about the blind date she's going on.

Five ten. It vibrates again, lighting up. Ali's still talking and I'm pretending to listen, rearranging the schedule, emailing clients, one eye on my phone, my mouth uncomfortably dry.

Five eighteen. As it rings, Leonardo is handing me a client's file, explaining why it's going to be a particularly difficult extraction tomorrow morning. Five twenty. He's back again, asking whether I'm feeling better this week because I look it. I don't have time to reflect on the irony.

Five twenty-five. I'm all alone, tidying my desk, struggling to hold my head upright. I could take the call, but want to speak to Jess before engaging any further with him. Perhaps it wouldn't harm to listen to the voice mails, though.

I wait for the message to be left, while gathering my things, shutting down the booking system. As I start to descend the stairs, I'm surprised to hear that I have eleven voice messages and sixteen missed calls.

Overheating in a rush, I hurry outside, immersing myself in the cold air, going a few steps away from work to listen to the most recent message.

I stop in shock. It doesn't sound like his voice. I wouldn't even have recognized him.

Stephanie, why haven't you picked up? Don't you love me anymore...? Oh, man...

His speech is slurred, labored. He sounds paralytic. I turn away as a couple comes out of a building—the one I'm standing outside. I walk off and then stop again, in the middle of the pavement.

Obviously, you don't care about me or you'd have come to the club. So now I…

I don't catch what he says next.

But you're not here. So…

He moans, fumbles for something. I press the phone to my ear, trying to hear. What is he doing?

…This is goodbye, then.

He stops talking. The line clicks. A voice says, *To listen to the call again, press—*

I close the case on my phone, staring ahead of me, my heart racing.

I'm about to open my phone again and listen to the other messages, when I realize that I don't have time to do that. I start to run, my coat flapping, my heels clunking on the pavement, echoing around the watchful buildings of the Circus.

———

My lungs feel raw as I lift my hand to ring the doorbell. I can taste iron; my ears are ringing. I took off my heels to run and my feet are wet. I stare at the *M* symbol on the brass knocker, willing the door to open.

I text Jess as I wait.

17.37 P.M. >
Come to the club. NOW

No one seems to be around. Does the club close on Thursday afternoons? Did Dan mention that once? I bang on the door with both hands. "Hello?" I shout, ringing the doorbell again. "Can anyone hear me?" I look at the buildings around me, above me, seemingly bending inward, blocking the light. I imagine how Nicky must have felt, abandoned here. And then I remember something from the diary: the side entrance.

Dan's father has access; he helps organize the stock for the bar. Dan sometimes borrows his key.

I stumble past a garbage container on wheels, a security light clicking on. The side door is propped open with a brick. From somewhere above, a cat is mewing.

Slipping through the gap in the door, I allow my eyes to adjust to the dark. The air smells musty. After several moments, I still can't see a thing. I've never been here before—haven't a clue where to go.

Using the torch on my phone, I head toward a staircase, my tights catching on something underfoot. I tug myself free, feeling the nylon rip, my bare foot meeting the floorboards. Along the corridor, I flash my phone, glimpsing photographs, paintings. I can't hear voices or see any lights anywhere.

Instinctively, I go where the diary went, where Nicky went, heading upstairs in the dark, my chest tight.

At the top of the stairs, I look left, then right, unsure which way to go. And then I hear the clinking of bottles and turn that way, heading toward the sound.

There's a splinter of light at the end of the hallway, and I remember this detail too.

I stop, hesitate. Do I go in? I haven't called out to him yet. Why is that? I thought I said he'd never hurt me. Do I really believe that?

He doesn't know I'm here. I could turn around, slip away. But I can't. I have to make sure he's all right, after what he said in his last message. If he was to do anything stupid...

Quietly, I creep forward, pushing open the door. I see his polished brogues first and then the rest of his hunched form.

He's sitting on the floor of the store cupboard, surrounded by boxes. Above him there's a bare light bulb, harsh on the eyes.

I drop my bag and coat, relief draining through me. "Oh, thank God, Dan! You're all right."

There's a bottle by his feet that he grapples for, taking a swig, slopping whiskey down his shirt. "Steffaffy, whaddya doing here?"

"I came to see if you were all right." My voice breaks with emotion and I well up, overcome, kneeling down in the small space before him. "I was so worried about you."

"Why?" He frowns, eyes swimming.

His right arm is stuck awkwardly by his side, hidden from sight, and I wonder whether he's injured himself. I look about for cut glass or a knife, but can't see anything other than boxes.

"Because of your message... Because of what you said." I shiver, soaked in perspiration. I still can't catch my breath.

"My life's ruined, Stefff..." He dribbles with the effort of trying to say my name. Closing his eyes, he takes another swig, missing his mouth again.

I hate seeing him like this. I saw my father drunk so many times, saying his life was over after a loss on the horses. But I never thought I'd see Dan so reduced, wretched.

"Stop drinking that," I say, trying to take the bottle from him.

"Leave me alone," he snarls, rapping my knuckle with the glass. "Whadda you care?"

I recoil, my hand throbbing. I'm shattered, ran across town for him, my foot is bleeding. And here he is, wallowing in self-pity.

"They're gonna put me in prison, anniss all your fault."

"You're not going to prison, Dan. And it isn't my fault. This is about what you did...in this room. That's why you're here, isn't it?"

This was where it happened. I haven't fully absorbed that yet. I look about me at the stacked boxes, imagining Nicky outnumbered, trapped.

My mood changes then from pity to anger, heat rising up my spine. "That poor girl. What did you do to her?"

"I don't know what you're talking about." He waves the bottle. I watch the liquid storming inside, a miniature sea.

"Yes, you do." I look about the confined space again, thinking how petrified she must have been. "You took advantage of a girl who couldn't fight back. She trusted you. She thought you were friends and—"

"Friends? You gotta be kidding." He waves the bottle again. "She was nothing, a cheap whore, out for what she could get. You're all the same."

I stare at him in disbelief. "Do you hear what you're saying? This isn't you. This—"

"Course it's me," he says, laughing. "Who else would it be?"

I'm still kneeling before him and suddenly it feels belittling. "I think I should go. Obviously, you're going to be fine." I can't believe I fell for it, running here at his summons.

Standing up, I retrieve my coat, looking around for my bag. It's near the door.

And I'm stooping to pick it up when he says it. Luckily, I've got my back to him. I wouldn't have wanted him to have seen the look on my face.

"It was jussa a game, a bet—who could screw her by the end of the night."

My hand tightens around the strap on my bag. "A game?"

"Yeah." The bottle sloshes. "Jack normally won."

"Jack, Lee and Brooke?"

"'S'right, yeah." Maybe he wonders then how I know those names. He pauses before continuing. "Nicknames. Made it more fun."

Fun. That word seems to linger.

"Had you done it before—played that game?" I ask, my heart hammering.

"No, not like that. That night was different. We all wanted

to win…" His voice trails off. I worry that he's fallen asleep. I turn to look at him; his chin is slumped onto his chest.

"So, who did win?"

"All of us… Quite clever of me, really." Cradling the bottle, his arms wrapped around it, he shakes his head as though recalling a great night. "I didn't think they'd do what I said, though. Didn't usually."

What *he* said? It was his idea?

Something peculiar is happening to me. I'm heavy and light; my eye sockets are on fire; there's a loud rushing sound in my ears.

He shifts position at that moment, moving his right arm from its hiding place, holding something up.

I freeze. Everything goes still and I can see clearly. I take in the dull black handle, the long silver barrel. I've never seen anything like it before.

"What are you doing?" I ask.

He doesn't reply, closes his eyes, the ghost of a smile on his face.

"Why have you got that?" I say, louder.

He has a firearms certificate for a shooting club, but I didn't think he went there anymore.

Is it loaded?

"Why d'you think?" he says. "You got my messages, didn't you? No point me living."

"Put it down, Dan. You—"

"She wasn't worth it." His mouth turns down contemptuously. "Wasn't even a good screw… Frigid as fuck."

I jolt, yet somehow stop myself from responding.

Remarkably, it doesn't take me very long to realize what I have to do.

Setting down my bag, I use my soft purring voice, the one he likes in bed, as I approach him slowly. "Come on, Dan… It doesn't have to be this way."

He points the gun at me, his finger on the trigger. "Stay back, Stefff, or I'll shoot. I mean it. There's nuffin you can do."

"Yes, there is." I smile comfortingly, lowering myself onto my knees before him again. The gun is right in front of me, almost touching my nose, but I'm not scared. "Put the gun down, darling. We can work this out. You know how much I love you."

I see the flicker of doubt on his face, the uncertainty. He wants to believe me.

"We can get through this." I place my hand gently on the inside of his thigh. "Just the two of us."

He looks into my eyes, lucid for a moment. "Really?"

I nod. "Yes, Dan."

The relief on his face. He smiles, his body relaxing in submission. He's about to lower the gun. I clasp my hand around his hand, lovingly, supportively.

And then I lift it upward, press it to his face and fire.

The noise is earsplitting. Something warm splashes my clothes and face. I fall backward, biting my tongue, hitting my head. Bottles rattle. There's smoke in the air, blood everywhere, pooling on the floor, seeping toward me.

And I'm trying to get up and away when I notice there's a shape looming in the doorway, someone blocking the light.

JESS

"Steffie! Get up!" I tug on her arm. "Get out of there, now!"

I can't get her to move. She's a deadweight. She's looking at me as though she doesn't know who I am.

"What happened?" I drop to her level, my hand on her shoulder. "Talk to me!"

"We killed him," she whispers, the color draining from her face.

I stare at her in horror. "No, you didn't." Then I realize what she said. "We?" I look around the gloomy room, catching sight of the gun lying in the pool of blood.

Kneeling before her, I clutch her arms. "Steffie, what happened?"

She doesn't answer.

"We have to call the police."

"No!" She grips the sleeve of my coat, her eyes wide, crazed. *"No!"*

I pull myself away, retreating into the corridor where I can think. The smell in the room... The blood... I retch, then hold my hands to my face, commanding myself to stay calm.

Stephanie has followed me, barefoot, tights ripped, bloodstains on her turtleneck.

"What were you doing here, Steffie?" She's freezing, trembling markedly; her lips are blue. I take off my coat, place it over her. "Why did you tell me to come?"

"I thought he was going to kill himself." She stares in the direction of the room.

"What? Why?"

She starts to whimper. "His messages."

"What messages? Where's your phone?"

She shakes her head.

I go back into the room. Her coat and bag are by the door. I grab them without looking around—can't stomach seeing it again. "Unlock your phone for me. Quick!"

She presses the button. I go to her voice messages. "Are they still here? You didn't delete them?"

"No."

I listen to the first one.

It's going to have to do.

Then I phone the police. It's a hell of a gamble. I've no idea what the other messages say. Beside me, Stephanie starts to cry. There's blood in her mouth. I hope for God's sake that it's hers.

"It's okay, Steffie. I'm here." I hold her hand. "I'm not leaving you. Everything's going to be all right."

While we wait for the police to arrive, I listen to eleven messages from a man who's dangerously drunk, desperation escalating, begging his wife to try to love him again. There's no mention of the letter, or Nicola Waite. In his final message, it was clear he was threatening suicide.

She tried to help him. She came as fast as she could, frantic, barefoot. Witnesses would have seen her—a strange sight. But he was too far gone and shot himself right in front of her.

Steffie is downstairs in the Green Room with a blanket and cup of sugary tea. She took a nasty blow to her head when she fell backward in shock and has a mild concussion. They've patched her up and the paramedic is speaking softly, taking good care of her.

There are police everywhere, but the situation seems clear enough. You can tell just by looking at Steffie in her turtleneck and fitted skirt that she wouldn't hurt anyone. Her distress at having been involved with this is so immense, she's almost catatonic.

The phone messages have been logged. We've given statements. Everything fits together, like the truth always does. A passerby has verified the time of the shot.

I can tell by the police's weary procedural faces that this will be deemed a suicide. There's no motive for anything else. No compelling reason for her to have fallen out of love with him, other than the usual breakdown of marriage. No reason why anyone would have wanted him dead. No reason to take revenge; no Nicky, no Holly; no crime, no proof.

Just the way the law wanted it.

———

When I get to bed at long last, I go back through those first few moments when I arrived, two questions circling my head.

I overheard a police officer talking into his radio. The gunshot wound was consistent with the statement given by Steffie.

She was taken to hospital to have her concussion checked out, so I didn't get a chance to talk to her alone. Yet I was dying to ask: Why did she think she'd killed him, when it was he who put the gun to his head and pulled the trigger?

And then there's the other thing.

She said *we*.

JESS

We don't see each other for a month, as per Steffie's wishes. I try not to overstep, but I find it frustrating. Zero involvement doesn't sit well with me—never has. So, I text every other day, asking if I can help. I'm desperate to know what really happened in that room, but she doesn't want to see me yet and I have to respect that.

I'm starting to wonder whether I'll ever see her again. And then, on Saturday 12th December, I get a text message from her.

09.11 A.M. >
Is there any chance you're free to meet today? S x

I'm so pleased to hear from her, but then I start tapping my teeth together. Why now? Is something wrong? I know they're not doing a postmortem, but there'll be an inquest—always is when a death is sudden. Yet from what the police led me to believe, there was nothing suspicious about the circumstances.

09.13 A.M. >
Yes, I'm free. Shall I ask Pree? J x

09.14 A.M. >
I'd rather not, if you don't mind. S x

On the way to the café—an upmarket bistro that serves morning coffee and always has pastel macarons in the windows—I
wonder why she didn't want Priyanka to come. Maybe, if I'm
honest, I'm worried she's going to corner me alone, point the
finger.

There have been nights when I've lain in bed in the dark,
wondering whether it was all my fault. A person's going to do
that. A man's dead. But then I didn't get the gun out of his safe.
I didn't pour alcohol down his throat. I didn't hold the gun to
his head. And I didn't rape Nicky Waite either.

I'm done with thinking this is our fault. And Steffie will be
too, someday, when she's got through this terrible patch.

In my right mind, I'd never be going to town in December on a Saturday. I've no idea why Steffie wants to put herself
through it. I'm having to fight my way through the throngs at
the Christmas market—coachloads of shoppers from Swansea
and Birmingham. The bistro she's chosen is near the abbey, the
worst possible spot. My scarf feels like it's choking me. I'm sure
both my feet are lifted off the ground at one point. The smell of
sausages and onions is overpowering, and a group of schoolkids
are singing a festive song.

The song reminds me of my girls at primary school and now
I'm upset, blinking back tears. The pain is with me all the time.
I wake and it's there. I laugh and then it's there. Crying is the
only time I feel authentic.

I didn't stop loving Max when I got that letter. It doesn't work
like that. I knew this was going to be tough, whichever way it
played out. He isn't dead, but may as well be. We tiptoe around
his name at home, freezing when we find one of his socks, navigating his empty chair at the table as though there's a ghost in

his place. I can't get used to sleeping alone. Maybe I never will. Maybe I'll be tired and brokenhearted for the rest of my days.

Was it worth it? I can't say. Some days, I don't even remember who we're doing it for, or why.

Max moved out—without my having to throw his suitcases out of the window—into an apartment in Bristol. I haven't looked it up online, am worried I'll balk at the state of it and change my mind. Eventually, he says he's going to relocate his mortgage company over that way too. He's agreed to continue to support us, but knows he won't have any access to the girls or be a part of their lives.

I don't know if I was expecting a huge argument on this point. In any case, I didn't get one. I think I might have preferred a fight, a small objection, even. Stand up and be a man. Defend yourself and your rights. But he just accepted my terms and walked.

He is and always will be the greatest disappointment of my life. No one will come close to it.

Someday the girls will understand that I had no choice. If I could have done it any other way, to avoid their getting hurt, I would have. Yet I couldn't have raised them in the same house as him, knowing what I knew; it wouldn't have been morally right. I've explained this to them over and over. But right now, neither of them is really talking to me.

Outside the bistro, it takes me several minutes to make my way through the queues of people streaming in constantly to ask about a table. There's no way we're going to get one. Then I spot Steffie sitting in the window, wearing a sparkly cream beret, and I catch my breath. She looks so gaunt, and she has someone with her.

I don't have time to think about it because she's spotted me too and is lifting her hand in a feeble wave. The doorbell tinkles as I enter, and I unpeel my scarf, my hair rising in static as I remove my hat and then my coat, losing weight by the millisecond.

"I'm afraid we don't have any tables." The waitress pounces right away.

"Oh, it's okay. I'm with…" I point, making my way over to Steffie, distracting myself with where to put all my woolen objects.

"Hello, Jess." Stephanie looks up at me, nudging her beret into place. It suits her, but she looks very pale. She's not wearing as much makeup as usual, and I think she's lost a lot of weight. "It's good to see you." She gestures to the girl beside her. "This is my daughter Rosie."

I don't know Steffie's family, but I know Rosie was the one who found the letter. She looks nothing like her mum—has a mean, angular little face, and I wonder whether she's thinking the same thing about me. She doesn't even say hello, but nods, pulling her sleeves over her hands.

"I ordered you an Americano. That's what you normally have, isn't it?" Steffie says.

I smile. "Yes. Thanks."

I'm not sure I could have ordered for her in return—never noticed what she drank. I was always too busy trying to get her to change her mind. And look where that got us.

"So, how have you been?" I ask, placing my coat and accessories on the windowsill. The café's busy, but the tables are placed at a civil distance. The couple at the table next to me are young, glamorous, feeding each other cream on spoons.

Max and I will never eat out again. We'll never share a moment again.

"Awful," Steffie replies.

"It's true." Rosie folds her arms. "She's been a total mess."

"How are things going with the inquest?" My question is badly timed, as the coffees have arrived, and we sit back in our seats, waiting. The waitress sets a place of macarons between us and Rosie takes one, putting it into her mouth whole.

"I'm not sure," Stephanie says, as the waitress moves away. "The communication's not been great, but then I haven't been chasing it as much as I could. I find it…difficult."

"I'm sure you do. But you know you can always delegate anything to me."

"Yes. I know. Thanks."

"It's good they're not doing a postmortem," I venture, stirring my coffee. "I mean, that's one positive thing, isn't it?"

Rosie looks up from her hot chocolate, watching us closely.

"Yes, I think so. From what I can gather, everything's straightforward, but there are procedures they have to follow."

"Course." I glance at the young couple again, who are kissing. Turning my chair slightly, I put my back to them.

"How's Priyanka?" Steffie asks.

"She's okay. Same as us, really. Taking it one day at a time."

"I'd like to see her, but not yet… You're the first person I've seen, other than my sister. It's hard, facing people. I don't know what to say." She sniffs and her hand trembles. "Work have been brilliant, though."

"You're not back yet, are you?"

She shakes her head. "Not yet. They've said I can take all the time I need. But I'm thinking of going in on Monday. I think it would do me good."

"She needs the normality. It's good for up here," Rosie says, tapping the side of her head. And then she links her hand through her mum's arm, rocking to one side to kiss her on the cheek.

I'm touched and look down at my lap, trying not to well up. Sugar might help. I select a green macaron, nibbling it.

"Did you ever meet him?" Rosie asks me. "Dan?"

"No. I'm afraid not."

"Well, you didn't miss anything. He was a bast—" She stops, still holding her mother's arm. "I didn't like him much."

"He's dead, Rosie," Steffie says quietly.

"Sorry, Mum."

I swallow the rest of the macaron, barely tasting it.

"We can't spend too long here, I'm afraid." Steffie sets down her cup. "We've got a lot of shopping to do. Christmas has caught me out this year..."

Christmas. I haven't done one thing in preparation for it yet. No word of a lie.

"...But I wanted you to meet Rosie. Because she has something to say to you."

"I do?" she says, frowning.

"Yes. Go on."

Rosie takes her time, eating another macaron. "Yeah, well, I just wanted to say, like, sorry about the letter. Sorry he found it."

"You don't need to apologize," I say. "Seriously."

"Yes, she does. None of it would have—"

"No," I say curtly. I glance about me, but everyone's wrapped up in each other and Christmas and pastry menus. No one's thinking about blame and guilt and death.

"I'm sorry, but I'm through with this." My hands curl as though I'm about to pummel the table. "We're not doing this anymore, Steffie. They're the ones to blame. We didn't do anything wrong—not Rosie or any of us. We've gotta get this right on the inside, in our minds. Okay?"

"Okay," she says.

Rosie gives a short laugh of surprise at my heatedness and I notice the glimmer of a stud on her tongue. "Mum said you were cool." And she nods slowly, respectfully.

"Can we meet again soon?" Steffie says, outside the café. It's impossible to have a conversation here. The Salvation Army band is playing "Silent Night" three feet away. Opposite there's a closed charity shop at the top of a couple of steps, so I steer us there, away from the main foot traffic.

"Yes, that would be nice." I hold on to the railings as I look around for Rosie, checking she's not within earshot, spotting her peering in the window of an expensive lingerie shop. I turn back to Steffie. "I'm glad you got in touch. I need to talk to you about something, but was waiting to hear from you first."

"Oh?" She removes a tissue from her pocket, dabs her nose.

I pause, unsure whether to press on. I don't know whether the timing's right, whether she's strong enough to talk about this yet.

"What is it? If you don't tell me, I'll only worry." A sequin is hanging by a thread from her beret, touching her hair. It makes her seem even more fragile.

"It's just...do you remember Lucy, Nicky's friend—the one I contacted?"

A look of apprehension comes over her face. "What about her?"

"Well, do you remember that she wanted to tell us something?"

"I don't think I..."

"Sorry. I shouldn't have mentioned it." I glance over at Rosie again, who appears to be taking photos of the mannequins for some strange reason.

When I look back at Steffie, I can tell she's torn between wanting to know more and protecting herself. She's pressing her gloved hands together, the hint of a frown below her hat. "What, Jess?"

"Nothing."

"Tell me." She touches the sleeve of my coat. "Please."

"Okay...well...she's desperate to meet and I've been putting it off. But I wondered whether we should hear her out. What do you reckon?"

She shuffles her feet. She's wearing sneakers, albeit gold ones. "I'm sorry. I don't think I can manage it."

"Of course. Forget I said anything."

"Why don't you meet her without me? I know you want to." She tries to smile, her mouth quivering.

"I'll think about it."

"You could go with Priyanka?"

"We'll see."

She touches my arm again. "You've changed, Jess."

"Me? How so?"

"I'm not sure… Do you still believe in the truth—everything out in the open?"

I hesitate, knowing she's hit on something vital, in the way that she sometimes does, surprisingly so. But honestly? When someone's dead because of the truth coming out, it's hard to tell how you feel about it.

"Dunno" is all I can say.

"It wasn't your fault. If it weren't for you…" She looks over her shoulder at Rosie before continuing. "Well, I never thanked you for what you did for me…at the club."

"What did I do?"

There's a funny expression on her face. "You covered for me."

I look at her intently. "Did I?"

As the Salvation Army starts playing again, she gives a little start, clutching her heart. She smiles up at me nervously. I know the moment's passed, the opportunity gone with it.

A crowd is gathering around the band. Coins tinkle into collection boxes.

"Are you okay for money, Steffie?" I ask, hoping it's not too personal a question.

"Yes, we're fine. Dan's business was in good shape and he had several investment properties. But we're going to move, downsize. The house doesn't feel the same now."

I reach for her hand, which is stiff in a leather glove. "Steffie, I—"

"Sorry to interrupt, Mum," Rosie says, appearing at the foot of the steps, "but I really think we need to make a move."

"Course," I say, smiling at them both. "You get going. We'll speak soon."

───────

When I get home to our Max-less house, the girls are curled up with books on the sofa. They don't say hello, but when I sit down beside Poppy, she doesn't get up and move away. And I accept this small offering gratefully.

I notice that Steffie has texted me.

13.58PM. >
Thanks for coming. Let me know when you're meeting Lucy. I'll see if I can manage it. S x

Two days later, I find myself in the Sicilian café where I originally read the letter, waiting for Duane Dee, my sculptor client, who was also with me that day. It feels like I've gone full circle, but I'm not back where I started because I'm not the same person now. None of us are.

I was worried how I'd feel being back at ground zero. Yet when I walk in and sit down at the same table on purpose, expecting some kind of out-of-body experience, I realize that reading the letter wasn't the moment when everything changed for me. And this sets me wondering when that was exactly...but then Duane appears and my thoughts are interrupted.

It's good to see him. Christmas is a nonstarter for me this year, and no one's less festive than Duane. He doesn't look like he even knows which season we're in, wearing a light summer sweater splattered with clay.

I don't listen to him today, any more than I did the last time. Ignoring the Christmas menu, he orders his usual calzoni and I order my usual Americano and almond pastry. And then he starts to tell me how difficult it is to make a living by being an artist and how that's part of its magic, because if it was a cash cow, then everyone would be doing it and it wouldn't be a labor of love.

On he talks, waving his hands around, the tassels of his Aztec scarf dipping in his sparkling water. And I'm thinking about how there were two parts of this that I've never put together before and how shortsighted of me that was.

Holly was an artist; and I work for the city's most prominent art dealer.

Duane is talking about Van Gogh now. I tune in. "…And he was, like, a total failure. He only sold one painting in his life-time and died in poverty. Can you imagine?"

"Yes, absolutely shocking."

He frowns. "What is? The poverty, or lack of acclaim?"

"Both." I'm not sure what I meant either. I shut up, finish my pastry.

When we part ways, I walk back to work, unable to get the conversation out of my head, which is unusual where Duane's concerned. And it comes to me then—I've got it: the moment when everything changed. It wasn't at the Sicilian café, reading the letter. It wasn't at the Montague Club, seeing Max's photo on the wall. It was when I unlocked Holly's storage unit and saw where she lived.

————

That afternoon, I persuade Gavin to take a trip across town with me. He's in a good mood, having just returned from a boozy lunch. As I drive, he searches for Christmas songs on the car radio, trying to get me into the spirit of things.

Not gonna happen. But I force a smile for the boss.

Giving the door of unit twenty-one its customary kick, I open it, waiting for the light to flicker on. Looking at it through Gavin's eyes, it strikes me afresh just how disgusting it is. I should have cleared up, but there's not been a chance, nor has it felt like a priority.

"Tell me again why we're here?" Gavin says, wrinkling his nose. It smells even worse than when we were here last.

"Because I wanted you to look at these." I gesture to the can-vases. I've never counted them before: there are thirteen. "Oh, and these." I pick up the sketchbook lying conveniently near us on a crate.

He flicks through it, hands it back, then gazes at the canvases. He doesn't speak for a few minutes, just stands there.

The suspense is killing me. "Any good?"

"Not bad. Who's the artist?"

"An unknown."

"Where is he, then?"

I smile at the sexism. Surely he's noticed the Tampax carton near his foot?

"It's a she. And sadly, she passed away recently."

"Oh." He scratches his chin. "Well, if you want to get rid of them, then I think we could find someone to buy the lot and look at framing them and selling them."

"That's not what I want," I say, looking up at him.

His lips purse in surprise. "Oh?"

"I want to do something a bit different—something that would set Moon & Co. apart."

"We're already set apart." He jangles the change in his trouser pocket. "We're the best in the city."

"Yeah, at doing the same thing as everyone else—dealing mostly with artists from privileged backgrounds. But this would give us a different emphasis—inclusivity, raw talent…"

"Raw talent, eh?" He smiles, whistling a Christmas tune, looking around the room at the paintings again. "Go on, then, Jess. I'm listening."

PRIYANKA

"Look, Mummy, a star!" Beau points out of the window, then presses his face against the glass, licking it.

"Don't do that. It's dirty." I pull him away, back onto my lap. We're on a crowded bus, going to town. The shops will be packed, but I can't leave it any longer and have to take Beau with me. Ironically, despite those times I lied about going shopping, I haven't bought a single gift and we're due back in the Midlands next week. My family doesn't celebrate Christmas as such but always gets together, giving presents to the children—fourteen in total.

I'm also going for my second and final tattoo removal session that Beau will have to sit through too. I didn't have anyone else to watch him, and that's something I've got to work on. I've no idea how to do this yet. Jess keeps offering help, but she's got her hands full already and I need someone at my disposal 24/7. Someone like Andy.

Beau feels very warm on my lap in his coat and hat as he wriggles, cooing at the festive lights. The strain of looking after him alone for the past month has exhausted me; I'm grieving too.

I've lost the only soul in the world who loves Beau as much as I do. Some days, cutting Andy out of my life feels masochistic.

In the New Year, I'm going to have to come up with a better plan for support. For now, I just have to get through the most miserable Christmas of my life, fending off the torrent of questions when I appear at my parents' house without a husband. I've considered staying home, just me and Beau, but I think that would be even more depressing than the questions.

There's only one person whose prospect of Christmas would have been worse, and that's Nicky. It was on this day—the last Saturday before Christmas—thirty years ago that her life was ruined. Whenever all of this feels hopeless, self-defeating, I remind myself of her and how we got here.

It's hard work, though, keeping hold of her. She's prone to disappearing, as impermanent as snow.

Which was why I asked Jess for the diary—whether I could keep it. And to my surprise, she said yes. So now it's on my bookshelf in the living room, right where anyone could pick it up and read it. No one will do that, though.

"Look, Mummy, another star!" Beau points, waves, as though the star will wave back.

"Yes, it's pretty," I say, planting a kiss on the back of his head absently, thinking about Andy.

He emailed last night with the address of the place he's renting, half an hour's drive away. I looked it up online and it's minuscule.

I've told him that I'm prepared to move to a cheaper house, given that he'll be keeping up our mortgage payments as well as paying rent. But he's adamant that we stay put, in order to minimize upheaval for Beau.

That's all well and good, but I'm worried the real reason is he thinks it'll be easier to worm his way back in if we stay where we are. There's no way that upheaval isn't going to occur on some level; Beau's already unsettled without him. And he knows that.

Everything's been disconcertingly civil, practical. We haven't spoken about Nicky since the night he broke down. I couldn't bring myself to discuss it any further. What was there to say? I couldn't even look at him.

I can't help but fear that something's brewing. It's all been too easy. He knows I'll do anything for Beau…and he knows I'm weak. Or thinks I am.

Still, I don't want to be tested, especially not at Christmas.

I don't know how to tell my family, whether I ever will. Meena said she always knew The Anorak was going to let me down. I haven't given her the full story. I said he cheated. Well, he did, didn't he?

———

When we get to the tattoo removal clinic and have to put on our goggles, Beau starts to cry because he doesn't want the man to hurt me. Dave, the technician, is so kind—making Beau laugh, reassuring him—that I start to cry a little, yet no one notices. Any tears will be put down to the fact that he's setting my arm on fire.

When we leave, I cry again because Dave tells me I'm a lucky girl—I'm not going to have permanent loss of color. I'm not going to be left with a ghost tattoo.

———

An hour later, we're passing the merry-go-round—right in the middle of the main street, causing bottlenecks and tension—Beau tugging on my arm, pleading to have a go, when I get the feeling we're being followed. I look about the crowds, but it could be anyone.

I pull Beau to the side of the thoroughfare to talk to him, squatting down to his level. "You're too little. I'd have to go on as well and my wrist's sore. Do you understand?"

His bottom lip wobbles. "Please, Mummy?"

"No, Beau. I'm sorry." I feel bad, but it can't be helped. If Andy were here…

My heart's aching as I stand up again, catching sight of someone lurking by the archway of the abbey courtyard, watching us.

It's Saffron.

"Come on, little man. Let's go." I try to lead him away, but he's digging his feet into the ground, making himself heavy.

"No, Mummy. I want a ride on the horseys!"

And then it's too late. There's a tap on my shoulder and Saffron is standing there, looking at me shyly. "Hello, Miss."

I grip Beau's hand, who transforms into a good boy at the presence of this stranger, tantrum dissolving. "Hello, Saffron."

"Nearly didn't recognize you." He points at my hair, shouting above the garish funfair music. "But then I saw those." He points downward at my Doc Martens.

I afford him a slight smile, tugging Beau's hand. "Well, we're short on time and—"

"I'm really sorry, Miss." He puts his hands in the pockets of his bomber jacket. It makes him look awkward, hunched, and with his cropped hair he looks very young. "I shouldn't have called you that."

"No, you shouldn't have."

Beau gazes up at me, blinking, then picks his nose.

"I was out of order. You didn't deserve it… I feel really bad about it."

I remember seeing him crying at the bus stop. But that's not my problem. I'm tired of defending them, excusing them.

"When do you start at the new school?"

"New Year, Miss."

"Well, good luck." That's enough. I'm not giving him anything else.

"Sorry I let you down," he says, lifting his chin to raise his voice.

I hesitate. And then I can't stop myself.

"I couldn't let it go, Saffron. What you did to that girl… I had to report it. Do you understand?"

"I know." He nods glumly and then shuffles away, jeans baggy on his skinny legs.

"Saffron?" I call after him, just as the music stops. He turns, looks at me. Something on his face makes me think that he's expecting a pardon. "Promise me you'll learn from it."

"Yes, Miss."

That's the last I'll ever see of him. I don't know if he'll learn from it. I have to hope so. I have to hope things like that or I'd never teach again.

As Beau and I go on our way, he skips happily alongside me. "Who was that, Mummy?"

"Someone you'll never be," I say, squeezing his hand.

———————

By the time we get home, it's getting dark and Beau is in good spirits, having forgotten all about the merry-go-round. We're talking about what to have for supper, so I don't notice until the last minute that the lights are on. And then I see Andy's coat on the banister.

"Hello?" I call, pushing our shopping bags to one side and picking up Beau, balancing him on my hip. The kitchen door opens and Andy appears, smiling cautiously. "What are you doing here?" I try not to sound aggressive, but this isn't what we agreed. He's not supposed to be coming and going as he pleases—not supposed to be anywhere near us.

Beau wriggles, reaching for him excitedly. "Daddy!"

I clamp him against me, not allowing him to move, waiting for Andy's response.

"Sorry to drop in unannounced, but I needed to see you and wasn't sure that you'd want to see me. So, I…" He trails off, apologetically.

Beau swivels to look at me, prodding my cheek as though

testing I'm still human, able to feel. "Why wouldn't you want to see Daddy?"

Andy looks appealingly at me. "It *is* almost Christmas..." he says.

My face burns. I can't believe he's doing this.

Only one month ago, he stood just yards from this very spot and confessed to the worst of crimes, yet now he's trying to make me falter, forgive. He knows I'll be struggling with parenting and work. His power depends on my vulnerability. He's counting on it.

I carry Beau through to the living room, setting him down on his beanbag, turning on the TV. "It's your favorite, look," I say, pointing at the screen. Beau, tired from town, is easily appeased, clapping in delight.

Leaving the door ajar, I return to the hallway, but Andy's not there. I hear the sound of the tap running, the kettle filling, and head to the kitchen. "What do you think you're doing?"

He turns to look at me. "I'm sorry if I'm overstepping, but I need to talk to you. This won't happen again, I promise. You can change the locks, but—"

"Damn right I will." I go to fold my arms, before remembering my sore arm. Instead, I unpeel my coat delicately, hanging it on the back of the chair. "I'll do whatever I like. You don't live here anymore, remember? And how dare you try to manipulate me in front of Beau?" I point at him. "I'm warning you. Don't use him as a pawn in this, or you'll regret it. Do you understand?"

"I'm sorry, but I was desperate. Please, just hear me out. We haven't really talked about..."

"Nicky Waite?" I offer. "Can't you even do her the honor of saying her name?"

He scratches his head, his tufty hair sticking up boyishly, and I momentarily recall the early days of our marriage, the happy ones.

"Would you like a cup of tea?" he asks.

"Uh, no!" I say, astounded. "I'm not just going to pretend that everything's okay. Honestly, it's like you've got no grip on reality!"

"Please, Pree," he says wearily. "Just a few minutes of your time. And then I'll be gone for good."

The way he says this makes my stomach churn. So final. But then that's what I want. He's lost all rights, including access to Beau.

I'm curious about what he has to say, though, so I take a seat, watching as he tries to find the tea bags. "Top right." I changed everything the other weekend in a fit of excess energy.

"Thank you." As he sits down opposite me, I set my gaze on him, taking in the details that I used to find charming, endearing. And it occurs to me then that eventually, further down the line, someone else may look at him exactly the same way.

What will I do? Warn her off? Do we have to watch them for the rest of our lives?

"Did Katie tell you where she and I met?" he says.

I think about the question. No, I don't think she did.

I shrug, like I couldn't care less.

"It was at the university…in Bath," he adds. "She was working part-time in the general office as a women's services counselor. I met her when I called in to see if there was anything I could do about finding…"

"Nicky Waite?"

"Yes… There was no one on the main desk, so she came over to see if she could help me. I didn't give her the real story, obviously."

"Obviously," I echo sourly.

He takes a sip of tea from his *I Heart Daddy* mug, the one Beau bought him. The manipulative attention to detail is wasted on me, won't work.

"I told her that Nicky was a family friend, a former student, and that I was trying to track her down. But Katie couldn't give me any information because of data protection. I think she felt sorry for me and we ended up going for coffee. And then for drinks a few times, and things went from there."

"I see." The fridge starts to hum, reminding me that Beau must be hungry—that we mustn't put ourselves out for Andy. "Why are you telling me all this?"

He gazes at me, his eyes tearing up.

I stare at the floor, noting a piece of dried pasta near the sink.

"Don't you see? I tried to find her. I wanted to help, to put things right. I knew what we did was wrong and the guilt was eating me alive." Holding his long bony fingers against his face, he begins to sob mutedly. "But I couldn't find her. She had disappeared and there was nothing I could do."

I don't know what he thinks this changes. Is he expecting me to be impressed, or to comfort him? How much responsibility am I supposed to take for him from here on?

These are the things we haven't discussed, Jess, Steffie and I. We never got that far in our planning before Dan shot himself and everything blew up and died down at the same time. I don't know whether I'm supposed to be offering him advice, support...

And then, finally, I get it.

This was exactly what Jess was trying to tell me that day in front of the tour bus in town—the day she said that she didn't have all the answers.

This is my choice. It always was. It's just that I didn't want to see it that way, wanted to be directed. But this is my husband, my son, my future.

I gaze at my bandaged wrist, thinking of Nicky's diary on the living room shelf. "You're wrong, Andy. There was something you could have done."

"And what was that?" he asks, uncovering his face, shuddering.

"You could have confessed, handed yourself in to the police."

He stares at me dumbly.

I smile. "I didn't think so." Standing up, I go to the door, open it fully. "You need to leave."

He looks crestfallen, a string of saliva between his teeth. Beside him, his mug of tea is steaming. "Pree..."

"Get out!" I shout.

He jumps up, the table wobbling, tea slopping. Coming toward me, his face is crisscrossed with shadows from the blinds, his gait stooped, begging. "Please, Pree, just tell me what I can do to make this right. I want to come home, to be a family again. We belong together. What about Beau? What about everything we went through with him? He needs me, and I need you. *Please.*" Clasping his hands together in prayer, he towers over me, crying again.

I shake my head, tightening my grip on the door. "I don't want to see you again. Ever. And—"

"You don't mean that. I know you don't."

"Yes, I do!" I shout, stamping my foot. "I don't want anything to do with you. In fact, I don't want you to pay the mortgage. We're moving out, cutting all ties."

"Don't say that, Pree. You're being rash. Think about Beau!" He reaches for me, his hand spindly, pathetic.

In a flash, I punch it away. "I *am* thinking about Beau! Get out! *Now!*" I scream.

There's a click of the front door and he's gone, his coat vanishing from the banister, the house falling still. Sinking onto the chair, I hug my good arm around my waist as I cry, the pain from my tattoo seeming to swell intuitively.

Somehow, amazingly, Beau is singing along to the TV. The sound pulls me to my feet, and I go through to the living room. Joining him on the beanbag, I wrap my arms around him, inhaling his innocence and bliss.

We sit like that for some time, until his tummy rumbles loudly. Turning on the fire and the Christmas tree for him, I gaze at Nicky's diary, and then head to the kitchen to start supper.

Andy's tea is still on the table. Clinically, calmly, I pour it down the sink, dropping the *I Heart Daddy* mug into the bin.

Someday, I'll tell Beau about Nicky Waite. I'll explain what his father and the others did to her. And I'll tell him about the butterfly too. I'll teach him that it doesn't matter how long ago it was, how deep the pain, there's always a way to fight back. And that when you're done fighting, you can set about repairing the hole in your heart.

Because someday, it *will* heal, and while there will always be a faint impression, it's a part of who you are now. And...you're okay with that.

JESS

"Thanks for seeing me so close to Christmas," I say, setting my bag on the table. I never got a chance to see inside the meeting room of the Montague Club before now. The decor's more to my taste: a white Scandi-style table, pale blue wallpaper. A vase of twigs lit with fairy lights. And at the head of the table, a female president: Florence DiMaggio.

"You're welcome… Gives me something to do. It's dead this week and I like to keep busy." Her smile seems genuine; she has a good solid handshake. When she's not here, she's a specialist recruitment lawyer, a professional who can wear oversize cat-eye glasses without looking ridiculous.

"I don't know if you heard about what happened." She takes off the glasses, rubs the bridge of her nose. "But last month, one of our long-term members took his own life, right here in the club."

"Yes, I heard about that. I'm sorry."

"Just between the two of us, it's been a complete nightmare. I'm not belittling what happened or being cold-blooded about it, but as far as trying to keep this place afloat?" She shrugs with her mouth. "Our numbers are the lowest since records began."

"Well, hopefully, that's where I come in." I slide my business card across the table to her. "I think I might be able to help."

"I'll admit, I took the meeting because I'm intrigued." She taps the card with her fingernail, smiling at me teasingly. "Let's hear it, then. Tell me how you're going to save me."

I like her, even though she's into this place. I can't help it.

But then I liked Max too.

"Okay, Florence, so here's the thing—recently, I acquired some art. It's been evaluated by experts who've been using words like *meaningful, original, impactful.* And if you knew these guys and how uptight they are, then you'd know this is high praise indeed."

"So, it's good stuff." She adjusts her necklace: three coins on a chain. "What's that got to do with the club?"

"Well, I need somewhere to showcase the artist's work. It's a she," I add, in case that matters.

It does. She smiles. "Excellent."

"There are thirteen paintings in total and a series of charcoal sketches, and I need to find somewhere to hang them. But more than that, I'd like to create an artists' hub—a local communal space to showcase artists from disadvantaged backgrounds. The idea would be to give them somewhere to talk about their work, somewhere where the right conversation with the right person could launch their career."

"Go on..." She's adjusting her clothes now—a black V-neck dress with a thread of silver woven through. Is she even listening?

"So, I'm proposing that you choose a day to suit and that every week, on that day, the artists' hub is held here."

"At the club," she says flatly.

"Uh, yes. That's right. All you'd be doing is providing the venue and we'd handle everything else... We'd need the usual facilities to be open so that the visitors could buy refreshments, and they'd have to be fairly priced, as many of them would be on modest incomes. But it would be enough to cover your expenses for central heating, cleaning and so on. And—"

"Let me stop you there." She frowns, fiddling with her necklace again. "This all sounds lovely. But why would we do it?"

Lovely? Helping the disadvantaged?

"Well, like you said, this place is empty, on account of one of your members blowing his brains out upstairs."

She lets go of her necklace, which falls onto her chest. I shift in my seat. Perhaps that was a little heavy-handed.

I wait, my eye resting on the portrait of a man at the end of the room; some dandy in a wig with very dark under-eye shadows.

"What's in it for you?" she asks.

"Quite a lot, as it happens. We'd put the word out in the industry—make sure plenty of local artists knew about it and, more importantly, lots of investors, critics, movers and shakers."

"Does anyone say that anymore?"

"I just did."

"Carry on." She picks up a fountain pen, playing with it, clicking its lid on and off.

"So, the artists would not only gather here to swap ideas, meet influential people and network, but they'd also exhibit work on a rotational basis in the Green Room."

"The Green Room."

"Well, yeah. That's the main room where the bar is, isn't it?"

What was she thinking? Put the riffraff upstairs? In some gloomy corner?

We're not putting them up there.

"Go on," she says.

"Okay. So, they'd exhibit their work and we would handle negotiations and acquisitions, taking a cut."

"I see. So, this is a moneymaker for, uh…" She glances at my business card. "…Moon & Co.?"

"Not really. I mean, it would generate profits, yes. But we're proposing to give them to charity."

"Which charity?"

"Rape Crisis." I don't even blink.

There's a tinkle of her bracelets as she lifts her arm, smoothing the ends of her hair. "What's your motivation for setting this up?"

I tap my teeth together silently. I guessed that she would ask this. "I knew the artist. She was a distant relative."

"Was?"

"She passed away recently. Didn't I mention that?"

I tap my teeth again, watching her. She's good at hiding her thoughts. I haven't a clue whether she's interested or bored.

"Then what's the point of exhibiting her work?" she asks.

"Because she was gifted, but she didn't have any money or connections."

"I thought you said she was a relative? Surely you were well-placed to help her in your line of work?"

Somehow, I manage not to blush. "No. I didn't know about her until recently."

"I see."

I look at the dandy in the wig again, steeling myself. She won't break me, get to me. Not here.

"Look, Florence, I know it's too late for the artist, but posthumous success is better than none. Van Gogh sold only one painting in his lifetime. Did you know that?"

"No," she replies. "I'm not exactly an art buff."

"Well, it's true. History's full of talented people who died in poverty and were only recognized afterward."

"So, your motives are altruistic?"

"Kind of," I say. "Although that makes me sound better than I am."

"Modest too."

I smile politely, shift position. The cushions are very padded, bouncy, perhaps to make people feel taller, more important, than they really are. I wonder whether Max ever sat in here, whether Florence DiMaggio knew him, fancied him.

"I still don't understand how this would solve my problem," she says. "Members may be slim on the ground right now, but memories are short. Once a few months have passed, if we can ride it out, we'll be back to normal."

"With all due respect, I beg to differ. I think there's an energy that hangs around places. I don't mean ghosts rattling chains. Just that people are more superstitious than you might think." I gesture around the room. "You can decorate with as many twig lights as you like. But there are plenty of other places in this city where posh people can meet, places where someone didn't—"

"Okay. I get it." She rests her elbows on the table, linking hands. "Look, all this is very interesting, but obviously I'm going to need to go away and think about it."

"Absolutely." I know when I'm being fobbed off. "Although there are some stipulations that I haven't mentioned yet, which you would need to hear before making any decisions..."

"What stipulations?" She raises her eyebrows at me.

"It may sound a bit strange but the—"

"Oh. I think we went past that point a while back." She smirks, laughing lightly.

I ignore this, keep my face straight. "Well, firstly, we'd insist on the thirteen paintings and the charcoal sketches being displayed in the hallway, with plaques identifying the subject and the artist. I'd need a legal guarantee that the artwork would remain there permanently, no matter what happened to the building in the future... So, basically, you could keep that picture of the club's founder, Sir What's-his-name, but—"

"Sir Graves."

"Yes, him. He could stay. But the others—all those photos would have to go."

She looks astonished. "Why?"

"Because they're all men, for a start. It doesn't reflect current times. There's not even a picture of you there, and you're the president. And besides, one of them is the man who committed suicide."

She gazes at me. I can tell she wasn't aware of that. "You seem very knowledgeable on the subject."

"Not really. I'm just thorough when I undertake a project."

"And possibly when you have a personal stake?" She cocks her head scrutinizingly.

"Only insomuch as I'm passionate about the idea," I say. "I don't like elitism. And the whole premise of this club is divisive, selective and exclusive."

"And yet you want to do business with us." She folds her arms. "I find that very strange."

"It's not for me. It's for the artist."

"So you keep saying."

She's tough; I can see that I'm going to have to be tough right back.

"I think you should know that the man who killed himself upstairs did it because…" I twist in my seat. These words never get any easier. "…He sexually assaulted someone here on these premises. And if word were to get out, well, you can imagine what that would do to the club."

Two perfect circles of red form on her cheeks. "I don't believe you," she says huskily.

"Believe it," I reply. "It's true."

Her tone changes to accusatory. "What is this?" She doesn't take her eyes off me. "What do you want?"

"For you to consider my proposal in good faith."

"Good faith?" She smiles in a way that I don't like.

I reach for my bag, setting it on my lap. "Look, you either accept the proposal or you don't. But I'd seriously think about it, if I were you. It's win-win. You keep the club alive and do something good for the community at the same time. The PR would be a dream—art, charity, equality… Clubs like this can't operate like they used to. You, of all people, must know that. Only a few decades ago, you wouldn't even have been allowed to set foot in here."

I'm on a roll now, stabbing the table with my finger as I speak, my tongue disconnecting from my brain. "And that's what this project's all about—opening doors for others. Not just the chosen few. Holly, the artist, knew all about that. The charcoal sketches I told you about? All of closed doors."

She pulls a silver thread from her dress, perhaps not meaning to. "You're obviously very invested in this, but would you be able to produce a legally binding agreement for the venture?"

"Being drafted as we speak." That's not quite true.

"Well, then, I'll take it to the board." Standing up, she flicks her hair over her shoulders. "We won't be meeting until the New Year, but I'll give you an answer as soon as I have one."

Her voice is icy, all camaraderie gone. We shake hands. "I look forward to hearing from you, Florence. Thank you for your time. Sorry if I went too far."

"You didn't." She gazes into my eyes, and I wonder whether I've shaken her world or whether it'll be business as usual. Impossible to say. "I still think there's something you haven't told me."

I smile briskly. "Isn't there always?"

———

Florence DiMaggio doesn't show me out. She remains in her Scandi-boardroom, adjusting her coin necklace, pulling strands from her dress. I walk in silence along the hallway, stopping in front of the photograph of the three men.

I'm sorry; of course I am. I make myself look at Daniel Brooke, taking in the juvenile acne, the army buzz cut.

I don't know whether Max or Andy will ever come back here again, but if they do, I hope the first thing they see is Nicky— her haunting eyes tracking them from her portrait on the wall.

Letting myself out, I realize with a start what day it is today.

Twenty-second December.

On my way back to work, I wonder whether the date will add extra power to my cause. It's a nice thought, but I know things don't work like that, not in the real world. All I can say is that I gave it my best shot. Sometimes, that's all the consolation we get.

JESS

We meet on a cold Sunday mid-January, frail snowflakes in the air. Lucy's running late, so we wait for her in the lobby of the hotel she chose as our meeting place. There's a massive log fire, and waiters dart about with silver trays as we stand in a circle near the curtains, trying not to get in the way.

"I can't stay long." Priyanka looks at her watch. "I've left Beau with a friend."

"I'm sure she'll be here in a sec," I say, watching the revolving door for her arrival. "I'm glad you've got someone to help, though."

"Only for an hour or so… Really, I could do with someone around the clock, to help out when I'm shopping or fancy a soak in the tub. It's the little things, you know?" She taps her boots together despondently, traces of snow sliding off the leather onto the carpet.

I do know, actually. I don't have a little one to look after, but kids are kids no matter the age. Navigating teenage boundaries by myself is terrifying. I miss Max so much, or the idea of him— the man I thought I'd married. There's no one to swap notes with anymore, no one to share the moments with, good and bad.

"You shouldn't have to struggle alone, Pree," Steffie says. She looks tired, drawn in the face, but otherwise better than when I saw her last. "I wish I'd had more people around me when my girls were young. Maybe I wouldn't have married Dan."

This feels like a big thing to have dropped on us, but Lucy is whirring around the revolving doors, wearing a gigantic multicolored scarf, kissing us like long-lost friends.

After wasting time over where to sit and who is hungry and who's going for the mulled rosé wine, which Lucy's raving about, we find ourselves sitting there, looking at her, wanting to pinch her to see if she's real.

She's pasty-faced, with dark blond hair and full lips. I remember the latter from Holly's painting. When she smiles, which she does a lot, her whole face changes. It's nice; she's nice. I can see why Nicky would have liked her.

I think things like that all the time now—how Nicky would have liked this or Holly that. Like I have a clue.

It's because Florence DiMaggio stunned me last week by saying yes; the Waite women are going to be setting up residence in the club. I've been convincing myself that this is what they would have wanted, saying things to Gavin like, yes, I think the artist would really appreciate that. But in truth, I've no idea.

"Thanks for coming, everyone," Lucy says, handing around the mulled rosés, placing a tiny bowl of roasted nuts between us. She has a chirpiness about her, an aura of authority. Even if she hadn't called this meeting, I think she'd be chairing it anyway. "I know you've been through a lot and I don't want to stir the pot...but it's just that there's something I wanted you to know. I thought it only fair that you have all the facts."

Steffie looks like she did when we first met: aloof, disinterested. It's a coping mechanism, so I've come to realize. She's possibly even holding her breath. Sometimes, I think she's changed more than any of us, and then she shuts down and I'm not so sure.

Lucy tucks her hands between her thighs, leaning forward

girlishly. "It's about what you said in your email, Jess, about Holly being conceived that night…at the Montague Club."

"What about it?" I ask, my heart bouncing uncomfortably. Beside me, Priyanka is sitting very still.

"Well, why did you think that, exactly?"

"Because Holly told us…in her letter."

"Oh." She picks up her drink.

I don't like this one bit. I glance at Priyanka, who looks back at me uneasily. I thought we were past this point, with no more surprises, but obviously not.

Lucy sticks her hair behind her ears, frowning. "Okay. Here's the thing… I don't know if this changes anything for you, but I know for a fact that she wasn't conceived that night."

I think about this, striving to take it in.

"What? That can't be right." I look at her skeptically. "How do you know that?"

She lowers her voice as a waiter hovers nearby, seeing to another table. When she looks at me, she's emotional—her eyes filling with tears—and I know she's telling the truth. "Because Nicky lost the baby."

I gaze in confusion at the glass of wine in front of me, the steam and spices tingling my nose. "How…? When?"

"At around twenty-two weeks. She miscarried and had to go to hospital." She pauses, wrapping her hands around her glass to warm them. "I went with her."

"Holly lied?" Priyanka says, turning to me.

No, she didn't. Surely not? None of this makes sense.

"I wasn't surprised about the miscarriage, if I'm completely honest. I thought something like that might happen…" Lucy sighs, hooking a grapefruit slice out of her drink, placing it on a napkin. I watch the wine soaking the paper, slowly spreading.

"…She was out late every night, drinking, smoking, which she'd always been very anti up till then." She looks at us each in turn, trying to catch Steffie's eye beside her. Yet Steffie's gone, off in her own world, staring out of the window. "Don't get me wrong. I'm not saying she did it deliberately. I think she was just out of control because of what happened to her, and losing the baby was a direct result of that. I don't think she would have loved it, though. I mean, how could you? So, in a way, it was a blessing."

A blessing? No, it wasn't.

None of this was a blessing. I hate it when people do that—try to find the silver lining. Sometimes there isn't one. There's a dirty top and a filthy underbelly and a rotten middle.

Still, I'm not going to argue. "What happened after that?" I ask.

"Well, she got worse. She dropped out of the course and fell behind with the payments on our flat. Kim had had enough by that point and left, and I was pleased to see her go because we were arguing constantly. So, then it was just me and Nicky, but eventually I couldn't take it anymore either. Alcohol, different men staying over… I didn't feel safe in my own home and I was worried about her. But when I tried to talk to her, she told me to mind my own business. In the end, although I hated going, I gave her my new address and moved out."

"And that was it?" Priyanka says, looking at me out of the corner of her eye.

I know what she's thinking: You left her? Twice? Once at the Montague Club, and then again when you left her to die a long slow death.

But that's too easy, dumping this on the lap of the nearest woman. Lucy wasn't responsible for her. She was a young student, with her own life and future to worry about.

"Where was her mum?" I ask. "What happened to her?"

"Not sure." She shrugs. "Nicky was always funny about her. I think she had mental health problems, from what I could gather. I did try phoning her, but she never answered. I got the feeling that once Nicky reached a certain stage, her mum couldn't cope with it."

"Poor Nicky," Priyanka murmurs.

"I didn't know what to do." Lucy plays with the bowl of nuts, turning it around. "If I could have helped her, I would have. But back then, you couldn't just go online to find out what to do and where to get advice."

"Did you see her again, after you moved out?" I ask.

"No. I wanted to, but I did my year out in London, and by the time I'd returned and got around to looking her up, she wasn't there. And no one knew where she was."

"She disappeared," Priyanka says quietly.

"And then, out of the blue, she wrote to me at my parents' address." She looks about for her bag, swiveling to unhook it from her chair. "I still have the picture she sent me... Here, look."

She takes a photo from an envelope, setting it down on the table. "It was the last time I ever heard from her."

These words seem to cut right through me. I'm frightened that if I touch the photo, I'll be breaking a spell—standing between Nicky and the last human connection with her. So, I look from a distance, like we always did, separated by time, by someone else's account of the past, never our own.

It's Nicky, smiling, holding a little girl in her arms. A happy little girl.

"You can keep it," Lucy says.

"No, it's okay," I say. "I think you should. I've got one, anyway. We found it among Holly's things." And I'm reaching for my bag, going to my purse to show her what I mean, when she turns over the photo on the table, tapping it with her fingernail.

"Look at the date." She makes it easy for me, placing it right under my nose.

I recognize the neat, methodical handwriting: *July 1994. Holly. 1 year, 10 months.*

"Oh my God. So, she was born in..." Priyanka does the math quickly on her fingers. "...September 1992. Nearly two years after the night at the Montague Club. She couldn't have been their daughter."

"Told you," Lucy says.

"Okay. So, she wasn't a blood relative," Priyanka says defensively. "I never thought it was a big part of this, in any case."

"But it was," I say. "I mean, we wouldn't have taken it so seriously if it hadn't been for the daughter claim, would we?" I look at Steffie, who's watching me attentively.

"Well, maybe that's why, then." Priyanka picks up her drink, wincing as she tastes it. It's not great; the ginger is way too much. "She knew the allegation would be stronger if she said one of them was her father."

"Who *was* the father, then?" I ask Lucy.

She exhales, cupping her face in her hand. "I'm not sure. She included a letter with the photo, but it was very vague. All she said was that she'd met a man at a party and that he was nice—an artist. But she hadn't told him about the baby—wanted to go it alone."

"An artist." I nod. "Well, that's the first thing that's made sense."

"And what happened after that?" Priyanka asks.

"Nothing. My career was taking off. I was traveling a lot. I always meant to try to track her down, but never did."

"Well, she followed you—you and Kim," I say, looking directly at her. "She collected press cuttings of everything you achieved."

"Really?" She flushes red.

I don't say this to make her feel guilty. At least, not consciously. Yet I can't think of any other reason why I'd have said it.

"I did try to help her, Jess," she says, brow furrowing. "We even spoke to a lawyer, but it was clear that she'd never be able to prove it… Of course, it didn't help that Kim kept saying it wasn't rape—that she'd seen it with her own eyes. I think that was what got to Nicky the most—the fact that no one believed her."

"I did," I say.

"Me too. Not that it made any difference."

"What do you think Holly wanted?" Steffie asks no one in particular. "Her mother must have told her there wasn't going to be any justice. So why do you suppose she contacted us?"

I gaze at her, in her fluffy white turtleneck and tiny white earrings.

None of us can answer that. I'm going to have to get used to the idea that we'll probably never know.

Yeah, like that's going to sit well with me.

I drink the overbearing mulled rosé, trying not to swallow a star anise. "By the way, Lucy, we never thanked you properly for saying you'd be a witness. We didn't threaten them with it—didn't have to. But it was handy to have in our arsenal."

"No problem. Anytime. It's always there if you need it."

"Thanks."

I won't tell her about the portrait of her that's going to be hanging in the club. It doesn't look much like her anyway, not anymore. I don't suppose she'll ever know it's there.

But we will. She's part of the story. Because she was there on the night at the Montague Club.

"The rosé's delicious." I raise my glass.

It was worth saying that just to see the look on Steffie's face.

––––––––

Lucy's the first to leave, then Priyanka, who sits for a few minutes with her coat on, her bag on her lap. She has to get back for Beau, but somehow can't move. I know how she feels. It's been a lot.

"Pree, I've been thinking…" I say, turning sideways in my seat. "We have five daughters between us. So that's eight women total. Couldn't we all look after Beau?"

She looks confused, jaded. "How?"

"I dunno, but surely we could work something out, if you were to tell us what you needed. We could come over on weekends and evenings, just to give you a break. What do you reckon?"

She fiddles with the stiff white tablecloth, biting her lip.

I look at Steffie for her input, opening my eyes at her. Thankfully, she takes the hint.

"I think it's a good idea," she says. "My daughters are definitely at an age where they could help."

"It's too much," Priyanka replies. "It's not your responsibility. This is my problem, not yours."

This really gets to me, after all we've been through. I stop her hand from fiddling with the cloth, pressing it firmly. "For God's sake, Pree. We're not offering to breastfeed him or pay his bloody university fees."

She blurts a laugh, tutting at me.

"It would just be a couple hours here and there, to see you through this tricky bit—or for however long you needed it. Whatever you wanted."

"Okay." She nods. "I'll think about it."

"Good," I say, sitting back in my seat, satisfied.

It may be my imagination, but when she stands to leave, she seems less burdened and I'm hoping I've lightened her load a little. But as I say, I could be imagining it. Sometimes, I give myself more credit than is due.

"I'll call you," Priyanka says, buttoning up her parka, taking her leave.

I feel very sad after she's gone. If I had my way, we'd all be living in some kind of commune, helping each other out. But people don't live like that—not in Bath, anyway.

"Are you all right?" Steffie asks.

I shrug; I don't want to go home yet. Both the girls are out. The house will feel lonely. "I don't suppose you fancy another drink?"

"Why not?" She smiles.

We order a normal wine without bits floating in it, and sit in silence. The snow's coming down thicker. I'm thinking about Nicky and Holly. When I'm not thinking about my girls or my mum, I'm thinking about them.

"I'm sorry, Jess," Steffie says, at length.

"What for?"

"I was watching your face when Lucy said Holly wasn't their daughter… I know you were upset, especially after all the work you've done for her at the club."

"Oh, that's okay. I think I'd have done it anyway."

"I'm not so sure," she says.

"What do you mean?"

"Well, it's not just about the genetics. It's the fact that she lied."

"I know."

Sometimes she's brighter than she looks.

I look at where Lucy was sat, her chair askew where she pushed it aside, the grapefruit segment lying on the napkin, a cluster of money tossed onto the table to cover the bill. She didn't even bother counting the notes. So financially fluid, so confident. Nicky must have longed for a bit of that.

"Jess, I need to talk to you about something," Steffie says.

"Yep. Go ahead." I'm still looking at the grapefruit, so it takes me a moment to grasp what's happening.

I watch her carefully, my heart picking up pace.

"It's about when Dan died…" She fiddles with her earring, selecting her words. "I…"

"Are you sure you want to do this?" I glance nervously around the room. We're not that far from the club. This place could be crawling with Montague cronies. "You don't have to say anything."

"But I want to." She stops fiddling, lifts her shoulders. "I killed him. He wasn't going to kill himself. I thought he was, at first—that's why I went. But I don't think he was the type. He was too self-preserving. He just wanted to scare me, or hurt me. So I placed my hand over his, lifted the gun to his head, pressed as hard as I could, and it went off."

I open my mouth, stunned. Again, I glance around the room, wiping my palms on my jeans.

"I did it in cold blood. I wanted him dead. He said it was his idea to assault Nicky and that she wasn't worth it." She wells up. "She was with me in that room. I felt her with me, Jess."

I reach for her hand. It's petite, soft, and it's then that I realize why she said *we*.

"Did he threaten you with the gun?" I ask.

She pulls her hand away to pick up her napkin, dabbing her eyes. "Yes. He said he would shoot me if I didn't stay back." She can barely say the words.

"Then it was self-defense. He got you there under false pretenses, threatened you with violence. He was a nasty bully. And you know what *else* he was."

She looks at me, a little smudge of mascara underneath her eye. "I know," she says.

I waited a long time to hear that. Sometimes, it's not just them we've got to hear it from; it's us too.

Picking up my wine, I sip it, thinking. The room has thinned out a little. The waiter is gathering plates and tips, his shoes squeaking discreetly.

This revelation doesn't change anything. No one knows but us. We could pretend it never happened. For once, I wouldn't have to tell the truth. For the first time in my life, it wouldn't matter.

"Do you know what, Steffie?"

She drops her napkin, tears dried, emotions checked. "What?"

I could say anything. She's waiting for me, hanging on my words, their unofficial leader.

I'll never know if I led them the right way.

"I think we should forget all about it. We should pretend this conversation never took place and that nothing untoward ever happened in that room, aside from in 1990. It's over, okay?"

"Okay," she says, and then turns to look out of the window, watching the snow fall.

STEPHANIE

I didn't kill him. He killed himself. That's what I tell myself every day, and there are plenty of things to back it up. I just focus on them and not the other details. I focus on what he did to bring me to that room, to that situation—not just that day, with the voice messages, the gun, the threats, but over the years when I was married to him, and what he did in 1990 too.

He's on my mind all the time. I'm not sure how I'll remember him in the long run, which aspect of his personality I'll choose. I can't even picture his face anymore. I always thought he'd never hurt me and I was wrong, because what he did and said to me the day he died hurt me more than he could have possibly imagined.

My sister, Fiona, came over yesterday, after I met Jess and the others at the hotel. She brought us a casserole for tea and stayed to eat it with me and the girls. She's been popping over on weekends, and it's been nice to have the support. I do hate the smell of dogs, though.

I've learned two things since it happened. The first is that my brain fog wasn't anything to do with the menopause. I woke up two weeks after Dan died and it was gone. The second thing is that I know why I hated Nicola Waite so much, why I couldn't see her as a victim, why I had to blame her no matter what.

When you married someone like Dan, part of the deal was that you played a game. And part of the game involved pretending you didn't know what was going on.

A fog descended to help you out. You told yourself it wasn't so bad, that everything was all right. He steered you away from relationships with anyone but him, and he wouldn't want you to work either, although that bit was up for negotiation. You might get away with it because the extra money would always be welcome, but friends and family weren't.

You weren't close to anyone, so you couldn't be sure what other people's relationships looked like. Judging by what you saw on TV and in the papers, you reassured yourself that there was no such thing as the perfect marriage. You didn't listen when people tried to set you straight. You thought it was because they were jealous, critical, even when it was your own daughter, shouting, pleading with you to open your eyes.

But it wasn't an easy thing to do. As soon as you stepped out of the game and called time, there would be consequences. Sometimes, devastating ones.

Was it ever worth it? Yes. I believe so.

Last weekend, I asked his family to clear his belongings. I said I wasn't up to the task. Before they arrived, I removed the military tag from his drawer and put it inside my mother's cocoa tin.

I think that's what I'll choose as my lasting memory of him. Just like Nicky.

———

At work today, Leonardo has been especially thoughtful. He's bought coffees and doughnuts, and we're having a ten-year anniversary gathering for me in the conference room. He's saying what a valued member of staff I am, and I'm smiling, pretending to listen.

I'm thinking about the day Shelley Fricker slid the sanitary pad to me underneath the toilet door.

I looked her up on Facebook recently and discovered she's an oncology nurse. I had to Google it and learned that it means she works with cancer patients. I felt ashamed.

Leonardo is handing me an apple doughnut. I don't normally eat things like this, especially not at work—the sugar sticks to my lipstick—but I want to make a show of being one of the team.

When Shelley comes in today for her final treatment, I'm going to ask her if she'd like to go out for coffee sometime. My little way of repaying her for a kindness long since gone, but never forgotten.

JESS

I'm alone in the office this afternoon and it's snowing again. I'm the only person at Moon & Co. who lives near work. Everyone else has made a dash for it. It's Friday; no one wants to be stuck here overnight. The forecast says heavy snow.

I like being here alone. The snow is making everything so light; the desks inside the office are glowing. I can think straight when everything's like this: simple, silent.

I used to stand out in the street as a kid when it snowed—right there in the middle of the main road, loving the audacity of it. I couldn't understand why no one else wanted to join me. I was always that person, wondering why I was the only one doing what I was doing.

Mum would carry me inside and defrost me by the fire, telling me I was a silly sausage. Not as silly as she is for arguing with Dad all the time, I used to think but not say.

I hope I can get through the snow to Beechcroft tonight to see her.

I've got a pile of filing to do, which Mary kindly left for me. Elliott left me half a packet of Custard Creams.

With a biscuit in my mouth, I take the stack of paperwork to the filing room, kicking the door open like I used to do at the storage unit. Leaning against the wall, I eat the biscuit, dropping crumbs on the first item: an application from one David Wellington. It needs to be filed in the Grants drawer, which I open as far as it'll go.

I don't like this drawer, hate it. It's full of people we've rejected. Moon & Co. hardly ever awards grants to artists, especially those who Gavin doesn't know personally. I've always wanted to do something about it, but nepotism is a sensitive subject to tackle, even for me.

This will be a great place to start when I'm looking for artists to target for the new venture, *#waitehub*. That's its name, by the way. All lowercase, because that's cool.

I'm putting David Wellington where he belongs, when something catches my eye and my heart stops. I swear it does.

I pull out the only other applicant in the *W* file and stare at the name at the top. Hurrying from the room, I sit down at my desk, putting on my glasses to examine the form. I'd know the handwriting anywhere: tiny, but in capitals. The quietest of shouts.

What on earth…? Holly applied to Moon & Co.?

There's scant information on the form, other than her name, the date and a return address at the YMCA in Bath. She sent it five years ago, shortly after I started here.

Did she know that? She must have. So she was, what, targeting me personally?

It doesn't look like much of a target. I didn't even know who she was at the time. Yet it would have been me who rejected her. Mary didn't work here then. It was my job—I'd have sent her the letter, telling her we were sorry but her application for financial assistance was being turned down.

She didn't fill out the sections about influences, stylistic preferences. But under the achievements heading, she wrote: SEE ATTACHED. Whatever it was, it's long since gone, tossed in the bin.

I hold my head in my hands, moaning. Why did she do this? Why apply for a grant here, to me? She needed money, help, for sure. But why also send us the letter about her mother, making one claim about that night that was true and one that wasn't?

I go to the window, squinting at the snow, wishing it would make things clearer for me, the way it did when I was a child. I don't understand any of it. The lie about her conception. The key charm on her bracelet. All those sketches of closed doors.

Which door? What was she trying to tell us? I go to call Priyanka, to talk it through with her, but then I stop, turning back to look at the snow.

Holy crap.

"You bloody clever girl." I laugh a little and then a lot. "Very well done, Holly." And then I'm crying a bit because it's the one thing we never really considered. Because people always make things so damned complicated. Whereas the truth is always simple, especially when you know what it is.

I knew she would work it out. I used to follow her, a shadow that she never saw. I knew she bought a hot dog and a coffee for the homeless man on the footbridge every day, and reported the bins when they were full. I knew she cared.

I didn't mean to use her and didn't intend for anyone to die, not even him.

All I wanted was to see inside the places that were shut off from us. All I wanted was to touch the velvet chairs and smell the lilies in frosted vases and bask in the cerise lighting—to know how it felt to be on the other side.

But that couldn't, wouldn't, happen. I knew that all along because of everything my mother told me about how the world worked—how there were people like them and people like us. And how we weren't welcome.

You see, to unlock the door you needed someone on the inside. That was the secret they didn't tell you. You didn't get in of your own accord, no matter how hard you tried. You had to get someone to open the door *for* you.

I could have read every self-help book, painted the most exquisite art, and all for nothing because I didn't know that one simple little truth.

Once I knew it, everything fell into place.

————

Ladies and gentlemen, let it be known that I, Holly Waite, am finally inside the Montague Club.

And it's every bit as sumptuous and bittersweet as I imagined it would be.

★ ★ ★ ★ ★

ACKNOWLEDGMENTS

This book wouldn't have happened without my editor Erika Imranyi, whose enthusiasm and insight made all the difference. Thank you to everyone on the team at Park Row, including Nicole Luongo in Editorial, Cathy Joyce for her thoughtful copyediting, and to all those in Editorial, Publicity, Marketing, Sales, Art and Production who had a hand in creating the finished product.

Special thanks to my agent, Nelle Andrew, who encouraged me to write the story that I truly wanted to tell. Nelle's a guiding light and one in a million.

Thank you to the online community of authors who make writing a less lonely business. I'd especially like to thank Neema Shah. A comment about representation that she made onstage at the Bath Literary Festival UK, when I was just beginning to write this story, really stuck with me and was the seed that created Priyanka.

Last, thank you to my friends and family for their love and support, especially Bec Vaughan, Johnnie Carey, Anita Rowden and Lisa Parker. They never see me without asking about my writing, and it's hugely appreciated. And of course to Mum, Dad, Nick, Wilfie and Alex, who have to hear about my writing whether they like it or not. x

QUESTIONS FOR DISCUSSION

Warning: contains spoilers!

1. The three main characters in the story are very different. Who did you relate to most and why?

2. Only one of the women, Priyanka, confides in her husband about the letter. Would you have done the same thing?

3. The theme of individual versus communal is explored in the book. Was Jess justified in pushing the others to consider the greater good? To what extent should they have set their own needs aside?

4. Jess's mother has dementia. Why do you think the author chose that condition, and what was she trying to convey by showing us Jess's visits to the care home?

5. Priyanka considers herself immature, the baby of her family, with a complicated past. Why do you think she decides

to get rid of the butterfly tattoo? What effect does this have on her immediate life?

6. Stephanie appears to be a woman who has everything her own way, but it gradually unfolds that this is far from the case. Did you like her? Why do you think the author chose to depict a character like her?

7. Art plays an important yet almost hidden part in the story. Given Holly's limited options, in the end she went for post-humous success. Did you find this comforting, or unfair, sad?

8. Doors and keys feature throughout, symbolizing the haves and have-nots in society. How much does disadvantage figure into the story? Would that night at the Montague Club have played out differently if Nicky had been from an affluent background?

9. "Nicky was out for herself and deserved what happened." Some people might say this about her or think it silently. Do you agree? Did you change your mind during the course of the book?

10. The women start out opposed but grow closer. Do you think they ended up friends? How much do you imagine they stayed in each other's lives?

11. What do you think is the significance of the book's title? Do you think the men deserved to be punished? Why or why not?